# Critic in Love

# CRITIC
## IN LOVE

· · · · · ·

*A Romantic Biography of*
## Edmund Wilson

· · · · · ·

by David Castronovo and Janet Groth

Shoemaker  Hoard

Front cover photos, left to right: first row—Edna St. Vincent Millay © Arnold Genthe, Edmund Wilson in 1930 and Elena Wilson both courtesy of The Beinecke Library, Yale University Archives; second row—Mary Blair © Francis Bruguiree, Dorothy Parker, Mary Pcolar c. 1970; third row—Mary McCarthy, Edmund Wilson c. 1940–1950s © Silvia Salmi, Margaret Canby in 1929. Back cover photo: Edmund Wilson in Talcottville courtesy of The Beinecke Library, Yale University Archives. Every attempt has been made to secure permissions. We regret any inadvertent omission.

Library of Congress Cataloging-in-Publication Data
Castronovo, David.
Critic in love : a romantic biography of Edmund Wilson /
by David Castronovo and Janet Groth.
p. cm.
ISBN (10) 1-59376-050-7 (alk. paper)
ISBN (13) 978-1-59376-050-2
1. Wilson, Edmund, 1895–1972—Relations with women.
2. Authors, American—20th century—Biography.
3. Critics—United States—Biography. I. Groth, Janet, 1936- II. Title.
PS3545.I6245Z5857 2005
818'.5209—dc22                    2005012692

Text design by David Bullen
Printed in the United States of America

Shoemaker 🔲 Hoard
An Imprint of Avalon Publishing Group, Inc.
Distributed by Publishers Group West

10  9  8  7  6  5  4  3  2  1

# Contents

*Introduction*                                          *vii*

  I.  Artists and Bohemians                             3

 II.  Proletarians and the Bourgeoisie                  60

III.  The Intellectual and the Cosmopolitans            89

IV.  Endings and Beginnings                            155

  V.  The Sum Total: Living and Writing               178

      *Notes*                                           195

      *Index*                                           217

# Introduction

EDMUND WILSON, TWENTIETH-CENTURY AMERICA'S MOST DIRECT and readable critic of literature and society, was a man of many loves. In his half century as a major force in American letters, he had an outsize romantic career that reflected the depths of his personality. Each woman he came to love was an alluring interpretative problem, an erotic and analytic challenge, a presence that fired his imagination. His Rabelaisian appetites, ardors, and vulnerabilities, and his conceptions of love and sex are a story in themselves.

Lacking the dashing appearance and glamour of Fitzgerald or Hemingway, Wilson far surpassed either as a chronicler of his varied, intense, and seemingly endless affairs. This man of prodigious research feats, author of several dozen works of ideas, was an uninhibited pursuer of desire and a recorder of its meaning. In his books and journals and letters, women are a mysterious and vital force. They came from the Greenwich Village of the 1920s, from his own upper-middle-class world of privilege, from New York's working class, from the high reaches of literary New York, as well as from the workaday world of Talcottville in upper New York State.

Who were they? They ranged from famous figures in American literature—Edna St. Vincent Millay and Mary McCarthy, to bohemians and people in the arts such as Anaïs Nin and actress Mary Blair, to upper-class women like Margaret Canby and Clelia Carroll, to writer pals like Penelope Gilliatt and Dawn Powell. Along the way, there were serious flirtations with poet Louise Bogan, with whom Wilson had deep intellectual affinities, and upstate neighbor Mary Pcolar, with whom he had an erotically charged and affectionate friendship. He was intimate with most of them and intense with all. The whole story falls into four parts: the artists and bohemians in his early life of the twenties, the proletarian and bourgeois women who were central to his life in the thirties, the intellectual who dominated the late thirties and forties and the cosmopolitans of the forties and fifties. Finally, there are the endings of old relationships and the beginnings of new ones—adventures and affairs of his later life.

Ultimately, it is not so much the number of Edmund Wilson's romantic and sexual encounters that distinguishes him from other artists and writers, but the fact that he left an exceptionally vivid and detailed literary trail. We throw these figures into high relief in order to show their essences. We profile their lives and interweave their relations with Wilson as a part of a romantic biography, in the course of which we give an account of a crowded social life and an intense inner struggle. That struggle is Wilson's psychomachia—his lifelong conflict between rationality and passion. The judgmental critic was always at war with the man of feeling. From his early years, Wilson was continually striving to break out of the limits of a strictly intellectual existence into a more expansive and passionate kind of life.

Wilson's affairs and friendships and marriages were by no means a matter of unrelieved torment. More often than not, he seemed to enjoy his varying roles as sexual performer, savorer of beauty, and connoisseur of personality. Leon Edel's remark about Wilson's enjoyment of "the zoo of himself" is totally on target—it only requires that we extend it to his emotional life as well, to include his brains and feelings as well as his glands. The four parts of this book follow the trajectory of Wilson's emotional development as it emerges in what he wrote about the women he loved.

In his recollections of growing up during the early years of the twentieth century, in Red Bank, New Jersey, Wilson recalls wheeling his bike to the edge of the property line, looking down the road and ruminating bleakly; he supposed he would "eventually have friends" with whom he would have "something in common." His emotional biography begins on this low note, when he had no real-life person toward whom he could direct his capacity for love. Childhood and adolescence were a time of discovering passions about the imaginary—about books and fictional characters—but there seemed to be a long stretch of time without intense feelings about people. The Wilson household was a dispiriting place in which to be young. It was long on lineage but short on warmth and affection. There was a distant relationship to the Puritan preacher Cotton Mather on his mother's side; another branch of the family built an old stone house in upstate New York at the end of the eighteenth century that was supposed to have hosted a memorial service for George Washington. An equally distinguished set of professional and ecclesiastical people on his father's side came over from Londonderry in the 1700s.

Edmund Wilson Sr. was a brilliant lawyer, a Princetonian, a success in the courtroom but a domestic disaster. Plagued with neurotic phobias, given to breakdowns and "eclipses"—as Wilson so dryly put it—he was emotionally elsewhere when the child and young boy was looking for companionship. Intellectually, he was there to deliver dinner-table pronouncements on politics and the arts, but he was a remote figure, often behind a green baize door. Strong will, fabulous analytic command, integrity, and public spirit were on display when he was in his emotionally stable periods, but the son's account registers respect for the father's principled way of life—and nothing more. Wilson Sr. had himself grown up in a depressing time—or so Wilson Jr. would have it. The Gilded Age—with most educated men having to serve the "money power"—was not exactly the springtime of imagination and creativity. Wilson Sr. was one of its victims—a gifted orator at Princeton's Whig Hall with a steel-trap mind who wound up using his talents not for some high purpose but for defending the railroad interests. He married a standard female type of the age—a patrician girl, educated at Abbott Academy, whose mind was bounded by gardening and gracious living and whose role as wife and mother was limited by very poor hearing. Mrs. Wilson—for all practical purposes—went deaf on a return trip from England with her troubled husband. She had just gotten bad news about his mental condition from a specialist. Young Edmund was therefore raised in a household of emotionally inaccessible people. In the immediate neighborhood, there was only one friend of any note, a little girl named Margaret Edwards. She was the daughter of a painter and Wilson found her a "sympathetic" companion—the trouble was that he was stopped from playing with her too often for fear that such an association was sissyish. This did not deter him from keeping up the connection for the rest of his life. A letter to Margaret written in old age is forthright and personal. But Wilson's Red Bank life was otherwise lacking in enjoyment and fun. Not inclined to sport—there is the apocryphal story of his putting on a baseball uniform and starting to read—Wilson was left with the only prospect: finding ways of escape.

Beyond the confines of Red Bank, there were the Wilsons in Shrewsbury and the mother's family, the Kimballs, in Lakewood. The father's family was most strongly represented by a grandmother, the widow of a Presbyterian minister. Edmund's memories of her are not fond, mostly because she exerted pressure on him as a child to learn the catechism. That little book was a grim series of precepts about sin and goodness, and fortunately his mother didn't approve of a steady diet of such lessons. Her family was worldlier and more amusing to the boy, consisting of lively and convivial uncles and aunts. Uncle Reuel Kimball was a terrifically devoted physician who was very well-to-do, well traveled, and altogether more relaxed in attitude than Wilson's father. He taught Wilson Sr. to enjoy beer drinking on a vacation in Karlsbad—and was himself given to periodic sprees. Wilson evidently had enough affection for him to name his own son by Mary McCarthy after him. Uncle Reuel's son Sandy was a childhood playmate—and from the start the boys were literary. They dictated short stories to Aunt Laura Kimball who then stitched their work into little books. Laura was a spinster for many years before she made a rather sad marriage to a local farmer. Edmund was always devoted to her, and she, more than anyone else in his early years, seems to be a lovable figure. Her "sensitive poetic nature" contrasted markedly with his father's hard-driving professionalism and his mother's conventionality. "I learned a good deal

about books from her," Wilson remarks. The sections about her in
*A Prelude* are also quite compassionate as they relate the story of
her isolation and disappointment. Laura belonged to a "pitifully
sparse" New Jersey gentry and suitable marital prospects were rare.
Her story has a poignant quality that is almost nowhere to be found
among Wilson's tales of his relatives.

It was his cousin Sandy Kimball who was responsible for Wilson's very early and thorough theoretical knowledge of sex. As a
doctor's son, Sandy had access to Havelock Ellis's *Studies in the
Psychology of Sex,* and the boys soon knew it better than the catechism, right down to the case histories in the back, printed in fine
type. Wilson remarks that it became as familiar to him as a preteenager as the Andersen fairy tales had been. He notes that the
result of sexual activity—no matter what the deviations (even
attraction to melons)—did not have nightmarish consequences in
Ellis's accounts. People didn't neglect their duty or forfeit their
rank. "The whole atmosphere of Ellis is reassuring." Edmund was
younger than Sandy, and soon the latter went off to prep school at
St. Paul's in New Hampshire, a very fashionable St. Midas school
(as F. Scott Fitzgerald dubbed the Old Money New England boarding schools). Edmund was piqued at Sandy's preppy airs and slang
when he returned; he himself was sent to Hill School in Pottstown,
Pennsylvania, a more severe and less ritzy place that was dominated
by the hated Calvinist spirit. There, he found a strange combination of humanistic learning, inspired teaching, and moral pressuring. His mother took him for the opening of term and let the other
boys hear that he was called Bunny. This nickname—given because
his mother thought that as an infant his black eyes made him look
like a plum bun—was humiliating and Wilson began by trying to
fight with the boys who used it. Eventually, he resigned himself—in
true preppy fashion—to the right of the group to label the new boy.
Like a character in Owen Johnson's Lawrenceville stories, Wilson
was known thereafter by the infantile nickname—part mockery,
part affection. Intellectually, Hill was demanding and ultimately the
bedrock of Wilson's humanistic outlook—Greek and good prose
were the order of the day, and Wilson took to both.

The emotional side of the Hill experience is movingly recorded in the long short story *Galahad,* published in 1927. Wilson said that he heard the story line at second hand, but he also admitted that the atmosphere is that of Hill, not of the New England, Episcopalian-sounding "St. Matthews." He also indicates that he was quite familiar with the sermonizing, the overwrought preachers, the warnings against sex and cocktails, and the ensuing degradation, insanity, and death. The story itself reads like a lightly encoded tale of Wilson's own feelings. Wilson may not have been the type to be president of the school YMCA like his protagonist Hart Foster, but like his character he too was a leader at school, a reserved and very studious boy who had almost no experience with girls. Edmund used his Hill vacations to visit with friends and avoid Red Bank; Foster does the same and visits the spectacularly rich family of his schoolmate Boards Borden in Greenwich. There he meets the imperious and magnificent Barbara, Boards's sister; she's a wild girl, a "barbarian queen," who flirts and drives a car and almost initiates him sexually—the problem being that he's afraid. The story was written by a thirty-two-year-old veteran of the 1920s sexual revolution, and it concentrates on what it felt like to be awakened, aroused, and confused by a somewhat older, socially superior girl. Its sexual scene isn't graphic, but it's by no means tame or evasive or filled with vague abstractions. Kimonos, thighs, and breasts—not to mention the male character's unmistakable excitement—are what the story is all about. The Amazon-like Barbara scares the young student, and he goes back to school; there he broods and fantasizes and soon runs away one night to tell her that he really wants her. The outcome is depressing and rather flat and predictable—but almost surely true to the spirit of Edmund's own young life. He's treated with condescension by Barbara—and walks off into the winter darkness. By the time Wilson graduated from Princeton, there is no indication that the drama of his romantic life had any further episodes. And, for that matter, there's nothing on the record in the journals and letters to suggest a disappointment of any magnitude at Hill.

What did mark the Hill years was the beginning of Wilson's

full-blown social life. Although there are few references to girls, there is friendship after friendship—and all the attendant holiday visits to classmates' homes, theater in New York, work with fellow editors on the *Hill School Record*. The visiting was often on the grand scale—to estates on the Hudson and to Manhattan townhouses and elegant residences in Brooklyn Heights. The *Hill School Record* gave Wilson his first chance to be published. From the start, Wilson was a writer who knew how to combine his own work with sympathetic understanding of others' work: no loner or cynic, he liked to discuss and to share and get friends' opinions.

Princeton may not have been a time of romantic awakening, but it certainly was a period of brooding about love, casting a cold eye on conventionality, and opening up to a wider cultural world. Entering the University in 1912, Wilson encountered a place that was still essentially a tame and fashionable institution—with strong traces of old-time fuddy-duddyism—only looking toward the modern, fast, and wild future. The students were still obsessed with their eating clubs, places for dining and socializing and lounging— "remarkably uninteresting" as far as Wilson was concerned. The ceremony and fuss that surrounded being chosen for a club— discussion called "bicker"—seems antique. The clubhouses were sometimes splendid—Cottage Club was designed by Stanford White—but other times "like a Hollywood set." At the end of the freshman year, the candidates paraded down Prospect Street (Wilson's own rooms were in Holder Court): "They saw the clubs all alight and the diners at the doors and on the curb, in the dress clothes of undergraduates or the fantastic soldier, sailor, artist and Arab costumes of alumni. Some of them held champagne glasses in their hands; and this touch added glamour to the paraders' impression that they were in the presence of arcana more mysterious and magnificent than anything else Princeton had to offer." But being chosen, according to Wilson, was a "disillusioning climax." From the beginning, he had a strong resistance to manufactured glamour, glitz, and standardized merriment. Princeton was not the best fit for this very serious young man. The professors varied a good deal, ranging from the brilliant humanist Christian Gauss, Wilson's

comparative literature teacher and mentor, to Dean West, a pomp-
ous classicist who specialized in humiliating students. Gauss introduced Wilson to French symbolism and to the idea that the scholar
was not an ivory tower onlooker but a vital force in the creative
world. As for girls, they seem to have been a poorly understood
species. There was a good deal of in-the-head eroticism, and there
were dances—which Wilson never attended because he couldn't
dance. *A Prelude*—a book filled with vivid impressions of the
university—offers this: "Some people call on and talk to girls as if
they were visiting the zoo and feeding buns to the animals. For
them, 'Calling on girls' becomes something entirely apart from association with other human beings." Despite all his Havelock Ellis
reading, Wilson seems to have been a bit terrified by his own phys-
iology, actually fearing chance arousal. "The Puritanism of the Hill
School had imposed itself to this extent. It was not that I had not
longed for women; but I was too shy with proper young girls who
were only just learning to be improper." In any event, he had no fantasies about the conventional girls of his social class, preferring to
dream about slender, intellectual brunettes, heroines out of H. G.
Wells. He and his friend F. Scott Fitzgerald had intense literary conversations, mused about life and art and society and their futures.
But sex was not particularly a topic. Wilson ends the Princeton section of *A Prelude* with a small incident that took place on Nassau
Street. He and Scott and a couple of friends spotted some girls; one
of the friends said, "They're hookers!" Wilson didn't even know the
word, had no idea that there were prostitutes in Princeton. Their
friends having gone off with the girls, Wilson reports that he and
Scott "talked of other matters."

Wilson sums up the Princeton experience by saying that the
"sublimation" of sexual abstinence resulted in a fine classical education. He had used his time well—studying Dante with Gauss,
keeping up his Greek, doing philosophy with Kemp Smith, learning
Italian, writing for the *Nassau Lit*. Fitzgerald called him the "shy
little scholar of Holder Court"; but he emerged as more than
that: He had already begun to function as Fitzgerald's literary conscience. He had supplied himself with the foundation of his life—

a knowledge of the classical achievements and a sound and sympathetic taste for modern literature. He knew that the smug middle-class Englishman Alfred Noyes, then a teacher at Princeton, was not much of a poet. He had developed his habit of following the new writers. He had been cool toward the predictable and the conventional—in ideas and literature, in ideals, and in friends.

In 1916, just out of Princeton, Wilson and his Hill School friend David Hamilton went together to a military preparedness camp at Plattsburgh in upstate New York. After a summer in which he found himself altogether unsuited to be an officer, he put in some time at the *New York Sun.* Wilson retained his slightly old fashioned air of classicism and Puritanism—and his virginity—through his early post-graduate days. Still, some changes were taking place: Arriving early for a dinner date at Wilson's digs in Greenwich Village, Fitzgerald saw him sauntering along in a brown suit and swinging a light cane. Fitzgerald had the distinct impression that he was no longer the "little scholar of Holder Court." He was right. By the time Fitzgerald had his glimpse, the now bon vivant and jaunty Edmund had moved into impressive digs in the most bohemian section of New York City, equipped, thanks to flush Princeton roommate Larry Noyes, with an oriental servant. Fitzgerald described it as a place where life was "mellow and safe, a finer distillation of all that I had come to love at Princeton."

During this period Wilson was gradually discovering that he was unsuited to be a daily newspaper reporter. And when the War broke out, he knew he would have to enlist or face the draft, so he went along with David Hamilton's plan to join the hospital corps. Before the two were ready to ship out, they spent some time at an army camp in Detroit. Wilson wrote his mother of "David's" shock at the rough language being bandied about in the tent by the other fellows after mess, and he expressed profound distaste for the army institution of KP, not so much the work as the dish towels, which were insufficiently clean and the dishwater, which was inadequately fresh. By the time he and Hamilton, still together—at least as far as their arrival in France—are crowding head to toe in Hamilton's bunk (Wilson's being too filthy for habitation), they are able to make

friends with several of the college educated among their shipmates
and with one fellow named Roy who, though he never went beyond
high school, was a clever artist. Together, they were putting out a
makeshift newspaper called *Reveille* (badly written in Wilson's fas-
tidious view, but the closest thing to a suitable task in his time in
uniform so far).

When later separated from even these companions, Wilson
wrote letters home from the hospital where he was orderly in the
winter of 1917. They indicate a kind of brotherly affection for the
nurses who shared hot chocolates over the brazier and a great
dependence on (together with a certain condescension toward)
John Andersen, "the little Dane" (again, not a college man) with
whom late at night he argues everything from Spinoza to Women's
Rights. But he and other cronies reunited near a French village and
took to patronizing a café in the town—more expensive than the
competition, not because the food was better, Wilson wrote home,
but because the proprietor knew the value of his English-speaking,
extremely attractive daughter Ninette. It is this daughter whom
Wilson tries hard to romance, walking out with her to visit girlfriends of hers at the hospital nearby. The ineptitude of his attentions may be inferred by the fact that, not only does Ninette ditch
him and sneak out the back way, but he doesn't even understand
that he has been ditched. (When he confronts her with his puzzle-
ment at having missed her, she admits slipping out the back but
blames her strict father and his displeasure at her being out alone
in the company of a male—a tale he reports without irony to his
mother in his letter home.)

If he was mystified about this first attraction, he was quite clear
about his views of the war. From the edges of the battlefield, he pronounced on the horror of gunshot wounds and mustard gas and the
endless waste of youth and idealism that went up in the smoke.
While many healed after repatriation, he and Hemingway and Fitzgerald and numerous others became what Gertrude Stein called
"the lost generation." Wilson's own idealism was so shaken that
never again—whether in the intellectual upsurge of hope for a
socialist revolution in the thirties or in the call to defend the world

against Hitler in the forties or in the retrospective look he gave the Civil War in *Patriotic Gore*—was he able to put aside that disgust for war or find just cause. He opposed all wars.

Wilson had certainly been friends with a number of party types at school: They looked upon him with a mixture of amusement and awe. When, in 1919, he returned to another convivial (slightly reconfigured) set of roommates in another Village apartment (slightly further uptown), he became something of a party type himself. His return from France found him taking a position, first as a writer and then as a managing editor at *Vanity Fair*. Wilson's Uncle Winfield Kimball—a wealthy and somewhat reclusive bachelor—described the goings-on of the four chums in their book-lined apartment: "Aw, they used to have the wildest dinner parties you ever heard of—every Thursday, about six or eight men, all Princetonians. You used to hear the inside dope on everything—all the gossip, all the scandal! I used to go along as the archaic old thing to lend some air of respectability to the party—I was the only one who didn't drink. . . . It's an awful bore for the man who doesn't drink, you know. It's amusing for about twenty minutes, but after that, they either begin to put their arms around you or they begin to curse you. . . ." Wilson may not have been one of the cursers, but he is on record as having to apologize profusely after a party five years or so down the line for having bitten one of his journalist cronies on the leg.

The scene described by Uncle Win came to an abrupt end when two of the more reticent members of the ménage—Larry Noyes and Morris Belknap—objected to Wilson's having given a tubless female friend the run of the bathroom for long steamy submersions. He and Ted Paramore, the fourth of the foursome, removed to quarters on Lexington Avenue at 18th Street which, situated above a furrier, struck them as always smelling of wet cats. However, this was offset by the railroad flat arrangement of the rooms—the bathroom-separated bedrooms allowed them to entertain women simultaneously.

The tubless female was Edna St. Vincent Millay.

# CRITIC
## IN LOVE

# I

# *A*rtists and *B*ohemians

EDMUND WILSON WAS A SELF-PROCLAIMED "MAN OF THE TWENTIES." He lived the frenetic life of the jazz age, mixing drink, parties, women, and animated talk with breakneck literary productivity and variety. His journal *The Twenties* chronicles his appetites—for books, sexual encounters, and friendships. The beginning of that passionate life—the story of a first love that preceded his first important efforts as a writer—takes the form of Wilson's love letters to Edna St. Vincent Millay, the flaming red-headed poet whose talent was one of the major media events of the era. The letters are a breakout from the restraints of an earlier period and also a vital clue in putting together the complex story of Wilson's career.

When Edmund Wilson set about writing "Epilogue, 1952," the shapely and affectionate tribute to Millay that forms the end piece of *The Shores of Light,* he wanted to contribute what he called a "counter-memoir" at a time when Vincent Sheehan's *The Indigo Bunting* was the only recollection out. Sheehan, after all, had come to know Millay only in the forties.

In "Epilogue," Wilson undertook to revisit his emotions about Edna and record his passionate response to her work and personality. He wanted to register the old "recklessness," the gin-fueled sessions in which he transcribed Edna's poetry, the "scorn for safe living," and "the need to heighten the sensations of life." As he set about reconstructing the summer of 1920—the period of their sexual affair, first in the Village and ending in Truro on Cape Cod—he did not have at his disposal the letters themselves, but only his journal entries of the twenties to guide him. He also did not have the desire to tell the unadorned truth in one of his full-dress essays. He sought, rather, to transform the inarticulate feelings of his youth into an altogether cooler record. Setting his love letters to Edna against the more reflective and discreet version of events he recorded in his memoir is revealing. Seen together, they show something of the workings of the writer's mind as he reshapes the raw materials, and the raw emotions, of what had been for him a significant rite of passage to adulthood.

The correspondence is sadly, almost comically, lopsided. Edmund, then twenty-five and a virgin, was in over his head. Edna, twenty-nine, had had, by this time, perhaps eighteen lovers, of both sexes, and had been the recipient of much more gratifying, far less tongue-tied love letters from several of them. Her pursuers included such established men of letters as the Nicaraguan poet Salomón de la Selva; the playwright Floyd Dell, a founder of the Provincetown Playhouse in Greenwich Village in whose one-act play, *The Angel Intrudes,* Edna had made an impact; and the poet-lawyer Arthur Davison Ficke, a married man from Davenport, Iowa, with whom she was to carry on a torrid epistolary romance for many years to come. Wilson complained that, for all the response they evoked, his nine letters to her might as well have been thrown "into the void." In the main, Edna's only reply was silence. The one exception is an oft-quoted August 3rd letter asserting that "I don't know how to write to you either,—what you would want me to write, or what you would hate me for writing." Its personal side is somewhat undercut, however, by an important business postscript. In it, she warns *Vanity Fair* to dispense with any illusion they may have had about publishing a "lewd portrait of myself" (a poem written during an evening spent with Wilson and his *Vanity Fair* colleague and former Princeton classmate John Peale Bishop). Wilson certainly had no illusions about Edna's past—he joked that her cast-off admirers should form an alumni association—and he was quite aware that, at the time he was polishing up his proposal of marriage to her, he was sharing her favors with Bishop. Even so, he seems oblivious, in these letters, of everything but his own naked need for her.

Yet, in spite of the impediments to a happy outcome, the venture was, for Wilson, far from an unmitigated disaster. As biographer Jeffrey Meyers put it, "Wilson had the great good fortune to lose his virginity to Millay. She, more than anyone else, enabled him to make that crucial leap from the intellectual experience of books to the sensual experience of life." And Wilson and Millay remained on friendly terms throughout her lifetime. "Epilogue, 1952" ends with the story of his last poignant encounters with her as she, in failing health, "somewhat heavy and dumpy," and he, portly and balding, pored, as intensely as they had used to do, over her latest verse. The visits were paid by Wilson and his fourth wife, Elena, to Edna and her husband Eugen Boissevain at their farm in Austerlitz, New York, when the Wilsons were attending concerts at the nearby Berkshire Music Festival.

Before he ever met Edna St. Vincent Millay, Wilson had half fallen in love with her by way of her poetry. He was particularly struck by her sonnet "To Love Impuissant," in which the poet issues a daring challenge to the god of Love and mocks him as impotent to conquer her. The poem concludes, "(Now will the god, for blasphemy so brave, / Punish me, surely, with the shaft I crave!)." Wilson memorized it and recited it to himself in the shower, admitting that his fascination for the poem was due partly "to my liking to think that one who appreciated the poet as splendidly as I felt I did might be worthy to deal her the longed-for dart. . . . How I hoped that I might someday meet her!" He was therefore all set up when at a Greenwich Village party of Hardwicke Nevin's he and a number of other partygoers listened raptly to Millay recite her poems. Wilson describes her in images of flame: "She was dressed in some bright batik, and her face lit up with a flush that seemed to burn also in the bronze reflections of her not yet bobbed reddish hair. She was one of those women whose features are not perfect and who in their moments of dimness may not even seem pretty, but who, excited by the blood or the spirit, become almost supernaturally beautiful. . . . She had a lovely and very long throat that gave her the look of a muse, and her reading of her poetry was thrilling."

Wilson was certainly not alone in his enthusiasm. Two ironic masters of modern verse—Thomas Hardy and A. E. Housman—

found a powerful presence in her poetry. Hardy thought she was as classically modern as the skyscraper; Housman pronounced her the greatest living American poet. "Renascence," her legendary poem set in Maine about breaking out and experiencing passion, made her a tumultuous emotional phenomenon forty years before Sylvia Plath. The public made her a bestseller and quoted her verse— especially the quatrain beginning, "My candle burns at both ends"— arguably more than that of any other contemporary. She would go on to become the first woman to receive the Pulitzer Prize. Meeting her that night, Wilson said, led him to "cultivate her acquaintance by way of *Vanity Fair*," where he and John Peale Bishop were working in the editorial department. "We published in *Vanity Fair* a good deal of Edna's poetry, and thus brought her to the attention of a larger public. . . . As for John Bishop and me, . . . we both, before very long, had fallen irretrievably in love with her." He claims this "was so common an experience, so almost inevitable a consequence of knowing her in those days, that it is possible, without being guilty of personal irrelevancies, to introduce it into a memoir." What's more, he says, "one cannot really write about Edna Millay without bringing into the foreground of the picture her intoxicating effect on people, because this created the atmosphere in which she lived and composed."

Wilson goes on to say this spirit so made itself felt that it overpowered any personal considerations: "There was something of awful drama about everything one did with Edna, and yet something that steadied one, too. Those who fell in love with her did not, I think, seriously quarrel with her or find one another at each other's throats and they were not, except in small ways, demoralized or led to commit excesses, because the other thing was always there, and her genius, for those who could value it, was not something that one could be jealous of." Wilson asserts that this presence-of-genius element "made it possible during the first days we knew her for John and me to see a good deal of her together on the basis of our common love of poetry. . . . I remember particularly an April night in 1920, when we called on Richard Bennett, the actor, . . . in the cheerful little house halfway downtown. . . . I sat on the floor with

Edna, which seemed to me very Bohemian." (A journal entry he
omits found Edna draped over both men's laps, delighted to listen
while Bishop and Wilson, holder of the lower half, debated politely
over who held the superior share.) Wilson remembers that "there
was also a trip on a Fifth Avenue bus . . . in the course of which
Edna recited to us a sonnet she had just written *'Here is a wound
that never will heal, I know.'* For me, even rolling up Fifth Avenue,
this poem plucked the strings of chagrin, for not only did it refer to
some other man, someone I did not know, but it suggested that
Edna could not be consoled, that such grief was in the nature of
things." The word *chagrin*, which is featured in several key locations
in these words of Wilson's, is used in the French sense of "sorrow,
grief, distress," yet it is worth noting that in English it more often
connotes mortification or humiliation.

Continuing his account, Wilson says, "I used to take her to plays,
concerts and operas. We saw Bernard Shaw's *Heartbreak House*
together, when it was first done in New York, in the November of
1920." He was, years afterward, to evince a special fondness for this
work of Shaw's, perhaps because he first saw it with Edna.

Without specifying when, in the time frame of their affair (April
to November 1920) it occurred, Wilson admits that "between John
Bishop and me relations were, nevertheless, by this time, becoming
a little strained," a characterization that proves something of an
understatement. As an example Wilson cites a stretch of several
weeks during which "I was more or less monopolizing Edna" in consequence of which Bishop "had collapsed and come down with the
flu. I went to see him, and afterwards told Edna—no doubt with a
touch of smugness—that I thought he was suffering, also, from
frustrated passion for her. The result of this—which I saw with
mixed feelings—was that she paid him a visit at once and did her
best to redress the balance. I knew that he had some pretty good
poetry to read to her, and this did not improve the situation."

One can see the disjuncture between Wilson's original feelings
and these of the recollected past by pausing here, to read the raw
desperation in his actual letters of the period.

8CRITIC IN LOVE

[no date, probably spring 1920]
Sunday

Dear Edna:

I must have left my pocket-book in your room last night. Will you look on the floor and see if it's there and, if it is, preserve it till I see you again?

E. W.

*Vanity Fair* letterhead
June 30, 1920

Dear Edna Millay:

[*Vanity Fair* editor, Frank] Crowninshield has acquired a strange passion for your poetry. In spite of the fact that he didn't care much for the Figs [Millay's recent publication, *A Few Figs from Thistles*] I showed him, he is now clamoring for more of your stuff and asks me every day if I have written to you about it yet. He wants to publish a page of you,—so couldn't you send us all the Ms. you can,—book, Figs, sonnets and everything,— published (except, of course, *Renascence*) and unpublished (though you might indicate which ones have been published). If you will do this, we'll send it back as soon as possible.

We [presumably, Bishop and he] receive with cries of horror and disgust your statement to the effect that you intend to stay [in Truro, on Cape Cod] until January.

E. W.

114 West 12th St., N.Y.
July 27, 1920

Dear Edna:

You must let me know when I can see you again. Couldn't you come to New York some week-end? Excuse this note—I don't know how to write you letters now—and please let me hear from you. I love you.

E. W.

114 West 12th St., N.Y.

July 28, 1920

Dear Edna:

I'm sending this on the chance that you're still in town. If you are, you *must* let me see you again before you go. Please be decent and call me up. Otherwise, you'll leave me pretty flat.

E. W.

114 West 12th St., N.Y.

August 1, 1920

Dear Edna:

I hate to keep pestering you, but could I come up to Provincetown this week-end? That is, would you let me see you, if I did? Unless you positively dislike me now, I wish you'd let me.—I suppose all this is pretty casual to you, but it's not to me, as you know. When you went you left me to a world of shadows: nothing seems quite real to me except you,—and you are gone. Even writing doesn't satisfy me; I can't even write you poems. I can only think about you. I want not only to love you, but really to know you and, except through your poems and a few things you have said, I scarcely know you at all. Until the last time I saw you I had always seen you on such silly terms. I used to curse myself for a fool while I was talking to you that I should be willing to exchange with you all those intelligent inanities.

—I see, upon rereading this, that it is a stupid letter. I'm sorry; it's not the way I want to talk to you but, since I haven't heard from you, I don't quite know how to talk to you.—I see that I say something about not wanting "only to love you" etc. And it has an earnest honest manly American sound that ill becomes me. Under the circumstances, I can't seem to write about my love for you without writing stupidly, so, for heaven's sake, let me hear from you,—if only to avert more letters like this. I have a horrible feeling now of throwing my thoughts and my correspondence into the void.

E. W.

114 West 12th St., N.Y.

August 12, 1920

Dear Edna:

You never gave me your Lake Placid address; consequently, I can't write to you except through Truro. Please let me know exactly when you are coming.—next Friday or Saturday, I hope. Everyone here will be away then and my vacation begins week after next.

I miss you horribly. I spend most of my time composing arguments to persuade you to marry me,—but I shan't attempt to lay them before you by letter. In fact, I can't do much by letter, anyway, except beg you to let me know when you are coming.

—F[rank] C[rowninshield] thinks *Passer Mortuus Est* too erudite for the man in St. Louis; but was greatly pleased with *Scrub,* which will go into the next number. Don't forget to send the other poems, will you?

—Oh, Edna, I wish I had something to cure your chagrin! You don't know how you tear my heart out sometimes,—because I feel that I cannot do anything to help you who have given me so much.—But I shall reserve the rest of this till I see you again.

You will pardon this abrupt letter,—but the ordinary language of love seems foolish to me,—and I know that it only bores you. I can't speak to you by letter.—But you know what honor I pay you and how terribly I love you.

E. W.

114 West 12th St., N.Y.

August 17, 1920

Oh, Edna, you desolate my evenings. I can scarcely tolerate the rest of life. You are necessary to the deepest part of me,—the part that has always been lonely before, the part that has scarcely ever felt dependence on another person. I always knew I could love, but I have never loved a woman before. I have loved only the nobility of art and thought and of a few men; but now that I can read your poems as I can read Plato or Dante your poems are not enough. I want to hold you in my arms; I want your terrible kisses which make everything else seem mean. You are the only woman I have ever known who could fill me with fire. — Do you think that you have accidentally broken down the self-repression of a respectable youth who is bewildered with the symptoms of first love at an abnormally advanced age? I can tell you that, though my opinions change with the years, the values in life change little for me. I may, — as I probably shall, if you tire of me and I cannot see you any longer, — be the lover of a hundred women and yet I know that they will content me as little as I have known they would in the past, when I have left them alone. Your memory will hurt my heart then, as it does now you are not with me, — though I should be the cleverest and the most learned and the ablest man in the world.

— Life already filled me with contempt and with impatience at its stupidity. And now that I have known you I am more contemptuous and impatient. I could enjoy it all with you, — if I had you to make life splendid. You have torn down the prison where my flame was burning and how, if you leave me or forget me, shall I ever get it back in its prison again and make it burn steadily alone?

— I love you, I love you, I love you! The memory of our kisses and of your beautiful throat gives me more pain than pleasure now, because I have not got them. All the harshness in my life seemed to melt when I first took you in my arms, and yet now things seem harsher than ever because my arms are empty. Your picture which I love exasperates me in the end and I want your living face that changes like a flame.

— Oh, my dear! — I can call you this as you have never called me, but remember, when you are away from me, what pain I suffer in your absence. God knows I have been thirsty all my life but never like this before. —

[no signature]

114 West 12th St., N.Y.

August 25, 1920

Dear Edna:

You *must* let me see you. I can neither amuse myself nor work. I don't care about anything now but you, and now you tell me that you probably can't come. Won't you drop me a line and let me know how and when I can see you?—I could come anywhere at any time. I could meet you somewhere on your way from Woodstock or go up to Provincetown and see you from there. Will you wire me (collect) if you can manage any such arrangement?—You will surely not be too ill, when you leave Woodstock, to let me meet you somewhere.

E. W.

114 West 12th St., N.Y.

August 27, 1920

Dear Edna:

I'm sending this to Truro, in case you should actually have left Woodstock yesterday and so have missed the two notes I sent you there.—Won't you let me know when and where I can see you? If it's possible for you and if you want to see me, I should like to come to Provincetown and see you from there. You should have known when you sent me that telegram that it is impossible for me to make any other plans, so long as the question of seeing you is unsettled. If you are ill and don't want to see me till later, I wish you would let me know so that I might, in case of necessity, put my second week's vacation off till later. You put me in a difficult situation by not answering any of my letters. I am sorry about whatever's wrong, but I do think I might have a line from you.—My days are empty, horrible.—But you must know all that.

E. W.

[Postscript] *Please* wire me (collect) when I can see you.

When he describes his hard-won trip up to Truro in August of 1920 in his memoir, Wilson says dispassionately, "She had me and John Bishop on different weekends," though of course his letters just before the trip evince anything but dispassion. The memoir goes on to describe being met at the Provincetown train station by a man with a cart who, "for some curmudgeonly Cape Cod reason," dropped him off an unconscionable distance from the house where Edna, her mother and two sisters were staying, "so that I somehow got lost in a field and dragged my suitcase through scrub oak and sweetfern in the breathless hot August night."

That he arrived thus bedraggled was not the only problem: "There were only two rooms on the first floor, with no partition between them, the only way for Edna and me to get away by ourselves was to sit in a swing on the porch; but the mosquitoes were so tormenting . . . that we soon had to go in again." After trying so long to get there Wilson was not inclined to abandon his mission so easily. "I did, however, ask her formally to marry me, and she did not reject my proposal but said that she would think about it. I am not sure that she actually said 'That might be the solution,' but it haunts me that she conveyed that idea." From the vantage point of time, Wilson can sum up: "I was not the solution, nor was anyone else she knew."

There is a curious condensation in the memoir at this point that only the journals can clarify. In the memoir Wilson says only, "I saw her in Paris in the summer of 1921." He reports her as "having, I think, a very good time." He goes on in rapid strokes to describe her return to America, her marriage to Eugen Boussevain, and a visit he paid the couple on Bedford Street in the Village in January of 1924.

But the end of the affair is told in *The Twenties*. Wilson's notebook entry from the trip says that, upon his arrival in Paris, he "found Edna very much allied with the Bohemians of the Left Bank, with whom I was not much at home. We walked in the Bois de Boulogne and joked." He remembers that Edna "was very broke at the moment and she asked me to take her to the South of France; but I knew that she was not to be relied on and would leave me for anyone who seemed more attractive. I did not want to have to worry and suffer again." He was conscious of another impediment as well, a commitment to a young actress with the Provincetown Players named Mary Blair, "who had promised to try to join me in France." (Wilson later married her.) "I declined to go away with Edna, and lent her money instead." Here, an interpolation quotes from a letter to John Bishop in which Wilson describes the encounter at length and goes into his own change of heart: "She can no longer intoxicate me with her beauty or throw bombs into my soul; when I looked at her, it was like staring into the crater of an extinct volcano. She made me sad; it made me sad, curiously enough, that I loved her so much once and now did not love her any longer. Actually, of course, I would not love her again for anything; I can think of few more terrible calamities; but I felt that, impossible and imperfect as she is, some glamour of high passion had gone out of my life when my love for her died."

He revisited that "glamour of high passion" in his 1929 novel *I Thought of Daisy*. His characterization of Rita Cavanaugh, the Greenwich Village poet, is charged by his infatuation, idealized— and only subjected to the most fleeting critical judgment. It's as if the nine years that had passed had not brought with them any skepticism or distancing. Wilson's narrator—unlike the Wilson of the journals—is still in the grip of his early passion. He's more articulate than the young man in the 1920s letters, but no less bedazzled. Wilson intended *Daisy* to be a novel of ideas—the Village ethos colliding with other styles of 1920s living and thinking, including those of the bourgeois professional, the jazz baby, the academic. Rita was to be the most creative embodiment of bohemia, able to stand forth as a genuine artist, but "an outlaw living from hand to mouth, always poor and often ill, bedeviled day and night by all the persons she no longer had the energy to excite to her own pitch of incandescence." Wilson's portrait—memory overwhelmed by sentiment—has an excessive, strained quality. The narrator meets Rita at a party and very soon starts to hang on her every word and gesture, finding piquancy and style in things that seem ordinary to the reader. We're led—with some amount of compulsion—through his excited perceptions.

At first he's got it right, capturing Edna's peculiar combination of allure and distance: "Rita Cavanaugh was a sharp-nosed little thing with mousy bobbed hair; she wore a shabby black dress. She was so small that I hadn't noticed her. But, as I shook hands with her, she gave me, from eyes of a greenish uncertain color, a curious alert intent look, as if of a fox peering out from covert." Soon thereafter he starts to lay on the observations a bit thickly—her seemingly artificial British accent, her staccato, precise puffing of her cigarette. When she reads her poetry, the narrator bursts into the essay form, giving us a discourse rather than a fictional rendering. Although there is sharpness of perception and some good phrasing, the pacing is off, and the response is elaborate rather than dramatic. We're told of the narrator's first experience as a reader of Rita's poetry: He recalls that the classic themes were treated in ordinary language and that the results achieved "boldness and austerity." We're then given his response at the party, which is his discovery of her gift for music: "I had not known . . . to what music these things had been tuned." And then he describes her imagery: There's a passage about a corpse lying on a shore, another about two afflicted children playing in a dismal city street. We're told that "on her lips" this material was "a song." Well, it may have seemed that way to her lover, but the reader of *Daisy* is likely to find the whole reflection a parody of Proust describing the effects of art and literature. It's arty when it needs to be immediate.

Things get even worse when the Wilson persona follows this fascinating woman around at the party. She critiques some modern drawings of Homeric subjects—and the narrator goes over the top. Although he uses his eye to see what the poet sees, he demands too much admiration for her. When Rita looks at a Pallas Athene— "Almost like a man!"—this is a pretext for her admirer to go into a rhapsodic fantasy about what is "austere and impressive," unconventional, and charming in both the drawings and Rita. The next thing you know, her way of saying "lovely" is referred to as having "disinterested and passionate conviction." If there is a touch of irony in this scene, it's all but imperceptible. And the Wilson figure is soon to take her back to his place on Bank Street where there's more of the same forced rhetoric as they talk together till morning. One truth about writing does come out: Rita-Edna is championed as the poet of rhythmic verse, nouns and verbs that can evoke strong feelings; the narrator, who tries his hand at poetry, is too adjectival.

In rounding off his portrait of Edna, Wilson creates what he's best at in fiction—a scene of loss. Rita is escaping to her aunt's in upstate New York, and our narrator rides with her in a cab uptown to the train. We feel his strong sense of abandonment, his intensity and tenderness. She's predictably talking about herself and her needs, and the you-just-don't-understand line she gives him rings true. She carefully carries her cactus plant from the taxi to the station: Whether this 1920s example of funkiness is all-too-cute is a matter of taste. The truth is that the portrait of Rita is not Wilson at his most subtle and penetrating. Ironically he's less insistent about a character's peculiar gifts and magnetic qualities when he's writing in the essay form: The personal reflection, the long review of a writer's work and nature, brings out his most creative side.

Take the instance of "Give That Beat Again," a piece that was first published in 1937 and then reprinted in Wilson's mammoth collection *The Shores of Light*. It's the next step in the story of Wilson's feelings for Edna. Written seventeen years after the sexual affair, it's a book review with some of the qualities of a love letter. He is fascinated by the woman artist and disappointed that the most personal side of her nature is submerged in her latest book, *Conversation at Midnight*. The book, he claims, is all witty banter among representative social types of the age—the Communist, the stockbroker, the liberal, the Roman Catholic. But what he calls for is "the noble magnanimity and bitterness" of the Millay of the 1920s. He wants the drama of Edna's personality, not the "fictitious personalities" of this book that "never give rise to any conflict half so real as the conflicts within the poet herself, as she has expressed them directly in her own person." Wilson's review is a curious blend of elements: a celebration of her great talent for self-dramatization, yet a lament for the decline of that talent; a sharply focused appreciation of Millay—the poet of sounds and rhythms and "beat"—yet an almost irrational claim that she has contributed in her latest volume to the muffling of "the old strong beat of English verse."

Reviewing his old lover, he becomes quite intense about her literary decline, blending her diminished achievement with the general fall in standards: "And now Edna St. Vincent Millay, one of the sole survivors of English verse, seems to be going to pieces, too." Never mind that Yeats, Eliot, and Auden were publishing. He has put Edna in their class, extolled her, then accused her of losing her way, and finally come out with a judgment that shows what this critic in love yearned for: "Yet I miss her old imperial line." The essay is as much about the subjective response, the critic's ardor, the encrypted story of his feelings as it is about literature. It is a mid-career example of how the critic's intelligence and the romantic spirit conspired. This time Wilson is right: Edna has substituted cleverness and talk for the beat. And he's kept his esteem for her without sacrificing his judgment.

By the time Wilson was writing his 1952 essay, even this note of bitter nostalgia has been transformed, as the following passage reveals, into a complex response—part balanced literary analysis, part rationalization of the mystery of love's failure. Honesty, sharpness, and sympathy come together.

He says of Edna's relations with him and Bishop "and with her other admirers" that they "had, as I say, a disarming impartiality. Though she reacted to . . . the men she knew . . . with the same intensely perceptive interest she brought to . . . a bird or a shell or a weed. . . . she did not . . . give the impression that personality mattered very much for her." He goes on to insist that "what interests her is seldom the people themselves, but her own emotions about them." She could and did, he says, deal in her sonnet sequences "with a miscellany of men without—since they are all about *her*— the reader's feeling the slightest discontinuity. In all this she was not egotistic in any boring or ridiculous or oppressive way." Still, he has to admit, "she was sometimes rather a strain, because nothing could be casual for her; I do not think I ever saw her relaxed, even when she was tired or ill. . . . But although Edna sometimes fatigued one, she was never . . . tyrannical or fatuous or vain. She was either like the most condensed literature or music, the demands of which one cannot meet protractedly, or like a serious nervous case . . .

whom one finds one cannot soothe." As a critic, Wilson pursues the question: "What was the cause of this strain? From what was the pressure derived that Edna Millay seemed always to be under?" And as a memoirist he interpolates a caveat: "At that time I was too young and too much in love to be able to understand her well, and I afterwards saw her only at intervals and in a much less intimate way. But I had found, when I had come into contact with the formidable strength of character that lay behind her attractiveness and brilliance, something as different as possible from her Greenwich Village reputation, something austere and even grim." Ultimately, Wilson finds that the central theme of Millay's entire oeuvre is to be found "in the astonishing *Renascence*." He characterizes the situation of the poet in that work: "She is alone; she is afraid that the world will crush her; she must summon the strength to assert herself, to draw herself up to her full stature, to embrace the world with love; and the storm—which stands evidently for sexual love—comes to effect a liberation. . . . yet it always leaves her alone again, alone and afraid of death."

In bringing Wilson's emotional and literary life into focus, the most useful phrase is "the demands of which one cannot meet protractedly." Wilson was to spend the next twenty years meeting the demands of difficult modern art, experimental writers, radical thinkers and actors of history—everything problematic and outside the bounds of his class, early training, and sense of order and coherence.

The origin of Wilson's passional life—the wound of youth—is contained in the letters: They are about a young, hardworking literary journalist—trained in the classics and disciplined by Protestant self control—who was suddenly out of control. His 1920s—and twenty-fifth year—began with the trauma of thwarted passion and desperate confusion. Edna was the flashpoint, providing the theme of torment conspicuously absent from the surface of his well-ordered life. The youth who had borne up so well against the trials of a troubled household—a deaf and emotionally unresponsive mother, a brilliant but chronically depressed father—sailed through the austere Hill School, stood up to the snobberies of Princeton, and went through the Great War without recording any break-downs or faltering of his solidly built ego. But his summer's worth of passion was perhaps the first real event to disturb his poise and set him on the road of exploring tormenting self doubt in books and people's lives.

.  .  .  .  .  .

HIS NEXT LOVE proved as problematic and disturbing as his love for Edna. In the summer of 1920, he was agonizing about the great poetess while up in Truro trying to woo her; by the summer of 1921 he was in Paris, still seeing her off and on—to all outward appearances pursuing her—but evidently the romance part was off. If truth be told (and he told it to Edna), he had a new girlfriend. He had not brooded too long and was in full swing by the time he went to Europe; moreover, he had made some kind of a promise to the new woman in his life. Mary Blair was an actress with the Province-town Players who starred in several O'Neill plays, notably *Desire Under the Elms* and *All God's Chillun Got Wings*. She was a signature performer of the times who excelled in controversial roles and was famous for kissing Paul Robeson's hand in *All God's Chillun*— a progressive act in the age of Jim Crow and the Klan. She acted the part of free spirit Bill in Wilson's first play *The Crime in the Whistler Room* and proceeded, in their marriage (which produced one daughter), to act in an unconventional role—no kind of mother and no kind of wife. Her story was really Act Two of his Greenwich Village phase: Enter the second bohemian, a wild thing who would fascinate and torment him nearly as much as Edna had. The embroidered story of their relationship, complete with a record of her feelings and his feelings, is to be found in the 1937 play *This Room and This Gin and These Sandwiches*. Here is where he gets to look back on the meaning of his second-most-important relationship with a Village character. The play, no masterpiece for sure, does manage to let a lot of facts and feelings hang out and provides a good deal of information about what he thought of one Sally Voight, an actress who is almost identical to Mary. The title of the play pretty much sums up the makeshift life that he and his girlfriend were having in the early twenties before they became man and wife. It's all about the conflict between a very middle-class, bespectacled, well-dressed professional named Arthur Fiske—in this play an architect rather than a critic like Wilson—who gets deeply involved with an actress on the edge; he's solid, in terms of income and occupation; she's lurching from part to part, trying to put together a career. He's bewitched, completely besotted by her winsome charm; she's trying to get him to cue her for her role.

He'd like to get married; she wants an open relationship and whatever adventure comes along with whatever man. She, like Edna, doesn't have a lot of patience with him and doesn't have her heart in settling down. Arthur's idea, according to her, is to install her as his wife in a steam-heated apartment in a building with a doorman. The mention of a doorman, however, ticks him off: He is, after all, a Wilson persona, someone who wants to be at least a fellow-traveling free spirit, someone who has been through the Great War and who has become disillusioned with all the bourgeois arrangements that war seemed to make a mockery of. But, in this play at least, Wilson has caught himself on the horns of a contradiction.

His sympathetic character Fiske would like to have it both ways —bourgeois and bohemian at the same time. There is a lot of dialogue expended on this problem, and he says that "gentility unfits people for being decent"; he protests when she says that his domestic yearnings would keep out her nonrespectable friends. He tries to draw the line between comfortable domesticity and bourgeois conformity. But the line doesn't seem that clear—and in Wilson's own life he was to make peace with a certain kind of bourgeois conformity, despite his fulminating. In this work, Arthur and Sally toss these ideas around and make us see what the central problem would be in Edmund and Mary's relationship when, in real life, they became Mr. and Mrs. Edmund Wilson. They both want to be outside the bourgeois scene, except that he would like to be a little bit inside. Meantime, a second theme emerges in the play, which is the theme of the Village itself. What are they doing there? What do they hope to accomplish?

The real-life story of the couple is quite close to the conflicts that come out in the play. It was all about Wilson's struggle to keep things together and her struggle to break them apart. Yes, he was to embark upon a career as a rakehell in the twenties and had already, as early as 1920, had a passionate affair that could obviously not be a settled union. But there was something in Wilson that yearned for Tea for Two by the fireside, and Mary Blair was not the right companion. Mary came from a Swedenborgian Pittsburgh family of five. Her father owned a pretty good printing business, and she was able to go to college. At fifteen, Mary entered the first ever drama class offered at Carnegie Tech. She left before graduation and married classmate Charles Meredith with whom she was briefly involved in exhibition ballroom dancing. They were divorced in California, and Mary headed back East.

After marriage to Wilson, the birth of a daughter Rosalind in 1923, and a second divorce in 1930, Mary wed Constant Eakin, a very well-to-do manager of the Frigidaire Corporation. They lived rather grandly in a duplex at 37 West 12th Street. Rosalind describes the scene: "The bedroom had been designed by Cleon Throckmorton, a famous set designer, with some help from Norman Bel Geddes, also a designer. There was a massive blond wood bed on a platform and a great bureau. In the living room was a huge portrait of my mother in costume painted by Djuna Barnes." Barnes, author of the experimental classic *Nightwood,* was a lifelong friend of Mary's.

Third husband Connie, as he was called, was also able to afford a summerhouse with a swimming pool and tennis courts in exclusive Redding Ridge, Connecticut. In one memorable photograph, Mary observes little Rosalind helping Connie out of the pool. But the good life didn't last long. Connie lost his job because of drink, Mary's health broke, and the couple wound up out in Pittsburgh during the thirties. Mary was in a sanitarium, and Connie struggled to keep a job at Gimbel's.

In terms of our story, Mary provided Wilson with his explanation to himself for breaking off with Edna. He told John Peale Bishop he had no intention of letting Edna get her hooks back into him and would brook no more bombs going off in his soul. One way or another, he felt committed to Mary and kidded himself that she would provide something solid to go back to after the turmoil. Mary Blair was about as solid to go back to as a piece of lake ice in late May. She was exceedingly charming, a glamorous figure in the Village, an auburn-haired gamine and a bona fide member of the avant garde. While not a Vassar girl like Edna, she was educated and cultivated and had, at the time he met her, definite star quality. Sharp, witty, and given to histrionics in personal life, she was the kind of handful that he relished.

She called herself a cynic and enjoyed making cracks about the bohemia that she herself was part of: The experimental theater in Provincetown needed "a good dose of Cascara," she remarked. Unlike the dizzy jazz babies of the time, Mary could provide a certain amount of intellectual stimulation and artistic camaraderie. She referred to Wilson's "great play that had not been written" in 1921 while *The Crime in the Whistler Room* was still in embryo. Her adulation for Wilson is evinced as a strange sexual, intellectual mix; a letter to Wilson in Paris, dated August 29, 1921, recounts, "I had a funny dream about you the other nite. I dreamt that I went to the Biltmore Hotel with you and you had a bottle of very precious liquid and you were bargaining with [the] hotel keeper for the bottle of liquid. Your only surrendering of it depending on their changing all the furniture to red plush." At Carnegie Tech, which throughout her short life she frequently and affectionately referred to as "Tech," she was engulfed in the study and performance of Greek tragedy and Shakespeare. In later life, she appears to have been an omnivorous reader and makes references to Lytton Strachey, Sherwood Anderson, Fitzgerald, and Hemingway. Although she did not graduate with the class of 1914, she had the training, skill, and knowledge to move from her classes at Tech without further preparation into her first professional performance in *Before Breakfast,* a one-act play in which she played opposite the only other actor, the play's author Eugene O'Neill.

Mary's rather narrow, provincial background didn't keep her from standing beside the most accomplished and sophisticated people of her time. She toured with John Barrymore, and such luminaries as Talullah Bankhead, Walter Huston, Ethel Barrymore, Eva Le Gallienne, Lee J. Cobb, Katherine Cornell, and Helen Hayes, who regarded her as an equal. Wilson had little taste for Broadway hoopla, and Mary provided something much more artistically solid. O'Neill thought that she had really given life to *Diff'rent* in 1920, and, after she had displayed her loyalty by coming back from a hospital bed to see through the opening of *All God's Chillun* in 1924, he never forgot to be grateful. In later years, even when he didn't have a part that was particularly right for her, he kept her in mind and then cast her in *Desire Under the Elms*. This—along with *All God's Chillun*, *The Hairy Ape* (1922), *Marco Millions* (1928), and a repeat of her debut part in the one-act *Before Breakfast* (1929)— was enough to secure for her a reputation as "the O'Neill actress." *All God's Chillun* received mixed notices. Heywood Broun, for example, called it "a very tiresome play. Caucasian superiority does suffer a little, because Paul Robeson is a far finer actor than any white member of the cast. . . . Mary Blair as Ella Downey, interested me very little, but this may be set down to the fact that the role that she plays is quite thankless." Other, more favorable notices abounded, however. In March of 1925, a Sunday *New York Times* review of her in O'Neill's *Diff'rent*, which she had first done in 1920, waxes poetic. In the role of a "girl who cannot and will not marry" a man who has proved unworthy, Mary is said to lift the character "into a terrible isolation and crude, lonely power of spirit." Defining her acting style as heightened realism that blends stylization with a "beautiful, natural directness and simplicity," the reviewer concludes by summarizing Mary's performance as "moving and unforgettable."

Her role in *All God's Chillun* may not have secured her that kind of ecstatic review, but it did secure her notoriety: By defiantly kissing the hand of a black man at every curtain call, she pressed the buttons of still-bigoted America. Mary was doing something electric in a controversial play. Although this all took place in Greenwich Village, one would never know it from the brouhaha: threats of violence, a bomb threat, the police called in, the KKK in the mix, and running denunciations in the press by the Secretary of the Society for the Supression of Vice and the Salvation Army. The Wilson who had turned to the left after the Great War and who shared its disdain for bourgeois pieties must have loved all this. He writes almost exultantly in his journals: "Mary got insulting letters," and O'Neill was called "so low that he'd have to take a stepladder to get up to a cockroach." Wilson himself provided some of the response and excitement by writing a review of the play for the *New Republic*. He praised O'Neill as an artist whose writing was sometimes crude, yet expressed "some impact directly from life." He said the play "gained intensity" by having "sheared away" all but the characters' relationships. And he made the broad-brush generalization that O'Neill's work was one of the best things that had been done about the race problem. At the time, the uproar looked rather frightening. But since the Provincetown Playhouse was not a legitimate theater, it was only ultimately responsible to its subscribers. Public censors could not shut down the show, but they did succeed in making Mary a poster girl for modern vice. In fact, the play was not a problem drama about miscegenation at all, according to O'Neill, but rather a tragic study of mismatched people in a marriage.

Meantime, Wilson was in his own mismatch. Mary was at the theater every night, went back to work one month after giving birth to their daughter Rosalind, and was generally unavailable for family life. There are accounts in Wilson's journals of idyllic times in Bellport and Brookhaven; and Mary's letters allude to a famous midnight frolic when Wilson, dressed in his pajamas and top hat, arrived on Burton Rascoe's doorstep with Mary on one arm and Talullah Bankhead on the other, ready to put on a show. He did his magic act; Talullah sang a song; and Mary recited a little something from Greek tragedy. But these are episodes rather than a way of life.

Most of the time it was Wilson at loose ends in the evening on the town; Rosalind, fairly permanently parked in Red Bank with Wilson's mother and a nanny called Frieda; and Mary merely monitoring marriage and sending wires from the Hotel Statler in Detroit and other points on the road. Wilson—while not a candidate for homebody of the era—was from his very early years attracted to the idea of domestic stability, pleasant surroundings, and amenities. Although he rarely had them in this period, except on cosseted weekends at his mother's well-staffed house in Red Bank, he wanted them, and the couple had a few good addresses but no sense of a real home. The closest thing to a signature place was 3 Washington Square North, an address that Mary later on was thinking of using as a title for her memoirs, sadly never written.

The marriage, not surprisingly, was brief, lasting from 1923 to a very amicable separation in 1925. When Wilson announced his intention of marrying the actress, his mother, conscious of the connotations of the word "actress," objected. His father, however, being somewhat more open-minded, endeavored to assuage her doubts and went up to New York to discuss the matter with, of all persons, Wilson's boss, Frank Crowninshield. Crowninshield thought it was a good idea, would settle Wilson down, and put ambition into him. That was evidently good enough for Wilson Sr., and the wedding took place on February 14, 1923. The bride was two months pregnant, and they had essentially been an item since the summer of 1921.

Back in August, 1921, she wrote to him in Europe, said that she planned to join him, but wasn't feeling well and thought that the "Winged Victory will have to wait to have a look at me." It turns out that she was delicate from the start and during that summer had two operations, one for a cyst on the liver and one for appendicitis. Her worries over her physical condition took a different turn in December 1921, when she wrote him from Pittsburgh that she wanted to talk about a problem that concerned the two of them, obviously pregnancy or fear thereof. Whatever the tension, it didn't break them up as a couple, and their marriage—while a patched-up job—came off in time for Rosalind's legitimate birth in September 1923.

. . . . . .

OVER A TWO-YEAR period as man and wife, they managed to make a go of it, and in fact they were both ambitious and hardworking. Mary was no less a driver than he. She was in three plays within a year of Rosalind's birth. Mary commented in April, 1925, "I'm determined to get somewhere in the commercial theater regardless of all sacrifices." She was tireless in seeking work, was always on the lookout for new plays, and thirsted to take New York by storm: "I want so much, I want so much, I want so much, it's terrible!"

Her energy was amazing. She played whores, innocents, natives in brown war paint (that took hours to apply and an hour's soaking to get off), and co-starred in an avant-garde venture with a stageful of ants. In short, she was not waiting for things to happen.

Wilson was furiously writing journalism for the *Dial, Vanity Fair,* and the *New Republic.* His productivity, pugnaciousness, and chance-taking were remarkable. In terms of covering classics, he wrote pieces on Byron, Stephen Crane, Boswell; with regard to the breaking news of the modern, he was starting to cover the ground— Stevens and Cummings, Carl van Vechten, Sherwood Anderson, Ring Lardner. His best and most memorable piece is probably "Mr. Hemingway's Dry Points," a breakthrough essay about Hemingway's economical style. When he was not writing about his impassioned reading he was covering shows, performers, photographers, painters and musicians. He pioneered (in a discerning way) the study of pop culture and took Houdini seriously, but he took issue with his friend Gilbert Seldes who wrote rhapsodically about the cartoon Krazy Kat. Wilson was much involved with critiquing rather than swallowing the whole scene: cartoons, Broadway shows, nightclub acts, and mass entertainment of various sorts.

From the beginning he forged an independent position between snobbish elitism and slavish acceptance. He was a true critic from the start, one who allowed performers and popular artists their unique being—if he found that they had one. A long section called "On and Off Broadway" in *The American Earthquake* has a landmark essay called "The [Ziegfeld] Follies as an Institution," a piece with plenty of edge—"a signal is given from the stage, and the audience responds like a shot." He analyzed Chaplin in 1925, and that same year he explained Georgia O'Keefe and Stieglitz for a wide audience. He loved Stravinsky and did the same for him. He also got into the issue of quality control in Louis Untermeyer's literary anthologies and said some pretty funny things: "The old veteran has withdrawn; his lieutenants are doing his work for him. There are two or three who re-edit his opinions in accordance with the principles laid down by the chief; and another who supplies the puns." Fair or not, this bit of roughing up was to become part of Wilson's style.

Meanwhile, the marriage didn't actually go sour; it collapsed for want of attention. Nevertheless, there were many good times. Mary had a wide acquaintance among party-loving girls, notable among them two nurses who were also freelance hookers. Peggy Lewis and Verna Tolley figure in Wilson's journals for their moonlighting and for their tragic deaths in a car crash. Wilson's catalog of their purses (he was charged with collecting their personal effects) is an example of his dry but evocative prose. After detailing the powder puffs, the cigarettes, etc., he mentions "a pair of cheap purple cuff links and an envelope containing the cards of a dozen or more salesmen, contractors, cloak and suit manufacturers and newspaper reporters." Mary and "Bunny"—she always used his preppy nickname—also traveled with his literary friends, and there are fond references in Mary's letters to Burton and Hazel Rascoe, Scott and Zelda Fitzgerald, and Eugene O'Neill and his second wife Agnes, a pal of Mary's. At the time when Scott and Zelda entertained the newly married Wilsons at dinner, Mary regaled the party with her imitation of Russian actors. Her letters recall visits to the Fitzgeralds in Great Neck and the time at University Place when Scott put one of Bunny's suits on his near comatose wife. And a good part of the good times was remembering plays and people who had figured in their mutual development. In 1940, Mary wrote Wilson a moving letter about Scott's death calling the old friend "one of the finest imaginative minds of our time."

When she and Wilson separated in 1925, it was by no means the end of their intense relationship. They had been through the challenges and thrills as professionals starting out in New York, and that bond proved to be enough to make them friends until her death in 1947, quite apart from the bond of their child.

As one looks back over their correspondence — some 1500

holograph sheets from her to him, which are the only side of the correspondence to survive—one comes to the odd conclusion that here (never mind that she had married again and that he had done so twice more) the two were doing a kind of penance to make up for their mutual sense of guilt over having muffed it earlier as spouses and as parents. We see it in the dogged soldiering on past disagreements, past hurt feelings, in the ever-present consideration for one another; she always ready with interest in his work and praise and encouragement for its every manifestation. We see it in her efforts to arbitrate a truce between him and Rosalind, who were always clashing temperamentally, and between him and his mother, who were always wrangling over money since he didn't inherit after his father's death in 1923. It's evident in her unflagging efforts to rally from a sickbed in order to interest and amuse him.

His own efforts came in the form of supplying the economic support and covering some of the expenses of Mary's prolonged medical care when Connie could not. (Wilson was always generous with the money that was doled out to him grudgingly by his mother.) His behavior with Mary puts paid to the notion that Wilson was a cold, unfeeling monster: He seemed here—and in many other parts of his life—to be at his best when friends were sick, depressed, or in trouble. The boxes of avocadoes and fresh tomatoes at Christmas, the cards and gifts on her birthday and, most touchingly, the Valentines, arrived without fail. In the thirties and forties, they are fashioning in however patchwork a manner, a shadow marriage. It has all the intimacy, the casual exchanges of inside jokes and gossip that married people enjoy and that sometimes provide the cement to glue things together. Each seems to have tried hard to repair or atone for the neglect of their de jure married years.

For Mary, as she wrote many times, their friendship was a lifeline without which she didn't know how she could have gone on. For Wilson, her friendliness and strength were the nearest to married conviviality he would come until he landed—almost concurrently with Mary's death—in the last and most fulfilling of his four marriages, with Elena Mumm Thornton. His final entry in *The Twenties*, telling of his and Mary's divorce (celebrated at the Lafayette), seems to say it all: "When I finally left her in her apartment, after dinner, —a look of understanding [passed] between us on a level away above our wrangling—I could count on her, she counted on me."

. . . . . .

WILSON'S WOMEN—those who shaped his views of femininity, won his affection, and stayed with him in spirit for years—were not always lovers. He was susceptible to more than sexual allure and found fascination in women whom he could admire, learn from, and draw into his imaginative-critical world. Sometimes he was seeking affinity with a sympathetic woman rather than sex. The special kind of camaraderie and companionship in question was simply not something he could get from a man. Vaguely erotic, it depended more on bonds of trust, on speaking the same language, on humor and wit, on flirting and performing intellectually than on going to bed.

Dorothy Parker was such a friend. She gave him his first break. They met after the Armistice when Wilson was shopping around his writing and Dorothy saw to it that one of his pieces came to the attention of Frank Crowninshield at *Vanity Fair*. When he was given a job on the staff, she continued to befriend him. She was pretty and stylish, and he "needed a girl," but the rather prim Wilson reports in his journals that he thought the overwhelming smell of Coty perfume was vulgar and made her not his type. According to the journals, the *Vanity Fair* office under Crowninshield was a very laid-back scene, particularly on Fridays, when "Crownie" and the other males on the staff enlisted the female secretaries in a game he called "The Rape of the Sabine Women"—a matter of carrying the young ladies in their arms out into the corridor. Evidently very enjoyable for all. But even the easygoing Crowninshield could feel the pressure of an obligation to please the players and power brokers. Dorothy's habit of ticking off big Broadway producers with her devastatingly witty theater reviews reached a crescendo in 1920 when she slighted the talent of Billie Burke, whose husband was none other than Florenz Ziegfeld. Crowninshield was forced to fire her. In the ensuing flap, her pal Robert Benchley (like Dorothy a member of the Algonquin Round Table), resigned in protest, as did Robert Sherwood. *Vanity Fair* had a brain drain, and Edmund Wilson was enlisted to fill in and do their work. Wilson was in the midst of a wonderful opportunity and soon rose to be managing editor of the magazine.

None of this affected the cordial dealings of Wilson and Parker; she and Benchley joked that he was a scab and took him over to the Algonquin for his first experience of the Round Table. Wilson never quite connected with the Gonk crowd, and he enjoyed taking swipes at those loud, aggressive, sit-down comics: "They all came from the suburbs and provinces, and a sort of tone was set—mainly by Benchley, I think—deriving from a provincial upbringing of people who had been taught a certain kind of gentility, who had played the same games and who had read the same children's books —all of which they were now able to mock from a level of New York sophistication. I found this rather tiresome, since they never seemed to be able to get above it." Evidently one of the children's books they had all read was Longfellow, as one of Wilson's samples is Dorothy's "Hiawatha nice girl till I met you"—which catches her at a low point. She was usually much better than that, and, at the top of her game, she had a special combination of qualities that set her apart from Woollcott and the rest. Next to her they seemed mere publicity seekers and makers of easy *mots*. Like Wilson, she recognized them for what they were; seeing them jammed elbow-to-elbow in an Oak Room banquette in the Algonquin, she observed, "This looks like a road company of the Last Supper."

Dorothy's definition of wit, manifest in all she wrote, is something quite different from wisecracking—wisecracking is mere verbal "calisthenics." Wit seeks truth. Although Wilson and Parker were never lovers, he had a special connection with her brand of caustic truth telling.

Dorothy, née Rothschild, was raised on the Upper West Side of Manhattan. Her father was a prosperous garment manufacturer. She was a rich man's daughter, but from an early age Dorothy displayed little tolerance for pretension and a great capacity for self-deprecation. Like some Jewish girls of her era, she attended a convent school; there she claimed to have learned little except how to spit on an eraser in order to remove ink. In her teen years, she went to Miss Dana's School for Young Ladies in Morristown, New Jersey, where she learned Latin and studied Horace, Catullus, and Martial (the last of whom might well have helped with her own epigrams). Unlike Edna and Mary, she never went to college. She became "Dorothy Parker" after a strange, ill-conceived marriage, contracted briefly in her youth, to Edwin Pond Parker II, a young stockbroker who boasted a good background but had a weak head for drink. After Franklin P. Adams used some of her poetry in his Conning Tower column, she had a poem accepted at *Vanity Fair* and then talked her way inside the Condé Nast organization.

Frank Crowninshield seems to have liked starting his trainees on garment description (he set Edmund Wilson to work writing about gentlemen's cravats); he was managing editor at *Vogue* before moving on to the new *Vanity Fair* in 1917, and it was there that he had Dorothy begin writing about ladies' lingerie. Her first caption, "Brevity is the soul of lingerie said the petticoat to the camisole," showed that she was ready to leave underwear behind. When Crowninshield assumed the editor's desk at *Vanity Fair,* he brought Dorothy along, bumped her up to doing features, and soon named her theater critic. Although she was no longer exclusively a poet, her ego ideal seems to have been Edna Millay: "I have slogged along in the exquisite footsteps of Miss Edna St. Vincent Millay, unhappily in my own horrible sneakers. Just a little Jewish girl trying to be cute. Miss Millay did a great deal of harm with her double-burning candles. She made poetry seem so easy that we could all do it—but of course we couldn't."

Actually, Dorothy could. And her verse has wonderful bite. She and Edna were two experts in the art of witty self-laceration and ironic regret: Edna the greater artist, but Dorothy the better entertainer. From the start, Dorothy proved her mettle as a generator of one-liners that are so much more. Keen to distinguish herself from high achievers, she described them as "People Who Do Things": "I don't do anything . . . I used to bite my nails but I don't even do that anymore." And just as keen to quash the popular view of romance, she wrote, "if nobody had learned to read very few people would be in love." Both lines are from a story called "The Little Hours" about a clever insomniac looking over what various wits like La Roche-foucauld had said. In her own self-deprecating way, she was, of course, putting herself in that tradition.

Wilson was a great lover of piquant anomalies in people; the desperately collapsing versus the bracingly strong side of Edna Millay and, in Dorothy's case, the combination of sexual innuendoes and prep school manners, the steely defensive wit and the thin-skinned weepiness. During the twenties, in his journals, Wilson collected slang, wisegirl remarks, and other bits of jazz-age flavor. Because he doesn't retail Dorothy's best remarks, his lists would be improved by such Parkerisms as the following: her passing reference to a London actress whose broken leg must have resulted from "sliding down a barrister"; her regret, after an abortion, that she had "put all her eggs in one bastard"; and her remark about a woman who wouldn't hurt a fly—"not if it was buttoned up." Wilson seems to be more of an appreciator of this kind of material than a generator of it himself. His *Undertaker's Garland* cultivates the same gruesome comic territory that Dorothy likes (she and Benchley subscribed to an undertakers' magazine called *The Casket*), but it's not the same. For all his irony and love of wit, she was the master here.

In "The Muses Out of Work" (1927), Wilson early on places her in good company, likening Parker's writing to the "cleanly economic" and "flatly brutal" work of the age of Pope. Elsewhere, put a little less politely, he refers to her sadism and "disgusting jokes." In the same passage in *The Twenties* he also quotes her as saying, "I am cheap—you know that!" Nevertheless, her name is at the top of his ideal party list. Although he could be grouchy about trivia and pop culture, he loved to dish the dirt with Dorothy. They were known to hang out together in her favorite speakeasy, Tony Soma's on West 49th Street, where they swilled Tom Collinses, the gin and tonics of their day. Carol Goodner, Benchley's showgirl mistress, had "thick ankles," according to Wilson. Dorothy brought out this side in him. When told that Claire Booth Luce was kind to her inferiors, she commented, "Wherever does she find them?" But there was a lot more than nastiness to Dorothy's banter.

In the 1930s, Dorothy went to work in Hollywood with her second husband Alan Campbell (a man who, after their divorce and remarriage, also became her third). But the movie industry was not, according to Wilson, her natural habitat—presumably, that was the printed page and the party. In the thirties and forties, he believed that a kind of "death of society" had set in, that people were beginning to worry about what they did and said, and that Hollywood and politics had inhibited writers and paralyzed "their response to experience." But Dorothy was never inhibited. She had been playing a fairly edgy part in progressive politics. She turned up at a protest for Sacco and Vanzetti in Massachusetts, walking to the police station after being arrested in strap heels (the adult version of Mary Janes) and a Hattie Carnegie cloche hat. During the 1930s, as a screenwriter in Hollywood, she was making $5200 a week, and thoughts of what the era was like for most people made her want to do something. She was active in the writers' union, several Communist-front organizations, and the Anti-Nazi League; later on, during the McCarthy period, she got in trouble with the FBI: "Listen, I can't even get my dog to stay down; do I look to you like someone who could overthrow the government?" After a life of parties, drinking, and (mostly unsuccessfully) seeking pleasure, she wanted her small estate to go to the NAACP. While not a cause junkie, nor a member of the Communist Party, nor an engaged writer and polemicist, she was, like Wilson, serious about social misery and injustice. She wrote a wonderful ironic story on race relations called "Arrangement in Black and White" that shows what it's like to receive the good will of nice white people. Wilson always admired figures who could distill political and social truths in their writing without getting sentential and preachy. Dorothy's literary politics, like his in *The American Jitters,* was a matter of showing readers scenes from American bad times. And like Wilson in *Travels in Two Democracies* where he described his travels in Russia, Dorothy went looking for signs of revolutionary hope—in her case, to Spain during the civil war.

When he came to express his thoughts more fully about her in 1944 with "A Toast and a Tear for Dorothy Parker," Wilson felt that her honesty and freedom from cant were a terrific "relief and reassurance." More than any kinship he felt with her progressive views, it was her writing itself that constituted the attraction. The clean lines and force of it chime with his classical sensibility. In an age of "imitation books," he admires Dorothy Parker's writing as the real thing. Her stories are originals, and, if he were writing about her today, Wilson might have identified her as the spiritual mother of Bridget Jones and *Sex and the City*. She initiated the naughty-to-raunchy style the movie and television series have only recently remastered. Unfortunately, most of the books in this genre are entirely lacking in Dorothy Parker's emotional range and substance. She most often deals with people pushed to their limit, usually women who are suffering from bad cases of man obsession. But instead of cheapening this and making it mere mass magazine entertainment, she gives it an acrid kind of wisdom. Like Edna, she raises her readers above her sufferers' victimhood. Then again, some of the characters in her stories triumph only in the sense that they see through themselves. A fairly desperate woman in the story "A Telephone Call" wants to avoid calling the man; it's a matter of pride: Finally, however, she comes to the conclusion that the real, the big pride is in having no pride. "I will be beyond little prides." More than a little bit like Hemingway, Parker wants to show her characters testing the limits of their dignity and endurance. And Wilson, always the champion of people who stand up to misery and personal misfortune, salutes Parker for presenting the struggle. Wilson does not make her a Brontë or an Austen, but calmly and movingly says that "she has been at some pains to write well."

A late-breaking story on Dorothy and Wilson is to be found in *The Higher Jazz,* a novel fragment recovered from his papers and published in 1998. Scholar Neale Reinitz has pieced together the pages that Wilson produced in the early 1940s about a twenties crowd of artists and bohemians and rich hangers-on. The character based on Dorothy, Kay Burke, is observed by a Wilsonian narrator, who is involved with a tony Canadian woman (of whom more later). Kay is a wisecracking Irishwoman with a wicked tongue, a taste for sadistic jokes, and a tendency to fall apart after the attentions of caddish lovers have been withdrawn. The narrative—a loose and baggy affair that's strong on atmosphere and weak on conflict— manages to show Kay in top cynical form. At one point when she is hospitalized because of a botched abortion, Wilson describes the scene; it's the great wit receiving—drinks, cigarettes, gruesome one-liners, and plenty of attention for her. He refers to the whole dynamic as if it were a session transplanted from the Gonk to the hospital room. "They all had their audiences in each other. Their sorrows became a necessary assumption one had to make for the right kind of humor: it was now one of the rules of the game, like the principle that the puns had to be bad in the days of *Hiawatha nice girl*. Life always let you down. . . . and I left Kay the queen of the court, throning with her one drink of the day which had already turned into three; and I realized that now she was happy: taken care of, admired, and amused."

Wilson's description of the scene is about the best that he does in evoking Dorothy's world, but one can see that he wouldn't have been anxious to have this particular self-involved and rather adolescent side of her on display when she was alive. The novel's close relationship to fact— sometimes cringingly unpleasant fact—made publishing it as much of a problem as the journals; but in the case of *The Higher Jazz* he never got the book out. It would have been his final say on the twenties and all that Dorothy, the Algonquin people, and the rich represented. Covering the same ground, it would have been a better book than *Daisy*. Its material, unshaped as it is, is a lot more lively—thanks to Dorothy.

. . . . . .

ELINOR WYLIE was another of Wilson's literary-platonic loves of the twenties; her brand of romantic appeal, for Wilson, was style rather than sex. Unlike Parker, she is now an all-but-forgotten figure, yet, according to Wilson, she was a kind of Edith Wharton. By this comparison, Wilson was trying to capture a certain elegance, class, graciousness, and freedom from commercial America that was always appealing to him. Wylie was an upper bohemian: none of Edna's makeshift apartments and ragtag life for her. Born Elinor Morton Hoyt, she came from a well-to-do Pennsylvania family and was so snobbish that she was ashamed of having been born in New Jersey. Although the family was not rich, her grandfather was governor of Pennsylvania, and Theodore Roosevelt named her father solicitor general of the United States, the kind of professional distinction achieved by Edmund Wilson, Sr.

Elinor was literary from an early age, reading Shelley at seven and writing poetry. She went to the Baldwin School in Bryn Mawr and finished her education in 1904 at Mrs. Flint's, now Holton Arms, in Washington, D.C. She married young—and disastrously. Philip Hichborn III was a Harvard man, but also mentally deranged and abusive. Elinor had a son by him in 1907 and abandoned both of them in 1910, a situation that has an ugly look, but is mitigated by the horrors of Hichborn. She ran off to England with Horace Wylie, a lawyer and a much older married man and father of three children. Since she had a growing reputation as a poet and was a socially prominent person, the affair was front-page news in American newspapers. Their time in England was marred by the scandal of their romance, and yet they acquired a certain glamour as a result, which made them attractive guests in several country houses. Although Wylie was obviously infatuated with her, she eventually tired of him. They returned stateside in 1915, married the next year, and had a tough struggle earning livings; by 1919 the marriage was over, and Elinor quickly took up with William Rose Benét, a writer and editor of standing who helped her get set up in the Greenwich Village scene. Wilson is not quite sure when they met, and says as much in a letter to writer Nancy Hale. In any case, by January 1921 we find her writing an apologetic note to him, half business (Wilson had taken her on part time and accepted some of her poems at *Vanity Fair*), half mild flirtation: "I was so sorry not to be able to type the poem when you asked for it—a terrifying chauffeur was waiting

---

for me at that very moment. . . . Can't you have dinner with us Monday (next week) . . .? Just ourselves, so don't dress up." By 1922, almost astonishingly, she was literary editor of *Vanity Fair;* Wilson named her his successor as he began straddling jobs at *Vanity Fair* and the *New Republic.* That made her a full-fledged colleague of Wilson's, and she signed off another note with "God keep you, Bunny, because you have a distinguished mind." Theirs was a mutual admiration society of two. In 1923, Wilson wrote in *Vanity Fair* that, next to Edna, she was "[p]robably the most remarkable of contemporary American women poets." Listing the Poetry Society's prize for her first volume of verse, he gives a plug to her second, due to come out that spring. Of it he writes: "Mrs. Wylie's poetry gives the effect of bright metals and jewels melted by a single intense flame," the molten residue of which she pours into rigorous molds, which, "when the fluid has cooled, stamp it with the hard mask of permanence." Seldom has any poet, even Edna, inspired him to such flights of fanciful praise. And she could do that to him in the office, too. He wrote her love letters from an imaginary fan named "Roscoe N. Wingo." This callow young fellow confesses "there is something inside me that just had to come out and which says write, she will understand." A poet himself, Wingo so far stretches his reliance upon the lady's good will that he favors her with a line or two of his own work, which, he modestly informs her, appeared in the January 16, 1922 issue of *Youth's Companion.* He ends with the somewhat impertinent question: "Will your heart beat a little faster knowing that your message has flown and nested in another's heart e'en though humble?" On another apparently slow afternoon at the office, Wilson writes her the fruits of The Voluptuous Pleasure Experienced in Writing the letter Z with a Soft Pencil; a sample assures her that "with azaleas and zinnias, azure and glazed," his "kazoo intermezzo" (composed in Arezzo) has left the zanzare dizzy, "the zitherists dazed." The soft pencil artist hopes to see her soon and give her "the opportunity of enjoying the inestimable treasures of my soul."

In short, in their friendship there seems to be enormous liking and plenty of light banter but no eroticism, and a letter of Elinor's to her mother indicates that Wilson, for all his geniality, was a bit distant: "Bunny is funny," she remarks, "I can't tell you what he is ever thinking." For her part, she declares that he's her favorite friend in New York. Wilson said he became "quite addicted" to Elinor Wylie, probably to her blend of high-toned living, liberated womanhood, and literary drive. He seems to have been very pleased to live in her near proximity and writes several friends enthusiastically that, having rented an apartment at 1 University Place, he is "living two stories above Elinor Wylie."

When he saw her set up there—silver candlesticks, a Sheffield mirror, and eighteenth-century chairs—he characteristically has some reservations, but also a good deal of admiration: The art and the furniture, "although rather grand, were a little bleak, but they gave her a civilized setting which is rather rare." Despite the silver gowns, the elegantly appointed apartment, and the total abstinence from the pedestrian side of New York, Elinor was a terrific worker, an indefatigable researcher, and, notwithstanding her slender formal education, a woman of considerable learning. She had developed a passion for Shelley at Mrs. Flint's, and he became her spiritual and poetic ideal. To Wilson, it was a case of both of them (Shelley and Elinor) being "spontaneous and baffled by the matter-of-factness of the world." Elinor's Shelley obsession was so strong that, according to one biographer, "she waved aside the sex difference and several times expressed the belief that she actually *was* Shelley." Which is not to say she was a rebel—the same biographer makes a point of telling us that.

Elinor was living and writing at a fast pace. She had married Benet in 1923; Wilson expressed his doubts about the union in his journal—"from a literary point of view he was so inferior to her"— and then, directly to Elinor. Her reply included a "harsh and callous laugh": "Yes, it would be a pity that a first-rate poet should be turned into a second-rate poet by marrying a third-rate poet." Elinor nevertheless found Benet a congenial spouse and a terrific promoter of her work.

Wylie's oeuvre is far from a slender body of poems and prose, and her social life was also formidable. She ripped off a profile of herself in verse for the *New Yorker* in March 1927 called "Portrait in Black Paint, With a Very Sparing Use of Whitewash," and signed it "E. W." Only when the author was widely believed to be Edmund Wilson and she overheard Wilson taken roundly to task for the unkind things the poem says about her did she confess that she wrote it herself—in about half an hour. It is indeed a remarkably unflattering picture of a fatuous, imperious social butterfly who "gives a false impression that she's pretty / because she has a soft, deceptive skin / Saved from her childhood; yet it seems a pity / That she should be vain of this as sin." But knowing she wrote it herself makes one like her a lot.

There is considerable evidence for the likelihood that Elinor Wylie's death in 1928 was preceded by a couple of earlier strokes. She wrote in her profile that she could "live on aspirin and Scotch"; her final stroke and death were seemingly brought on by stress and burning the candle at both ends—like Edna. When she wasn't entertaining and being entertained, she kept a very disciplined work schedule, using every spare moment, even when "relaxing" in her home in Connecticut. She left behind eight volumes of poetry and prose. Her apartments in New York, always exquisitely decorated, were not wide open to drop-in visits from just anyone, but Wilson and Dorothy Parker were two people who could and did penetrate her inner sanctum. In her sister Nancy Hoyt's biography we learn that "Dorothy Parker, vivid, sympathetic, never showing the caustic side which is in many of her poems and stories, would spend the afternoon in the back [room on a chaise longue] between the table with the typewriter and the bookshelves, a place where few penetrated." Hoyt also wrote that "Bunny Wilson would not come if anyone else was there, but would talk half the night to Elinor long after Bill had retired, giving her a savage criticism which she accepted from no one else."

In their time her novels—especially *Jennifer Lorn* and *The Venetian Glass Nephew*—were quite popular, got good reviews, and were evidently to the taste of an audience that liked the gothic, fantastic, and exotic. *Jennifer Lorn* is partly set in Persia and involves the heroine spending some time sequestered in a harem where she is wait-listed long enough to permit a satisfying dalliance with one Prince Abbas; the hero Gerald (who is briefly presumed dead, apparently killed by robbers) seems like a mix of the Byronic and the more sinister side of Henry James. He and Jennifer have some chaste bedroom talk, and a great deal is made of their shopping trips to Paris and the exquisite outfits they'd purchased. Elinor's hothouse material puts one in mind of James Branch Cabell's *Jurgen,* another enormously popular fantasy of the twenties. Her next novel, *The Venetian Glass Nephew,* is even more whimsical, being populated by characters made of porcelain and glass. While to contemporary tastes this may all sound as if it were made out of lead, in the twenties it was all the rage; *Jennifer Lorn* inspired a torchlight parade in Greenwich Village, and parties were thrown just to utilize the menus devoured in the novel. Wilson, too, had a taste for Wylie's material and wrote her "A Letter to Elinor Wylie" (1925), setting down his firm opinions and signing the letter Sam. Johnson. This witty bravura piece shows Wilson going Wylie one better in the historical mode, but using his common sense and directness to bring the faux eighteenth-century style down to earth. He apologizes to the author for not having read *Jennifer Lorn* when it came out, but in "a moment of tranquility and leisure," he has taken up the book and is prepared to render judgment. He takes wonderful shots at "criticks" Carl Van Vechten and Mark Van Doren, two opinion makers who were riding high in the twenties and whose extravagant praise Wylie was in the habit of flinging out in her defense whenever Wilson was disposed to be harsh. It won't do, he tells her in his Johnsonian mode. Van Vechten is so eccentric in his choice of books to praise, and Van Doren so entirely indiscriminate in his, that "[p]osterity must be as little persuaded by the . . . caprice of the one as by the universal patronage of the other." Wilson then gives it to her straight. *Lorn* is good entertainment, but *The Venetian Glass Nephew* is ultimately unsatisfactory because of its jumble of fact and fiction, its "luxuriance of phrases" that obscure the story, and its lack of narrative interest. Wilson slaps Elinor for not knowing much about Venice, a sin among the cultivated, and hardly the same thing as not knowing a lot about Persia. But the tone of the letter—its jocular courtesies and Latinate diction— make it a memorable tribute and make more of Elinor than is perhaps warranted. The piece is a little gem.

Elinor had become, by this time, something of a fashion icon, both copied and parodied for her hats, her dress, and her carefully marcelled waves, which fell in ripples from a severe center part to the point at her neck at which they were drawn back.

She was also thought to be exceptionally vain, and when Louis Untermeyer, visiting her during a hospital stay in 1924, told her she looked "lovely," biographer Stanley Olson tells us she shot back: "Have you ever seen me looking any other way?" The professional vanity on display during a visit with Virginia Woolf in London did not fail to produce a reaction. In a 1926 letter to Vita Sackville-West, Woolf does a job on Wylie the self-promoter: "Oh, what an evening! . . . a green and sweetvoiced nymph—that was what I expected, and came a tiptoe in the room to find—a solid hunk: a . . . patriotic nasal thicklegged American. All the evening she proclaimed unimpeachable truths; and discussed our sales: hers are 3 times better than mine, naturally." It was a case of one very celebrated aesthete stepping on the toes of a greater but yet to be fully recognized artist. And Léonie Adams wrote Wilson in 1928 of the Bloomsbury group's revenge: "Had you heard that the Sitwells persuaded Elinor Wylie to declaim her own works by moonlight from a high seat in Stonehenge? I felt a little depressed by the idea of furriners making game of her." In another context, Wilson was miffed by what Wylie reported of a snub from Virgina Woolf: The great novelist told Elinor that she should avoid literary English and instead write like an American, in the style of Ring Lardner. Wilson, whose career was based on taking a writer's natural gifts as a given, was appalled.

But Wilson did not regard Wylie as a mere self-promoter, famous for being famous. In one of his imaginary dialogues, "The Poet's Return" (1924), the voice of Matthew Josephson is pitted against that of Paul Rosenfeld, and the argument has a good deal to say about Elinor Wylie. The first voice denounces Wylie as irrelevant to modern American culture: "Of what use is that to anybody?" says Josephson about one of Wylie's poems on a Nocturne of Chopin. Rosenfeld, a special friend of Wilson's and a prodigiously cultivated man, calls Wylie "the Edith Wharton of our poets," by which he means an exposer of the hard surface of wealth and gentility. Josephson hammers at his own philistine point—obviously losing the argument—by saying that modern people find subways and bathroom showers "more magnificent poems" than Goethe.

This cynical line is important in Wilson generally and can be found also in the hilarious things that he imagines Henry Ford spouting, e.g.: "How can you set up these trivialities [art and literature] as rivals to the electric sign. . . . [w]hich slings its great gold-green-red symbol across the face of the heavens themselves and tells the world that it has made a new Chewing Gum or a Pickle or a Cigarette that will give you a new sensation. I tell you that culture as you understand it is no longer of any value; the human race no longer believes in it." Any reader of Wilson's masterly dissection of Henry Ford in "Detroit Motors," a 1931 essay he reprinted in both *American Jitters* and *American Earthquake,* will recognize that, although the quote may be imaginary, the sentiments are truly Ford's. Elinor looks good in the midst of such things.

February 1928: Wilson mourns Elinor's passing in a short piece that puts her in his gallery of vulnerable but persevering artists. With her death, he says, it is almost as though "the intellect that orders, the imagination that creates" has been immortalized in "the lovely lines" of her books, where they continue to exist for him, like "magnets" by which to set "our compass in this sea without harbors." (Wilson, rarely carried away, mixes magnets and compasses here.) Her life seemed possessed "by some strong and non-human spirit, passionate but detached . . . laughing with unbiased intelligence over the disasters of the hurt creature it inhabited, and the mistress of a wonderful language in which accuracy, vigor and splendor seemed to require no study and no effort." The remarks about the strength of the poet should be compared to his remarks about Edna's spirit. This is about the highest praise that he gives to an American artist, although not Wilson at his critical best. He also says that, with her death, we may well be abandoned in a "pig-headed," herdlike world.

Wilson considered Elinor Wylie a really close friend. He was on terms of easy familiarity with her from the start, and liked to spike their relationship with silly humor and gentlemanly courtesies. There are ornate blandishments in his letters, but no sign of passion. Nevertheless, her particular blend of grandeur and artistic struggle earned her a permanent place in his romantic imagination.

. . . . . .

THE POET Louise Bogan was a friend of Wilson's from the early twenties, and, while they were never lovers, he was in many ways her mentor. Louise Bogan was raised in the hardscrabble environment of Livermore Falls, Maine, where her Irish father was foreman in a paper mill; the family moved on to mill towns in New Hampshire and Massachusetts, and Louise was subjected to a rough upbringing. Wilson was evidently so struck by what Louise told him about herself that he uses it in the character Sally Voight in his play *This Room and This Gin and These Sandwiches* (1937)—a character otherwise based on Mary Blair, with touches of Edna Millay. Sally describes her life at home this way: "My mother used to have love affairs and take me with her and make me wait for her out in the hall, and my father would threaten to kill her, and my brother would fight with my father. *You* never had poverty and fighting at home and no prospect of ever getting away from it!"

This perfectly characterizes Bogan's somewhat sordid upbringing. In real life Bogan did manage to escape from her background by attending Girl's Latin School in Boston. We have yet another relationship with a woman who knew the classics—at this point one might almost say it was a prerequisite for bonding with Wilson.

Bogan spent a year at Boston University in 1915 before getting married to Curt Alexander, a man of German ancestry; she had her one child in 1917, a daughter Madelaine whose name was changed by Louise to Maidie. The baby was soon planted with Bogan's (by now somewhat more reliable) parents, and Louise headed for New York and a job selling books at Brentano's. Not raising a child under her roof, she had the scope to be a bit wild; she put in some time as a gangster's moll, even going on jobs and waiting outside in the get-away car.

When she was being her literary and bohemian self she met Wilson, sometime between 1921 and 1923. She had another boy-friend who was a friend of Mary Blair's, and by 1923 she and Wilson were good friends. During this period, Louise had been writing, and her first volume of verse, *Body of this Death,* had been published. Leon Edel reports that by 1924 Wilson was on record as finding Louise "a lady poet of remarkable achievement." By the time Wilson wrote his freewheeling evaluation of the era, "The All-Star Literary Vaudeville," he was making brief remarks about her work, indicating that, as a poet, she "plucked one low resounding theme on tensely strung steel strings" but that her recent poems demon-strated "the vibrations" of that one theme "rather than a further development."

This comment about a want of further development is not exactly the bouquet-throwing effusiveness and false praise that could get a young poetess into bed, which should quiet down critics who have said that Wilson praised women in order to seduce them. Wilson's critical commentary about Louise's work was sparse and rather sober, considering that he wrote a whole essay on the West Coast poet Genevieve Taggard—and it was hardly like his hymns of praise for other female poets. Moreover, he never expressed any affinity for her ideas of feminine identity or the poems that deal with her feelings about womanhood. Early on, she showed a predis-position to (perhaps) disparage her own sex; in her first volume, a well-known poem begins, "Women have no wilderness in them, they are provident instead, / content in the tight hot cells of their hearts / to eat dusty bread." Wilson kept his own counsel about this part of her work, and we may conjecture—without going wild— that he was too life-loving and women-loving and familiar with pas-sionate women to buy into this. Bogan herself wanted to escape from what she perceived as the negative side of her femininity: but more of that later.

Wilson's relationship with Bogan was doubtless platonic, but charged with intense emotions as well as bitter and tender feelings and rivalry. Suffering from childhood trauma and from disorder in her personal life, Louise was not an easy person to get along with. After her early affairs, she married Wilson's old Princeton classmate Raymond Holden, an editor at the new *New Yorker* magazine, although Wilson had nothing to do with introducing them. This union was rocky and included a good bit of physical abuse on both sides. Louise was given to tantrums, depressions, and physical outbursts, and this side of her found its way into her relationship with Wilson himself.

For a pair who were not lovers they managed to do a remarkable amount of fighting over art, politics, and their conflicting feelings. They were both aware of the toll their temperaments took on their relationship. She wrote, "as for his friendship and mine, and my opinion of his middle-classness—some of this was thrashed out, and more will be. We have been having knock down and drag out fights for twenty years now. And more to come, I have no doubt." These remarks from a letter of 1943 pretty much cover the whole span of their friendship. The evidence is most abundant in the 1930s, when Wilson was at loose ends after the death of his second wife Margaret Canby. They were busy tearing each other down and building each other up. He protested in a letter that he did not do the one but only the other: She replied, "I don't know why I fall for your epistolary gifts, and am willing to make up with you.—You do give me such a pain sometimes, that I'd like to cut your throat." But it should be remembered that in 1931 at the time of her first nervous collapse Wilson was there with his support: "I'm terribly sorry you've been in a bad state—I sympathize profoundly, having been there myself. . . . You are one of the people that I value most and count most on . . . These are times of pretty severe strain for anybody. . . . Still, we have to carry on, and people like you with remarkable abilities [however vulnerable to nerves] are under a peculiar obligation not to let this sick society down. . . . The only thing that we can really make is our work. And deliberate work of the mind, imagination, and hand, done, as Nietzsche said, 'notwithstanding,' in the long run remakes the world." Louise writes in reply, "Your letter came just now. It made me laugh and cry, so you can see that I have been separated into my component parts."

Edna Millay had been ethereal and elusive and exasperating; Mary Blair had hardly been on the scene; Dorothy Parker had not been intensely involved with Wilson; Wylie was an elegant phenomenon; but Louise was a character who got under his skin and made him deeply angry and deeply sympathetic by turns. Her poem "Evening in a Sanitarium," one of her best, certainly must have resonated with someone who had spent some time there himself: "The free evening fades, outside the windows fastened with / Decorative iron grilles. / The lamps are lighted; the shades drawn; the nurses are / Watching a little. / It is the hour of the complicated knitting on the safe bone / Needles; of the games of anagrams and bridge, / The deadly game of chess; The book is held up like a mask. / The period of the wildest weeping, the fiercest delusion, is / Over. / The women rest their tired half-healed hearts; They are almost / Well. / Some of them will stay almost well always."

In the thirties especially Wilson stepped in as pal, confidante, fellow-student of German, and all-purpose literary guide. In a letter from the *Berengaria* on May 13, 1935, he wrote, "I have never had this kind of companionship with a woman for any length of time ever before in my life, and I became so addicted to it this winter that maybe it's just as well that I'm going away: you and I really have too much fun together. I'm afraid that if I had a little more money I'd decide to spend the rest of my life drinking beer and stout with you." They did a lot of this in actuality, and Bogan retails a hilarious incident of Wilson cursing the lack of gin in the house at Trees in Connecticut and vowing to buy a case that would see them through their evening discussions. The subject matter of these discussions was wide-ranging but essentially literary. A terrific price on a set of Heine provided the impetus for twice-weekly sessions of reading and study in German, which Wilson needed anyway in preparation for *To the Finland Station*. (As always he made work out of play.) "After twenty minutes or so," Wilson writes in his journals, "she would say in a childlike tone, 'Would you like some cake? I'd like to eat some cake!' And I'd have a hard time keeping her to it for half an hour before I went out to Ugobuona's for cake. And she and Maidy [sic] would make me good little dinners and afterwards play me piano duets."

At one point, longing for a good German session, he wrote from Provincetown in 1934—warning that this time it would be non-alcoholic—"So come along wunderschöne Mädchen, with your Eisenblinken and your Augenfunken, and we can go to the beach in the afternoons and have a go at Heine in the evenings."

Wilson's mentoring involved career advice and urging, as well as the laying on of his erudition. As far as the first is concerned, he advised—he insisted on—Louise taking up literary criticism. She was not, by her own admission, a natural critic; while proud of what she had done ("I'm a professional, I can turn it out") she was "a slow writer, and there's no one lazier than I. I hate every minute of it. . . . I remember, in the beginning, sitting at that desk with the tears pouring down my face trying to write a notice. Edmund Wilson would pace behind me and exhort me to go on. He taught me a great deal, at a period when I needed a teacher."

In an act that strangely foreshadows his behavior with Mary McCarthy, he got a woman to sit down and write in a genre that was not her first choice. The pattern was exactly the same: The would-be writer balked but produced. Bogan cried: "I can't, I can't," but Wilson would have none of it. She went on to have a phenomenal run as poetry critic and editor for the *New Yorker*, producing steadily from 1931 to 1969. What she wrote is strangely reminiscent of the Wilson approach to contemporary literature—omnibus pieces that take in a great many new works and are not especially concentrated on any one figure. One particular example is a piece that he suggested to her about anthologies of verse by Victorian women poets; at his urging, she wound up doing the job. The essay in question was also rather Wilsonian in that it contrasted the positive view of marriage he found in the Victorian women poets with the gloomy perspective of modern women poets whom he once referred to as the "Oh-God-the-Pain Girls."

Bogan also absorbed another lesson of the critic, a commitment to literary structure. She didn't want to be just another emotive writer, someone whose work was held together by no structure of "fundamental brainwork." Here, she starts to get into that tricky sexist area that probably ticked Wilson off: "I am a woman, and 'fundamental brainwork,' the building of logical structures, the comparisons, are not expected of me. But it is only when I am making at least an imitation of such a structure that I am really happy." In short, Wilson prompted her to forget about her own prejudices for a while—a state of affairs that proved to be productive for her, though in time she had to fight her demons all over again.

Bogan published a highly praised volume of criticism, *Achievement in American Poetry 1900–1950*. Alas, Wilson the mentor found the volume dull. His disapproval signals a problem in their relationship, something that came up fairly early on. She admired him: "Edmund is the best all-around brain I know," she said in a letter to Theodore Roethke, but she chafed under his authoritarian rule. They fought about taste: He called her ignorant; she called him a snob. And she couldn't stand the political slant to his writing and his sympathetic take on what then seemed like a Marxist revolution: In a letter to Rolfe Humphries she puts down proletarian art and culture, takes swipes at proletarian writers like Mike Gold and Granville Hicks, and mocks the public spectacle of the Stalinist era as "a senseless and blatant kind of mass-gymkhana." Her mockery even extended to Wilson's post-Russia mannerisms: "Edmund has picked up an SU [Soviet Union] form of embrace, rough yet chaste: he sits upright, talking diligently, and grasps your neck with his whole right arm in a sort of bear hug."

But she found him very funny, too. The same night (when all the talk of his trip to Russia had set her off) was a night that found Wilson, Rolfe Humphries, and Louise drinking Tom Collinses on Wilson's bed at the Lafayette Hotel. She wrote Theodore Roethke that "Edmund is *wonderful* on Russia. His story of how Poland . . . looked is priceless." And, she says, his account of Sir Alfred Lyle's poems "was so immense that I slipped out of the bear-hug and rocked on the counterpane with mirth."

Their friendship, emerging from their mutual love of the aesthetic and the craftsmanly, was very durable. Wilson always liked to dwell on the pleasure of her company. Seeing her off on the *Berengeria* in 1933 he does a one-sentence portrait of her that says a great deal: "—In her new brown traveling suit and round brown hat tilted on one side (Do I look like a Lesbian? I don't look like a Lesbian, do I?) she looked like a Steichen or German photograph, standing behind the glass of a window half slid to the side—shy, self-consciously good-looking and proud, making occasional gestures and expressions in answer to our signals."

Those signals never stopped, and Wilson continued to be interested in her in later life. The woman who had once been a gun moll and a svelte bohemian in slacks had become an institution: Dressed in schoolmarmishly conservative clothes, poetry editor of the *New Yorker* since the 1930s, she rejected young poets—John Berryman, whom Wilson admired, among them—and later rose to become a member of the American Academy of Arts and Letters. Wilson never had much use for august institutions (he refused the Academy's offer of membership) and literary lionism (he mocked the public roles of Macleish and Frost); but he stayed true to Bogan when she was a venerable figure rather than a vigorous force. In the sixties, Wilson made it a point to get up to Louise's place in Washington Heights on a number of occasions. In 1961 he dropped in on a Sunday night looking "ghastly," Louise noted. "A little J. Walker helped, but when we went out for a taxi he could hardly *walk*. We pledged fast friendship, however. Time!" There was another rendez-vous with her and Léonie Adams in 1963. The evening was filled with animated talk and, as usual, a big disagreement, this time about Robert Frost, whom in his old sage guise Wilson considered a fraud. Not a lot had changed in some forty years.

· · · · · ·

BY THE TIME Wilson became intimate with the poet Léonie Adams in 1928, he had not had sexual relations with a poet since Edna. For all his adventures in bohemia, his literary contacts, his constant party going, he was essentially a lonely man. Between the de facto end of his marriage to Mary Blair in 1925 and the time of his marriage to Margaret Canby in January, 1930, Wilson's moral compass

was far from steady. He was passing through a period of considerable turbulence. He dallied insincerely with good-time girl Magda
Johann (styled Katze Szabo in the journals); ventured into working-
class territory with Frances Minahan (an affair which had, in Marxist terms, uncomfortable similarities to the sex-for-money exploita-
tion of a peasant by a member of the master class); and wound up
in the compromising position of a marriage to Margaret Canby—
a woman with whom he shared nothing intellectually.

Wilson allowed himself, in the midst of these criss-crossing
liaisons, to become the classic deflowerer, impregnator, mental
deranger, object-of-first-love-and-heartbreak in the life of an important American lyric poet. In her day, Léonie Adams was regarded as
the near equal of Edna Millay. Viewed from certain angles, Wilson's
brief love interest in her was no surprise; they had something in
common. She was an accomplished poet of the symbolist-aesthete
sort, and he was at work on *Axel's Castle,* a book about literary symbolism. She was a Barnard graduate and a friend of his friend Louise
Bogan. She, Bogan, Wylie, and Millay pretty much were Lyric Poetry
Ltd. at the time. But while the others were showy, histrionic, tough
ladies and memorable talkers, Léonie, a gentle mix of the Anglo-
Saxon and the Latin, was shy, sensitive, fragile, vulnerable, and
wholly inexperienced in adult relationships.

Wilson always loved ambiguity and complexity in women, and
there is certainly enough of that in Adams. Her poetry is always
compared to the metaphysicals, but when you look closely, it's not
the images that stand out, but rather the landscapes and the moods.
Wilson praised her for her craftsmanship, writing in the *New
Republic* that her first volume of verse, *Those Not Elect,* was "a very
remarkable book, of which the language . . . seems to branch
straight from the richest seventeenth-century tradition." He goes
on to say that Adams's imagery of "the bright-washed night after
rain" manages to strike "music from the calm summer starbreak,"
but he notes that a solitary gull or a pigeon "seeking freedom in that
space and clarity, is lost in a confusion of cloud and light." Now this
is not a type of verse in Wilson's natural orbit: Although he loved
nature poetry, there are no people here; there is no highly dramatic

scene, no vivid stamp of personality. His strongest responses to literature generally involved all three. Even the language in which he couches his praise seems un-Wilsonian in that it is vaporous and strewn with poetic rather than concrete diction. The praise for Adams's language is certainly not irrelevant to what was on his mind at the time; yet it is forced and strangely weightless. And this is also the case, despite a good deal of tenderness, with the relationship as far as he was concerned. Neither critic nor lover was fully committed.

The facts are these: Wilson knew Léonie before he was separated from Mary Blair; she was at a party that he and Mary hosted at 3 Washington Square and was so drunk that she was put to bed; by her account the bed commenced to spin. Sometime in 1925, according to Louise Bogan in a letter to Rolfe Humphries, "Léonie informs us that the Great Wilson made some hearty passes at her, inviting her to stay at his house." Yet Léonie seems not to have been horrified; on the contrary, she told Louise Bogan who told Mary Blair, "Léonie thinks Edmund is wonderful." Whether it was Wilson's then-married status or Léonie's shyness, nothing came of the first moves in her direction. And when, in 1928, the move did get made, it seems to have been more of an accident than a design on Wilson's part; and this time it seems to have been he who had had too much to drink—for reflection that is, not for amorous action. Léonie appears in *The Twenties* as Winifred, a difficult conquest. He records an episode with Léonie/Winifred that emphasizes his partner's shyness and inexperience, her "little moth flutterings and rabbit startings and soft, tender cheeks and a touch of Spanish sensuality, and obedience and readiness and fright"—and the whole thing causes him to be unsettled and remorseful.

The uncharacteristic flightiness and flutterings of his prose here registers that Wilson was doing something out of character. Although Léonie was an aesthete, she was not the kind of strong personality that he had the most fun with. And furthermore she was a virgin. Wilson also had not anticipated her emotional neediness. The consequences, for her, were quite considerable: She had a miscarriage, suffered from depression, and the confusion of the affair haunted her during her Guggenheim year—so much so that she made a return trip to New York midway through in an effort to clear matters up.

In her letters from Europe, she unpacks her troubles. It seems that when they were lovers she was not sure of him, felt he was not being honest about his feelings, and then felt that she was in the awful position of forcing him to feel more than he did. She was in love, but she was wise to the fact that it was recreational sex for him. Léonie's moth-to-the-flame immolation on the pyre of Wilson's accidental passion resembles nothing so much as Wilson's own short-lived love affair with Millay eight years earlier. Like Wilson, she was the only child of a protective household—in her case, less socially exalted, but with an equally repressive cultural dynamic. She had a Spanish Catholic mother and a strict overseer of a father who actually accompanied her on the subway from Brooklyn to her every class at Barnard College. Brilliant at her studies, after graduation she followed her parents to a farm in Rockland County outside New York and seldom left the family home except to oversee the transformation into print of her well-received early verse and to visit her friend Louise Bogan in Bogan's Village digs.

Sometime in the late spring of 1928, probably in May, Wilson was renting a dismal flat on West 13th Street—little more than one room and bath. The place was like the one described in his play *This Room and This Gin and These Sandwiches*. It was there that he threw the fateful drinks party that found him spinning unreflectively into Léonie's arms; they were together on his bed at evening's end. Then began a comedy of errors that was to be played out all over again, ten years in the future, with a much more experienced but no less psychologically fragile Mary McCarthy.

Wilson compounded the mistake of his one-night stand by attempting to parlay it into a full-blown affair. He wrote in his journal that, if he hadn't been too drunk to really know what he was doing, he wouldn't have gone to bed with her in the first place. When he found out he was the first, he was overcome with guilt. He sought to redeem matters by asking her out again and again over the several weeks remaining until she was slated to sail to Europe on a

Guggenheim. (Wilson also wrote her letters of introduction to John Bishop and Allen Tate, friends already in Europe who could prove useful to her.)

His mailbox must have been a veritable Pandora's Box of worries for Wilson during this period, the eighteen months of August, 1927 through February, 1929. Mary Blair was writing worried letters from hotels on the road about bills and about their neglected daughter, Rosalind; Maxwell Perkins was writing gentle urgings regarding his overdue manuscript of *I Thought of Daisy;* the working-class girl Frances was sending urgent imprecations not to leave messages at her mother's house, messages that her brutish husband could hear about and beat her up for; she was also writing to fix trysting times, "I can come by Thursday at 3:30—need money something terrible"; Magda Johann, aka Katze, whose boyfriend Franz had committed suicide, made a claim or two upon his sympathetic shoulder; Margaret Canby was writing on S.S. *Majestic* letterhead from Southampton of her imminent arrival and of her expectation that they would meet in her hotel for drinks. By the time she got back home to Santa Barbara, he was "Bunny," and she was pinning him down to come out and spend the autumn in a rented beach cottage. Meanwhile tiny, crabbed, handwritten tearstained missives—interspersed with panicky cables—came from the suffering Léonie. They were like small explosions of conscience in Wilson's soul, not the large bombs that Wilson complained Edna had tossed in 1920.

Léonie was now in Paris and asked to be excused for taking him to task, always assuring him that she didn't for a minute mean to suggest that he was a no-good bum who had hurt her miserably—on the contrary, she knew he was the best of men, a prince of a fellow, but she did just have to tell him how fiendishly she had been hurt when she had come in to see him on one of their last opportunities to be together, before she sailed and he had, oh how hurtfully, just gone on reading his proofs from the *New Republic.* Did she mean nothing to him? Well, she cared for him, and she wasn't sorry. No, she wasn't a bit sorry. She didn't want him to think it was necessary to berate himself, or call himself to account. No, that isn't what she wanted at all. But, how she wished he would write to her, by special mail, now that she was in Paris and was, thanks to his having put them together, getting to know his friends the Tates. "THEY WILL NOT HEAR ABOUT IT MY DEAR," she telegraphs him (vaguely referring to her affair). She wrote again the next day and asked him to forget she had ever been so indiscreet as to suggest that the Tates would ever be allowed to get wind of things.

A key letter of hers, dated February 15, 1929, from the Café des Deux Magots in Paris, is a cat's cradle of tenderness and old resentment, noble renunciation and memories of blame. She once thought him "horrid" and "callous" but now does not. What is clear is that it's over and over without acrimony. "Good-bye Edmund dearest. I love you very much and am not sorry about it. I wish I could have talked to you more and been happier with you when we were together. But that was as much my fault as yours." She explains that, although she had suffered a miscarriage in August, only in the fall, when she was resting in England, and thanks to a wonderful doctor there, had she understood the physical distress she had been through. The problem, dating from New York, was caused by "the little organism [that] had gone west some time before." The helpful woman doctor had plucked it out and made a new and much calmer person of her.

Now, Léonie lays it all out: She truly hadn't meant to be so mysterious and so melodramatic. She actually (incredibly, to us) hadn't known she was pregnant or understood what was happening to her body—to say nothing of her nerves—all that fall. Now that the miscarriage was all behind her, although she had always insisted on wanting a child, she could face up to the situation quite serenely. Not only that, but she wanted Wilson to know that she didn't blame him for the mess. Not one bit, and he wasn't to blame himself either. She had recognized all along what it was he was doing. It was simply a matter of his not caring for her as she cared for him. Making more occasions for intimacy with her before she sailed had been his way of letting her down gently. Now that she had told him, she didn't know if he would ever want to see her again; it would be so awkward. But more than anything else she wanted one more interview, when she came back to New York, in the spring, before returning to Europe. The Tates had been awfully nice, but of course, she told them nothing. She would never tell them or anyone. The following August, back in France, she refers to the pain of seeing him again. After that reunion, Wilson confided to his journal that there had been not one interview but a series of "harrowing" interviews with Léonie, from which he had come away with the impression that her miscarriage hadn't been "a miscarriage after all." He was later to contrast Léonie's travails with Frances's. Frances, while gallantly making wry reference to how funny it would be "to have a little Edmund" running around her house, went through the pain and suffering of an abortion and welcomed him back to her arms. He tipped his hat to her in his journal over the classy way she handled it, noting how different it was with Winifred.

None of this reflects particularly well on Wilson, who comes off as a gentleman cad. It must be said in his defense that he never intended to produce this kind of pain—and few cads do. What's more, very interestingly, Léonie is one of a number of women who actually thank him for his grisly contributions to their self-knowledge. A letter from Paris credits him with having "made me be more honest with myself than I had ever been before and I do not know what more you could have done with me." She goes on to say more: "I don't want you to feel that you have done nothing but make me miserable. There were a good many things that I did not know about, and now I feel older. I was pretty undeveloped emotionally for my age and I had no conception of the actual conduct of mature people. I do not know any better way to put it than to say that I am aware for the first time of myself as an absolutely separate creature and of the hostility that must underlie every human contact. So I guess it was good for me after all." Now, understanding the world as full of mature people whose every human contact is full of inevitable "hostility" may not be everybody's idea of a salutary world view. But it does serve as a fair template of the mature artist's tragic vision, and there is no reason to doubt Léonie's sincerity when she says that she believes him to be "on the whole the best person I have known." Wilson, for all his flaws, and for all the dubious merits of his relations with women, must have been doing something right.

Finally there is the Bow to Léonie's Wound to consider: her poetry. She included in her tiny handwriting (for all the world like one of the Brontë sisters') a copy for Edmund of "High Falcon," one of her best poems. This lyric is surely one of the reasons that she, along with Louise Bogan, was given the Bollingen Prize in 1954:

> Send forth the high falcon after the mind,
> To topple it from its cold cloud.
> The beak of the falcon to pierce it, till it fall
> Where the simple heart is bowed.
> In wild innocence it rides
> The rare ungovernable element,
> But once it sways to terror and descent,
> The marches of the wind are its abyss,
> No wind staying it upward of the breast.
> Let mind be proud of this,
> And ignorant from what fabulous cause it dropt,
> And with [how] learned a gesture the unschooled heart
> Will lull both terror and innocence to rest.

After it was all over with Wilson, Adams went on to a distinguished career as teacher and poetry consultant to the Library of Congress, though not as a prodigious writer. Her second volume, *High Falcon,* was published in 1929, the year of her great wound; it was the last to be heard from her until *Selected Poems,* 1954. She wrote a bit in the intervening period, but her time was mostly occupied with jobs at NYU, Bennington, and Barnard. She had married the critic and academic William Troy, an Irish Catholic who brought her over to his faith and taught with her at Bennington. Theirs was a happy—though boozy—union, and Wilson uncharacteristically took a shot at Troy for, supposedly, dragging down a lovely woman with his drunken Irish ways. When, in the last decade of her life, Wilson met her at Louise Bogan's, he unchivalrously blew her off in his journal with the remark that she looked like an unattractive middle-aged English teacher. She is not a presence who rings down the years for him the way Edna did. But as her letters and cables attest, her love for him went every bit as deep as his had for Edna Millay in 1920. For his part, he remembers her in *The Twenties* ("she was so sweet, so dear") with deep affection and reverence for her love: He may have been caddish in some ways but he did not fail to see the strong feelings she sent his way.

. . . . . .

THE WOMEN Wilson had been spending most of his time with through the mid-1920s had been in his sphere. They were cultured, professionally accomplished, and exceedingly talented. But beginning with the breakup of his marriage to Mary Blair, there was a lot of time he had to kill, and at this juncture, we start to see a wilder and less gentle Edmund Wilson. It could be argued that Wilson had seen a good bit of sexual hijinx and post-grad cutting up when he lived with Ted Paramore in 1920—and Ted and Ted's doings will play a part in our story before long. The immediate question is how Wilson moved from the company of a delicate beauty like Léonie Adams to the less romantic regions of the New York sex scene. The answer to this is that the realm of culture and the New York party scene were all part of the same thing.

There were no firm divides between gatherings of intellectuals and gatherings of jazz babies, wild girls, and empty-headed flirts. Wilson, in fact, was socializing with one Katze Szabo—identified by Lewis Dabney in *The Sixties* as Magda Johann, who was apparently a middle-class girl out for a good time—when he was at a party given by Norma Millay. Norma, of course, was Edna's well-informed sister, and Katze was someone who "wouldn't know a line of poetry from an old piece of kindling wood." Wilson fell pretty hard for this rather conventional, long-legged, well-dressed tease. Her profile, so far as we can establish it, has only the faintest traces of culture and the arts.

Gentility and yearning for gentility is there, as is her *"jeune fille* respect for her mother," needlework, the violin, and studied manners. From the get-go Wilson wanted to improve her, giving her a copy of *Vathek,* an eighteenth-century work of prose that he described jokingly as an "improving romance." What he could do to improve this girl is not at all clear. She was notable for antics, public displays of affection, yes-no come-ons, and irritatingly conventional remarks and clichés. Of course, Wilson loved it and considered her phrase "I haven't the foggiest" worthy of recording in his journal. Yet on the positive side this girl appeared in evening clothes, wore alluring white stockings, and provided just the right amount of encouraging banter to keep him going.

He took her to the theater: "Awfully nice of you to drag me along." And she amused him with tales of her childhood and her experiences in a Catholic school. One point that seems especially significant is that she told him about an instance of being socially mortified because she wasn't tended by a hired nurse, like the more well-to-do girls. Anyone who knows Wilson's temperament and sociological imagination knows that he thrived on such details and found great interest in what the women in his life went through. Here, the pickings are slim, and the relationship itself—seemingly protracted for a while by his hope of sex—never amounted to much.

But he did get her to the couch, where she came forth with a surprisingly responsible remark—and the first sensible one in their relationship. The passage in question shows Wilson, probably in the earliest phase of sexual boldness, getting to third base: "When I carried her to the couch—we both had been drinking—she succumbed completely till I began to address myself to her bloomers, when she made me stop—'Why?'—'Because we're both being foolish—We're neither of us in earnest.'" Wilson, of course, was perfectly serious about what he wanted, but she was dead right in suggesting that it was just an adventure for him. "I used to say 'You're so sweet.' or 'You're such a darling!' . . . but I didn't mean it—I felt strongly at the time that that was just what she was not." The relationship was filled with nothing but hot air, a few caresses, and frustration; it turned nasty, and she wound up belittling him, calling him woodchuck-cheeked and shoe-button eyed. This added to the considerable hurt that he had accumulated to date.

The unpleasant episode did not make him cynical, however; and it's important to note that his response was a kind of disheveled chivalry—not a code, but some finer instincts. While thinking about Katze as a "cynical, self-centered and cruel girl," he remembers seeing "her face, with the ordinary consciousness of expression and her make-up relaxed" and is moved to a mood of male protectiveness. He writes of his deep tenderness and pity for women and— "however unamiable the girl"—of his desire "to respect her confidence, protect her reputation and lend her money when she is in debt."

But, as of 1926 or so, about the only good memories were selective memories of Edna and Mary Blair, with some comradely times in the company of Parker, Bogan, and Wylie providing a piquant supplement.

# II

## Proletarians and the Bourgeoisie

"I TOLD HER THAT SHE WAS THE BEST WOMAN DRINKING COMPANION I had ever known," Wilson wrote of Margaret Canby in *The Twenties,* and her letters to him confirm the observation: "Write me on your third slug of Scotch," she says in a 1928 letter. The references that year to "gallons of gin" and drinking on the beach in Santa Barbara are plentiful. Wilson's relationship with Margaret is, as it were, a roundabout story. He knew of her from his early days on Lexington Avenue with his wild friend Ted Paramore, a chum from Hill.

If Wilson was F. Scott Fitzgerald's literary conscience, Ted was Wilson's id. Although he was hardly ever serious, it should be mentioned that Ted did a good bit of writing in his life, beginning with the comic "Ballad of Yukon Jake." A Californian from a very rich old family, he went Hollywood and worked for RKO and Paramount; he wrote the screenplay for *The Virginian.* But like many another he didn't achieve any enduring fame or accomplish anything major. Ted's talent was for partying, epigram making, and orchestrating wildness. Part of the wildness was Florence O'Neill, the model for Wilson's Daisy in *I Thought of Daisy;* she was in Ted's party gang, and is depicted in *The Twenties* in a variety of dizzy and frenetic scenes. She is one of the jazz babies who passes through the journals, though not nearly as memorably as Ted himself. (Her behavior and remarks should be contrasted with the brilliance on display when F. Scott Fitzgerald describes the drunken girls found at Gatsby's house. They're shadowy, but they live.) Strangely enough, Wilson later took Florence's antics and made Daisy into one of the best things in his novel.

But he did an even better job, which is to say, a more authentic and vital job, when he depicted Ted's "jazz high spirits" in his diaries and retailed his pal's out-of-control stories. Ted and his friend Leon Walker occupied a room at the Yale Club. The management tried to get rid of the two of them "because the room was always swimming in gin and garlanded with condoms." Ted and Leon occupied twin beds, with a cocktail shaker on the nightstand. Ted's May Day party had enough "stuff here for a brawl" and "a punch bowl as big as a man." He was famous for a faded art form, living room theater, as well as for singing crazy songs and reciting absurd poems. Margaret Canby reports that Ted composed a version of "Button Up Your Overcoat" in German, and her remarks about him make him sound Cole Porter-like in his louche behavior and polymorphousness. Wilson, the quiet scholar of Holder Court, apprenticed to him.

As for Margaret, she was very much in the picture that far back, evidently visiting the squalid place that Wilson and Ted had set up on Lexington Avenue. The arrangements—which permitted them to entertain females in separate parts of the apartment—allowed Wilson to get away from the proprieties of his old Village pals Larry Noyes and Morris Belnap. Before setting up with Ted, Wilson had been the elegant but chaste bachelor; it's not entirely clear that, like Ted, he was going wild on Lexington Avenue, but the atmosphere was definitely not scholarly bachelor hall.

The arrangement freed him from inhibitions, at least theoretically. In fact, we hear of his reading *Ulysses* and *The Wings of the Dove* "with my feet on the gas heater" and chortling about Ted's exploits and risqué one-liners. But the scene was set. And, for Wilson, during the twenties, there was pretty much no turning back to the monastic life. The decade, despite Wilson's grueling work schedule and the change of jobs and the constant proving of his talent, was a montage of women: Edna, cut to Mary, cut to Louise, Elinor, Léonie, cut to middle-class Katze, cut to women of the lower classes, cut to Margaret. These relationships are very often simultaneous rather than serial. There is evidence that Edmund was seeing Margaret, who was to become his second wife, at the same time that he bedded Léonie, had a growing relationship with a dance hall girl/waitress named Frances (of whom more later), not to mention Marie, a plain streetwalker.

The whole situation is as dizzying as a film told through jump-cuts —at times we don't quite know where we are. The journals do not give precise dates, and Wilson's head must have been so filled with images and sensations of women that he could not quite separate things out into sections. But the one relationship in the late twenties that was to be a real union—the one with Margaret Canby— probably produced as much anxiety as consolation, simply because he found himself, at the end of the decade, in a terrible state of confusion and indecision.

Perhaps his makeshift life as a journalist and his failure to come out with a few solid books in a decade disturbed him, but the truth is he had not been professionally uncertain about his goals and desires. His novel *I Thought of Daisy* was finished, and his first masterpiece, *Axel's Castle,* was well underway, parts of it already published in the *New Republic*. This is not to mention the enormous amount of solid reportage that he had behind him. When he landed in a sanitarium at Clifton Springs, New York—after a couple of hallucinatory episodes—it was not professional indecision, failure, or frustration that had landed him there. The idea is abroad that he was a dry critic without any access to real life and living people, without any ability to create. The fact is that his journalistic pieces are filled with personality and flavor, and he was at work on a book that would make Proust and Rimbaud and Joyce living presences to a generation of readers.

Although not strictly a creative writer, he was more talented than celebrated imaginative writers such as his friend Elinor Wylie. His critical work of the period has aged better than the creativity of most of his contemporaries. And, as a matter of fact, he worked very well on *Axel* when he was in Clifton Springs. What was eating him had to do with the shape of his personal life: fragments, episodes, brief encounters, frustrated yearnings, and nothing amounting to much. He had been a thwarted lover and a married man who wasn't leading a married life.

And now came Margaret; they appear to have gotten serious about each other in 1928, but a remark of Wilson's about her says all we need to know: He writes, in *The Twenties,* that "we did not have enough in common." It does not take a psychiatrist to know what the frightening isolation that he felt was all about. He couldn't decide whether or not he belonged with this new, highly sexual, upper-middle-class, congenial woman who was totally unliterary and unintellectual. The hook between Wilson and Margaret was essentially a matter of sex and class. They connected in bed, and she was from a Scotch-Presbyterian family with Philadelphia roots that was more than a little bit like his own background: the gracious living, the proprieties, the family stories. As he put it in *The Higher Jazz* when referring to Caroline Stokes, the Margaret-based character, she was "a lady as none of my fast little girls had quite been. She was in fact the only available lady that it would be at all possible for me to live with." He also liked, as he says of Caroline, "her piquant combination of dignity with child-like jollity, of rakishness with the British coolness that is the only thing perhaps in the long run that makes rakishness in women tolerable."

His diaries take great pleasure in retailing legends of Margaret's family. She had a nutty, dandified uncle who owned a portrait by the nineteenth-century artist Sully. She also had a wild father who was remarried to a Floradora girl and had been painted by Mary Cassatt. Margaret comes alive against this background, and indeed is in some ways metonymic for it. Wilson swept up the details of her life and made them into a portrait of a class and an era in his journals and in his unpublished novel. It was a world he knew well and was actually more at ease with than that of Edna Millay's tough, plain-spoken mother. Much as he mocked and derided the commercial compromises of his class—and tried to escape—we find him always coming back to their traditions, creature comforts, and networks of relationships. And in Margaret's case, there was the added attraction that she was in Ted Paramore's set, one of the people on the Coast who was connected with the movie business—went to parties with Helen Kane, the "Boop-Boop-A-Doop" girl, and Clara Bow, the "It" girl, the "it" being sex appeal. So there was some diversion —at least for the brief time they were married—to compensate for the lack of intellectual stimulation.

Edmund and Margaret's story really begins as a Ted and Margaret story. Margaret was Ted's old girlfriend and had gone to Yale dances with him. They had been an item before she broke it off to marry James Canby, a Californian like Ted. Ted agonized about the marriage, wrote her a letter professing love, then retrieved the letter, and wished them all the best. But no sooner did they meet again than they "swooned away." Wilson gives us Ted's words: "As soon as we got together it was like an electric current—it used to come over me periodically while I was away—I used to miss her terribly." Nevertheless the union with Canby went forward with all its instability and emotional emptiness. Margaret had a son, Jimmy, in 1918, but the marriage was certainly on the rocks by the early twenties when Ted entered the picture once again.

The object of Ted's (and soon Wilson's) affections was a small, sturdily built and curvy woman of no particular accomplishments, yet possessing definite genteel sex appeal, good humor, and a general buoyancy and friendliness. "I'm a Western girl!" she was fond of saying, and there's no question about the fact that she was straightforward, uncomplex, and ready to get to the point. Wilson always liked this about her.

In 1924 Wilson was out on the Coast trying to promote a script that he had written for the Swedish Ballet. On a trip up to San Francisco, he met Margaret and her roommate Paula Gates, two women on the brink of divorces. Ted fixed it so Wilson would go for the sultry Paula—and he did. But the fling didn't have any particular consequences, whereas Wilson's acquaintanceship with Margaret led to no end of consequences. Of course Wilson was a married man, living with Mary Blair between 1923 and 1925. But, after that, he was on the loose, and although nothing happened during that San Francisco meeting, he evidently formed a bond with Margaret. If Edmund, as a journal entry suggests, "thought her preempted by Ted," he appears to have been undaunted (and perhaps emboldened) by Ted's involvement. In any case, it appears that Ted had spoiled his own chances, even for a solid affair, by having made a fool of himself when drunk at a ball in 1924.

By August 1928—evidently by this time knowing her pretty well —Wilson received a letter at Red Bank from Margaret saying she was "charmed and delighted" that Edmund "can come." He's about to spend the fall at a beach house in Santa Barbara that Margaret had rented for him near her place. This was a culmination of what had been going on earlier in the year when she wrote him that she missed him "terribly" and enjoyed his books. She was saying her "prayers for a bigger and better life."

At the beach Wilson got to work on revisions of *Daisy,* formed his opinion of the California scene, and started getting used to life with Margaret. Her down-to-earth qualities were what Wilson was experiencing while he was depicting the down-to-earth, all-American Daisy. In the midst of all this, he was struck by the colors and light and easy living, but turned off by what he perceived as the monotony of it all. Eventually, Margaret was to accuse him of not liking her hometown, and there is plenty of evidence that he found it "tepid," and that the easy life reminded him of life among the wealthy in Rumson, New Jersey. Nevertheless, he and Margaret had a gin-filled October on the beach; by Christmastime he was back at the *New Republic* and Margaret wrote that she was "feeling like Madame Butterfly."

After New Year's she reported that Ted Paramore felt a Bunny and Margaret union would be "a grand combination." Margaret was nervous about Edmund and wondered whether he was seeing the new year in "blowing a trumpet or trailing a strumpet." They were pretty frank about each other's pasts: "When I boasted about my amorous adventures at the beginning, she asked 'Ever been a fairy?'" And they were equally frank about their infidelities, Margaret knowing from the start about his relationship with the dancehall girl and refusing to be jealous or hypocritical. Edmund didn't have to worry about Ted at this point—he was married, for one thing. 1929 was a bad year for Wilson, his emotional crash preceding the Wall Street crash. He was also not doing well financially, and Margaret characterized them as "a couple of washouts." Added to the tension was the fact that they could not be together on a full-time basis. According to Margaret's divorce settlement, young Jimmy, who was placed by the court in her charge for six months of the year, could not be taken out of the state. The situation resulted in constant shiftings, rented places, and eventually a marriage that was as chaotic and unsettled as his union with Mary Blair. Typically, it was a question of who would be where when.

When they got married in May 1930 in Washington, D.C., there was really no change in their style of life. They spent that summer at Provincetown, taking their flask of "alky and water" to Race Point. Rosalind and Jimmy were with them—Jimmy evidently by special arrangement—but the family group split up by fall. From the start the newlyweds appear to have loved each other; Margaret, Wilson reported in his journals, said she would rather be married to him "than to anyone living she knew." Wilson, although critical to the core of his being, filled his journals with praise of her. A lot of it is physical description. He loved her "turtle paws" and "trim though full figure." She's "a little short plumpish Venus," and is "like a little pony." He was taken with her good manners, "her fine nobly distinguished face"; he pronounced her "a thoroughbred." But the praise didn't clear away a troubling aspect of the relationship: his mind was far away from hers.

This was the period when his journalism was most concerned with the crisis of the Depression, and Margaret was completely elsewhere. Wilson's mind was on the suffering of little families in Brooklyn, the dehumanization of Detroit auto workers, the despair of lost people in San Diego who had come West with hope but who ended it all at "The Jumping Off Place."

She was evidently depressed about his temperament and said, "How can you worry about humanity and see somebody who's so unhappy?" His "great big beautiful masses" were nothing to her. It turned out that the best person in the world to be married to was pretty creepy: "You're a cold fishy leprous person, Bunny Wilson." He was also called "Old Man Gloom Himself." Worse yet, he was a loner, married to a very sociable woman: "Why don't you take me out and jazz me once in a while?—I like people!—You don't like people." The latter remark isn't quite so—it's triviality that gets to Wilson: "the silly sort of life they [Margaret's friends and family] lived in Santa Barbara" is a remark from a minor character that Wilson quotes with some enthusiasm in *The Thirties*. Now Wilson didn't mind reporting on silliness—he is one of the masters of recording L.A. and Hollywood glitz and trashiness—but he didn't like being engulfed by it: "Los Angeles (the goozly-floofy beach, flou, floozy, goosy, goozley, goofy, floozant, flooey, floozid, foozled, the floofy goosey beach." Or "—a pink morocco camel—a pure-white marshmallow of purest driven snow—a peanut brittle pagoda—a Moorish nougat with embedded nuts." And it is also true that he understood his own grumpiness and felt guilty about it: "Perhaps I had gotten more like her [Margaret's] father: extravagance, drinking, arrogance, and tyranny." And, in addition to this, there was the question of children for the new couple. Wilson didn't want them. Margaret mordantly remarked that he should have his warnings about precautions written on his tombstone.

Part of the tension-filled marriage played itself out on West 58th Street, where they had an apartment a floor below the drama critic Harold Clurman, who gave an ugly account. He said that they were nonstop drinkers who fought bitterly and noisily. When Wilson came up to Clurman's place for some reason, he muttered something and collapsed. Back in his own apartment, Wilson pulled down the curtain rods—and generally, if this be true, foreshadowed his abusive behavior with his third wife, Mary McCarthy. There's also evidence that Wilson was a rough lover and that poor Margaret had to endure his sadistic expressions. As per usual, he reports it, complete with perversity: "Used sometimes to make her get on top of me, which she did self-consciously and awkwardly . . . though she had dreamed when she was young that she was taking the man's part with a girl—finally, however, one night she got on top of me and did it with some enthusiasm, but this excited me and I came almost immediately—I told her this and she said, 'Oh that spoils everything!'—had never before me done anything but normal intercourse —I telling her she was like a boy." Elsewhere she complains that he hurt her, that he didn't need her, that she was strictly "a luxury, like Guerlain perfume." Wilson, having done something brutal, was cool enough to report Margaret as saying, "I needn't put any cold cream on either." (He was also enough of an exhibitionist and an obnoxious sexist to refer to his "pink prong." The ugliness of "prong," however, was mitigated by a later reservation. Toward the end of *The Thirties,* he said, "It's very hard to write about sex in English without making it unattractive." He hated the word "*come.*") There's evidence that his unattractive side involved verbal abuse and criticism as well: "Her nightgowns that I used to object to." But she was wise to what was awful about him. He remembered that she liked the old music hall song by Richard Carle, "I Picked a Lemon in the Garden of Love."

In September 1932, Margaret died a horrible death as a result of falling down a flight of stairs in Santa Barbara. Her skull was fractured at the base of her neck, and she succumbed at the hospital after being worked over for several hours. The couple was separated at the time, and she'd been out partying after an illness. The steps were wet, she was wearing heels, and had been drinking heavily. Wilson cried for the only time on record, according to Rosalind. He was in a complete state of shock in New York, and had to fly to the Coast and hold himself together for a funeral and for the formalities with her family. Leon Edel notes that in his characteristic manner Wilson decided to make the flight to California an occasion for recording his surroundings, a way of taking his mind off his grief. It's amazing to see Wilson's powers of control while in mourning, to hear him surveying everything from the rather stiff manners of Margaret's mother to food and erotic episodes enjoyed in the desert with Margaret to "two Hollywood pretties in pink Pierrot costumes opening the covers of an enormous book that said 'Harold Lloyd in Movie Crazy.'" That such a piece could have been written is a testament to Wilson's devotion, the special kind of devotion that he had to offer, his exacting writing. And this writing, at first blush a dispassionate series of non sequiturs, in fact carries considerable emotion, perhaps like the hard-boiled style of Hammett and Chandler. Even when looking at an airline stewardess, Wilson read into the woman's life and imagined a "happiness . . . that I could never know." The very long "Death of Margaret" passage combines obsessive detail, romantic recollection, social history, and soul baring. This may well be Wilson's offering to Margaret: a bouquet at the graveside.

. . . . . .

WILSON PAID a stunning tribute to another woman in his life from the 1920s and 1930s in his notorious novel *Memoirs of Hecate County*. Written in the 1940s with an eye to making money, this erotic classic is a recollection—in turmoil rather than tranquility—of what he had once been through as a man and lover. Written when he was in an upheaval with Mary McCarthy, it deals with other upheavals. Margaret Canby is essentially a minor figure here, a woman named Jo Gates who is his "regular girl" and who is off in California a lot of the time (as Margaret was in real life). When Jo is not around, the narrator-protagonist of the famous section "The Princess with the Golden Hair" takes a walk on the wild side of lower-class New York and has an affair with Anna. She's very closely modeled on Frances Minahan, so closely that Wilson's journals of the 1930s provide sounds and textures that are almost identical to those of the novel. Frances's story is Anna's, for all practical and most literary purposes: The emotions and dialogue are those of Frances and do not involve much imagination or invention on Wilson's part. But what does come into play in the novel is the narrator's feeling.

One of the women in Wilson's montage of the twenties, Frances was very much on his mind—and over at his apartment—during the period of his courtship and marriage to Margaret Canby. Frances was a working-class woman whom he had met in 1927 at the Tango Gardens on 14th Street. She was one of the dancers who entertained men on the town, often men up to no good. This was not exactly a familiar venue for Wilson. The encounter came out of a combination of boredom and curiosity on his part. One night, he wandered downtown, and shortly after that he was in a relationship with a girl who was part of another America. Wilson had of course seen some wild times with Ted, but this was entirely different. And it must have been a terrible shock to his system to be balancing Frances's world—a teeming, sweaty, workaday, and sometimes sordid scene reminiscent of a Reginald Marsh painting—with the dressed up, cocktail-drinking world of middle-class playgirls and boys.

Frances was a "daily worker" at the dance palace and at several restaurants, including Schrafft's and Child's. She was not by any stretch of the imagination a freelance hooker. A married woman, Ukrainian by background, she was living in Brooklyn with her mother and stepfather and her little girl. Her husband was often not on the scene, even when not in prison for car theft or forgery; he was a skinny, upstate Irishman named Albert Minahan from a more middle-class background who had gotten in trouble with the law and who was a menacing presence in her life. When Wilson first knew her, she was willing to make dates, but only late at night. She was also scared of being found out. The "Sam" of Wilson's journals —Albert in real life and Dan in Wilson's novel *Memoirs of Hecate County*—beat her, berated her, and gave her gonorrhea, which she was to pass on to Wilson in that bad-luck year, 1929. Wilson had his nervous breakdown in February, and in September Frances had an abortion; apparently it was Wilson's child. His Christmas present was the crabs.

The affair went on for about ten years. They had quickly become intimate, and stayed that way until the brink of his marriage to Mary McCarthy in 1938. In the meantime, they saw each other irregularly, sometimes were tender and loving with each other, and sometimes were ready to break it off. Trust was strained by the VD incident and, inevitably, despite Wilson's solidarity with the working classes, by the class divide. Frances wanted help, money, sympathy, attention—and ultimately, it would seem—commitment, though not from Wilson. Her "new boy friend" Jerry had serious intentions in January 1934, and Wilson was a year away from being in Russia on a Guggenheim Fellowship. His career was perking, and he had already started on a mammoth project about socialist development and struggle, *To the Finland Station*. Margaret Canby, of course, was a haunting memory, and he refers to the period of 1932 and 1933 as a "sordid" one. The remark refers not only to sex but to the general unsettled, disheveled quality of his life.

Frances provided comfort and a certain amount of reassurance in his essentially cold world. The situation with his mother and money was as tense as always—she doled it out. His journalism, while well known, did not allow him any freedom from anxiety. But Frances was some compensation. She was easygoing, daintily built, humorous, and intelligent. He describes her emotional responsiveness, her sexual readiness, and her freedom from middle-class hang-ups and neuroses. She was no whiner, despite the essentially hideous life of standing on her feet all day as a waitress and having her husband Albert's threats to contend with. Her family worked for furriers and were basically a bunch of low-lifes. Wilson's journals indicate that she worked hard doing the cleaning and housekeeping while her mother—completely indifferent to Frances's welfare—carried on with her own boyfriend, a hugely fat, sebaceous fellow who turned their rented place at one point into a whorehouse. Frances, although not a vestal virgin, was not promiscuous and had middle-class aspirations, ideas of beauty and ugliness, and a general sense of Wilson's worth and the value of having him for a friend and lover.

And they were real friends to each other. She was concerned about his drinking, his crazy habits, his depressions—and she wanted to do something for him. At odd hours, they would be together sharing much more than sexual pleasure. She had opinions of his friends from having heard about them, and by his testimony she was very astute. He credits her common sense, logic, and ability to see through things—qualities that set her apart, of course, from the playgirls. For his part, he offered her help in emergencies, even when he was far away, and small sums of money for necessities; he went shopping for her and her little girl at Bloomingdale's to buy them shoes, and got her treats such as a high-grade line of cosmetics. Most important of all, he came through for her when she had a serious gynecological operation. He was there at the hospital and ready to do everything that his slender means permitted. As usual, he was good in a crisis. It goes without saying that they went out a good deal; he took her to the Russian Ballet, which she enjoyed very much, although she felt the man performing seemed "like a fairy."

The journals of the twenties and thirties have many passages of graphic sexual expression, most of them clinically recorded and by no means slanted to make Wilson look good. He depicts himself as hungry, a bit brutish, rather gross. "Fucking in the afternoon with her dress on—different from anything else—rank satisfactory smell —peculiar zest, on these hurried occasions, added by shoes and stockings and dress, which would be discouraging and undesirable at a regular rendezvous at night." Although in the midst of such stuff he records her joshing him about an occasional bout of impotence, he invariably depicts her in a favorable light. Always the gentleman, strange as that word may seem, given the context, Wilson shows Frances as a life-availing, honest, and truthful individual. Despite opportunities to be devious and grasping, she comes across as an essentially loving and decent person in a pretty loveless and indecent environment.

Wilson's basic account of her in the journals is in keeping with what he writes about his fictional dancehall girl Anna in *Memoirs of Hecate County*. But the journals, while graphic and exhaustively informative, do not quite carry the emotional weight of the story of the two lovers. In *Hecate* Wilson has the scope to warm to his theme—which is nothing less than the intersections of sex, art, and society. The journals, while by no means devoid of feeling, are notes: The fiction is a more coherent presentation of the whole affair. *Hecate* attempts to straighten out the chaos of the journals. The journals give a vague sense of Wilson's conscience, misgivings, fears, and realizations about himself; the fiction gives a full picture. In the novel, Wilson has a chance to depict the two lovers in many intimate scenes, to inject those scenes with his ardors and dejections, and to make it all seem like more than one long fling.

But, if the truth be told, the degrees of intensity are difficult to measure. Both the journals and the novel reveal Wilson's capacity for tenderness as well as his characteristic ability to question his own motives and behavior. In the novel, he appears this way: "I asked her whether she didn't want to sleep, but she put her arms around me and we went to bed together; and that night I felt a satisfaction of possessing her perfectly, completely—my arms around her slim little figure, my tongue in her soft little mouth, and her slender legs twined over mine." This may not be Wilson at the top of his prose game, but it does put paid to the notion that he was a "cold, fishy, leprous person." A scene from the journals—pillow talk 1933—has the same flavor; the two of them are comfortably tucked in, exchanging the relaxed conversation of old lovers and showing their friendship for each other. This is hardly—in either case—the world of using and being used, of brutal transaction.

Nevertheless, Wilson is always complicated and troubled, and almost always honest. In *Hecate* he had the chance to spin out the full story of his anxieties. In fact, there were things that disturbed him about his relationship with Frances/Anna, and foremost among them was the way he mixed politics and eroticism. His affair with the real Frances and his affair with Marxism had reached the high-water mark at about the same time. The sexual affair described took place largely before he visited the Soviet Union in 1935, when he was writing lots of journalism about the travails of Americans during the Depression. At the time that he conceived his great work on the origins of the Russian Revolution, he also misconceived his own motives about Frances. In his journals he speaks of the initial impulse for *Finland Station:* Nobody had ever presented Marxism "in intelligible human terms." And he was excited when he found in this working-class girl his window on Big Ideas. It all seemed perfect from the proletarian point of view: the actuality preceding the ideas, the material conditions undergirding the relationship and the thought processes—the only trouble was the factitious quality of it all.

Frances/Anna, like most Americans, did not want to be a proletarian abstraction, an exhibit of victimhood. And Wilson's narrator in *Hecate*—despite all his fantasizing and fancy talk about going to live in Brooklyn and getting real—comes clean about the situation. Somehow ideology and romance don't mix that well: "I began to feel silly and insincere." He realizes that he has made his proletarians into people who are "practically outlawed from humanity" rather than "meeting on equal terms." Marxism here is not only "bad taste," but does "violence against everything that was good between us." He dropped the subject with Frances/Anna, but we cannot for this reason: Wilson's aesthetic in *Hecate County* and his attitude in real life are strongly colored by socialist realism. He may recognize the contradictions in his position, but the gritty realistic style is perfectly suited to both the book he is writing and the woman he is writing about. That style is essentially naturalistic, obsessed with material conditions, and insistent upon close observation of economics and class. Although his occasional lapse into cheap Marxism in his narrative is heavy-handed and distorting, his focused attention on the real world helped him break through as a writer. And Wilson has also, in the process, become self-critical and has shown that there's more to Marxism than slogans and formulae.

In *Hecate County* Wilson went far beyond his twenties vision. He finished celebrating the Kingdom of Art in *Axel's Castle*; in the novel he took a long, mocking look at debased art, artiness, and upper bohemian pretentiousness in the person of Imogen Loomis. Based on a girlfriend of his named Elizabeth Waugh, she's the woman that our intellectual hero, an art historian, hangs out with when he's not with Anna. She has allure, class, come-hither mystery, and is a walking art object, complete with period costumes; Anna, of course, is a woman who wears a shabby dress and can't afford a girdle. Imogen ultimately fails the test of life and love (as we shall see), and the hero of *Memoirs of Hecate County* gives pride of place to his working-class dream girl, the woman whom he has mistreated by making her an object of pity and a category, but with whom he has discovered his best instincts. Wilson the narrator of the story has told how he entered a new phase of life, one which in his real life would last through the decade and color his relationship to women.

He was the reporter as artist who is wise to pretensions—be they aesthetic or Marxist. In *Hecate County* he wrote that he had left behind the concepts of Clive Bell, the British critic who emphasized the autonomy and significant form of modernist art. That vision was essentially highbrow, cerebral, and devoid of the sweat and pain of humanity. The passion that the narrator had for painting —his way of seeing it as an expression of man's whole condition in the material world—carried over into his relationship with Anna. That passion "had brought me to her through the prison of the social compartments, across the clutter of the economic mass . . . [and] had kept me with her, happy, so long." He has found that there was something deeply satisfying about Anna's way of looking at life and his old Kingdom of Art was a dead end.

The problem is that Wilson, the writer and man, knew himself too well in one sense, understood his own tendency to be carried away by beauty and by love of ideals; what he didn't understand— and what was never resolved in the 1930s—was that there are sur- prise combinations in the romantic life and people who embody them; these can be as dangerous as worship of beauty or humani- tarian ideals. There are also such things as heedless passion and naiveté. After Wilson got through early middle age—with misad- ventures involving the wrong women—he found another dream girl, Mary McCarthy, a young woman who had it all. Or so he thought. But that story is preceded by a number of experiments of the flesh and mind.

. . . . . .

ANOTHER DEAD END, like the Kingdom of Art, was the relationship with Elizabeth Waugh, the woman on whom Wilson modeled the character Imogen in "The Princess with the Golden Hair." She was a beautiful, highly romantic, and mannered woman in real life (and in the fiction), and her emotionalism and tendency to poeticize was a headache for Wilson, something he wanted to escape from—even as he was tempted by it. Elizabeth Waugh came from a solid upper- middle-class New Jersey family, DAR on her mother's side, and, on her father's, business people who had amassed considerable wealth in the manufacture of valises and steamer trunks. Her father was something of an oddity for his class in that, having lost his inheri- tance in a photography venture with a dishonest partner, he forsook money making and became involved in arts and crafts, gaining a name for himself as a silversmith. From an early age, Elizabeth was encouraged to think of herself as an artist, and benefited from her father's connection with painters and craftsmen at Woodstock, New York. She studied with the American painter Robert Henri and at age eighteen married the son of a major marine painter, Frederick

Judd Waugh. Coulton Waugh, the son, was himself a talented artist, somewhat in his father's shadow but nevertheless capable of doing successful commercial work in New York. He drew the popular comic strip "Dickie Dare" for Associated Press. He and Elizabeth also had a good business in Provincetown called The Hooked Rug Shop. They were collectors of rugs and ship models, and their place was a Provincetown institution.

Wilson knew Elizabeth as far back as 1930 because of a connection with another local shopkeeper. He developed a strong passion for her—to all outward signs merely a friendship—by 1933. We have little of his side of the correspondence but a great deal of hers. Although she is not among his most intelligent passions, she could now and then turn a phrase, and seems to have gotten something right in a December 1933 letter: "You are a guileful lover and straight thinker." She supports those who insist upon Wilson's cold side by referring to his "hard heart." He is obviously importunate from the start, but he had years ahead of him before the affair was consummated.

From the very beginning, she was head over heels in love with his mind, his accomplishments, and his judgment. "If you were just prose I'd be mad about you!" But Wilson was never just prose, and the whole package was compelling, but too much for her. She had an essential emptiness in her life, despite the work in the shop and her painting and writing. The last of these yielded a book on rug weaving and some stories for young people. Her marriage was stable enough, but doesn't seem to have been particularly rich in companionship. Her career was not quite a career, but not mere time filling either. She was an artistic and erotic wannabe, and Wilson filled a gap in her life. Her epistolary blandishments, endearments, compliments, fancy language, cuteness, professions of loneliness, and mooniness are of monumental proportions. These are to be contrasted with what she called Wilson's "stark epistolary style" and its "crystals" of meaning. Her letters are filled with the kind of excess that he deals with in "The Princess with the Golden Hair," and she at one point gave a good characterization of herself: " I have always been medieval essentially." She loved aesthetic Catholicism, would have liked to live in a nunnery and illuminate manuscripts. This sort of thing is exactly what Imogen Loomis in Wilson's story embodies and talks about.

Wilson's Imogen lives like a period piece, dresses in antique costumes, resides in a faux Tudor house in Hecate County, and is bewitching. She has Arthurian language on her tongue, and, propped on a table, a framed Elizabethan ballad about *The Story of David and Berseba*. The Wilson persona in the story is enchanted by this flummery, goes along with the game, and essentially is under her spell. This is not of course the only illusion in the book: Anna, as exhibit A for the proletariat, is Imogen's opposite number, also a figure to build false dreams on.

In real life, the facts of Edmund and Elizabeth's four- or five-year romantic dalliance are abundant enough, but often swathed in her fanciful terms. In sheer wordage, she has a lot more to say in her eighty-some letters than he does in his scattered few; but though what she produces is much bulkier, Wilson gets many more crystals out of his journal entries and passages about Imogen in the "Princess." To her, he is "Ed, dearie," something almost unthinkable to people who know Wilson and his work. He's also someone that she routinely sends "pink love" to—this being love from a baby girl. While being about as up in the air as it is possible to be, she was also not without insight, and remarks on how "the flesh and the devil meet so charmingly in your [Wilson's] person."

She was a no yes-no girl from the start, and must have exasperated Wilson with remarks like, "You have . . . made me come to life," (when, to his mind, she had thus far allowed him to do no such thing). She probably employed every method of praise and pulling back known to womankind: The letters are a torrential downpour of affections and fears. "No doubt my letters are an annoyance": no argument about that. "There are cleverer women," but none who love Bunny more. Wilson refers to her "adolescent romantic illusions"—one of his crystals.

The affair got hot, yet still was not consummated, by 1936, or so our sources say. She became the aggrieved beloved, saying that "even your damn plays get into my fallopian tubes." He was enjoying his rough love play with her, but she complained, "My lip is very sore and red . . . where you bit it, you beast!" They were frank with each other in conversation, and she knew about Frances, his friend Louise Fort, and his brief fling with his cousin Helen Augur (about whom more later). There was a good deal of anger and pain on both sides. She said, "You close up tight." She referred to her "mental agony," pain that was worse than birth pain, that caused her to want to lash out and bite. The last references, from January 1937, strongly suggest that this was the period of consummation. The places in question were Wilson's house in Stamford and a hotel in Concord, Massachusetts, where they seem to have been skulking around and having sex on a dirty weekend. The flavor of this material—at least as expressed by her—is full of strife, but there's also plenty of language out of the cliché warehouse: "Darling, After I saw you, I was carried away on a flood of passion such as I have never known. . . . When you didn't call up, I knew that it was all off, but I took the shock like a good soldier." And, following one of her several break-offs: "Don't hate me. I couldn't stand that." She says she is ready to leave him "free to love someone else. . . . I've had enough agony."

Wilson's journal entries on the affair are in the raw and frank mode, and Elizabeth comes off as a more sexual creature than does the essentially frigid Imogen in "The Princess with the Golden Hair." "I was surprised to find her completely naked . . ." "[H]er sex was the only beautiful as distinguished from sexually stimulating one that I had ever seen." When, after a not very satisfactory first entry, he goes at it again, he found her "brimming" with "female fluid . . . her buttocks were at once lovely looking and hard and tight instead of soft." On yet another try, "when I beckoned to her, . . . she said 'Now you want me to make love to you.'" She accuses him of looking "like one of those monks in Boccaccio." It was somehow a little wounding to his vanity to be likened to a lecherous cleric. The literal sense of her remarks, however, is quite complimentary. "I never saw such virility. You're so masculine. . . . I'm only used to once." And she wasn't frightened, just excited. "It's all new to me!"

In a September letter, we get the aftermath of her feelings, and the inhibitions and fears expressed seem very similar to Imogen's in

"Princess": She complains that her nightgown was covered with bloodstains. "It was as if you had been sleeping with a virgin." This suggestion of innocence is perfectly in keeping with Imogen's coy manner in Wilson's novel. And the same letter has the accusatory tone of Imogen: "Are all the others like that too?"

The end was in sight, and you're-so-woven-into-everything was her theme. She still loved him, but late in 1937 she wrote that she couldn't do "the sin part"—evidently because she "had a winking eye." Meantime Wilson had been making other plans, ones that included Mary McCarthy from October onward. In November, he paused to reflect in a poem called "November Ride." The piece combines a bleak and elegiac quality with some luxurious descriptions of Elizabeth. They sometimes went horseback riding at the house in Connecticut, and Wilson has composed a suburban version of Browning's "The Last Ride Together."

> And you run with me still
> In the stones and the cold
> Till all I can feel
> Is for round and for gold—
>
> Gold white, gold, red, round arms, rose-dotted breasts,
> That long space between hip and knee, the striding thighs,
> The vase-line of the throat that answers to the waist's,
> The great round-lidded, heavy-curtained eyes;
>
> The short dear feet that firm the perfect line,
> Red ringletted gold hair that harbors hidden angers,
> White skin like goldleaf beaten smooth and fine,
> Soft as the goldsmith's chamois to the fingers—
>
> . . . Back home—dark now—
> High eaves—hard light—
> Dogs bark far
> On dark farms—
> Hard now—bad tonight!

Although Wilson's diction is a lot more Yeatsian than Browning-esque, the occasion that prompts it is the same as the Victorian poet's. The big difference is Wilson's tone at the end, that devastating end. Browning was an optimist. The poem of course gives no explanations, but "The Princess with the Golden Hair" tells us what, in the end, the problem was. Imogen is a witchy neurotic whose neurasthenia (taking the form of back complaints rather than a winking eye and a fear of the "sin part") is too disturbing for the narrator to handle. He gets the impression that she's not a physically fragile woman but a mental case, and this fear is even more powerful than his fear of Anna's venereal disease. Somehow, the narrator pulls himself together and gets back in bed with the proletarian. In real life the breakup with Elizabeth was probably caused by a combination of elements: the exigency of a new love, the fear of madness, and the weightlessness of the affair. We can only suppose that Wilson is feeding off fears from the period of his breakdown, perhaps fears of being like disturbed people that he knew. Elizabeth Waugh, be it remembered, was not a neurasthenic poet; she was the neurasthenic owner of a craft shop. Somehow, the advice that he dispensed elsewhere about the artist overcoming psychic wounds did not seem to apply to this case. Elizabeth's neurosis was not the attendant circumstance of any real creativity.

The affair was over.

Elizabeth's life was to be a short one. But before she died in 1944, there was a chance for a few cordial exchanges: Her New Year's greeting in 1939 congratulated Wilson on his "cute little red-headed son" and sent good wishes "to you and the little society." Subsequent notes politely ask after Mary and the boy. He wrote her mother a letter in 1947 in which he took loving stock of her qualities; these included her gift for friendship, her promise, and her ability to help him "through some difficult years."

·  ·  ·  ·  ·  ·

THE IMOGEN in "The Princess with the Golden Hair," based so closely on the life and times of Elizabeth Waugh, is a wonderful foil for Anna, but also an important contrast with several other women in Wilson's life from the late twenties through the thirties. These minor players—a middle-class friend Louise Fort (styled "K" in *The Thirties*), a mysterious "O" also in *The Thirties,* a prostitute named Marie, a colleague Betty Haling and Wilson's second cousin, a writer named Helen Augur—brought out Wilson's earthier side and, when described, have little of the adornment that he gives Imogen. Whether proletarian or bourgeois, they are raw physical presences from start to finish.

An old friend like Louise Fort, someone Wilson knew from the Sacco and Vanzetti period, became a fairly straightforward sexual partner. Louise, from a well-to-do Boston family, was one of a number of women whom Wilson identifies by a letter preceding that of her first name (a system that was to break down by the forties); whether out of chivalry or fear of lawsuits, the treatment of these characters by initial does not preclude their being discussed in nicer contexts by name. The Louise affair has some of the familiar Wilson ingredients, including alcohol, out-of-control behavior, and crazy blandishments. They spent time holed up together in his house on 53rd Street (a rented old frame structure, still standing, that he took for himself, subletting portions of it to friends of friends). He was shut off from the outside world, even, weirdly enough, for a time, from work. "I gave up trying to do anything. And would succumb to cocktails late in the morning." He was made so "vibrant and delicately sensitive by love that I snapped like a violin string." He was pronounced by Louise to be "the best sleeper-with" there was; his reaction to the affair was fairly absolute in terms of what he was going through in those days: "It seemed to me at the time my most animal, though most extraordinary, experience of the kind."

The whole thing was part of the creepy side of Wilson's romantic life, and he recorded the sadomasochistic and fetishistic pleasures they were trying to enjoy. She liked to be spanked, and Wilson was willing to oblige, although without much enthusiasm. "I had some inhibition about hitting her and could only seem to do it clumsily, not landing my blows squarely." He fantasized about buying a whip but that quickly passed. Meanwhile, she was satisfying his lifelong foot fetish in a big way. This little kink in his nature is most notably seen in *I Thought of Daisy* where he compares Daisy's feet to "little . . . cream cheeses." On the present occasion, Louise stimulated him with the tip of her foot. "After that we went upstairs." The Louise Fort as "K" encounters show us that Wilson did not necessarily have to be enjoying the sex in order to enjoy recording it:

I, having the night before had very little sleep and being weary
with my drinking and exertions, kept tending to fall asleep; but
she was full of interest and ideas—wanted to know what "funny
way" I'd like to do it, kept getting on her knees and presenting
her rump, which I was quite unable to cope with. She said that
she had been liking it that way lately. She sat up and dangled
the nipple of first one breast then the other for me to suck,
which I did in a moribund manner (they seemed to hang more
now that she was thinner.) She kept talking about doing it
"funny ways" and I said, trying to calm her, that there weren't
very many things you could do. She finally got up and dressed.

Figuring in this unintentionally funny sexcapade were also Louise's
general bawdiness, love of obscene lyrics, and sexual grandiosity.
She fancied herself an Irish queen and felt that she "ought to be
carried around in a bed." True enough, this mixes fantasy with sheer
lust, but it's different from the Imogen affair in the sense that this
woman did not have the delicacy and idealism of Elizabeth Waugh.
She was uninhibited: "When I told her how well she looked in bed
she said it was because it didn't embarrass her the way it did some
women. She could never see why you should be embarrassed." And
she also commented on Elizabeth Waugh as "this quince," "this
bitch that won't sleep with yuh." In full recognition that he was
doing so in front of a nonliterary person, Wilson recited Yeats's "On
a Political Prisoner"; the high romanticism of the poem caused him
to break down in tears. Louise's reaction is not recorded.

Someone styled "O" in The Thirties, a woman with a dark bang,
is also middle-class and, while there are references to her "fineness
and distinction" and "beautiful dignified manner," the passages
involving her are pretty much a matter of sexual transaction—and
not very satisfactory at that. Wilson was shaken by his inability to
perform, even though he was terribly drunk at the time. He was
capable of recording her complete self-possession, apparent coolness, and what sounds like her upper class "drawling voice," when
the encounter is pretty much a humiliation for him.

At a different end of the social spectrum, he encounters Marie,
a call girl from his lonely days in the middle twenties. With moments

lagging and no regular girl, he picked up an olive-skinned, apparently Mediterranean woman, and quickly got down to business. But business as usual for him always included social profiling, artistic comparisons, aesthetic musing, and thorough stocktaking of the woman's charms. Wilson could never be accused of having anonymous, meaningless transactions: Raw as they were, his sex scenes were always full of humanity. In Marie's case, he found out that she had a Catholic upbringing in a convent school and was the victim of what we would call sexual harassment of minors—a priest kissed her passionately; she told him it was a sin. "Father James don't you know that's a sin?" but his response only "stunned her with some technicality that she didn't understand." With Wilson, there were no technicalities. He was interested in details, apparently for their own sake, and in experience, apparently for its own sake.

The attitudes that undergird his dealings with Marie are by no means simple. Yes, it's all about sex but, at the same time, in the passages that involve her, he tries to explain his philosophy of writing and his view of reality. He's disturbed by the fact that "literature" often distorts and misleads; he's trying in the journals to record a nonthinking world of sheer physicality. This 1920s musing was written right before *Axel's Castle* where there's a great deal of material about breaking through into life. Wilson wants to do that, and his gross, rather off-turning descriptions of Marie are a seeming attempt to get to the substratum of things, the naturalistic condition of people. He always critiques people, and Marie gets compared to the whores who probably posed for madonnas in the work of Italian Renaissance painters. But the burden of what he's writing is about his strange encounters with nonrationality and sexual abandon. With this call girl, he gets what he wants by lip-biting, and by entering the "obscure and meaty regions" of her body. The word "obscure" says a great deal. This is some kind of an adventure in the unknown, and a short vacation from thinking. Wilson seems to be trying to do that very modern thing—recorded in writers from Eliot to Beckett: get out of his own consciousness. But soon—actually, just after his call girl has left—he's back reading. Who does he read? Matthew Arnold, of all people, the poet of agonized consciousness.

Just as he can't entirely stop thinking, Wilson can't seem to close his aesthetic eye. Much as he wants to be caught up in the moment, he can't help giving a full report of what a 105th Street call girl's headquarters was like. Marie was evidently having her talent managed by someone of means, and the appointments in the apartment, department store fresh and slick, catch Wilson's eye. There's a raspberry red satin bedspread that seems to have been put on like shellac and an array of photographs, evidently introduced to give the place a homey touch. Wilson the anthropologist is interested in pictures of youth and the convent school. Now, all this seems to foreshadow his curiosities about Anna, the problem being that the emotional affect is rather faint here. About all he can come up with in terms of Marie's endearing ways is her neatness in hanging up her clothes and his suit. The portrait therefore stands as a strange mix of wanting to submerge himself in the underworld and to keep a close eye on it at the same time.

His instincts were more generous—and his crude side was not on display—when it came to an old gal pal Betty Huling. Betty had put in years at the *New Republic* and they had known each other from the mid-1930s. She was not one of their writers or editors, but her proofing and research were extremely important skills, which Wilson availed himself of, both at the magazine and when he had severed his ties with it. Betty was from an upper-class family in Larchmont, graduated from Vassar, and was in close touch with her fuddy-duddy mother and father. The father was a rich man who had never worked a day, but started to hurt during the Depression years. The mother was a DAR, and there was a good deal of talk at home about sports, country clubs, gardens, and class distinctions. This narrow atmosphere was not all that far from things that Wilson knew about from his younger days in Red Bank. He spent some time with the family and from the start developed a friendly, hearty, and essentially untroubled relationship with Betty. Although they had a couple of bouts of sex in the thirties and after he left Mary McCarthy, there was something not quite serious about his romantic attachment to her. Betty's world was one of work and serious playing and drinking and tennis. Wilson joined it with good humor and good grace, always stuck by her, but realized that some underlying problems she had—mental fragility and plain old lack of beauty—made her vulnerable and somewhat sad. In "The Princess with the Golden Hair" she's a very minor character named Helen Hubbard—one of the strapping girls ("always hearty," "a real Amazon") who were in long supply in fashionable suburbia and going no place maritally. For all Wilson's retailing of sexual adventures and romantic yearnings in his journals, there's not a word about Betty in this regard.

She's known for her "tremendous cocktails" (the best recipe consisting of applejack, gin, and pink grenadine); her Stutz (which was in dangerously ramshackle condition and given the nickname "Lambie"); and her 1920s holdover antics and excitability. She evidently had a terrific figure, but a rather thick-featured face. She was a sport and incredibly *sportif*, besides being an extremely reliable worker.

In 1937, Betty was active in trying to get a union at the *New Republic*. She "agitated the old ladies in the subscription department, pointing out to them the advantages—of old-age insurance etc.—which would accrue to them under the contract and of which they had never dreamed." By the early forties, things had evidently gone wrong for her at the magazine, and she was out, looking for work. Wilson, as usual, took part in the search, tried to help her to get on the *New Yorker* (but without success); he was delighted when she got a job on a cheesy, short-lived slick magazine named *Atlas* and held it for a while. In the fifties, she did some proofing for Wilson that involved fairly high level attention to errors; he succeeded in getting her paid by Farrar Straus. But her life situation was pretty grim at this point, in that she had mental problems, health problems, and no decent man on the scene. Wilson had always been disappointed in what she came up with in the way of boyfriends, mostly vulgar seducers who were quite below her standards. She went along with such characters, but nothing ever worked out. Her dating and relating was mostly a question of twenties style wildness—such things as being found by her father on the floor biting a boyfriend's ankle. It goes without saying that she was thoroughly juiced on such occasions, and the father was shocked by the fact that a daughter of his would drink gin; the mother was equally shocked that a daughter of hers would drink whiskey. Wilson, playing the role of Dutch uncle, shook his head and offered sensible advice.

Wilson's loyalty to Betty Huling is touching and true and in character. When she was sick and hard up in the late sixties, he proclaimed himself rich from a prize and paperback sales (hardly the truth), and pressed money on her for hospital bills. She died shortly after, in 1969, three years before Wilson. With her death, the old crowd from the *New Republic* was gone.

A minor episode in Wilson's romantic career comes to the fore in *The Thirties* and in *Upstate:* his relationship with his second cousin, Helen Augur. The descriptions of Helen in the books are not sensual or anatomical, and there is no attempt to escape the critic's role: never for a minute lost in a "nonthinking world," Wilson has a fling with someone he dissects. Helen was a historical novelist of considerable accomplishment. She also wrote magazine pieces and books for young adults. During a full career she wrote material for the WPA and worked as a foreign correspondent. She was certainly an intellectual, yet Wilson only grudgingly allows her this distinction and never refers to her writing. In point of fact, he is irritated by the idea that she's an intellectual, saying that she's "not enough of one." But her letters are quite literate, filled with references to reading, writing, and thinking about issues. At the time she was reading *To the Finland Station,* she was also rereading *Ulysses.* Nevertheless, there's something about her that gets his back up.

Helen was a beautiful blond, and cut out of the same social cloth that he was. Her family ties with him were through the Bakers. Thomas Baker was an enterprising man up in Talcottville in the first third of the nineteenth century. He was a Jacksonian Democrat, against the old feudal way of New York State, and a business go-getter. Helen—no slouch when it came to forging her own destiny and making a living—signs a 1935 letter "very Baker-ish." She also knew how to maneuver herself out of a bad marriage to a rich man and land on her feet (in her case, in a penthouse on South Stuyvesant Square). She and Wilson had their fling in 1937 and 1938, and, as in the case of Elizabeth Waugh, there appears to have been more intensity and a greater emotional investment on her side than on his. "I've missed you, monkey," is not matched by any unusual term of affection from him.

She's terrified to be away from him in the aftermath of their love-making, feels that he has done a great deal for her, and is especially grateful for the fact that their love had made her less venomous. Evidently, Wilson had provided her with her first orgasmic success. He gets a lot of credit: "You're the only person in my whole life that has ever wanted me to be the kind of woman I want to be." She credits Wilson with "an instinct for what is true and what is phoney" —and this rings true for people who know his writing. He evidently was able to put his finger on her egotistical nature and the way it blocked her happiness. She admits to being "unsatisfied all these years," and that sense of emptiness does seem to come from being self-absorbed and stubborn. She was also a controlling person who has the idea of control on the brain: She credits Wilson with being able to keep a woman in line, live up to the strong traditions of great-grandfather Baker, and generally run the show.

Whatever the truth of this, the fact is that he reports on her manipulative behavior when, years later, she's up in Talcottville for an extended stay. When these two cousins are together—with romance long in the past—they drive each other crazy. She's the Baker woman, bustling and vigorous and interfering, and her man-agement technique in the household "affects me like my mother's." She's at this point a "substitute sister," but one who is not simpat-ica. Wilson the critic indicates that she "doesn't grasp what's going on around her," and that "when she tries to get in touch with you by finishing your sentences, she always gets the sense wrong." Wilson, with his nastier side in the ascendant, refers to her "failure as a woman," an extreme judgment for someone who often seems like an egotist himself. He's also extremely hard on someone who called him, in 1950, "my favorite critic." She had said from the start—back when he was her "monkey"—that she was proud to be related to him, even distantly. She was glad to get any lecture on ideas from "the old hand." And she had the self-knowledge to be envious of his settled life in the 1950s: "I'm such a stray dog." But his portrait of

Helen tends to be peevish, resentful, and bitter. He has time to read and praise a lot of minor work by acquaintances, but somehow she's brushed off. Again, as is the case with Elizabeth Waugh/Imogen Loomis, one gets the impression that her temperamentalism turned him off.

At the time of their affair, her problems were significant enough for her to see Dr. Sandor Rado, the psychiatrist who would treat Mary McCarthy a few years later. Helen wanted to discuss "this ego-business" with him. And this seems partially to be the problem in her relationship with Wilson; in addition, there wasn't enough bulk, in terms of talent, to compensate for her difficult nature. That said, Wilson's relationship with Helen does not show him at his best. She gave him, when they were together as lovers, a good deal of affection, wanting to be with him rather "than just *thinking* myself under you, in every sense." Her crude pun is a concession, an emotional cry, but hardly the reaction of a bossy narcissist. Wilson gets this one wrong.

. . . . . .

AT THE END of the thirties Wilson was feeling certain letdowns and trying to brace himself up with prospects of new career triumphs and greater romantic satisfactions. Nothing had quite satisfied him, not even his marriage to Margaret Canby. During this period, he had found at times sex without intellectual companionship; at other times his life was all intellectual strain and overwork without any truly satisfying release. Wilson, like many an American writer or American male, was determined to have it all. The prospect of all was on the horizon in 1938.

# III

## The Intellectual and the Cosmopolitans

"A MAN HAD BETTER BE FEELING FIT WHEN HE TAKES HER ON," William Carlos Williams commented about the prospect of a relationship with Mary McCarthy. Edmund Wilson at forty-two—wounded veteran of two marriages, one ecstatic romance, numbers of affairs with women of his own class, and assorted transactions with women of the underclass— thought he was prepared to satisfy and be satisfied by a complex, troubled, and brilliant young critic. She was only twenty-five when they met, but already a practiced player of the sex and the city game. Divorced from actor Harold Johnsrud whom she had married right out of Vassar, she had put in some serious time as a love object for the leftwing set associated with the *Partisan Review*. She was by her own admission promiscuous, the kind of young woman who could remark on entering a room that she had slept with most of the male guests. At the time she was introduced to Wilson, at a lunch meeting, she was the girlfriend of Philip Rahv, the magazine's editor and a top-notch intellectual who concentrated on literary modernism and Marxist criticism. Rahv was an autodidact, an immigrant, a graduate of the Providence, Rhode Island Public Library, but this new older man was upper-middle-class and reminded her of the world of Vassar and her own lawyer grandfather. And she in turn made the established critic think of what he had been missing—a young and beautiful woman of his own sort, both socially and intellectually. She was a drinker and a terrific talker, spoke his language, shared his aesthetic values, loved the same books—and wanted to get ahead in the literary world. But when their affair started they were both in for some shocks. He was getting ready to be pleased and comforted and sexually gratified by a completely new kind of woman—a partially formed intellectual with solid bourgeois credentials who fit his specifications. The trouble was that Mary was not the discriminating critic's dream fusion of mind and accommodating emotion. Impulsiveness, high-spiritedness, volatility were more a part of her makeup than warmth and dependability.

Her incisive mind also cut through his selfish motives, spoiled his romantic illusions, and refused to handle him as a good middle-class wife should. She matched him as a dominant personality and was every bit as demanding and critical. And she added guilt and disappointment and bad family memories to his fund of faults—his high expectations, his nasty drinking, and sarcasm. This was not to be the household of George Eliot and Henry Lewes.

The mismatch began at a lunchtime meeting in October 1937. Wilson had been invited by the *Partisan Review* "boys" (as Mary called them)—led by Rahv and Fred Dupee—in order to get him to contribute to their first issue. And they brought a beautiful young woman who was inappropriately dressed to the nines for a simple business meal in a downtown eatery. Wilson was not very animated (having hit the bottle pretty hard the night before) and chose club soda. But he was evidently taken with the girl. A couple of weeks later he invited Mary to dinner along with Margaret Marshall (who had co-authored, with Mary, in 1935, a series for the *Nation* entitled "Our Critics, Right or Wrong"—Wilson being the only critic to make the cut into their first category.) Dupee, anticipating a dry evening, took Mary to the bar of the Hotel Albert beforehand for fortifying cocktails. Mary had three daiquiris. Tiddly when she arrived at the restaurant—a well-known Village establishment called, as if Wilson's choice had already been made, Mary's—she found Peggy Marshall was already there. Wilson compounded the bibulous comedy by ordering several rounds of double Manhattans. At dinner, he filled his glass and their glasses again and again with the cheap house Italian red. He polished the evening off, in more ways than one, with B&Bs all around. (Mary later commented that Wilson always believed in getting thoroughly and systematically soused.)

During the proceedings, Mary evidently talked a blue streak and managed to give Wilson her life story—orphaned at six, convent bred, living rich on one side of the family, poor and abused on the other—all to be famously reported in her later blockbuster *Memories of a Catholic Girlhood* (the Presbyterian-Jewish affluence of her mother's family got left out of the title). Not surprisingly, as they left, Mary fell unconscious to the pavement. Wilson checked the girls into the Chelsea Hotel, paying in advance, after which he took himself home to Connecticut in a taxi. Mary awoke the next morning exceedingly puzzled to find herself with a female roommate.

Wilson evidently liked the ploy of courting in twos, and before long he took the young women to a second dinner at Mary's, after which he invited them to come back with him to Trees, his rented guesthouse in Stamford. The talking marathon began again, fuelled, as usual, with drink. Marshall retired to her room. What Mary did then is open to question, and exactly why she did it is still a matter for conjecture. Unlike Margaret, however, she was unwilling to conclude the evening so abruptly. She sought Wilson out in his study, either because she wanted to "talk" with him, or, in a different account, to get a book to read. In any event, wrote Mary: "When he firmly took me into his arms . . . I gave up the battle," and things went on from there. The motivation and the meaning behind it is not at all clear. Did she intend to seduce him? Did she intend to impress him with her verbal prowess? With her sexual prowess? McCarthy herself always spoke of her confused and mixed motivation in times of crisis. She had a habit of doing things and then justifying them later. Everything that followed the deception she practiced on Philip Rahv—and even her decision to enter into a disastrous marriage with Wilson—was in consequence of her confused and drunken acquiescence that night on the studio couch at Trees.

Things started off well enough, if one is willing to overlook a bewildered Philip Rahv, waiting in the sublet apartment he and Mary shared on Sutton Place. He had already spent one night worrying about his AWOL girlfriend, the first night she dined with Wilson at Mary's. She'd called him to come and get her in a taxi at the

Chelsea; this he had done, and had made excuses for her for the next two days in the offices of the *Partisan Review* while she played hooky at home, recovering from her monumental hangover. On the occasion of the second dinner at Mary's, he heard nothing from her or about her all night long until Wilson rang him up the next morning explaining that he had brought Mary and Margaret Marshall up to Trees and inviting him to come up for lunch. "And Philip *did*," reports Mary, with some awe.

In Mary's opinion, only when he saw her leaving Trees with Rahv for the same destination did Wilson get the picture. He had just slept with this man's girl—a man who had admired him inordinately and had been exerting considerable effort toward getting Wilson to contribute to his fledgling magazine. Well, that's by the way. McCarthy seemed to believe, years afterward, that leaving Rahv, who loved her, for Wilson, who most probably merely desired her, was just a matter of class warfare—for her, Marxism explained, almost sanctioned, her move up the ladder from the working-class, self-educated Rahv to the Princeton-educated patrician Wilson. (However weak this rationalization may seem, it was Mary's.) Once done, though, the ambition behind her move rather escaped her attention. In later life, she felt free to sneer at Simone de Beauvoir for having ridden to literary fame on Jean-Paul Sartre's coattails. She exempts herself from any such charge on the grounds of having married, after Wilson, a man eight years her junior who was at the time working as a checker at the *New Yorker* magazine. Still, jilted lover and modest choice of third husband aside, the thing began well enough. In *Intellectual Memoirs* McCarthy remembers that, after going into Wilson's study and thence into his arms and thence into his bed, he wrote to her, she wrote to him, and their affair was off and running.

In point of fact, she wrote first, and much more frequently, and at much greater length than did he. But write he did, and he even inquired in his first note "how about those letters you were going to write me?" McCarthy readily obliged, tapping out a steady stream on the typewriter in her office away from the *Partisan Review*. At the time, she also worked at Covici-Friede publishers; the job provided cover for her missing dinners with Rahv when Wilson could get into the city for a rendezvous. He teases her in one of his early letters about Peggy Marshall coming up to Trees without her: "I don't expect to hold her on my lap, though" (as he had done the first time she came up, at the Sunday lunch with Rahv). At the time, Rahv had seen Mary turn quite livid with jealousy. But McCarthy, later telling Wilson about this, is certain Rahv suspected nothing sexual; she thinks he interpreted her jealousy as a loss of master Wilson's attention, a literary loss of face in this *Partisan Review* world. Another subject undertaken is Lord Byron. She wanted to resuscitate him; Wilson assured her this was unnecessary—Byron was not dead. But Wilson nevertheless offered books and other help if she wanted it. On one of their trysts, they wrote a poem about Stalin together and submitted it to Dupee for publication in the *Partisan Review,* still keeping Rahv, Dupee and Mary's other *PR* pals in the dark about the true nature of their collaboration.

She was amusing about the comings and goings of the busy office around her, and said—because there was a plastic surgeon in the office at the time—she was getting all mixed up with "Fanny Brice's nose and Peaches Browning's legs"; or, again, "Having just finished writing a business letter to . . . a deaf man on the *New Republic,* and a literary letter to a lesbian in Columbia, Missouri . . . I am now all wound up to write a letter to you." She found the keeping of secrets from her friends thoroughly enjoyable—shivered with the shock of Eunice Clark's suggestion that she might try her hand at literary criticism and knock off without too much difficulty another *Axel's Castle.* "It is wonderful," she insists. "Such conversations have a kind of pleasing dramatic irony." When Margaret de Silver, Wilson's benefactress at Trees, wondered aloud in her presence what to do about letting "Bunny" stay on in her guesthouse, Mary was filled with the special delight of hearing the name of her lover spoken by a third party who had no idea of the truth. Isn't this straight out of *Madame Bovary?*

It was Madame de Stael not Emma Bovary with whom Mary seemed to identify, however. She protested that she had no intention of writing him the letters of a *femme savante,* but her letters are

full of French phrases, polished witticisms, self-conscious turns
of phrase, and quite a lot of literary gossip dished up with relish.
"Philip was right—Delmore Schwartz *is* just another precocious
Bronx boy . . . but still a monster. . . . So intellectual he is inhuman.
If D. H. Lawrence were to hear of him, I'm sure he'd come back
from his grave to evangelize against him."

When Wilson shows signs of conscience, she is, by turns, archly
regretful: "I have a feeling that you've gotten awfully strong-minded
and sensible and renunciatory after I left . . . I should be very sad if
you carried it into stern practice. Oh, very." And pouting: "Do call
me or write me a note, so that I can feel in touch with you. I confess
I don't, now." And coy: "This not-going-to-see-you is very painful,
more than I can bear quite stoically. I am full of such wonderful
things to say to you. God!"

Neither went in for much in the way of love talk. Wilson attached
four asterisk kisses to an early short note—adding in the margin
"though you say they mean comparatively little to you"—where-
upon she sent back the word "kisses" and explained that it wasn't
that they meant nothing to her, it was just that she thought of them
more as hors d'oeuvres. Then she expressed the desire to be with
him again soon, presumably to partake of the full meal. In another
letter, she went further still: "My dear, I miss you so much. I hope
you will come to New York. I had a lovely time with you last night.
. . . You must write to me and reassure me or I shall languish away.
Kisses, Mary."

Begun in October, the correspondence seems to have hit a dry
patch by late December and early January—Grandfather Preston's
death for her, holiday and family obligations in Red Bank for
him. But then matters picked up, postally speaking. Two letters
apiece over a four-day period January 16–20 contain notes of
mutual longing. She: "It's nice that you called me. I was feeling
rather sad and up in the air about you." He: "I've been sleeping horribly all week. Look forward to seeing you Saturday."

On February 10, 1938, they were married before a county clerk in
Red Bank, a ceremony followed by lunch at Wilson's mother's.
McCarthy reports with dismay being left to a postprandial chat with

her new, deaf mother-in-law—whom she describes as "a wart-hog" —while her husband of several hours slipped up to his old room for a nap. The couple evidently went away with a substantial cash gift. That night in the New Weston Hotel in New York, she was treated to one of Wilson's drunken rages, this one spectacularly paranoid. He accused her brothers, Kevin and Preston, with whom they had had drinks earlier in the evening, of being agents of the GPU (the 1930s version of the KGB). She realized she'd made a disastrous mistake and made it, in her view, out of an embarrassed desire to avoid acknowledging that she'd initially gone to bed with Wilson as an accidental consequence of too much to drink.

This explanation seems disingenuous, to say the least. In her courting letters, Mary had alluded to herself as being "a little bit in love" and confessed, twice, that she thought he was "wonderful. I must just say it, naively, like that." She was to write later that, reading them over, "I am surprised by the intimacy and friendliness of my tone. . . . Apparently I liked him much more than I remember, more than I ever would again."

Well, never mind. Marry him she did. And the whiff of playacting, greasepaint, and the theatricality of playing to the gallery became unmistakable throughout. It began as early as her second letter when, critiquing her performance at the lunch she had participated in, with both her old lover and her new one present, Mary wrote: "Sunday was a bad day for me. I was giving a very poor impersonation. The trouble with it was, from the theater standpoint, that, instead of creating a role, I was merely deleting certain rather prominent features from my character of the moment. The result was highly artificial and unconvincing, a hollow characterization."

Once ensconced up in the country, this time with benefit of a county clerk's license, Wilson encouraged McCarthy to write fiction —he shut her, in fact, in a room where she was to do it, the room once used as a guest room by Margaret Marshall. McCarthy lost no time blending her real and her imaginary lives by quickly dashing off "Cruel and Barbarous Treatment," a story about a very strategic woman trying to get rid of her husband. She may have smiled as she waved the finished manuscript under Wilson's nose. Randall Jarrell

—drawing on Mary's smile for his character Gertrude Johnson in *Pictures from an Institution*—likened it to a "skull's grin," and said of it: "Torn animals were removed at sunset from that smile."

As for Wilson, he may unwittingly have added fuel to her stored up resentment by being enthusiastic about the story and refusing to take it personally. She added five more stories, all with Meg Sargent as a heroine much like herself. Most famously and most successfully, she wrote "The Man in the Brooks Brothers Shirt," another seduction story, this time gaining erotic suspense by its setting on a transcontinental train. It involved, as so many of her stories and novels were to do, sex with a middle-aged man, a seduction ambiguously initiated—or at any rate participated in—by Meg in a drunken daze. Wilson admired this story too and wrote to his mentor Christian Gauss that it made him think she might be the female Stendhal.

By May, the female Stendhal was pregnant. By June 7, the Wilsons had as overnight dinner guests Wilson's old friends Caroline Gordon and Allen Tate. Mary, not feeling up to a long evening of reminiscences that would not include her, and finding no charm in the many glasses of wine making the rounds, rose from the dinner table to retire early. Wilson, according to Gordon, insisted—over the Tate's protests—upon reading a long Pushkin poem to them, in Russian. At three A.M. Wilson, snockered and out of sorts, arrived in the marital bed chamber where Mary had asked Hattie, the maid, to make the bed with then very newfangled colored sheets "as a surprise." In fact, they were blue. Enraged, Wilson ripped them off, tumbling his pregnant wife onto the floor. She, writing of this fifty years later, does not say if the two of them then bedded down on mattress ticking or if white sheets were brought out and applied. She does congratulate herself for shutting up and thus refraining from further annoying the raging bull. But she also chastises herself mildly. Why? Because, failing to see that he was still drunk, she accosted him in the morning with an outraged "How *could* you?" and more verbal attacks in the same vein, along with, she admits, a certain amount of hitting and pushing, in the course of which she received from him (whether deliberate or not was a bone of contention between them) a black eye. That set off in Mary a fit of hysterics. Somehow, in the early stages, the Tates came downstairs and took themselves off. But Mary's carryings on became so pronounced that Hattie called a local doctor. He, according to Wilson, prescribed a rest. According to Mary, he suggested a rest all right, but when he wanted to fix her up in the Harkness Pavilion in New York, Mary insisted she preferred the curtains in the rooms at New York Hospital. And so that is where, in a taxi, Wilson took her, admitting her to a side pavilion, the mental wing, in what she would insist was a subterfuge.

Wilson's committing her (if that is what he did) was not an event he was likely to view as a heinous act of punishment and betrayal, which tended to be Mary's lifelong view of it. With a similar stretch in a Clifton Springs clinic behind him in his early thirties, and with friends like Louise Bogan and Edna Millay doing similar hitches (to say nothing of pals in the future like John Berryman and Robert Lowell, who rather traded off drying-out clinics and loony bins), it must have seemed to him a virtual rite of passage. The upshot of Mary's landing there was a three-week stay (in a nonviolent area with her own room and therapy sessions with Sandor Rado). Wilson wrote her to counsel ending the pregnancy as too much for her in her "generally stirred-up condition," and urged her to think only of coming back to the summer place he had rented on Shippan Point just opposite her therapist, where she could have fun and get well at the same time. "I don't think we've made such a false start . . . I love you as ever, my dear, and I miss you and want you back with me terribly for as much of it as you can stand." Mary refused to end the pregnancy, but she did go back to Wilson and continued with the therapy.

A period of relative calm and a great deal of literary work ensued. The baby came on December 25, necessitating another taxi to the hospital in New York City. (Wilson did not drive and was always having to take expensive cab rides or talk people into taking him places.) During the following winter and spring, the two wrote voluminously. The pattern of productive work would hold throughout their time together.

By the end, between them, they had written six books and numerous articles. Wilson's output consisted of *The Triple Thinkers* (1938), *To the Finland Station* (1940), *The Wound and the Bow* (1941), *The Boys in the Back Room* (1941), *Notebooks of Night* (1942), and *The Shock of Recognition* (1943). He had also edited Fitzgerald's posthumously published *The Last Tycoon* (1941) and *The Crack-Up* (1945), and written most of the four stories making up *Memoirs of Hecate County* (1946). In addition, he had produced a manuscript that never saw the light of day in his liftetime, later published as *The Higher Jazz*. Mary had published four short stories and written two more, the six of which were gathered into novel form and published as *The Company She Keeps* (1942); she also wrote a number of theater reviews for the *Partisan Review,* which were later included in her theater chronicles, published in 1963.

But, as the summer of 1939 loomed, pressing financial needs forced Wilson to accept a teaching job at the University of Chicago. Baby clothes were provided by sympathetic friends and a baby carriage, which Wilson railed against as unnecessary, was finally got out of Mrs. Wilson Sr. In June, baby, nursemaid, and McCarthy in tow, Wilson arrived in Chicago to take up what would be stormy, cramped, and steamy residence in the five-room faculty sublet they rented near Lake Michigan. Within weeks, notwithstanding a couple of rather pleasurable lake shore picnics, things had come to such a pass (the police were summoned twice, called by neighbors fed up with the noise generated by the vocally gifted couple) that when Rosalind was added to the mix, Mary beat a strategic retreat with baby Reuel to her Grandmother Preston in Seattle.

Wilson's letters to her out there are determinedly upbeat and chatty: "I haven't been doing much except the—very pleasant— bike ride [yesterday morning with Rosalind] and taking Rosalind and the Evanses to the circus." There is an amusing anecdote about Mrs. Evans, who evidently talked a lot about kindness to animals, mentioning in the same breath that they had just had a "tragedy at home: Malcolm, the rat, had eaten Venus, one of the canaries, and they had had to chloroform him." Occasionally, they border on the sentimental, alluding to "how cute [their son Reuel] looked on his hands and knees in the upper berth," how broken his health is on account of his enforced celibacy: "I miss you, and think that part of my decline has been due to trauma caused by your departure" and how chastened he is by her absence: "I'll be seeing you soon; have been missing you dreadfully; didn't know how much you meant in my life till you left." Some of the letters tell a different story, though, and hint at the sources of family disputes. A flap arises over a fur coat, over some unpaid bills and some prematurely cashed checks. "You have very strange ideas of economy," huffs Wilson. But he is clearly looking forward to their reunion on the Cape at the close of the summer term. Then a frost descends. Rejected again—Mary makes it all too clear that she is returning only because she has no other place to go—he quickly retreats from plans to come back a day early. "By all means stay till the 7th. But be sure you make the connections on the Hyannis train. You know how tricky the Cape Cod timetable is."

Still, the purchase of the Wellfleet house (a loan financed once more by largesse from Wilson's mother) made a stage on which the two played out, from 1939 to 1942, a semblance of domestic harmony. The spring of 1942 found the couple sharing what in Wilson's journal is made to seem an afternoon idyll of transcendent pleasure and significance. Here, at some length, is his account of a day with Mary in the fifth year of their marriage:

> *Gull Pond, May 21, 1942.*—The lady's slippers were out, . . .
> deepening in a couple of days from flimsy stooping ghosts as
> pale as Indian pipe to a fleshy veined purplish pink . . . , the little
> white violets with their lower lips finely lined . . . , their long
> slim rhubarb-purplish stalks and their faint slightly acrid pansy
> smell, grew with thready roots in the damp sand . . . As one
> walked in the water one encountered pines putting out their
> soft straw-colored . . . bunches of cones and smelling with a
> special almost sweet-fern fragrance. The baby cones seemed
> almost embarrassingly soft, almost like a woman's nipples. . . .
> On the other side of the pond, the stretch where there was a
> screen of tall pines, a new and grander note, almost theatrical—

and then the little screen of scent-pines . . . —in there we used
to make love while all kinds of little birds rustled and twitched
and sang behind. Today we cleared a place under the low
branches of the pines so that we could get a little shade, and
the light openwork shadows rippled on Mary's white skin—her
waist and abdomen where she lay naked—as the breeze stirred
the branches, also fish splashing. Afterwards, Mary put her feet
up and grabbed a branch with her long square-tipped prehen-
sile toes—she giggled and snickered about it, enjoyed the idea
of being able to do it, one thing she wasn't sensitive about—
stretched up further and seized the branch again and, rather
to my astonishment, pulled her whole body up while only her
shoulders rested on the ground. She said then I couldn't do that
—I replied that I was in a little more advanced stage. She said
that her ancestors had been kings of Ireland—I said, yes: in the
trees.—When I was trying to keep my mind off it, in order not
to come before she did, leaning on my hands, I was able to look
out on the lake and the afternoon landscape, where only the
cries of the gulls were heard.

Even the contents of their picnic lunch seem bathed in the light of
this special mood:

For lunch we had had from the brown picnic basket the classical boiled eggs, bean salad in glass jars, cucumber sandwiches,
and sandwiches filled with some mixture of green chopped
herbs and white cottage cheese (and there were bananas,
tomatoes, and sliced sweetish green cucumber pickles which
we didn't get around to eating); and had iced lemonade out of
the thermos bottle and white California wine out of a glass jar
that had been cooled in the refrigerator and that we tried to
keep from getting tepid by standing it in the water.—Before
lunch, we had gone in for a dip: not too cold to be uncomfortable. Mary had gone in naked, I had put on my old brown
trunks. Mary looked very pretty and white. But she was ripened

by the summer sun where her face and neck and arms had
been exposed while working on her garden, and the tan of her
forearms and the reddening tints brought out in her rather pale
skin were in harmony with her blue suit of overalls and made
her seem almost luscious. When I seized her after we'd eaten
as she was lying in her new rather shiny pink latex bathing-suit,
with its skirt cropped smartly off just at the base of her buttocks
(it was when she was standing up, though, that you noticed
this)—the shoulder straps down so as to leave her breasts bare,
I kissed her wide red fleshy and rather amiable mouth, which
had character, while she shaded her eyes from the sun with her
hand, it (her mouth) seemed to me naked and made me think
of the lips below. At this point we finished the yellow wine and
went on to the screen of the scrub-pine.

For some time after the love-making has ended, the sense of sexual
excitement suffuses the remainder of the scene:

—I had a sense of adventure in exploring the other bank of the
pond and . . . when we came back from our walk around it . . .
the water had a leaden look that was at the same time perfectly
limpid—and lovely.

Wilson makes it quite explicit that it is Mary who has invested the
scene with its magic for him:

—When I went back to get the towels, on which Mary had
been lying, I saw a little orange-and-black bird, like a finch,
hopping around in those scrub pines just where we had been.
The little yellow buds . . . give out [when you shake them] a
lemon-yellow dust that looks like lemon-colored smoke.
      —. . . just opposite where we lay [a] yellow-and-black butter-
fly (monarch?) . . . was flying over the pond. . . . .

The Gull Pond entry is followed by this melancholy marginal note:

—All to be followed by violins
     quarrel the next morning and her running away to New York.

Yes, on May 22, 1942, Mary left once more. This time for what
would, over the next three years, be a series of alternate digs in New
York; both the rented rooms and the trips into the city were osten-
sibly needed for Mary's therapy sessions and Wilson's visits to editors' offices. (In 1943, he took on Clifton Fadiman's job as senior
book editor of the *New Yorker*.) But from time to time, there were
still sexual encounters pleasurable to them both; one in particular
is detailed at length in a journal entry from January 1, 1943: "I asked
her if she enjoyed it, and she answered, 'Couldn't you tell?'" He'd
invented a sexual technique he'd engaged in for the first time: ". . .
first, a trick of running my tongue around on the inside of her lips—
then, a smooth unbroken rotary motion that didn't have the element of jerkiness that brought you down to the ground—it was
wonderful, almost like flying in a dream, and it carried her along,
too. I began to intensify it by speeding up a little and pressing in—
and she came before I did. Then I doubled up her knees and put her
legs back over her body, and drove in from above." He describes it
in his journal [omitted, like the rest of this entry, from the published
version] as: "A wonderful transporting discovery. Afterwards my
penis did not lose its stiffness and still felt as if it had some kind of
enchantment on it, as if it had been dipped in an invisible magic
fluid that could prolong in the organ withdrawn the magic that was
in her—only gradually fading off. I am happy tonight."
     And they still had some jolly social times, with the Nabokovs
and others. The Bunny-Volodya letters of the period almost always
include cordial greetings to Vera and Mary. Wilson wrote to Nabokov in November of 1943, "We are absolutely counting on you for
Thanksgiving. To let us down would be inexcusable." But Nabokov
replied with such a hair-raising account of his tooth troubles that
Wilson softened: "We are terribly sorry to hear about your crisis of
dentistry." The two couples went on to have other sociable times
together.
     The next big blowup occurred in the summer of 1944, again

precipitated by a drunker than usual Wilson who, perhaps in a jealous rage over some perceived indiscretion of Mary's during a dinner party they had been giving, refused insultingly to help her when she asked him to take out the garbage.

As Mary tells it in her legal deposition of 1945: "I slapped him— not terribly hard—went out and emptied the cans, then went upstairs. He called me and I came down. He got up from the sofa and took a terrible swing at me in the face and all over. He said: 'You think you're unhappy with me. Well, I'll give you something to be unhappy about.' I ran out of the house and jumped into my car."

Rosalind's version is not quite so dramatic—she reports never having seen her father hit Mary, and says that on the incident after the dinner party the two—that is, she and Mary—jumped into the old Chevrolet Mary had by that time acquired and drove out for a swim in Gull Pond, a project that foundered when the car ran out of gas. Wilson had pursued them on his bicycle, and, when all three had returned to the house, he somehow managed to put his hand through a glass panel in the front door. Next day, gas in car, Mary took off yet again. This time the letter Wilson wrote her is a shaft of light throwing the marriage and its wounds and fissures into quite laceratingly high relief.

Wellfleet, Mass.

July 13, 1944

Dear Mary:

I have decided that there is no point in my going down and am wiring you. . . . —I make this suggestion: come back up here for the rest of the summer on a purely friendly basis. I promise you that I will not drink anything all summer. I think it is hard on Reuel to wreck the family in the middle of the summer like this. It would be easier for you and me to set up separate establishments in the autumn when he will be going to school. If you could get a cook in New York, the household itself would be easy. (Miss Forbes, by the way, however, seems to expect her vacation soon.)

I feel terribly badly about this, and I know that it was my fault that things got into such a mess. In spite of everything, I thought we were pretty well off in the earlier part of the summer. It is always true that Rosalind upsets the balance of the family when she comes; and the heat . . . and my own bad habits did the rest. But it may be that you and I are psychologically impossible for one another anyway. I had already got discouraged about everything before I left New York in the spring; but I have never wanted things to be as bad as that because I have really loved you more than any other woman and have felt closer to you than to any other human being. I think, though, that it is true that, as lovers, you and I scare and antagonize each other in a way that has been getting disastrous lately (though sometimes I have been happier and more exalted with you than I have ever been with anybody). And when you make me feel that you don't want me, all my fear of not being loved, which I have carried all my life from my childhood, comes out in the form of resentment.

Wilson goes on to give a remarkably objective list of their problems:

I know that the difference in our ages is a real difficulty between us. I prevent you from doing things that are no longer to my taste but that are perfectly natural for you to want to do; and you don't sympathize with the miseries—like the death of old friends, bad habits and diseases of one's own, and a certain inevitable disillusion with the world that has to be struggled against—that hit you when you get on in your forties.

Wilson also made a sincere attempt to give credit where credit was due:

I want you to know, too, that I know that you have made an effort to keep house for Reuel and me, and to be good to Rosalind, and that we all appreciate it. You have been wonderful except when you turn the whole thing into a kind of masochism that is calculated to make other people as uncomfortable as you are. There is no question, though, that you have been very much better this last year. There have been long stretches when you seemed to me to handle things better and to be a great deal happier than at any time since we have been married—isn't that true?—and I am sorry that I have sometimes been demoralized myself and let you down when you were doing your best.

The letter concludes with a suggestion for a temporary truce:

Come up and stay here and let us make a modus vivendi for the next two months. It wouldn't work out in the long run; but we could make other arrangements in the autumn. I'm entering a period of sobriety and work (have even initiated a diet) which may be tiresome for you; but I will do my best to be considerate and not nag you. In the meantime, I want your company, which, aside from other considerations, I prefer to anybody else's. . . .

Love, Edmund

She *did* come back — presumably on the terms Wilson outlined — but by September the pot was boiling over again. Mary's retreat was to New York, to their last shared address, a little cul de sac near Gracie Mansion off 86th Street called Henderson Place. Cunning to glance in at, the street is cast into shadow by the surrounding high rises so that they must have been residing in a place of deepest gloom. When, in December, Mary left the "note in the pin cushion" announcing her final decampment with Reuel to the Stanhope Hotel, it came as something of an anticlimax. And by the time the two drew up their respective affidavits for the lawyers, the gulf between their initial understanding of what they promised to each other and what they found in the real union was both comical and very poignant.

Mary's affidavit, filed in February 1945, is a curious document that contains some ideals, some truths, and some lies. "Before we married he gave the appearance of a man of quiet habits with an interest in books, pictures, and music. He was well-known as a literary critic and I had admired his works even before I met him. During his courtship he held out great promise of a quiet settled life and the rearing of a large family." They both loved the ancient classics, she from her days at St. Stephen's in Minneapolis and later at Forest Ridge Convent of the Sacred Heart in Seattle, he from the Hill School years. Although no teacher, he had always been a kind of mentor to friends, and we have no trouble imagining the young woman eager to listen and question and debate. She'd expected to read Juvenal and live a gentrified life in the country, but instead got —according to her—knocked around and subjected to humiliation in front of their son and their friends.

He, too, envisioned a settled, quiet life, one in his view they on occasion actually achieved.

She insisted that she had been deceived about his violent temper, his drinking, his inability to provide for them in a manner she had been led to expect. All well and good—as is the idyll of enjoying pictures (she was strongly interested in art history), though Wilson's love of music couldn't have counted for much—she hated it. And that little irrelevancy makes us wonder about other things— his drinking, for example. A well-known rake of the 1920s shocked her with his drinking—this, after she had experienced the full force of it on their first evening together. Elsewhere, looking back, she enumerates some other hopes and expectations: They were to take nature walks and identify the wild flowers and fish for trout. But could this very self-aware young woman have completely forgotten the life she had been leading? The men, the drinking, the affairs, the publishers' lunches, the evenings of theater and parties—all of this to be exchanged for a house in the country with a brilliant, boozy older man. The affidavit and the memoir evocation have a false ring —and yet they ring true to something about Wilson. He did prefer the country to the city; he had already had his fill of literary Manhattan and was looking to hole up and write.

Wilson insisted that he had been deceived about her emotional problems. (As a young woman of twenty, Rosalind was told by Rahv that Mary's "illness" was the reason he had never considered getting a divorce and marrying her.) Wilson's basic point in the legal deposition he filed was that McCarthy was crazy, subject to mood changes, and dangerous: "I discovered shortly after my marriage to plaintiff that she was a psychiatric case. In May of 1938 [*sic*], during her first pregnancy, she developed an acute hysterical condition and I took her to the Payne Whitney Clinic at the Medical Center. She was there confined to the ward for violent cases for a period of time. She remained at the Payne Whitney Pavilion for a number of weeks."

In a retrospective note on his marriage (only the first sentence of which made it into the published journal), he wrote: "I made fewer entries in this journal during the years I was married to Mary, and those usually about other people. She was a hysteric of the classical kind who makes scenes. . . . I could not bear to write about it."

Wilson says he covered for her from the start. "In her spells of hysteria, she would be likely to identify me with the uncle by marriage whom she had hated and with whom she and Kevin had been sent to live after her parents' death. She was under the impression —which must have been exaggerated—that he had beaten her every day."

In spite of everything, he fought the divorce, made unsupported charges that she was deranged in order to get custody of Reuel, then, finally, succumbed. A letter that Katy Dos Passos wrote to her husband during this period gives some idea of Wilson's outcries of pain:

I am in bed because of being worn out by a midnight visit from Wilson [nicknamed "antix" in the original] who came unexpectedly to dinner and stayed all hours. He called a taxi twice and then sent it away and finally I took him . . . in the car long after twelve. I am just like Cinderella, you know. After twelve the Ball is over and I *haf* to go home. But could not as poor Wilson talked all evening about his domestic sufferings which have indeed been frightful beyond belief. He told me his life with Mary from the beginning—it was hideous for years I guess and a good thing they have parted. Wilson said she wanted to destroy him and his work. She had indeed undermined his work. (I thought so myself some time ago.) She kept telling him it was worthless and getting worse. Oh I felt sorry for both.

Anaïs Nin's diary of winter 1945 contains this entry: "Edmund Wilson invited me to lunch. I felt his distress, received his confession. Even though not an intimate friend, Wilson senses my sympathy and turns toward it. He is lonely and lost. He is going to France as a war correspondent. He asks me to accompany him while he buys his uniform, his sleeping bag. We talk. He tells me about his suffering with Mary McCarthy." Wilson made similar *cris de coeur* to Helen Muchnic and Betty Huling about his wretchedness.

In mid-March he left for his European assignment for the *New Yorker*. After taking an unsuccessful run at Mamaine Paget, he set about convincing a married woman to leave her husband and marry him—his single-minded goal being to find a compatible mate who would build a home for him, and nurture him and his work and his children. To a large extent he succeeded in finding all that in the person of Elena Mumm Thornton.

The next part of the story is creative stocktaking. McCarthy, as we have seen, turned to fiction at Wilson's urging. The results— as far as they concern the story of this marriage—are four novels: *The Company She Keeps* (1942), *The Groves of Academe* (1952), *A Charmed Life* (1954), and *The Group* (1963). Extending from the early forties to the early sixties, they constitute a payback time in fiction: Here are the dark sides of their relationship, direct unflattering portraits of Wilson, caricatures, encoded stories of their troubles, as well as lies and revealing truths about herself and her husband. Wilson himself was enthusiastic about the enterprise—at least at the start. Remember, he wrote his old Princeton mentor Christian Gauss that Mary might well be the new Stendhal. At first blush such a comparison seems wildly off the mark; yet one has only to look a little more closely at *The Company She Keeps* to see its force. Mary was, like the French master, mocking, scaldingly ironic, relentless in her pursuit of motives, cool, and passionate at the same time. And her subjects were Stendhalian—seduction and status. The best chapters in *The Company* are close to what McCarthy and Wilson had been living out since 1937. "The Man in the Brooks Brothers Shirt" is a minefield of sorts: Everywhere you look something explodes about them. To begin with the story is about age and youth, and all the incompatibilities that go with this. Mr. Breen is forty-one, set in his ways, but determined to pick up a sophisticated young thing of twenty-four on a train going from New York to the Coast. He's physically unattractive; despite his elegant Brooks wardrobe he resembles a "young pig." Yet he's vaguely alluring because of his neediness, his persistence, and his power in the real world. Meg Sergeant's many boyfriends have been rather wimpy and unsuitable for a woman of her strong character and high standards—lame-duck bohemians, barbarians with bad table manners, limp-wristed and vaguely homosexual types. Bill Breen is a take-charge steel executive, someone who knows his way around cities and clubs and social scenes, knows how to tip porters and conduct an affair with brisk efficiency. And Meg is swept along—flattered, even, by the attentions of a man of the world. When they go to his compartment for whiskey, they keep the door open at the start—and she enjoys acting the part of the bohemian girl with the commanding new friend: "It was exactly as if they were drinking in a show window, for nobody went by who did not peer in, and she felt that she could discern envy, admiration, and censure in the quick looks that were shot at her."

Being with Breen produces a kind of high—and a lot of confusion as well: "Gradually, now, she was becoming very happy, for she knew for sure in this compartment that she was beautiful and gay and clever, and worldly and innocent, serious and frivolous, capricious and trustworthy, witty and sad, bad and really good, all mixed up together, all at the same time."

Strangely enough, her locution in a bit of dialogue directed to Breen—"I like to *talk* to you"—comes right out of her remarks to Wilson. And Breen also talks Meg into bed—not because they have much in common as people, but because she is swept away by a sense that she is important to someone important. Meg says it was essential that he should "believe her a woman." But once the belief leads to bed there are dark thoughts: Seduction "never failed to disconcert and frighten her: I had not counted on this, she could always whisper to herself, with a certain sad bewilderment. For it was all wrong, it was unnatural: art is to be admired not acted on, and the public does not belong on the stage, nor the actor in the audience." Meg takes Chaucer's heroine Creseyde's line as her motto "I am myn owene woman, wel at ese." She thinks of herself as a classic, a work of art, and somehow her own passions have damaged her. The idea is to regain balance and mastery of the situation, but unfortunately the older man has fallen in love, and she feels an obligation to comfort him for a while. She was "a little bit in love," again an echo of a letter to Wilson. But more to the point she hugged him "with an air of warmth that was not quite spurious and not quite sincere." At the end of the line in Sacramento, she would get off the train, and resolve her ambivalence—an act that would take McCarthy seven years.

The other version of the McCarthy-Wilson conflicts in *The Company She Keeps*, "Ghostly Father, I Confess," is blunter in its psychology, concentrating on an overbearing husband who doesn't bring out anything in Meg but guilt and rage. The tenderness and doubt of "The Man in the Brooks Brothers Shirt"—not to mention the attractions of the older man's power—are missing in this story of the effects of domination. Meg's latest husband is a modernist architect and an out-and-out bully. Once again an older man, he is nevertheless far from appreciative of her youthful self-absorption and preening. Meg, like Mary, has scruples of sorts, carried over from a Catholic upbringing: She knows how to examine her own conscience, sort out logical from illogical, question her own conduct. But her psychiatrist tells her that her conscience is getting in the way of self-acceptance and normal living. And her husband sees her moods and fears and ambivalences as excuses for acting like a "bitch." He wants her to "behave decently. Instead of telling yourself that you oughtn't to have married me, you might concentrate on being a good wife." Wilson's pleas for decency and common sense (and the importance of their marriage)—hollow as they are in the light of much of his own behavior—are clearly audible in this remark. He—and fictional husband Frederick—wanted Mary/Meg to stop the ambivalent antics, the acting out, the moods. But neither Wilson nor Frederick ever quite got the fact that love, so far in her life, was a problem more than a passion and a commitment, something she wanted but also something that always seemed a bit forced and strained—spurious and sincere at the same time.

McCarthy's next major look at Wilson is *The Groves of Academe*. Here, again, there is a plentiful lack of subtlety as she makes him physically loathsome—pear-shaped, with vague red hair, bad tailoring, and bad breath—and hypocritical and calculating. The Wilson link is the main theme of the book: ruthlessness, the willingness of a small-time Joyce scholar to sacrifice anything and anybody to get his way. McCarthy was always insistent about Wilson's mastery of the art of manipulation—and this novel takes that insistence over the top.

Henry Mulcahy is Wilson degraded—what McCarthy in her most vindictive mood thought Wilson could be all about. The book is not so much about actuality as about McCarthy's version of potential. She lets Wilson's controlling nature run wild on a Pennsylvania campus, making him a master manipulator whose dissimulations—especially his ability to talk his way into people's confidence—practically destroy a college. Meantime, there's Domna, a chic Russian girl—a scholar and a sympathetic heart—who falls for his line: She believes him when he says that he's been dismissed for political reasons. The book is a nightmarish view of Wilson on the loose—he corrupts people's thinking, makes his self-pitying into something precious, sacrifices truth to self-interest, uses his love of Joyce to make himself look like the bedeviled, suffering novelist.

Henry, it must be said, has a certain fame on the campus because he's a humanist and man of general ideas in a college where most of the teachers are interested only in narrow questions of literary form. Educated by the Jesuits in "an older mold," Henry commands a certain respect; McCarthy turns this distinction into a horrible defect as Henry pursues his philosophical universal—himself.

Wilson once remarked to McCarthy that she had the ability as a theater reviewer to assemble a crushing brief against a play. The wit and mockery and dismissiveness are directed against Tennessee Williams and Thornton Wilder among others. When we turn to *A Charmed Life,* the brief is assembled against Wilson: The novel is a sustained, often amusing attack that tells as much about her as about him. Her fictionalized Wilson in *A Charmed Life* is the rather unattractive Miles Murphy. She covers the negative ground here, retailing just about everything that had been or could be said against Wilson—the truths, lies, suspicions, prejudices, and put-downs circulated in his time. Miles Murphy, admittedly, is a character who strongly resembles the man who lived—and yet the resemblance has a cartoonlike wildness and lack of subtlety. If *The Groves of Academe* is an out-of-control fantasy, this book is a lurid comedy with an intellectual-as-villain dominating the story. Martha Sinnott, the young woman who was formerly married to "the Monster" (to use Mary's name for Wilson), has settled in the Monster's New England town, New Leeds, with her new husband John. She's working on a play and trying to sort out her feelings about why—of all places—she settled on New Leeds. But Murphy's presence raises the reader's suspicions from the start; and the magnetic Monster exerts his hold until the end. At one point, Martha declares that people tended to do what they wanted in life, the exception being her marriage to Miles in which "she had done steadily what she hated." But what she hated was also compelling and dangerous and sexually charged.

Miles, true enough, is fat and freckled, with reddish curly hair, and "small, pale green eyes, like grapes about to burst." He eats like an Elizabethan, drinks like a fish, and conducts his relationships with others—wives, neighbors, friends—like a Renaissance aristocrat. Miles was educated by the Jesuits. (McCarthy, as in *The Groves of Academe,* has a bee in her bonnet about the Company, making it the tricky, dishonest order of anti-Catholic legend.) At twenty-three, he wrote about his old teachers in a hit Broadway play. Thereafter he has been a writer, magazine editor, lay analyst, adventurer, boxer. He's always been attracted to intellectual women, but as Martha comments, they disagree with him in more ways than one. His crooked nose and swollen belly and peremptory manner, however, are attached to "a brilliant mind." Yet his intellect is capable of "astuteness, cunning, and clarity" rather than original achievement. He set out to be a Goethe, but, Martha cattily remarks, wound up a rolling stone. (The backhandedness and disparaging tone give credence to Katy Dos Passos's remark that Mary always said Wilson's work was pretty bad.) Miles has become a prodigious researcher, a man who "roamed" into the history of ideas and "might yet" achieve something. Now the elements of Wilson's life are just below the surface—the devotion to teachers, the journalism and scholarship, the psychoanalytic interests, the intense living, the monumental tasks like *To The Finland Station*. As for the boxing, that's Wilson's aggressiveness and the punching out Mary supposedly received.

The charge of brutality is everywhere. Dolly Lamb, a character based on the artist Mary Meigs, pronounces him " a stone-crusher." Martha remembers the "bulldozing" that led to marriage and calls him "selfish, brutal, and dishonest in his domestic life." He's accused of conducting frightful campaigns against his wives, calculated to break their spirits. At one point, he's likened to a Renaissance condottiere, "pillaging the countryside from his stronghold." The following statement covers just about everything, including taking candy from a baby: "He made his wives his accomplices, that was why they could not escape him. They had to stand by and watch him abuse the servants, hold back their wages, eat their food, accuse them of robbing him. He insisted that his wives lie for him, to his creditors, to the insurance company, to the tax people. He had no sense of limit of other people's rights. Nothing was safe from his meandering appetites: the maid's time off, her dinner, her birthday box of candy, the cooking sherry, the vanilla. He slept in every bed and commandeered every bathroom. He even, Martha remembered, used to eat Barrett's lollipops."

But when all is said and done Martha "did not like Miles, but she did not dislike him either." She assembles the brief, but she also exhibits her own ambivalence. He had a hold over her and continued to exert it. Her senses awakened to his touch in the late and fatal love scene. McCarthy gives him a certain terrifying grandeur, making him like Robert Browning's Duke of Ferrara in "My Last Duchess." In a scene in which Miles is vying to buy a portrait of Martha, we see him rendered as the witty connoisseur, sardonic but nevertheless impressive as he looks at the work of art. Martha always said that he would enjoy seeing her stuffed and mounted, yet there is something alluring about someone who regards you as a work of art. At the heart of things is Miles/Wilson's love of art and beauty and beautiful women, his sometimes gruesome but also reverent attitude toward what and whom he loved. McCarthy captures this, even as she mounts her attack.

Miles also regards Martha's mind as a fine instrument—capable of standing up to his own. In a kind of love scene cum lecture—in which they turn each other on with their insights—the two of them hold forth brilliantly about Racine's play *Berenice*. A group of intellectual innocents and half-literates listen as Miles and Martha talk about love, passion, and tragedy in a neoclassical mode. The play is about the breakup of a romance and the steeling of the self against the consequences. McCarthy has Miles explain Racine's microscopic look at love, his vision of tragedy, his idea of the dignity of leadership. And Miles also derides conventional love. Martha adds her own point—that action in tragedy is ambivalent, can mean different things and produce different outcomes. This last point of course is at the heart of the McCarthy-Wilson relationship—the strange and incoherent things we produce by following our passions. Miles's love of beauty and Martha's love of power and commanding intellect—not to mention of her own brilliance set off by another's—produced a sordid mess. Martha sleeps with him on the night of the discussion and thus must face the ugly possibility that this man—the Monster—may have made her pregnant. McCarthy has Martha, supposedly a reasonable and normal woman when compared with Miles the terrifying phenomenon, crack up in a car while running off to get an abortion. In the theater of McCarthy's mind—if not in real life dealings with Wilson—the only thing left was to die.

*A Charmed Life* also touches on the very controversial matter of Martha/Mary's mental stability, or lack thereof. McCarthy is willing to air the Wilsonian charge that she's a mental case—"Martha is a very sick girl," Miles pronounced. She was a pyromaniac, someone who needed to be watched carefully. She needed a "steadying force," a man with a mind. "I now think I mishandled her . . . I thought I could teach her self-knowledge." We, however, notice Martha examining her own motives, reasonably considering how to behave, being skeptical about her own actions, and trying to out-maneuver her fairly depressing situation. Rather than madly and belligerently asserting her right to be herself, she wants to be "normal"; she turns away from Miles's "I'm different" code of behavior.

McCarthy depicts Martha talking about "a mistaken premise," which is to say that Miles misinterpreted their first kiss. She admits being confused, but is sure about one thing: It was not romance that was behind the gesture but rather an attempt to get him to pay attention to her talking. All of this sounds tricky, bitchy, skittish, a bit weird—but in the end rationalized in a fairly sane, self-justifying way. Dishonest, for sure. Mad? Well, there just isn't enough detachment from reality to make us think so. Plainly put, McCarthy makes her protagonist a troubled woman trapped by mixed motives and a crushing opponent.

The next rendering of the Wilson problem is McCarthy's most famous novel, *The Group.* Here she has a chance to enlarge on the madness-rationality theme and pick through the incident of her own hospitalization in Payne Whitney. McCarthy is up to some fairly predictable tricks in her portrait of the marriage of Kay Strong and Harald Petersen. Kay had been a socially ambitious eager beaver at Vassar, a girl from the far West who wanted to be in with the in crowd—fascinating and interesting. She's the first to get married and the groom is—to say the least—interesting. Outwardly modeled on McCarthy's first husband, actor Harold Johnsrud, he's part bohemian, part harum-scarum: He's an against-the-grain struggler who hates the bourgeoisie and has theories on every topic—especially sex. He's a practiced seducer who can dispense advice on the etiquette of birth control and all matters related thereto. Kay, a trainee at Macy's, does most of the earning while Harald messes up in his acting jobs—and goes to bed with her friend Norine. What places Harald firmly in the Wilson drama is his betrayal of Kay when she's overwrought, not to mention the way his nasty temper leads to violence: The incident of committing Kay to Payne Whitney gives McCarthy a chance to heap abuse on a man who flies off the handle when he's annoyed over nothing. This man is identical to Wilson when he tore the blue sheets off the bed. Kay and Harald had been entertaining at cocktail time just before the trouble broke out; both were high. Kay, in true McCarthyesque fashion, then had ticked Harald off by wanting a pickle for a dinner sauce. After storming out and not returning until morning, Harald beat the poor woman; he then used her girlfriend to help convince her to be hospitalized. He signed the papers for her committal and was out of the picture for many hours, drunk and oblivious of her suffering. Kay, like McCarthy, made the best of her stay and managed to get out for good behavior. But McCarthy makes Harald's damage the fatal factor in the unhinging of a hardworking, essentially loving, and devoted young girl. He's had her branded as a mental case —and McCarthy implies that this is just what she becomes. She dies after a fall from a window at the Vassar Club. This may have been an accident, but her flighty state suggests suicide. Stigmatized, humiliated in front of her friends, robbed of her precious ambitions (among them a happy marriage), Kay is the wreck that McCarthy could have become. Kay has a number of McCarthy's traits—perfectionism, pushiness, intense beliefs—but she lacks McCarthy's survivalist instincts, her hard-as-nails defenses, and, of course, the solace of her talent.

What was Wilson's literary response to this unsavory brew? The short answer is not much. His writings—particularly *Upstate* and the journals—are filled with luscious dreams of work, nature, and love. He needed someone to make the third dream real. The curious fact is that he never gave a clear and extended account of the disappointment. McCarthy was to depict him in several novels, in her memoirs, and in good gossip. While he might issue a plaintive cry to old friends and girlfriends, old and new, for the record he was always tightlipped, laconic, if not silent. This lover who delighted in writing about his sexual performances—and this deeply emotional man who recorded his reactions to girlfriends and wives with such copiousness and precision—would only represent Mary in minor works and glancing ways. There was something about her—and something about the dynamic of their relationship—that made him go silent. He seemed to have lost his desire to criticize, exhibit himself as a romantic character, and analyze motives. For his other women writer friends, he always managed to write an essay that set down what he thought of them. But with McCarthy the level of acrimony was too great.

When he wrote the little that he did write about her, he became allegorical and weird rather than characteristically precise. His interesting but flawed play "The Little Blue Light" in no way stands up to what his wife achieved in literary revenge. A curious, strained, *Twilight Zone* sort of fantasy, the play is about betrayal, the force of evil in the modern world—and a woman with a center part and a bun and a determined manner.

Wilson concocts a preposterous plot about a country-based newspaperman named Frank Brock whose wife Judith is part of a large conspiracy to shut him up. "She is tense, with a habitual tensity that never relaxes." Judith is also a perfectionist who is never satisfied with life. And she's an adulteress, cheating with Frank's assistant Ellis—a man who tells Judith that's she's beautiful and has the brains of a man. She and Frank had met long ago when he gave a lecture at her college and she came up to him afterwards— "with her panther eyes." In the mix is also Gandersheim, a short story writer who has premonitions about modern totalitarianism and expresses them in his fantastic plots about Shidnats Slyme, a personification of evil (almost Miles Standish spelled backwards). Gandy, as he's called, is a preppy with a profile like Wilson's— including resentment of a controlling mother and yearning for an older America. Post–World War II America—Frank and Gandersheim feel—is in the grip of terrible destructive forces—power units, especially the Peters (the Roman Catholic Church), the Elitists, and the Teniakis organization. This last bills itself as a benevolent organization, handing out jobs and giving security to little people. It's actually a bunch of mobsters headed by a pseudo-Periclean strongman.

Frank thrives on the thick conspiratorial atmosphere, wants his newspaper to fight for free speech, hopes to be a real force for opinion making in the *Time* magazine-dominated postwar era, and especially hopes that he and Judith can be a team of browbeaters carrying the truth to the world. But Judith sees him as a small-time tyrant, and he eventually sees the full picture about her cheating, posing for indecent pictures(!), and collusion with Teniakis. This, of course, is McCarthy on the loose—his weak equivalent of Mulcahy in *The Groves of Academe*. The little blue light is an unintentionally farcical ray that is beamed when evil is in the ascendant. Needless to say, Judith sets it off. What the play amounts to is no more than ventilating—and trying, unsuccessfully, to connect the spirit of McCarthy with the spirit of the oppressive pressure groups. That's perhaps all that Wilson hoped to accomplish—a linkage of his own traumatic experience with the huge and undigested subject of a nation entrapped.

Wilson's ability to write so little about McCarthy is direct testimony to the depths of his hurt, the depths to which she could shake him. He looked into dark corridors where she would lead him and found himself unable to go there. Yet it seems important to notice that in the end he was able to turn these hurts—wounds, if you will —into art and, so, it must be said, could she.

· · · · · ·

THE OTHER woman writer who played a significant part in his life in the late thirties and forties was Dawn Powell. She was a provincial who became a cosmopolitan. Born in Mount Gilead, Ohio, in 1896 (she always pretended it was 1897), she traveled a hard road. Her mother died when she was six years old, and four years later she had a stepmother who, among her many harsh qualities, didn't like literary children. The woman burned thirteen-year-old Dawn's early stories and drawings, and the youngster ran away from home and sought refuge with her sympathetic Aunt Ophra in Shelby, Ohio. This was the beginning of the Powell story—disaster and destruction, eventual landing on one's feet and endurance. Lucky to have gotten to college at Lake Erie, she graduated in 1918, and soon headed for New York City, where she was to spend the rest of her life.

Although she started out on the Upper West Side, Dawn became pretty much a permanent Greenwich Villager. Wilson's essay on her in *The Bit Between My Teeth* focuses on the Village, celebrating her urban vision and the types she observed. Her own type was most definitely elfin—she had been properly cast back in college as Puck in *A Midsummer Night's Dream*. She was fanciful, witty, and satiric from the start, and although no raving beauty, had an active romantic life. Rosalind Wilson, later one of Dawn's editors at Houghton Mifflin, commented that she had two modes of behavior with men: the flirtatious and the buddy-buddy. The latter defined her style with Wilson and is the obvious cement that kept her relationship with him going for so long. They were never lovers, but they had an intense friendship that began rather quietly in 1933 and lasted until Powell died of cancer in 1965.

The Powell-Wilson relationship had a surface amiability and more: Their correspondence, for example, was a matter of ritual joking, assuming comic personae, and exchanging stories of humorous incidents. Their friendship contained a good deal of supportiveness on Wilson's side, and a good deal of gratitude mixed with resentment on hers. Dawn Powell's work has a significant place in American satire, and a few of her novels about Manhattan are classics. In them she pillories its trendiness, and the savage climbing of artists, writers, and business people, especially in the advertising and public relations games. With such subjects, one would think she would have hit a live nerve with readers, but what essentially happened was that book after book didn't quite connect with the popular taste. She did a good bit of railing and whining about the fact that the public couldn't take wit, especially when mixed with mordant subject matter. But, as we have seen with Dorothy Parker, this excuse won't wash. Wilson, after knowing her for about ten years, got down to the job of telling her a thing or two about craft. Take it as you will, Dawn took it badly. In a 1943 letter Wilson told her the truth of the matter—of course, as he saw it. "I had definitely made up my mind years ago that you could not be any good as a writer; and after telling you frankly, I believe, on the occasion of our last supping at the Pickwick, I decided that I ought to check up on my

intuitions which have very seldom betrayed me. Imagine my amaze-
ment at discovering how good your novels are and that I had been
taking you all these years for an incompetent!" He was delighted by
the humor, wit and "lively observation." But the rough stuff in the
evaluation still stood. The dynamic here—what was going on
between the two of them—not only had to do with literary quality
and liking a friend's work, but also with the peculiar kind of relationship that they had set up together.

Wilson was here addressing her in his fictional persona as Ernest
Wigmore, a down-at-the-heels literary man and she was often cast
as Mrs. Humphrey Ward, a real-life Victorian worthy. Later on, the
two adopted the characters of a raffish couple, Aurore and Raoul.
This permitted a good deal of mauling (to use Wilson's expression
about the Nabokov correspondence), joking, ridicule, and plain
ordinary offensive frankness. On Wilson's side, it allowed him to
throw across a remark that's quite hard to swallow. It also allowed
him, in other letters, to tell her (hold the diplomacy) just what was
wrong with her work.

In 1948, he put it this way, addressing her as "Dawn" but signing
himself "love,/Wig." He had the best of both worlds here, directness and his mask. "About your book [*The Locusts Have No King*]:
I had the feeling that I often have with your novels—that you
brought it out at a stage when you had merely got the material lined
up so that you could see what problems still had to be dealt with. It
is full of holes that ought to be filled. Sometime you must give a
book six months more and turn out a masterpiece."

This thought about half-finished work was nothing new. Wilson
had told her about it publicly in a review published in the *New Yorker*
in 1944 of *My Home Is Far Away*. There his phrases were lapidary
and perfectly to the point: "Three of her recent novels—*Angels on
Toast* and *A Time to Be Born*, as well as this latest one—have all
been in some ways excellent but they sound like advanced drafts of
books rather than finished productions." He goes on to make his
precise generalization: "Miss Powell has simply not allowed herself
enough time to smooth these gashes and hummocks out . . . [she]
has not yet done the sculptural rehandling which is to bring [out] its

self-consistent contours and set it in a permanent pose." This is Wilson at his most sober, with no mauling and no joking. Powell's reaction immediately was that the book was killed with guarded praise. She wanted more about her wit and less about her sloppy craftsmanship. But that reaction was only the beginning in the dynamics of their friendship. In her 1945 diaries, she vented about Wilson, the man and the critic. The trouble with him, it would seem, was everything. "All relations with Bunny are dictated by him—he is the one to name the hour, the place, the subject of conversation. After knowing him slightly several years I finally realize he is not at all what he seemed—he is totally unaware and violently allergic to whatever is going on. He is mystified and annoyed by the simple process of creation; he is furious at the things he does not understand—furious, blind and bored. What he does not understand is all life that is not in print, so he sees people, invents a literary category for them, then locks them up in it, occasionally peeking at them through the iron bars of the peephole to say: 'There you are, you in-love-with-father, hate-mother type, reacting exactly as your type does and any other way you act will not be observed by me.'"

The justice of this, of course, is a matter for argument. Philosopher William Barrett accused him of the very same thing in his memoir *The Truants*. When he led Wilson around Rome after the Second World War, Barrett said that the critic could see nothing but what was already in his mind. The trouble with this is that we have observed Wilson in the very act of changing his mind about people—in his diaries, his fiction, and his essays. One of his typical critical ploys is to change his mind.

Powell's venting about rigid Bunny goes on in the 1945 entry and also goes off into the realms of resentment and rancor—not to mention gross inaccuracy: "Freud served a purpose for this type of anxious-to-know-what-they-can-never-comprehend intellectual. For they can fasten a ready-made label from the printed book on anyone without even trying to study them. Bunny resents women being friends with each other, and since he is positive they cannot be friends, he tries to make trouble between them by resorting to such a bludgeoning type of bitchery that it unites them against him. He likes all conventional things but fancies himself a revolutionist. There is no popular opinion he does not share, no unsuccessful artist or writer he does not berate, no Book-of-the-Month he does not praise. He wants to see his ladies alone so he can attack them, leave them chastened and feeling limp, hopeless, unloved, unattractive. He has told them that they are looking well, that usually they look so unkempt, so dowdy; he has told them on seeing their latest work that he always felt their best work was done when they were twenty; he has told them that everything they like is impossible; everything they dislike is perfect and a test of intelligence and taste. He beams with joy and well-nourished nerves as he leaves, like a vampire returning from a juicy grave."

Parsing this muddled mouthful is heavy work if one were to take it quite seriously. Yet, since it's part of the legend and lore of Wilson the Monster, one must proceed to refute the ridiculous. Yes, there's a tincture of truth in the accusation that Wilson could be high-handed, but the rest of it, despite an air of plausibility, is pretty much guff and hot air. First of all, Wilson specialized in overthrowing the readymade and the reductive, and was famous far and wide for not sticking to theories and principles in criticism and evaluation. He had a very light touch as a psychological critic, for example, and his journals, when they psychologize about people, like to show them in the raw, give various sides of their character, and refrain from concluding.

As far as making trouble among women goes, this was a strange charge to level against a man who liked to mix and match people socially, didn't mind having his old girlfriends meet his wives, and insisted that his wives accept his women friends. We can think of no example of Wilson stirring up trouble and playing one woman against another. If she had been at all on the mark, Powell would have noticed his real game—pressing the buttons of his wives, making himself more and more attractive to more and more women. This is quite different from attempting to make one woman hate another. He didn't want rancor; he wanted attention. Notice the trouble he went to get Margaret Marshall and Mary McCarthy up to his place Trees at the same time.

He could be argumentative, and was, on many an occasion, but he characteristically combined the argumentative and the genial, as he did in his relationships with Louise Bogan and Léonie Adams. Such examples can be multiplied. To accuse Wilson of conventionality—to accuse the refugee from Red Bank of being a conformist—is like accusing F. Scott Fitzgerald of being too calm. It makes no sense whatsoever.

As for popular opinions, in a long life he hardly shared any of them: He didn't like Roosevelt and was against America's entry into the Second World War, and he hated detective fiction, most pop culture, and entertainers, including, in his last days, Barbra Streisand. As for berating unsuccessful writers, the charge is silly. He championed obscure talents and had a tendency to take shots at big moneymakers like Somerset Maugham. All of which is to say that he had no use for the to-do and hoopla that attended most bestsellers and the book clubs that marketed them. As for being unchivalrous and putting women down, his journals are a kind of literary tribute to beauty, femininity, style, and allure. Unlike many men, he seems sensitive to the clothes, grooming, and social presentation of his female companions. Wilson, of course, was first and foremost the intellectual, but that never kept him from noticing the whole world of appearances.

It doesn't do Dawn's screed much good if we consider what she wrote in her diary two years before about the stimulating effect of cocktails with Wilson. She was excited to hear about the story of Frances in his journals—"his comments on the woman and his varying opinion of her. . . . He said he had put down everything she said, they did, etc., and the result is the 'greatest love story ever written,' in pornographic detail. . . . It was exhilarating to spend time again with a sharp, creative, literary mind, a balance so necessary in the hoodlum world I live in."

So where does Dawn's tirade of misperceptions and misjudgments come from? She was an exceptionally incisive observer of human foibles. Her novels take on the follies of many different types of New Yorkers, most of them venal and grasping. Her depressing provincials are also rendered with a keen eye. But she was caught in an all-too-human situation: that of the neglected writer. Her resentment, raillery, mockery, and nastiness work well when she is taking on hustlers in the art world, nonproductive writers, and do-nothing bohemians in one of her best books, *The Golden Spur*. They work less well when taking on a friend who did her a lot of good, was responsible for a Viking contract, wrote one essentially laudatory review—and would in 1962 celebrate her and put her in a class with Evelyn Waugh, Anthony Powell, and Muriel Spark.

But the fact remains that Dawn Powell was not a prophetess, and had taken some roughing up in letters, life, and reviewing. There was also a long period in the 1930s when Wilson didn't react to her work at all. And the letter quoted above suggests that for a long time he considered her an incompetent. Sorting all this out— justifying his remarks, justifying her resentment—is a difficult task. On his side, there was the characteristic bluntness; on her side, there was peevishness and shooting from the hip. Their relationship, however, managed to endure, despite such things. Not only did it endure, but there was considerable warmth on both sides once they became older. What had started off as a rather troubled friendship between a high-powered critic and a neglected novelist became the relationship/friendship of two old pals who had seen fads, writers, and movements come and go.

By 1962, they were well used to each other, and they were also able to handle a blowout and still remain friends. A diary entry of Powell's indicates that she exploded at him in a taxi, accusing him of standing behind his wife's negative feelings about her. It seems that Elena, according to Wilson, had grown to like Dawn and Dawn was humiliated by the fact that she had always liked Elena. This mishmash then prompted Wilson to say: "I wish you weren't so jealous of me, Dawn. It makes it very hard for you." She replied that what *was* hard was being kept "on that little back street," apart from the mainstream of his life and his other friendships. They had evidently had an essentially one-on-one friendship, and Dawn wondered why. Wilson said yes, it had been hard for her. They parted on that note without any "real embarrassment." The next day she made it up with him by sending a daft Aurore wire: "Darling, what happened to us? Was it my money or your music? Was it the Club? Where did we go wrong, dear?" Raoul replied, suggesting that they not "see each other for awhile. The strain of our relationship is becoming difficult." Wilson's later reply—lest it be said that he held a grudge or was peevish—was the November review praising her in the *New Yorker*. At this late date, it turned out that what he wanted to say was that for all her lack of glamour, for all her failure to suck up to the literary establishment, and for all her lack of sentimentality, she triumphed as an artist. The piece, called "Dawn Powell: Greenwich Village in the Fifties," catches her as she plays her strongest suit, extols her "kaleidoscopic liveliness," and offers her some of the highest praise that he can give anyone. Her "mind is very stout and self-sustaining," which is to say she has the solidity and enduring quality that he values most. In other words, she is a classic.

· · · · · ·

ANGELA ANAÏS Juana Antolina Rosa Edelmira Nin y Culmell— known to the world as Anaïs Nin—was as far as you can get from Dawn Powell's solidity. Wilson, in starting off his relationship with her, commented on the fact that he could never read her stuff: It was too "ethereal." He met her at the Gotham Book Mart on 47th Street when he was married to Mary McCarthy. Frances Steloff, the legendary proprietor, put Nin's *Under a Glass Bell* into his hands. But it's his eyes rather than his critical judgment that would be doing the work thereafter. "The first time I saw you, . . . you were wearing a little cape and hood. I thought you were the most exquisite woman I had ever seen. I was so enthusiastic that I went and told Mary McCarthy. I had praised another woman so much, Mary was irritated. When we began to be estranged, to quarrel, among other things she accused me of being in love with you."

Nin was yet another whiner and complainer—one of those

brilliant women that Wilson ultimately found to be "neurotic." She
felt that he didn't appreciate her enough: This judgment was
threaded through her diary entries of the forties and took on a life
of its own as she found every way imaginable to put down the critic.
He was "purely intellectual, unemotional." He was likened to "older
people who fall into rigid patterns." He was quoted as saying, "I hate
young writers. I hate them." First he was accused of being a stodgy
part of the "English tradition," soon thereafter, he was a "Dutch
burgher." He was "a dictator" with "no magic" and "no poetry" in his
makeup. He was all criticism and no spontaneity. The charges take
on a physical cast as she lashed out at him as someone who was not
attractive enough in his person and his style. Furthermore, he
chose the wrong settings—Longchamps, "the most banal of restaurants." (Rather incoherently she is fascinated by the orange walls in
the place, which were "beautiful as fruit, and the noises and the
lights of the summer gay and wonderful.")

　　He was the wrong kind of person for her, no emotionally unbut-
toned Henry Miller. The latter boyfriend—no devotee of scholarship, criticism, and meticulous judgment—was poles apart from
what she discovered in Wilson. "To me he seemed to have this hard-
ening of the arteries I find in men of achievement. The florid skin,
the satiated flesh, the solidity of the earth, and its heaviness. He is
didactic; he has conventional ideas about form and style; he has
scholarship. He is all brown: brown earth, brown thought, brown
writing." (She forgot the brown suits, but she may well have been
echoing James Joyce's putdown of the fuddy-duddy desiccated Mr.
Browne in "The Dead," who is "all brown.") The fact is, however,
that this hopelessly out-of-it man was the critic who reviewed Nin
four times in two years in the *New Yorker,* praised her work, and
referred to someone who was coming from nowhere in a literary
way as "a very good artist." In his review of *Under the Glass Bell* in
April 1944, he took note of her gifts for imagery and her superiority
to most of the Surrealists. But he evidently did not manage to satisfy her in his response to the work. She thought the review was
"well-intentioned . . . but inept and inadequate." She also had no
idea of the company she was keeping: Gore Vidal, one of her friends

Edna St. Vincent Millay
[Photo by Arnold Genthe]

Edmund Wilson in 1930
[Courtesy of The Beinecke Library, Yale University Archives]

Magda Johann

Mary Blair
[Photo by Francis Bruguiree]

Louise Bogan
[Amherst College Archives and Special Collections]

Léonie Adams
[Photo by Blackstone Studios]

Dorothy Parker

Elinor Wylie

A drawing of Elinor Wylie
from the *New Yorker*

Margaret Canby
[Courtesy of The Beinecke Library,
Yale University Archives]

Wilson and Canby in California

Margaret Canby in 1929

Louise Fort

Anaïs Nin
[Photo by Carl Van Vechten]

Elizabeth Waugh
[Courtesy of the Waugh family papers
1838–1971 in the Archives of American Art,
Smithsonian Institution.]

Edmund Wilson c. 1940–1950s
[Photo by Sylvia Salmi]

Mary McCarthy

Mamaine Paget

Leonor Fini

Elena Wilson
[Courtesy of The Beinecke Library,
Yale University Archives]

Dawn Powell
[Collection Tim Page]

Mary Pcolar c. 1970

Penelope Gilliatt
[Photo by Zoë Dominic]

Edmund Wilson in Talcottville
[Courtesy of The Beinecke Library, Yale University Archives]

at the time who later came to see her limitations, summed up the situation. "At no point is she aware of having been in the presence of America's best mind. But then," Vidal adds, "Wilson represents all that she hates: history, politics, literature. To her, mind and feeling must be forever at war."

Behind her peevishness and snapping in her journals is of course the sexual subtext of their relationship. He evidently reminded her of a patriarch, and her own father, a composer-pianist and Cuban-born bohemian, had been the kind of patriarch who perhaps was involved in child molestation. Wilson had this ugliness projected on to him, and the Nin journals went to great lengths to make him the oppressor.

Whether in relationships or in the literary life, he weighed heavily on all those around him, and was completely unlike Nin herself, who enjoyed describing the fact that "Wilson's writing never gathers up oxygen and flies into space. It always follows earthy gravitation and rolls downward." This is true. Wilson had little hot air in his books. But despite his frankness and grounding, his literary-sexual relationship with Nin exhibits some real loss of honor and integrity. For the first time, he overplays his hand in evaluating a woman whose best work, the *Diaries* (legendary in the 1940s, but published from 1966 to 1980), had yet to appear. She gets star billing for fiction that is often slack, and that has a pretty face behind it. Nevertheless, the compromised Wilson couldn't help trying to show her something. Her *Diaries* even indicate that he wanted to combine literary guidance with marriage—that toxic formula that we know from Mary McCarthy. "I would love to be married to you and I would teach you to write." His gift of Jane Austen's novels was meant to provide a model, but only further antagonized her. She wanted rhapsodies about her work when she was way ahead of the game with Wilson's overrating. His false praise boomeranged on him, and Jeffrey Meyers has rightly highlighted a snarled sentence that Wilson wrote about her—a syntactical mess, because Wilson's own feelings were a mess. "She has worked out her own system of dynamics, and gives us a picture, quite distinct from that of any other writer, of the confusions that result to our emotions from the uncertainty of our capacity to identify the kind of love that we tend to imagine with our actual sexual contacts, and of the ambivalent attractions and repulsions that are so hard on contemporary nerves."

Wilson's nerves were frayed in the mid-forties, mostly as a result of his acrimonious dealings with Mary McCarthy. One thing Nin is right about is that he was a desperate, lonely, and forlorn character —a state that did not do much to sharpen his judgment of a beautiful woman. Unlike his response to Edna Millay's work, this writing is insincere, clouded, and informed by a combination of infatuation and frustration, rather than genuine passion. Back in the twenties Wilson was also taken by an alluring young writer, but the difference is that he never lost his head in losing his heart.

Writing about an evening he had with Nin in 1967 afforded Wilson an occasion to review her case. Recollecting what he had written her about her work in a letter back in the forties, he notes, "She had not understood, and still, I think, does not understand, that I was trying to tell her that she would not attract attention or even get readily published if she continued to offer thin slices of a larger more ambitious work which ought to be more comprehensible." There speaks Wilson the critic. Unfortunately, when he was actually in her presence he tended to leave his critic's hat at home. During their evening together, they compared notes on what had gone wrong in their relationship. She complained again that he had not supported her work as warmly as she thought he should have. Wilson, going easy on her, admitted that he hadn't done her early novel *Under a Glass Bell* justice. An odd thing to say, when he had twice praised it in print, each time beyond its slender merits.

In his journal, Wilson turns to her life situation as well as her writing; he seems to take in stride his recent discovery that all the while she has been portraying herself in her diaries as a free spirit Nin has had a husband, Ian Hugo. Wilson might have been a bit shaken to learn that there was yet a second husband out on the West Coast, one Rupert Cole (making her an unapprehended bigamist). But probably not, given his ability to campaign, show off, and be stimulated in the midst of complications. And from the start he had been a sucker for her prettiness; he still maintained that even in the light of the Princeton Club, she "didn't seem to look any older" than she had in the forties.

Wilson and Nin met again at the club to go over what she had written about him in the diaries of 1944–1947, which she was preparing for publication. She told him that he wouldn't recognize himself and said she had portrayed him as a Dutch burgher in too-large shoes. Wilson seems to have been undismayed by this, and asked her to change only a few matters of fact about Mary McCarthy and about the author of the set of books he had given her—"as if there could be such a thing" as a "set" of Emily Brontë. Perhaps he was so sanguine in the face of her portrayal because she pleased him at the same time by telling him that it was of course impossible to write "the best things in our relations." Like so many of Nin's remarks, this doesn't make much sense upon close examination, but as usual Wilson cut her a lot of slack. Summing up the two hours they had spent together he said mildly, "I had forgotten what good company she could be."

Wilson and Nin—the intellectual who loved evidence, the embroiderer who loved fancies—did have a few things in common. The first was their love of bohemian life in the palmy days of the twenties and thirties. They were major players, knew many people, and their prickliness notwithstanding, managed to make a great many friends and lead a kind of literary life that is no longer possible. They wrote about their contemporaries memorably, but here is a similarity that leads to a crucial difference. As indefatigable journal keepers, they both had an energy and determination that remains impressive and that is a permanent part of the twentieth-century literary record. Nin, however, was given to doctoring her journals, excising passages, and not letting the immediate response stand. Her friend the critic Maxwell Geismar allowed that she was as famous as Pepys, but he was not pleased with the tinkering, reshaping, and falsification. Wilson is famous for his remark to Leon Edel: "I don't want to cut any corners." Edel reminded him that he could do what he liked with his own writing, but Wilson preferred putting things in shape and letting his old faces from the twenties and thirties and forties look at us without a lot of makeup.

And then there's the matter of the erotic component. Nin was given the chance to read *Hecate County* in manuscript, and one of the few positive notes in her responses to Wilson and his work is her comment that this novel could be a breakthrough for American writers and a blow to censorship. But the concession to him doesn't bring them very close together. Nin is airy-fairy, mystical, and very much into what she believes is a kind of feminine discourse that rebels against the heavy hand of Maleness. Wilson is very down to earth, very much involved with fact checking and letting the sometimes ugly record stand, even with its confusions, huge cast of characters, and undoctored dramatic moments. So in the end the two erotic journal keepers are separated by an aesthetic and a whole way of recording experience. No one would go to Nin for facts and chronicling, but Wilson is one of the source books of American modernism.

·  ·  ·  ·  ·  ·

JUST AFTER seeing Nin in March of 1945, Wilson was on literary maneuvers again. He got an assignment—his first lucrative one—from the *New Yorker* to look at ravaged Europe. Beginning in England, he went to Italy and eventually to Greece. His travels were, as usual, flavored with romantic activity, both physical and platonic.

In terms of his own critical art and love of artistry, an important woman during this period was the Roman painter Leonor Fini. In *Europe Without Baedeker,* her aesthetic and her personality are thrown into high relief and serve as a curious counterpoint to the horrors of the period. Fini was born in Argentina in 1907 of an Italian mother and an Argentine absentee father. She came to Italy and earned a reputation as a Surrealist painter, her particular brand of the style featuring elongated female figures and bizarre juxtapositions of imagery. Typical is an image that Wilson describes in *Baedeker:* a beautiful and voluptuous girl emerging from a distorted plant. Fini's art is by no means simply tricky, cheap, and kitschy: An accomplished draftsman, a strange orchestrator of compositions, and an offbeat colorist, she produced striking and original work—

although it should be said that the work has a certain Gothic decadence and witchiness. Her female figures are slender, haunting, and look haunted. Wilson's attraction to Fini's aesthetic—especially her taste for the grotesque—foreshadows his admiration for the Italian literary critic and connoisseur Mario Praz and his themes of eroticism, spirituality, and cruelty in *The Romantic Agony*. Like Praz, Fini deals in Romantic agonies, freakishness, sadomasochistic material, and the sinister side of aestheticism. Such hothouse, weird subject matter takes us as far back in Wilson's career as *Axel* and points forward to Wilson's admiration for Edward Gorey's world of the comic grotesque and to his fascination with the monsters of Bomarzo.

In *Baedeker* Fini is a revered figure—and someone he wants to be friends with. In London, in the spring, he speaks of buying paints for her and of his delight in being offered his choice of any one of her drawings. Fini was, let it be said, a *grande dame* and a glamorous figure of real magnitude. "She's magnificently and generously Italian." He said that she was "a handsome and voluptuous woman" with large eyes and "abundant dark hair." When he gets to Rome in midsummer, he devotes a whole section of his travelogue to a visit with her. The scene in which she is depicted is, to say the least, a bit eerie. The "enormous old palace in the squalid Piazza del Gesu" seems to echo Wilson's earlier reference to what Rome looked like—something out of Piranesi with exposed staircases, labyrinthine passages, and an intricate, menacing aspect. In residence amid the "disorderly elegance" was Fini the intrepid artist, "unshaken in morale" in the midst of post-war destruction.

Wilson had a good number of things to say about her art, some of them a bit contradictory. In a certain sense, he seems to be overwhelmed by her, but not cheaply infatuated in the way that he was with Nin—maybe because of an in-residence *marchese*. (Not a lot is made of this man, however.) Wilson proceeds to spin out his impressions. The praise for her devotion to painting is diminished somewhat by his comment that she is "entirely a *female* artist." This remark—in its time and place—is not exactly meant as a compliment, in that Wilson expands on it and says that it entails being more concerned with dreams and her own personality than with craftsmanship. His descriptions give one the sense that he doesn't quite know how to process what she is doing: Yes, her work has the strange juxtapositions that he frequently values in art, in this case, "brokenness and deadness" with "a warm and rich physical life." Wilson, the lover of paradoxes and tensions, gets this one right. But his basic reservation about her as an artist, her narcissism, seems both wide of the mark and unfair in evaluating someone whose work is as carefully crafted as hers. Fini was a meticulous worker, often producing only ten pieces a year.

At the bottom of the problem—Wilson's problem—is undoubtedly the fact that he was fascinated by the creepy quality of her work and also repelled by it. Fini had illustrated Sade's *Juliette* and obviously had a talent for depicting sadism and other nasty acts. Wilson pulls back from this whole world of relished violence, understandably in the age of Buchenwald. He comments on her "amused astonishment" at a *Vogue* article on the concentration camp juxtaposed with "smart bathing brassieres." Wilson does not accuse her of being insensitive, but he does impart a moral lesson—in the mode of his essays on social suffering in *American Earthquake:* "The Surrealists had cultivated deliberately a sadism of the parlor and the gallery; but now the times had overtaken and passed them in a manner so overwhelming that it was impossible for Leonor Fini not to be shocked at the impropriety of juxtaposing these wretched victims with the refinements of Saks Fifth Avenue." Fini's art triggers such thoughts in him and brings out his divided nature: the moralist faced with the frightening depths of the imagination. Meanwhile, sex does not appear to have been in the mix with this beautiful woman, yet sexuality certainly was.

· · · · · ·

BEFORE WILSON had his memorable encounter with Leonor Fini, he had spent some time in London, where he took in the grim sights of the ravaged city, ate some pretty bad meals (including what probably was crow passing for duck at a great London restaurant), tangled with the Labour MP Harold Laski, and groused about what was on offer in Picadilly and Green Park in terms of street romance. He was billeted in what was probably "a converted brothel" and was in sour humor. Actually, the main gripe was that English tarts, for all their pertness and piquancy, didn't offer the smooth, gracious service of their French counterparts. In Chapter 8 of *Europe Without Baedeker*—a section that would of course have been too frank for the *New Yorker* or any other popular magazine of the period—Wilson complains about the blowsy, often rude, rundown, Rowlandson-like quality of the streetwalkers. Always involved in cultural matters, he quotes Alberto Moravia, who attributes the bad service to the fact that prostitution was not, in England, as it is in France, a recognized profession. The whole British scene was just too brusque, transactional, crude, and sordid. He admitted that "a tough, short and stocky blonde wench" was good-natured enough when she approached him, but not to his liking.

A French prostitute named Odette is made much of both in *Baedeker* and more graphically in *The Forties* because she has just the right blend of efficiency, manners, and human depth.

Wilson, always sensitive to paradoxes, was taken by the fact that this woman of the street also has her decent and domestic side. On the one hand, she conducted business in a totally skilled way, getting her clothes off and a rubber condom on him; on the other hand, she had a story to tell, as he hears when he paid her extra to stay and talk. The talk gets more time than the sex, and we hear that she works for the Red Cross by day, folding bandages, and is knitting a stout sweater for the director even as they speak. In this overtime period he seems to enjoy the particulars of her career plans, a future running a lingerie shop back in the old country. Opportunities for graphic description—taken of course in the diaries—are in *Baedeker* bypassed in favor of sociology. (The journals refer, in addition to the condom, to a purple girdle, her "black bush," and her nakedness except for rolled down stockings and shoes.) The *Baedeker* material concentrates on setting and characterization rather than transactions. We even hear about the Parisian prints in her room.

The sour note struck in London never quite disappears from

*Europe Without Baedeker.* Wilson fulminates about Roman corruption, the fetid atmosphere, the open-air brothel aspect of the streets, and the fact that people seem "like lumps of flesh and fat in a cheap but turbid soup." It is true that his spirits pick up a bit when he sees the smart shops of Rome and the well-turned-out women who make even their cheap clothes seem chic. He loves the attractive footwear—in keeping with his mild foot fetish—and he is better humored for a time. But soon the grouchiness apparent in London returns and presently things take a turn for the worse. He becomes downright exasperating about human weakness, the badness of the species, and the lowdown sordidness of Neapolitans particularly.

At his very worst, he is pretty awful: "The Neapolitans seem to me to have as little relation to people as small octopi, crabs and mollusks brought in by the marine tide." This passage, by no means isolated, feeds into his wooly speculations at the end of *Baedeker* about eugenics. This bad bee in his bonnet is all about wanting to create a better world order after World War II. Sad to say, such thinking—about the awfulness of real people and scientific hopes of making them to his liking—is a minor but distinct note that runs through his later writing. Yet it should be said that this cold and fishy part of him is always accompanied by lapses into feeling. Sympathizing with the plight of the soldier, he does a wonderful little analysis of the signature World War II song "Lili Marlene." About lost love and pain, the song seems to him one of the good things on the popular scene in Naples.

. . . . . .

THE SPRING AND SUMMER of 1945 were active periods for Wilson, romantically speaking. To begin with, his intense and passionate attraction to Mamaine Paget was in full bloom; at the same time he was managing his feelings for two other attractive women, Darina Silone and Eva Siphraios. Elena—the woman who was to be his fourth wife—had not as yet come on the scene as any more than an acquaintance. This tail end of the war was a time of experimentation and sorting out. Prostitutes, acquaintances, other men's wives—all figured in Wilson's internal drama.

Darina was the wife of Ignazio Silone, author of *Bread and Wine* and legendary intellectual of the left. She was one personality that Wilson engaged with and was to have strong feelings about later on in his life. She was a magnetic Irish Catholic who had had a puritanical upbringing. Temperamentally charming, she is a shadowy figure in this period but someone we need to watch later on. In *The Forties* there is a reference to an astute remark about politics interjected in a gentle voice, and not much more. Silone was a somewhat dour character, and some reports indicate that their marriage was a sparse affair, sexually speaking. Wilson came into the picture —and provided his own brief picture of what they were like. Always methodical, he seems to have been laying the groundwork for future flirtation, and of course documenting it.

The same can be said for his remarks about a charming guide that he had in Athens, Eva Siphraios. She appears in *Baedeker* as Eleni, a young wife married to an older man and the mother of children of ten and thirteen. Darina and Eva probably should be categorized as what Truman Capote would call "backup girls," there for moments of boredom and, in Wilson's case, for teasing his last wife. Wilson was never a complete cad, and does not fit Adam Gopnik's definition of men who rate women like wines on a numerical scale; but he was a connoisseur, collector, and scrupulous maintainer of ties who always had a well-stocked cellar of memories in reserve.

. . . . . .

ON JULY 4, 1945, Wilson wrote his pal Betty Huling from Rome: "Your question about heart interest came apropos, as what I wouldn't have thought possible at my age, I fell terribly in love in London with a young English girl [Mamaine Paget]—twenty-seven and one of the brightest I have ever known and—need I say?—rather neurotic." This was the real thing, powerful emotion in a period of dalliance. Wilson was at one and the same time sure of himself and not quite clear about what he was doing: He loved this ethereal socialite and glamour girl who was a dominant presence in the London scene around Cyril Connolly's magazine *Horizon;* yet he also knew that he was being more than a bit foolish and observed himself in his extravagant futilities. He was, after all, dramatically older and no-where in her league in terms of physical attractiveness. This widely admired British beauty also had a boyfriend, the ruggedly hand-some (in the beat-up tradition of Bogart) Arthur Koestler, author of *Darkness at Noon*. He happened to be away at the time when Wilson was in Britain, but Wilson probably didn't even need this incentive: he was, be it remembered, not easily discouraged. He went into deep waters with this woman, probably sexual waters. (In *The Forties* he speaks of "Intoxication after making love," and speaks of "G," i.e., Mamaine: This may be wish fulfillment, but if it is, we can find no other case of it.) The passages in the candid Chapter 8 in *Europe Without Baedeker* have the flavor of intimacy: The two are together in the evening, conversing intensely, and he is even prompted to ask her to "keep still" in order that he might draw a verbal sketch of her. This does not sound like a casual date. Nevertheless we have her testimony—perhaps a bit tainted—that there was no sex.

One thing is for sure; there was a good bit of intensity and she went along with his routine: accepted the compliments, held up her end of the flirtation, and permitted him the time and scope to produce some remarkably heartfelt descriptions of her. Whatever you want to call this, it was not simply being friends. The language, not to mention the gifts and blandishments, tells a lot. She has a volatility of mood that "always enchants me," Wilson writes. Her feet—invariably an erotic indicator—are not small but they "added to her piquancy and revealed a firm base in substance for solid qual-ities of intellect and character with which I was coming to credit her." If this seems a bit coolly evaluative, it should be noted that Wilson could be coolly evaluative and erotic at the same time.

He never insisted on physical flawlessness and found beauty in her "very fine though rather irregular features. Sharp and longish nose, with a hump and a dip in the bridge, that is assertive and shows curiosity." The description itself should dispel notions that Wilson was merely besotted by conventionally sexy looks and pres-entation. "G" (as she is called in Chapter 8) is in a gray suit and white blouse at the time—hardly a negligee—and the one extravagant detail, "her little diamond bright blue eyes," is elucidated by saying that they might be used "as points for Johanssen gauges." (For sure, his mistress's eyes were nothing like the sun.) One needs to get a technical manual to unpack Wilson's response, and one needs also to remember that he specialized in the off-beat critique of women he loved. He didn't idealize her figure—with its "disproportions of largeness and longness with smallness and shortness." He found the whole presence an expression of "her complexity."

In addition to that, the material in Chapter 8 on Mamaine shows a fascination with the English response to things. Her matter-of-factness and dry thank yous for gifts—silk stockings, an antique fan, earrings, sparkling wine, cigarettes, a book by Silone (one of her favorite authors)—were part of what interested Wilson. The "British phlegm" was something that he hadn't to date experienced in a relationship. No "transports of delight" that he had been getting from American girls who had received his gifts. Wilson always liked edge, and here he has it, complete with Mamaine "G" sweeping up the loot and putting it away.

The Mamaine relationship played out over a very short period of time—the spring and summer of 1945. Mamaine told her twin sister Celia to get Wilson's book "and read about me." Although she admits to being "G" and says Wilson "very clearly hints that I was his mistress," she adds an emphatic, "which God forbid!" Those who collect lore on parallel lives led by twins might wish to note that, in the same year, 1945, in which Mamaine was turning down a marriage proposal from America's foremost critic, Celia was turning down a marriage proposal from his British counterpart, George Orwell.

By the fall, Wilson was back in the States and sending Mamaine a few desperate letters meant to protract something that was dead, or perhaps, in her mind, never alive. In any event, June and July were active months in Wilson's imagination, and there's also no doubt that their many meetings fed his desires. The spring segment of the "affair," if that's the word, contains plenty of ardor and professions of love and yearning that couldn't have emerged from nowhere. We do not have any record of Wilson fabricating romance out of whole cloth or from vague, at-a-distance attractions: This seems similar.

On April 28th, he'd just left London, told her he missed her, and did confess that he might be having "daydreams that can't correspond with any reality." He wants to avoid these things, but he still feels that there's some reason to tell her "[p]lease don't fall in love with anyone else before I see you again." In Italy, in the middle of May, he wants her with him, has avoided the sights until she, too, can enjoy them. He pleads with her to be in contact, a complicated matter in post-war Europe. A few days later he says that he doesn't want to tear up (as she has asked him to do) "your pictures": These are "all I have to feed on." He had taken them, wished he had taken more—and the reader of the letter doesn't quite know why they have to be torn up.

There was no break in their relationship at this point, no fight, but there is evidently something about those pictures. Koestler was not on the scene, and in any case he would not have been likely to rifle Edmund Wilson's picture gallery. Less than a week later, Wilson offered a marital proposal through the mail and, while not on bended knee, was prepared to say, "I've never felt a natural understanding with any woman come so quickly as it has with you." This is not the stuff of discouragement, reserve, and coolness. It is not necessary to engage in wild conjectures to assume that there was some warmth of feeling on her part. So what was the problem?

Years later, according to Jeffrey Meyers, the all-too-obvious came out: Celia indicated that Mamaine was never physically attracted. This definitive explanation, however, was not enough to shut down what was going on in 1945. Wilson was laying siege to her and bringing out his strongest artillery: his crusty interesting self, his ardor, and his incredible persistence. Just as no literary project, no matter how big and complicated could daunt him, no woman, no matter how glamorous and remote could quite discourage him if he had the desire.

He did his usual, told her about the scenes that he had observed in his own ironic, off-center way. It can't have been uninteresting to her to hear a major critic critiquing the English public, the celebrations at the end of the war, and the mood of the time. He found the VE Day crowds "idiotic," and while we find him at the pretty awful top of his obnoxious form, we still have to admit that a young woman might have been flattered by his candor and privileged to watch him showing off with his ad lib remarks. She was also a grade-A socialite, had been presented at court, and, with her equally beautiful twin sister, had been written about in gossip columns and papers ever since her debutante days. His high-horse remarks—that snobbish side of Wilson that always looked down on populist outpourings— were what he wanted to communicate to her. Besides that, he enjoyed sharing his more private perceptions about puppetry, children's imagination, and by implication his own lonely childhood. What was the response he got?

The above-mentioned phlegm was only part of it; he was also given a warm hearing. By mid-June, however, unable to convince her to come to him, Wilson breaks off his European tour to return to her in London. When there, "in spite of our snappings and snarlings," he still felt closer to her than to anyone else, although he admitted that this was "(perhaps an illusion)." He also had a strong intimation that there was something problematic—which is to say unsolid—about her reactions: "I think you live a lot in cobwebby relationships with people based on unrealized possibilities—but sometime, you know, you'll have to try seriously to realize one." This Wilsonian solidity evidently stopped the whole thing on a dime. He's rejected in an unambiguous way at the end of July—not that that kept him from the end of a well-fought campaign.

Back stateside, he renewed his marriage offer and threw in the possibility of a job as his secretary. He also sent along a pair of navy pumps. By the middle of September, he was still mooning about her and fantasizing about their being together, selecting furniture and other things. In an early October letter, he tried to press her buttons by telling her about a new secretary, half-Russian, who had in fact helped him buy things for his apartment on Henderson Place. Since Mary McCarthy had pretty much stripped the apartment, he could honestly play the role of bereft bachelor. Another letter jocularly referred to "a Greek rival" (Eva Siphraios) whose story should be reserved for a "later installment." What does he get from all this? "Am I the victim of English understatement [?]" he asks, after remarking that her last letter rather chilled him. Having reached the end, he nevertheless soldiered on. He said, in November, that he was still in love, always trying to get her to a country where he is and she isn't, saving up shows in New York so that they can see them together, and monitoring her moods in his correspondence with Cyril Connolly. Instead of being despondent, he paints himself as a liberated tiger by virtue of being separated from Mary McCarthy. But there is no response from her.

. . . . . .

WILSON GAVE himself very little recovery time. Brooding and mooning were of course always a part of his personality, but they didn't inhibit action. The forward march of his passions took the form of a sudden assault on Elena Mumm Thornton, the "half-Russian" married secretary. By mid-fall of 1945, this campaign was in full swing; by winter it was an affair. And, by spring, it was a moody, dreamy theme in his letters. "I'm going to write in my notebook some more descriptions of you," he told her in a letter in April, 1946, "so that I can never lose the images of how you looked at certain times." This innocent-sounding, romantic remark belies the flaming sexuality in the journal descriptions. At Henderson Place they were competing for who could get a tongue down whose throat first; he's adoring each breast Andrew Marvell-style; she's crying out "I'm so pleased" and turning him on with just the right blend of the animal—she takes a "wolfish" bite of his arm—and the European lady. In another image, she's clothed in a towel, and he's doing (in words) a Vermeer-like study of her coming out of the bathroom. Wilson, the language freak, takes in the French nuances, the German "r," and the British accent in her speech—the latter giving the piquancy that he likes.

    Besides the romance and sexuality, she presented him with an attractive package for a stable future. In spring letters of 1946, she is gracious, "straight," and quite specific about what she wants to do as his life's companion. She seems to sign on for "cooking and cleaning," averring that she excels at them. She's forthright about her money picture—and dissipates any confusion there might be on his part as to whether she is a monied woman—when she says that she doesn't have "one single, solitary penny." What she does have is the desire to sit "for the rest of [her] life" on his left when he is correcting proofs, imagining that he will keep one hand on her knee while hard at work. This is the unbuttoned version of Agnes Wickfield sitting next to David Copperfield as he writes his books.

The late forties were a period when Wilson wanted to clear away old conflicts, the cobwebs of his past life. He wanted her to do the same, and, from the start, urged her to get on an honest footing with her husband, Jimmy Thornton. By "honest" he meant forthrightly pro-Wilsonian: "How could you live with Jimmy and be having a love affair with me at the same time?" He also gave a nod in the direction of fair play by asking how she could do justice to Jimmy's feelings "if you still cared anything about me?" Wilson wanted her "to put it through," his business-like prescription for decisive action. Practiced in the nasty art of breaking up, he gives some fairly sane advice. Within a month or so, she took it. He didn't complain.

The only complaints are lover's complaints about being separated. He was up on the Cape longing for her, and she was wrapping things up in Manhattan. The best letters that we have are laments of one sort or another—Wilson, located at a great distance, sometimes a continent away, writes with considerable ardor. Sometimes he's only a few states away, when he's in Talcottville, and she's in Wellfleet. Distance makes his pen grow sharper. Their marriage was to have plenty of the excitement and edge that comes from not being together all the time. Recall that Mary Blair was touring a lot of the time, Margaret Canby was in California with her son Jimmy, and Mary McCarthy was on the wing in the Pacific Northwest when he was beached in midsummer Chicago. For Wilson the writing table seems to have the same weight in these romances as the bedroom.

This tall, lithe, sophisticated woman—one of the heirs to the Mumm champagne fortune—was not just a trophy won by a rather bearish, distinguished older man. She fed his imagination as well as his ego. Yes, he wanted to clear off old business and old unpleasantness; at the same time he had a curious way, for better or worse, of weaving his passion for Elena with thoughts of the past, past loves, past experiences. She reminded him of everything he loved best and triggered many associations. If one sorts out extraneous things from basic responses, one sees that Wilson enjoyed—indeed, was overjoyed by—the experience of connecting with beauty and Europeanism. The latter had been a theme from his college days on; he was a very American writer who was nevertheless always looking to the Continent. His first book-length triumph was about Europe. Elena, in a very definite way, returned him to something successful. He felt instantly at ease with her cosmopolitanism, and the life that they built together, with its home base in Wellfleet, was a life that was populated by European intellectuals as well as by American writers and thinkers. It also allowed him to forget his fatal attraction to Irish beauties, types that he got on with, as he said of Darina Silone, "like a house afire," but who ultimately demoralized him. Elena could understand his strong emotional connection with European writers like Nabokov and Malraux; she could speak four languages, make the perfect champagne punch, and talk easily about all things Continental. When he wasn't traveling, she was. And then, they traveled together. It's almost as if the Continent was their third home.

Who was this striking combination of sexuality and European cosmopolitanism? Elena Mumm Thornton was half-Russian, half-German, born in 1906 in Rheims. The German Mumms, of course, were one of the legendary champagne families, and after the First World War their interests had to be relocated to Johannisburg, Germany. As Michael Macdonald tells us, Elena grew up "in a town house near Frankfurt, as well as hotel suites in Paris and Switzerland." She was privately educated and briefly attended art school in Munich and Paris. In 1931, she married James Thornton, a shabby genteel scion of a rich Canadian family in the railroad business. They met in Frankfurt, had a son named Henry, emigrated to Canada, lived in Montreal, and came to New York just before the Second World War. Wilson himself says in *The Sixties* that it's "sad to think" of the gap between Elena's "eagerness" for the New World —with the Marx Brothers, skyscrapers, and *le jazz hot* (all the focus of "the smart people in Paris")—and the reality of stuffy Montreal. The Wilson-Elena story began well into her time in the United States. She first ran across Wilson (who was married to Mary McCarthy) when she was a boarder at Nina Chavchavadze's in Wellfleet. Elena worked at *Town and Country,* and her editorial assistance on "Glimpses of Wilbur Flick" from *Memoirs of Hecate County* brought her together with Wilson after the war. The literary and cultural connection was strong. Wilson writes in his journal, "I love going to theaters and such things with Elena—she is so sensitive and responsive to everything, and her criticisms are always definite. This makes one of our best relationships." We find that while out in Nevada, waiting for their divorces, they plowed through Faulkner's "The Bear"—not exactly light reading for excited lovers. Once they were married (December 11, 1946), they began a life together that always had the flavor of books and book talk. Mary McCarthy's putdown of Elena as merely a hausfrau doesn't wash. The doormat portrait she gives in *A Charmed Life* of "Helen" takes no account of the literary side.

Elena could provide the German language skills that Wilson so much enjoyed drawing on with Louise Bogan. She could read of an evening with him—Goethe, Schnitzler, and Wedekind, the Russians, especially Turgenev and Pasternak—and do so in an exquisitely orchestrated setting that she created at Wellfleet out of family heirlooms, little money, but real taste and flair. The domestic results took time, but they're well described by Wilson's old friend Louise Bogan. She commented that "Elena has really effected a tremendous change in Edmund's way of living"; she remarked that by 1954 the house had become a kind of show place of Elena's handiwork (scraped floors and handmade curtains): In addition to a Federal parlor in yellow and a dining room in blue, full of Staffordshire and silver, there was a "middle room . . . with more blue walls and blue chintz" and Edmund's "magnificent study, with a bathroom attached, and a stairway to an attic, filled with overflow books." She concluded that "for the first time poor E. has attention, space and effectively arranged paraphernalia of all kinds. . . . Now all moves smoothly; tea on a tray for his 'elevenses'; absolute silence in his

working hours, and good meals at appropriate intervals." Poor
Edmund was no longer alternating between fending for himself
(canned turkey a la king and peanut butter sandwiches) and enduring the tensions of Mary McCarthy's kitchen theater. Elena was
balanced and, if such a thing were possible, she tried to balance
him. Yes, his drinking continued apace, but it did not involve pulling drapes off windows or blue sheets off beds. In his new blue
heaven—with a wife who favored man-tailored denim shirts in the
country—he could get down to business, calm himself somewhat,
and think about family rather than parking children.

The family included Elena's son Henry of whom Wilson was very
fond. Wilson offered advice about Henry's education, recommend-
ing St. Paul's for a gentle boy who would probably have found
Andover or Exeter too "hard-boiled." Wilson's own son Reuel was
on the scene every summer, with his friends, including Dwight
Macdonald's son Michael. Rosalind was in and out; and, in 1948,
there was a new addition, Helen Miranda Wilson. She is referred to
along with Elena in a 1954 letter as "you two darling ladies." Once
again, Wilson saw to it that a child of his was the recipient of close
supervision and tender caring. Despite his drinking, his uncertain
temper, and his workaholism, he always had time for children's con-
cerns and pleasures. He was not a literary father from hell, sealed
off or indifferent. The study was sacrosanct, of course. But unlike
him, Wilson's children knew what it was to be part of a home, to
have a father who, even fueled with before-dinner drinks, wine, and
after-dinner drinks, had time to read *David Copperfield* as a good-
night story. Elena, according to the record of Wilson's letters and
diaries, was a kindly and active stepmother to Reuel, and certainly
a conscientious mother. As far back as their courting days, Wilson
made mention of Elena's attempt to smarten up Reuel with a gift of
clothes. Rosalind, off on her own most of the time, always seemed
welcome. Wilson duly recorded the details of all this, never brush-
ing off his children's conflicts, tastes, and desires. Exasperated as
he could be with them when he couldn't bend them to his will, he
nevertheless listened to them and helped them along. His means
improved during his marriage with Elena, but he was never a rich

man, and the help that his children got was help from a struggling
writer who had to begin anew, financially speaking, each time he sat
down to the writing table.

In 1946, when Wilson was out West getting his divorce, he was
also embarking on something new, marriage to a woman who
seemed to want to be married. His thoughts were sometimes quite
optimistic, and he mused on Americans who went out West: "the
frank, free, the first, the adventurous who had lived in the society
that Jefferson had said was something new under the sun." Wilson
definitely projected his sense of excitement and newness onto this
marriage; despite being over fifty he was anxious to be in top form
sexually, to experiment with his new mate, and to enjoy the sensual
and intellectual life with this very right person. *The Forties* records
plenty of rather frank, indeed, somewhat raw, episodes. "On one
Sunday afternoon, we did 69 first. She responded to it. Flushed
darkly—which is rare with her—put her legs up so that I could
push it down into her. I was terrifically swollen and hot—'You were
so big!' she said afterwards—and she got that green wolfish look in
her eyes that is so unlike her ordinary blue-eyed and sweet expression." His bigness and her wolfishness aside, there is also evidence
in this period of anxiety and slowing down. He refers to himself
as "getting slower in coming." And old memories sometimes are
braided with new experiences in a none-too-pleasant way. He
dreams of Edna and Anna and relates the "experience" (evidently a
disagreeable one) while describing a love scene with Elena. Yes, he
wanted things to be new romantically, but he couldn't help colliding with old injuries and physical limitations.

In *The Fifties,* he enjoys recounting their lovemaking, but there
is always a certain note of sadness and diminishment mixed in with
the pleasure. On a picnic in October 1950, in Wellfleet, "we made
love on the sand" and "I gave her my old hat as a pillow." Well
and good, but we get the impression soon thereafter that sheer will
and just enough wine were necessary "as I felt myself driving the
charge home." Intensely pleasurable, certainly: filled with tension,
assuredly. The fifties was a period in which Wilson was battling
not only his aging body, but also his somewhat changed sense of

pleasure. Almost every instance of lovemaking has a tincture of criticism, reserve, or doubt. Up in Talcottville, they tried a venerable
old bed, a family heirloom, and Wilson sours the episode for us
(doubtless intentionally) by saying that it "reminded me . . . of my
more satisfactory experiences with prostitutes: a simple enjoyable
moment." We as readers are not particularly in on the joy when he
further distinguishes the episode as quite different from the more
"romantic" "kind of thing." The infelicity of expression ruins the
scene, and perhaps Wilson, never one to slap down a phrase, knew
just what he was saying. Soon thereafter, we see the rising tension
of things in a dream he had in which his father has more of a right
to go to bed with Elena than he does. This Freudian mix of old guilt
feelings and new worries is typical of the anxiety dreams that
Wilson had during this period. It's also typical of his braiding of past
and present. Wilson, a terrific saver, appears to fit Freud's idea that
everything exists together in the subconscious mind. He doesn't
seem to have much capacity for denial: He faces everything.

By the mid-fifties, he is still enjoying himself with his wife but
dark thoughts start to enter the picture. And a fairly new theme
emerges: Sex seems less importunate, and he is now of an age when
he wants to concentrate on "more intellectual and dignified things."
Worse than that, sex is "an elderly malady," "something like gout,"
and it becomes "sharper as you get older." Sick with desire, Wilson
does not, however, seem to want to get well. Ten days after his six-
tieth birthday in Wellfleet, he's again the sexual *plein air* man with
his companion lacking a pair of panties. This picnic excursion to
Duck Pond included delightful lovemaking, a lot of wine, but inevitable exhaustion. Wilson had an "awful dream" upon returning
home, and confessed to his journal that "my sexual powers must
be definitely flagging." The contradictions—between delight and
terror—are a vital part of the story.

Wilson also has a tendency to be very idiosyncratic in his descriptions of passion and arousal. Surely his description of a radio speech
by Adlai Stevenson and a bout of intense lovemaking is one of the
most curious examples of the sexual life on record, written of course
after Kinsey. Wilson refers to his "period of erotic revival" which

# The Intellectual and the Cosmopolitans 147

started in Europe in 1956. Back home, he and Elena keep up the European tradition while listening to politics: "One night we sat on the couch and listened to Stevenson on the radio, campaigning in Madison Square Garden. I began to feel her . . . and she opened her legs and loved it." It was "the high pitched speech and applause" heard from the Wellfleet study that "created a sort of excitement."

Almost as strange as finding Adlai Stevenson a turn-on is Wilson's naturalistic look at himself and his desire in later years. The sharpness of desire had by no means been destroyed or even diminished. What had changed was his relation to his desire and performance. He was observing and critiquing and concerned with how the sexual function fit into the larger scheme of things. In talking about how Elena was unique and not just a product of her family (i.e., an "animal brood"), he generalized about the confluence of the creative and the sexual in a way that reveals a lot about him as well as about her; he seems proud to have played a part in the formation of her personality. That all this stimulates is both weird and typically Wilsonian; he's turned on by his conceptions. "It is not the family I love but the unique person Elena. This gives me an erection as I write. It is somehow associated with the unique products of art, love is creative as well as art." Sexual excitement and literary excitement are closely allied in him.

Not only is his thinking aesthetic, it is also "scientific." A combination of windiness, *weltschmerz,* and observation of animal and plant life, his discourses in the journals, *A Piece of My Mind, Patriotic Gore,* and *Upstate* sometimes border on the ugly and annoying. This turn to nature and biology is partly about himself and his decaying body and by extension about the entropic state of life on earth. Everything has been built up in order to run down. It's normal enough to hear that "the last lusts gutter out." It's also not extraordinary to hear that "all this fuss should be made about getting one's penis into a woman." But our protagonist could never be content with anything as matter-of-fact and sensible as that. He has to take the long biological view of things, talk about futilities, sea creatures whose penises detach, and the disgust that he feels on seeing advertisements featuring lovers dining and on vacation. In 1965 in the midst of this dour biological look—he is "getting a little old for l'amour"—he also wants to protest that "melancholy has not gotten to him." It's not Shakespeare's "expense of spirit in a waste of shame," he hastens to assure us. What it is, apparently, is a case of naturalistic stock-taking combined with the urge to question himself about what it all means.

He is, after all, at this point, in his forty-fifth year as a lover—and feels he wants to communicate something. That communication is not exactly grim, but it's not quite hopeful either. About time, impermanence, and personal assertion, it has something in common with Montaigne's musings on the subject. It's about his animal-spiritual nature, watching it heat up and cool off. A good example of this from *The Fifties* is an episode that takes place at Gull Pond, always a favorite spot for Wilson. This al fresco lovemaking scene contains meticulous descriptions, comments on Elena's clothes and charms, and recollections of what has just taken place. "Afterwards, I walked around the Pond, feeling perfectly happy—enjoyed the sight of a painted turtle swimming from the shore to the depths. I looked back at Elena from time to time—she was taking a nap: I loved to see her—her bare legs and blue clothes (skirt and sweater) —and know that she was still with me, and that we could still be happy together in the open air on the beach." Wilson was amusing himself about his adult career, its waxing and waning, and now, the somewhat sad course of the latter. He has said plainly that passion is guttering out in the mid-sixties. But anyone who is about to look closely shouldn't count on that.

Wilson's marriage was fraught with problems of various sorts— and one of the most thorny was his eye for every lady in his vicinity. A combination of teasing, keeping himself amused, fighting off depression and old age, this series of escapades, head trips, fantasies, and some realities took its toll on his relationship with Elena. These things, which would be enough to trouble any woman, should be seen against the social backdrop of Talcottville and the general clip at which Wilson was writing and meeting literary demands. During the fifties, he had pretty much set up summer shop in Talcottville; that old stone house, in the family since the early nineteenth century, was to become the moral and intellectual center of his later life. It was remote, unfashionable, and about as American as the Eastern seaboard gets. Elena hated it. She considered it spooky, boring, tacky, and altogether unlike the gay and bubbling fashionable summer scene at Wellfleet. Wilson enjoyed solitude and raking over family memories and escaping people who made demands on his time and doubtless wanted favors. Elena enjoyed parties, the future, new friends, and involvement. The conflict was serious. There were hysterics on her part, shouting matches, periods of alienation. But to Talcottville he went—and to Talcottville she was lured and sometimes forced. In his periods of separation from her, he had time for looking around and dalliance. This was his pattern whenever they were not getting along too well. It's seen especially in Cambridge, Massachusetts, in the winter of 1957, later on, when he was alone in Manhattan, and often in Talcottville. In short, tensions ran high after the forties.

Elena described the long stretch of their marriage as "hell with compensations." Wilson did not go in for lapidary phrases about marriage, unless we count a greeting card that he sent to her for their anniversary. It begins, "That we've been twenty years together I forget;/Some married men are bored, I never yet." He obviously created his own excitement from fantasies about her, his literary outpourings, and the flirtations and strayings that punctuate this alliance. But if it's a summing up that we seek, we'll find it in this remark about his and Elena's sex life: "Looking at her beautiful body, which does not show any signs of aging, I told her that making love to her had been the most wonderful thing in my life."

Notwithstanding this absolute statement, made in the mid-sixties, there had been a lot going on. Beginning in 1954, there was the reappearance on the scene of Mamaine Paget. When the Wilsons were in London, his attentions to Mamaine obviously pressed Elena's buttons, causing her to create "a jealous scene." The threat seemed a bit real because Mamaine had just divorced Koestler and was at loose ends. Wilson, playing the role of Mr. Innocent, soberly said that she "didn't have any real designs on me." But he was anxious for the dinner dates and said, upon her tragic death only a few years later, that there was no London for him without her. Wilson referred to her as having possessed "so much energy, brains and charm." He also made this odd comment: "I never talked to her about anything personal." But the use of "personal" should not be thought of as synonymous with "intimate." How could you be deeply in love with someone without having exchanged any personal talk? Maybe Wilson meant something like what Gatsby meant when he said that Daisy's love for Tom Buchanan was "just personal." In any case, Mamaine loomed large.

Others were about to take their place in the list of irritants. Wilson was a very susceptible man, and this later period of his life, settled though it was, saw him casting around for amusements and stimulants. He found them in every locale. While Elena was doing her wifely best to keep a home, keep his drinking under control, and manage a social life for them, he was looking in a number of directions. By this time, he and his wife were an older couple, and he reports, a bit ruefully, that she had taken to wearing a shapeless flannel nightgown known in the dreary annals of domesticity as a Mother Hubbard; underneath was her still beautiful body, but the fact that she wore the nightgown was not exactly an aphrodisiac. Ever on the lookout for spicy bits, Wilson found them where he could.

When left unattended in Talcottville, he needed help and he also — God knows why — needed to learn another language. Mary Pcolar, a neighbor and married woman, stepped in to provide a little help, a little chauffeuring, a little tutoring in the Hungarian language, a little typing, a little gossip, and plenty of erotic excitement. Elena, departing from her urbane manner, got a bit huffy about it, and lapsed into sarcasm. Mary was the Madame Bovary of Lewis County. Wilson got an April Fool's card in which he was asked to judge a Magyar beauty contest. In Cambridge, the sarcasm became rage when Wilson worked well with a young woman named Frances Swisher, his student at Harvard, briefly his crackerjack secretary, and (in Elena's mind, at least), perhaps more. Elena's temper was out of control, and Wilson so recorded it.

But Wilson certainly was making a contribution. An entry in his journal in 1961 lists all the women for whom he was at that time experiencing an extramarital yen. Five names appear; four of them will figure to some extent in this biography. A word should perhaps be said about the fifth, Suzanne Hughes, a woman who occasionally gave him rides. She and her husband Stuart, a Harvard history professor, socialized with the Wilsons, both in Cambridge and in Wellfleet, where Stuart was the source of the term *"La Plage des Intellectuels"* for the beach frequented by the Kazin-Schlesinger crowd, one which he himself did not use. That Wilson should have included Suzanne in such an intimate remark might, in another man, be thought significant. Here, it is more likely to be the result of his loneliness that summer, all by himself at Talcottville, and the bleak social scene at Cambridge, where a recent evening with the Hugheses would have been enough to ensure that she was, although fleetingly, on his mind—and therefore on his romantic agenda. In another entry he refers to her "coquettish mannerisms," which seem to have consisted of dropping her eyelids and looking up at him from under them. If this was flirting, Wilson was doing a bit of flirting of his own, and not just with Suzanne. Mary Grand (called Grant in *The Sixties*), who often attended the Wellfleet parties, liked to tell people that Wilson had "made a pass" at her too.

The early sixties was a period in which Elena had been—or so he maintained—neglecting him. In his journal of that decade, he talks about the times when Elena let him down: after his mother's death, when he was at Harvard giving the Norton Lectures, and when he was thrashing out his problems with the IRS. These three lapses, it might be noted, correspond to three locations that she wasn't particularly fond of. Red Bank and Talcottville are obvious enough; Cambridge was a place where Wilson was under the gun, the weather inclement, and their domestic arrangements not the best. The dreaded Swisher, of course, was the big problem, and Wilson fully admits that he talked "so much about her" that he might have provoked Elena. It's not too much of a stretch to say that he *wanted* to provoke Elena, and yet he said that he was "too sexually fond" of her to start a love affair. But he was starting something by another name with a number of people in the last fifteen years of his life.

The very worst of it all appears to have taken place at Talcottville, referred to by Elena as "the abyss." (She mispronounced the word as AB-iss but meant what she said.) On her birthday up there, they had a big fight, and she spat at him about Mary Pcolar and berated him for his "spongy body." Wilson, ever the naturalist, conceded that the latter might be a point; nevertheless the nasty incident didn't keep him from having cordial and more-than-cordial relations with Mary. But that is a subject for later.

Looked at from the outside, Wilson's relationship with Elena was laced with some unpleasant and unattractive elements. Mary McCarthy, not exactly an objective reporter in *A Charmed Life*, nonetheless provides some corroborative evidence about the marriage that seems to ring true. Her bullying intellectual and polymath Miles Murphy has found himself the perfect wife in "Helen." This woman is pretty much a McCarthy special, which is to say a lightly encoded version of the real person. Not a Russian, she's the child of rich Greek Americans and has a relative who is a Metropolitan. She's studied art and prepared herself for the career of being Mrs. Murphy.

That job has a number of specifications, according to McCarthy: You must be somewhat older, although of child-bearing years; you must never have been married before (a good piece of disguising); and you must be "submissive, pleasant-spoken, and moderately pleasant to the eye." (McCarthy at her back-handed best.) Helen Murphy appears in a characteristic pose on the beach up in New Leeds; having been married two years, she still retains the "hovering air of ingratiation." As observed by the narrator, she knew how "to efface herself in the European way": Bluntly put, "he came first." McCarthy's narrator nevertheless concedes that Helen is "all woman." That said, she also depicts her as being a supreme "manager." Helen knew instinctively just what Mary McCarthy and McCarthy's surrogate Martha in *A Charmed Life* could never learn —how to handle the great man, how to get him to concede, back off, and be a little considerate. This velvet glove managerial style, as described in the novel, seems to fit a good deal of the time in real life, though it breaks down as the couple gets older.

What comes through—even in bad times—is that they both knew how to back off and mitigate their worst traits. There was something in their attraction that caused them to create an ultimately gentle dynamic. His self-absorption never went too far in his marriage; her strong likes and dislikes never prevented concessions. It should be remembered that Wilson, in an early letter, told Elena not to make too much of his letters or save them or start treating him like a great man. In fairness to Wilson, there is no sense in his diaries that he thrived on flattery. For someone who had a rough time getting recognition and money during his career, he seems not to have been anxious to retail praise of himself or his work. Another witness, Wilson's daughter Rosalind, registers the turbulence as well as the deference. But Rosalind shows us that praise was there on the home front, not just in an occasional remark but as a real pattern of behavior. "Yes, dearest, you're brilliant, dearest" was Elena's mantra. Jeffrey Meyers's interview with Rosalind also yielded this variation—paid in front of W. H. Auden, when she remarked, "as Wilson cringed—'Oh, dearest, you're so brilliant, you know so much.'" Rosalind takes all this to be a shield, a way of coping with and mitigating Wilson's nastiness and the hypercritical behavior that he showed with Mary McCarthy. Rosalind, in McCarthy style, refers to the times when he would "set about destroying a woman." She's not clear about whether it is conscious attack or the expression of a deep, unconscious need. But she does tell what it is: constant criticism, morning till night. Rosalind reports the way Elena endured it—"not to be completely numb" in the face of it but "still have some reaction." As we've seen, Elena's reactions—to his nagging about Talcottville, his general bullying, and his baiting—were a good deal more pronounced than that understatement would suggest. She threatened him with an eggbeater in Talcottville and, in Wellfleet, directed a kick at him that sent her shoe through the ceiling. Maybe she didn't give quite as good as she got, but she definitely let him know that she was not a doormat. And, for all the "dearest-darlings," she knew very well that he had a strong sadistic streak and said as much to Rosalind.

For all the ugliness that we see on Wilson's part, we don't see a cover-up or an attempt to make himself look good. We also *do* see plenty of instances in which he attempts to make Elena feel better. Wilson's account in his journals and in *Upstate* did not contain an apologia for himself: He lets us see him drunk, nasty, willful, and selfish. In other words, he creates a portrait of himself that no woman could stand. As compensation, he offers the truth; he is not a monster of denial. He doesn't beat his breast, he doesn't plead or whine; he reports.

# IV

## $E$ndings and $B$eginnings

THE SIXTIES USHERED IN A PERIOD OF LOSSES FOR WILSON, who had become inured earlier in life to the deaths of such male friends as his cousin Sandy, Paul Rosenfeld, John Peale Bishop, Scott Fitzgerald, and others. Now he was saddened by the deaths of Dawn Powell, Louise Bogan, and Betty Huling. But, romantically speaking, the sixties was also a period of new beginnings.

The trouble in the Wilson marriage was, of course, a matter of a number of things—Wilson grown increasingly grouchy, a conflict about where to spend time, and a serious problem about how he was spending some of his time. Maybe his daughter Rosalind put it best when Wilson told her of a gift of petunias the charming Hungarian woman, Mary Pcolar, from nearby West Leyden had brought him up in Talcottville. They were Hungarian petunias, according to Rosalind, and could mean trouble.

Mary Pcolar was married to a rather bland man named George, was the mother of three children, the attentive daughter to an elderly mother, and a terrific go-getter and worker. Along with raising her family, she took various jobs in the Talcottville area, most notably a responsible and demanding position at a thriving drugstore in Boonville. That's where Wilson first met her. He came into the store, looking for the New York papers, was his disagreeable worst with her when she couldn't oblige, and repeated the performance a couple of times. The owner, a man named Kramer who had taken over an old business, told her that Wilson was a big man in the neighborhood, and before long, she warmed to him and was willing to take on some work that he offered her—characteristically without fuss or ceremony or preliminaries. Mary's duties at the drugstore were only the tip of the Pcolar iceberg; she was into community affairs, night courses, and moonlighting in a number of capacities with Wilson.

She worked for Wilson as chauffeur, sometime-secretary, and Hungarian language tutor. Dashing from one task to the next—and performing a variety of different duties at a high level—she seemed to Wilson to be a kind of superwoman. From the early 1960s until the end of his life, Mary figured as both a practical helper and a highly charged romantic presence. Obviously bored with her marriage ("she says that she has never been in love") and yearning for something beyond the routines of a small town, she was ripe for the attentions of a distinguished old man who was somewhat neglected by his wife. While doing a thousand things, she made time to do plenty for him. And, as the sixties went on, he developed a strong emotional dependence on her that had a definite sexual element. "Even though I don't make love to her I like to have her body around." He speaks of her "naturally and beautifully developed" ability to do things. After stealing a kiss, he finds her body "hard and solid" and is turned on by the usually incompatible combination of femininity and ox-like strength. Added to this growing passion for a woman who had an array of qualities—the ability to raise good children, grow flowers, make her own clothes, excel in business, be charming and alluring, and take on a certain amount of reading and serious reflection—was Wilson's undeniable neediness and projection. He went so far as to rhapsodize about the Hungarian community from which she came: "self contained and self-sustaining" like Talcottville in the early days of the nineteenth century. Things Magyar were romanticized and charged with excitement and exoticism. He was in love and in need, and he would find all kinds of qualities within his new beloved. But his emotion had to grow in an atmosphere of discretion and outward formality. And being in love in this way was a terrific juggling act for someone in his mid-sixties suffering from angina and in the midst of Herculean writing tasks. He had to get into the spirit of a new woman's life, discover her tastes, adapt himself to some of her idioms, and find a way to get more and more affection by so doing. The man who wore his father's "Ben Franklin" gold-rimmed glasses took an evaluating and admiring look at a young woman who wore an "orange sherbet" dress. It became his favorite. He became a connoisseur of outfits and a commentator on the aura of yet another woman.

She felt important, and, in turn, developed a certain dependence on him; he was a writer of recommendations, confidante, a career advisor, host, and a squire. (At one point, when she was about to travel abroad, he wrote her letters of introduction to virtually everyone he knew—perhaps because she asked for them, perhaps to let others see what he was seeing.) Mary's husband evidently did not perceive the old man as threatening, and she was available not only to drive him around and do chores but also to dine and go to the movies in the area. One of their favorite dining spots, an old-time Italian restaurant called the Savoy in Rome, held enough sentiment for her that she broke down when she revisited it with the writer Frederick Exley.

Exley took her to the Savoy to find out everything he could about the last days of his master. (He had the kind of catholic tastes common in Wilson admirers; his books *A Fan's Notes* and *Pages from a Cold Island* stand as eccentric classics, the first lauding football star Frank Gifford and the second Edmund Wilson.) Exley, who virtually worshipped Wilson, wanted to get the traces of Wilson's nature that he felt Mary would carry with her. On the occasion, he got some of them: She broke down when she got her ritual daiquiri, the drink that Wilson always, half-humorously (DIKE-her-ree) ordered for her.

Wilson's activities with Mary ranged from seeing movies, some of which he hated but tried to enjoy for her sake, saying that she made even the bad movies seem better, to picnicking, country drives, some work, and plenty of conversation. At one Sidney Poitier picture Wilson was not able to hear a word or follow the plot at all; Wilson the critic commended Mary's after-theater plot summary and commentary, a model of lucidity. When something good was around, like *The Godfather,* he wanted to go with her, and he did. This was four nights before he died.

He was always impressed by her quick-study nature, enthusiasm for knowledge and general curiosity. Yet he was acutely sensitive— strangely so, for him—to her inferior intellectual position: He was on his guard about condescension, fearful that she would feel patronized. He encouraged her to take college courses at night and was disappointed when she dropped out. He didn't want her to venture into *Patriotic Gore,* knowing full well that it would be rough sledding for someone with no background. But he was quite willing to hear a negative and fairly ill-informed view of his own work. She didn't like his favorite among his works, *Memoirs of Hecate County;* he laughed it off.

Not surprisingly, it is her beauty and feminine charms that dominate his perception of her. At this period in his life he admits to *le béguin,* that yen for attractive women; he knows it's ridiculous, but he also knows himself. Mary stepped in with just the right combination of looks and flirtatiousness. She was shy about defining the word *"megláttam."* The Hungarian word means a sensual touching with the eye. After a bit of hesitancy, she admits that if she were down in New York she wouldn't use the word on just anyone, but *"megláttam,* Mr. Wilson." In short, he received encouragement.

Things got pretty far, considering his health, her married state, and the fairly nosy-body atmosphere of Talcottville. Wilson during this period was moaning and groaning and grouching, complaining that he lived "the life of a monk." This monk would surely be out of Boccaccio. "While whining about the infrequent beautiful things up here," he knew at least one. He could talk with her, evidently talk about naughty things, such as *Fanny Hill,* and they could kiss enthusiastically. She let him get a bit physical, although he did not get beyond the foundation garments. "I never knew a woman so armored with bra and foundation garment."

In the fall of 1969, he was quite glad to have had an erection and to know that their relationship had passed to something "hot and physical." We can only surmise that she was a bit excited, fueled with drinks, and flattered by the attentions of a famous writer (who had gotten the Medal of Freedom from John F. Kennedy), and yet her decision was firm: "I want to, but I won't."

He took it good-humoredly, and more than good-humoredly; her "thanks for trying" "cheered and bucked me up." All of which is to say that the sheer experience of it, having carried his desires through to a point, was almost as satisfactory as consummation. Along the way to this somewhat sad finale, there were numbers of piquant moments, little incidents and details that he registered in his journals and letters. He wrote a touching, clumsy birthday poem for her, part in Hungarian. One of the lines says it all: "You walk the earth like woman." The poem, which is by no means very short, praised her high cheekbones, her "full-bodied grace," her feet ("whitened in our clear quick-running rills") and, having listed them at length, the skill of her hands and her "mastery of everything that's going." One of the things she had going—and which fascinated him utterly—was a charm school that she established and made a success of: He admired her "teaching the girls of Rome to look attractive." Not only did she get poems but Valentines—one features an ice-cream sundae he averred that he would "like to eat." He played the role of "Ödön Bácsi" (Uncle Edmund)—sending stamps from foreign lands to her son Eddie, inquiring about the date of the Hungarian picnic—but he was in his heart, and in the privacy of his diary, something else altogether. He even got huffy when Mary kiddingly said that she had a crush on Wilson's publisher Roger Straus. He knew, as we have said, that he was a bit ridiculous, but he was seriously ridiculous. In *Upstate* he wrote: "I never leave Talcottville without an uncomfortable feeling of never being able to do justice to my relation to Mary Pcolar."

Nevertheless, so successfully has he given resonance to this flirtation-friendship that outsiders, readers aware only of "the Hungarian woman" who runs like a *leitmotif* through his book *Upstate*, reacted strongly. One reader from Washington, D.C., a person of some sophistication, wrote Roger Straus and highlighted Mary's place in the volume; he called her fascinating and professed an intense desire to know her, writing, "she's by far the most interesting person in the book." Magyar fever is evidently contagious. It could spread to as cynical a character as Anita Loos, author of *Gentlemen Prefer Blondes*, and a friend of Wilson's. She too wrote

Straus and said that she got "tearful" at every paragraph about Mary Pcolar. She also said that *Upstate* had a quality that particularly struck her: The "tone of the book cancels out all the moral smog we're forced to breathe today." Coming right after the remark about Pcolar, this seems to apply as well to the relationship; it is frankly depicted throughout the work and is what it is, the frustrated but touching passion of an old man with a poetic soul and a clear eye.

. . . . . .

A LESS SERIOUS diversion from the journey of marriage was Clelia Carroll. Wilson's infatuation with her, dating from 1958, was essentially a matter of fantasizing, doing some literary work together, and exchanging sentimental, chatty letters. Clelia was the editor of Jason Epstein's Looking Glass Library, a children's book series at Anchor Doubleday, and Wilson, W. H. Auden, and Phyllis McGinley were consultants. A strong attraction soon developed, at least on Wilson's part. Clelia, a vibrant beauty connected by marriage to an old and distinguished Maryland family, had a curious appeal for Wilson—she was married to Philip Carroll of Carrollton, Maryland, a descendent of a signer of the Declaration of Independence. Wilson said she reminded him of a young woman of his own generation, come to life as a delightfully contemporary presence at midcentury. Her quiet stamp of money and breeding didn't hurt either.

When Clelia repaired to the country to give birth to her third child, a son, Philip, who was born in December 1961, Wilson sent the new mother one of his individualized Valentines—this one claiming "There's a cabinet particular in my heart / Just for You" and ending with the hope that she would "always keep a corner / in the Algonquin / JUST FOR ME!" Thus began an extended epistolary flirtation that involved compliments, confidences, and the sharing of gossip and dreams with another impossible love.

Reading the two sides of this cache of letters between Wilson and a woman who was, at the time of his first fervid Valentine to her, the mother of a two-month-old boy by another man, one sees that this attachment was of a piece with those Wilson formed to Mamaine

Paget, Darina Silone, and Eva Siphraios—a fine and tender madness. It was also a feast of idle, gracious talk—uncharacteristic small talk for Wilson—enjoyed by two patricians. Wilson delighted in swapping stories with someone connected to an older America that he yearned for in the age of TV and Madison Avenue. She was his type, a lover of old furniture, good manners, and non-fast-track living. Our critic—who had his romance with Marxism—never gave up his attraction to an older America, the pre–Civil War country of landowners like his mother's people. This man, who had at least a twenty-year affair with socialism, later enjoyed being the grand seigneur of Talcottville, and liked to talk about his tastes with a sympathetic listener. Clelia's husband was an admirer of Wilson's work and an enthusiastic seconder of Clelia's frequent invitations.

Actually, one bond between them was that both their families had ties in the South, and Clelia and Wilson got a hoot out of what they called Southern Belle stories. Wilson chortles over the lady who offered him whiskey sours as a "very nice" drink in the morning; Clelia told her husband's story of the woman who ignored everything he said and ended every conversation with, "Naow, . . . you know I just *love* your mother."

Through the years they came to know—and evidently like—other things about each other: the way seasons and holidays were noted by each, the opera they loved to listen to, the gossip they exchanged about the other members of the Looking Glass Board—Jason Epstein, Brendan Gill, Edward (Ted) Gorey. Their respective families entered the picture, sometimes as points of reference, sometimes as irritants, sometimes as useful reminders that they were not free.

They discussed a possible rendezvous in Nantucket, the Baltimore area, the Boston area, New York at the Algonquin; but except for two or three longish cocktail hours at the Gonk, when Elena and the board were variously in attendance, no such meeting ever materialized. This led to mutual laments and protests of continued affection. From her, there's-no-one-I-think-of-more-often-and-see-less-of; from him, I-have-never-so-much-missed-anyone-I-see-so-little. He gave her pathetic pictures of his life in Talcottville (where his menu ran heavily to baked beans) and boastful ones of Wellfleet (where he crowed over his purchase of an orange rug). There was more detail than he gave to anyone else. And she—while quietly preferring brown chairs to gold to coordinate with the rug— sympathized with his homeowner's pride. She and Phil had been restoring at great expense something called "the manor," the dimensions of which took on specificity when she detailed a fire in the outbuildings. In addition to a horse barn and five sheds, these included a corn-holding barn a half mile away. There were mentions of stable boys and servants. In fact, her gracious living must have made Wilson salivate as she mentioned the books she wanted to catalog in the family library, some of them "untouched on the shelves since circa 1721," together with hundreds of beautifully bound law books and a sizeable library of books in French.

Wilson, not to be completely outdone, talked about culling his library, and dropped the information that he had kept every scrap of the reading he had done in preparation for *Finland Station* and was giving the whole thing to Yale. Laced though the years like Valentines are the Valentines themselves, plus his wounded I-sent-it-and-you-sent-me-nary-a-word; but in the end all was well; it had simply gone astray. He commiserates with her flu; she with his gout, shingles, and strokes; they compare notes on drinking (it speeds things up for her, slows things down for him), and they tell each other their dreams—at length. This latter is the tip-off that, under all the chitchat, a serious, prolonged flirtation was going on. Her salutation "Dear Edmund" never changes, except once when it is "Edmund, love." His "Dear Clelia" is always signed off "As Ever Edmund"; but, in one of her last notes, Clelia broke out into a full "I love you," and it might be said of him to her as well.

· · · · · ·

JUST AS QUIRKY, touching, and even odder, is the long correspondence Wilson conducted with an artist named Mary Meigs. Beginning with her purchase of Mary McCarthy's place on Pamet Road in Wellfleet in 1958, and throughout her long tenure as neighbor-in-chief to Edmund and Elena, she played a part in Wilson's fantasy

life. She was a lesbian who lived with activist Barbara Deming.
That Wilson found her a woman of interest was to Mary "inexplicable." She professed bafflement, even as late as the Wilson centennial forum at the Mercantile Library in New York in 1995.

Quite apart from anything else, Wilson's affection for her may be
accounted for by the charm of her letters and the pencil sketches of
the Cape that frequently accompanied them, by her good humor
and evident love of good living—she suggested that they celebrate
Edmund's seventieth with oysters and champagne and caviar—as
well as by the devotion she showed to the natural beauty of the
Wellfleet area. (She turned down his invitation to spend a summer
in Talcottville because she could not bear to miss "a procession of
natural happenings, that I have to watch.") For his part, Wilson
made the foundations of his profound feeling for Mary quite plain
in his journals of the fifties and sixties. "What I feel for Mary Meigs
is love," he said in the first of these volumes, though he added that
he was not "in love" with her. And again in the second he wrote: "I
really love her and I always shall."

The fascination he felt for her seemed to rest on not being in the
least sexually attracted to her. He found her boyish body a turn-off
turn-on. She reminded him of his cousin Sandy as he looked in the
years when they were closest. And that would be that, if he did not
insist that his every moment alone with her is precious to him. This
happened with suspicious infrequency, and it was entirely possible
that Mary had instructed Barbara to stay close by; for whenever he
was alone with Mary, he showered her with kisses, an act we have
no reason to believe the polite and shy Miss Meigs would have
enjoyed, but we have every reason to think her too courteous to
protest about it. She did, however, early in their correspondence,
protest Wilson's use of the term "girls" when referring to her and her
companion. "I am 41," she reminded him, and asks if he would
please fight the temptation to so address her.

Now the reference that links Mary Meigs to Sandy and the
intimate friendship Wilson enjoyed with him—virtually his only
intimate friendship in the days of his youth—comes as near as any
buddy movie or locker-room bonding story might in introducing a

homoerotic element into Edmund's otherwise relentlessly hetero-
sexual romantic career. In drawing attention to it in his journal,
Wilson underscores the "uniqueness" of the note struck here. But
the yearning for reminders of Sandy was largely nostalgic. The two
boys did, after all, read Havelock Ellis together. Wilson's feelings
for his cousin, and his later penchant—however prolonged—for
Mary Meigs never rose above a kind of grateful warmth, a dreamy
platonic romanticism with a touch of the polymorphous perverse.

. . . . . .

ANOTHER SYMPATHETIC encounter—one that shows him connecting with someone off the beaten path of the literary scene—
was Wilson's friendship with a Seneca woman named Betty Crouse
Mele. This time, the thrust seems to come much more from her
side than his. She first came to Wilson's attention when the eloquence and emotion of her letter to him upon reading his *Apologies
to the Iroquois* broke through his barriers and won her, instead of
one of his preprinted Edmund Wilson Regrets cards, an actual letter in response. (These cards were an all-purpose refusal to deal
with the public. They enumerated the twenty things that Wilson
did not do—including most of the things that famous authors do. A
sample—"it is impossible for him to:  . . . Give talks or make
speeches . . . Broadcast or appear on television . . . Supply opinions
on literary or other subjects . . .") He was in fact, deeply impressed
by Betty's story—she was thrilled to be reintroduced to her Sene-
can roots, to be given a positive self-image of her birth heritage.
Before reading Edmund's sympathetic treatment of her people,
the only experience she had had with white American response to
Indians had come to her in the form of schoolyard taunts of "squaw."
For six formative years when she was growing up, her family had
lived off the reservation. Because of his sensitive portrayal, she
wrote Wilson, her life had been changed. "*Apologies to the Iroquois*
presented us with dignity and intelligence. . . . It removed us from
the archives and attics of anthropology and archeology and portrayed us as a viable cultural group."

Wilson's response to Betty's letter went even further—to the unprecedented length of sending her an invitation to visit him personally, either in Talcottville, in Cambridge, or at the house in Wellfleet. In addition to the eloquence of her letter, one other reason that Wilson's defenses broke down was the intermediary who knew them both, William Fenton. Dr. Fenton, an authority on the Iroquois, had been adopted into the Seneca Hawk clan by Betty's grandmother, and he vouched for her to Wilson.

She found him and paid him a visit on the Cape. Mrs. Mele, who was married to an Italian psychiatrist practicing in Princeton, brought her three children and their German nanny to Wellfleet. In the course of a delightful afternoon of conversation, she told Wilson that his book had done more for her than her years in analysis had. "I was very much touched by this," he wrote.

Their meeting was so successful that Betty began a campaign to have Wilson made a member of the tribe. But this Wilson could not permit; he said that he did not deserve it, as, he said, Fenton had. Nevertheless, Betty found an ingenious way to express both her idolization of him, and her gratitude. She named her baby boy Antonio Edmund Wilson Mele, thus ensuring that Wilson's name would appear on the Seneca rolls of the Iroquois Nation. Wilson's only comment on this was that he thought the boy had too many names, and she berated herself in a last letter exchanged, saying she now wished she had just named the boy Edmund Wilson and been done with it. In addition to the book dedications, the poems, the flowery letter tributes that came his way from women over the years, Wilson could stick a Seneca feather in his cap.

. . . . . .

IN 1969 WHEN she came into his life, Anne Miller lived as close to a hippie existence as Wilson was ever to come across. Though she was to go on to more conventional attitudes in a later, second marriage, at that time in her life she was experimenting with what had been called, in Wilson's day, free love. In this respect, being with her must have reminded him of the grand old bohemian days in Greenwich Village.

Anne, "a small and pretty brunette, with vivacious black eyes," was a nature lover, married, with four children, and well-off. Her dentist husband, from an established family in the region, had not only his Lowville home-office but a camp on nearby Crystal Lake and was in the process of building a second home in Jamaica. Her husband's single earring, said to signal a participation in wife-swapping parties, may have seemed incongruous in view of his profession, but it was not unheard of in the Adirondack region, certainly not in those years toward the end of the Vietnam era.

Anne at length convinced him not to wear the earring around his office, but in other ways, she was the very model of a flower child. She lived in rustic surroundings, baked whole-wheat bread, raised her own organic vegetables, and talked a lot about peace, love, and happiness.

Signs of the age of Aquarius abound in her letters to Wilson—in the disdain they express for the "rat race," in their frequent references to happiness (Wilson quizzed her about this, asking her, in effect, why she was so fixated on it), and in their professed love of nudity. In her life, the zeitgeist asserted itself in her and her husband's practice of open marriage. Evidently, before Wilson became more than a patient in her husband's life and hers, Anne had had a fling with a local clergyman, with the result that the clergyman had been called, rather suddenly, to another parish. And so we find a close-to-classic situation of a man in his mid-seventies enjoying a few sexual favors thrown his way by a hippie in her forties who became very excited by the fact that her elderly swain was written up in *Esquire* as one of the 100 most important persons in the world. (Wilson rather touchingly denies this, saying she'd paid him attentions before the piece appeared, but his status would have of course preceded him.)

Somewhere between dental appointments Wilson found himself getting involved with Anne and her poetry. He wrote in his journal that he intended to warn her the poems were best thought of as keepsakes for her children, and as usual he tried to improve her: "I . . . suggested her trying a sonnet." Anne, however, after taking Wilson lessons to no great effect (the sonnet "didn't come out right"), continued to write poetry and send it to him; she even asked him to advise her as to some noncommercial, nonestablishment publication where her work could appear. She said she wanted to publish. But she was just as interested in holding her head up among the vegetables she grew outside her north country home— weeding in the after-the-rain mud with nothing on but her black rubber boots.

Rosalind was appalled, and no doubt said so. But Dr. Miller was only upset by the sorry state of Wilson's teeth. After many of Wilson's appointments, he and his wife offered the patient a sociable cocktail and listened to him hold forth. That Miller was able to save any of Wilson's decayed mouthful was strong evidence that he was a gifted dentist, and Wilson was thankful. He relished the Millers' conversation, literate talk in short supply among the locals.

In the next few years, Mrs. Miller began bringing some of her poetry over to Talcottville, taking nature walks, and having long talks about meter, poets to be read, and the meaning of life. She was a tempting prospect, offering Wilson stimulation plus the work he always had a taste for, playing Pygmalion.

She let him know she was feeling quite uninhibited, both in their wine-drenched afternoons and in the letters she wrote him in her best schoolgirl penmanship, to the point of feeling free to confide in Wilson her innermost thoughts and feelings—telling him what kind of person she was, free and unfettered by convention and unlike the dull souls who voted for Nixon. She had enough insight to be able to say, in letter after letter, how bored he must be by her flower child ramblings, but she did not blush to send him more. At the same time, the fact that there are so many of these letters and free verses can only be accounted for by postulating some encouragement from Wilson. Consider that she was, in spite of four children, a fit and trim and tanned figure, who often appeared in white shorts and a kind of tennis attire. And she was an eager recipient of his cultural commentary.

For his part, Wilson seems to have made a game try at teaching and seducing—there are references both in his journals and in her letters to how much he'd told her about rhyme and meter and how he had gotten her to read Keats and Pope. And, for one summer, at least, she and Wilson had steamy sexual encounters of the kind that render intelligible his putting up with some amount of silliness. She allowed a lot of kissing (only what any warm person would do, she seems to have said); this was accompanied by her doing some skinny-dipping in his presence, and, on one afternoon up on his bed, when their usual two bottles of wine had stretched to three and been followed by some scotch for him and some gin for her, they went a good deal further.

She wanted to know the reason for pubic hair (evidently displaying some), and made a pretty good argument that protection didn't account for it because how about a man's chin hair? He wanted to know what the deal was with all the open-mouthed kisses he'd been seeing on the screen in recent movies (not a feature of the films of his era); she promptly demonstrated for him the art of French kissing and the importance of running your tongue lightly around the tongue in your partner's mouth. Wilson kept his garters on, which she found a little at odds with his generally courtly behavior—he assured her that he knew of men who kept their shoes on as well. Not for nothing does Wilson remark of this interlude, "The situation has comic possibilities."

Patiently he would, after receiving page after handwritten page of verse—full of references to the sun and the moon and the stars and the wind and the sand and how loving and being loved was so much better than money because money could only buy *things,* and an occasional bird or flower—invite her to send him more. She did and he read and he asked for more, but he may, after a season or two of intimacies, have gotten one more poem than he bargained for; in that year's batch, there was what amounted to the poetic equivalent of a Dear John letter. Well, not quite a Dear John, more of an "It's not you, it's me" letter. Entitled "Sorry Answer to a Request," it begins, "I think I have made love with you for the last time" and goes on to assure the man addressed that it was "Not because it was unpleasant./Not because you were demanding./Not because of strength of virtue. And not because I want to hurt you"—no, it was just that she saw him as a friend, not a lover. It is much the strongest poem of the lot. But after that her letters focused much less on her sun baths in the altogether and much more on news of Ned and the children.

In the summer of 1971, she and two of the children paid him a call in Wellfleet, after which she wrote, telling him how pleased she was to have met Elena—something she'd been wanting for a long time. Wilson put on one of his puppet shows for the Miller children. Dr. Miller sent letters to him in the off-Talcottville season, warning him that the whole lower jaw was in jeopardy and imploring him not to forget to rinse. Only that, it seems necessary to say on Wilson's behalf, could account for the fact that, once there was no more hanky-panky, social cordiality continued on both sides. Maybe it was even a relief. "I don't want to spoil, by my attentions to his wife, my relations with the best dentist I have ever had," Wilson wrote. More and more, his contact with Anne became automotive and cinematic in nature and sexy in memory only. The same week he and Mary Pcolar took in *The Godfather* in Rome he got Anne to go with him to *The French Connection* in Utica. But the lion was now nearly toothless and far from at his best.

. . . . . .

WILSON'S LAST girlfriend, the English critic, fiction writer, and screenwriter Penelope Gilliatt was, like his first, a redhead. Like Edna, she was also capable of throwing romantic bombs, grabbing press coverage, and being outrageous. Important men were like the air she breathed. Her combination of beauty and significant literary production—stories, essays, reviews—had brought her into the orbit of playwright John Osborne, Mike Nichols, film critic Vincent Canby, and Wilson himself.

Gilliatt's father, Cyril Connor, was a noted barrister and judge; her mother, a Douglass, was from an established shipbuilding family in Northumberland. When the parents' marriage broke up, the country comfort of her early years ended, and she began a gypsy existence, moving with her mother and new stepfather first to London, and then to New York. She studied at Julliard for a time and then at Bennington College. After a year, she won a writing prize that carried an internship at British *Vogue* in London.

The job began inauspiciously—Penelope was stuck in the needlework section, a misfit of a job reminiscent of Wilson's early stint covering men's cravats at *Vanity Fair*. Although she was soon doing more exalted jobs in journalism, she was also moving up the highly stratified rungs of London society. In 1954 she married Roger Gilliatt, later himself caught up in a scandal but at the time of their marriage always described as a brilliant neurosurgeon and member of the wedding of Princess Margaret. Her new status brought with it the perk of lovely accommodations in a flat in Knightsbridge, but seems to have fallen short in the emotional security side of things. While she could easily have turned society matron and lived a life of leisure in considerable luxury, Penelope continued to work with all the energy, productiveness, and fanatical attention to detail that were to mark her entire career. She wrote for *The Spectator, Queen, The Guardian, The New Statesman, The London Review of Books,* and *Encounter* to name only the most prestigious of the many organs to which she contributed. With her vivacious wit, vivid coloring, and active participation in left-leaning antinuclear protests, she became a well-known figure in the swinging London of the sixties. With its heavy concentration of free-love types from the worlds of publishing and theater, it was the best time livers of *la vie de Boheme* had seen since the Paris and Greenwich Village Wilson had enjoyed in the twenties.

In 1963, the lovely redhead hit the papers not as a producer of copy but as the subject of it, many column inches, in fact. It took a lot to make an impression on the press of the period, but Penelope did the trick with her rather public departure from her near-royal husband's roof for a country cottage tryst with the so-called "Angry Young Man" playwright John Osborne. The press turned out in numbers, cameras in hand. The awkwardness of a public love affair between two people married to two other people found another parallel in Wilson's life—his trip to Reno in 1948 with Elena, where each would shed a spouse to pave the way for their nuptials. (Still another was that Osborne put a portrait of her in one of his plays, the character Margaret in *Hotel in Amsterdam,* as Wilson had done with more than one of his wives in more than one of *his* plays.)

Gilliatt already had tabloid journalists gunning for her because of a scornful article she had written in *Queen* called "The Friendless Ones," in which she depicted them as the scum of the earth (and inaccurate scum at that)—an article that cost at least one *Daily Mail* columnist his job.

Osborne, on his side, had not won any points for diplomacy, seemingly determined that all should recognize in him the epitome of his play's angry young man. He was roundly scolded for choosing the amorous, rustic idyll with Penelope over a trip to the hospital to visit his new daughter. The jilted wife—and now mother—in question was the respected and well-liked actress Mary Ure, whose blonde prettiness cast her perfectly in the role of the innocent woman wronged, while the flaming redhead was equally right as the femme fatale. The upshot was that the lovers endured weeks of sensational press, the tone of which was unfriendly in the extreme. They survived, divorced their respective spouses, married, and, about to become the parents of a daughter of their own, the couple bought (and Penelope's sister Angela spectacularly decorated) a Georgian mansion on Chester Square.

Penelope's position as regular movie reviewer for *The Observer* and the sheer glamour of the circle she and Osborne moved in—the likes of Kenneth Tynan, Tony Richardson, and Vanessa Redgrave—made life spin by with the color and speed of a kaleidoscope. Penelope, who was happily dividing her time between her writing and her daughter Nolan, was, by all accounts, devoted to Osborne. But Osborne reverted, in time, to what was to be for him a continuing pattern of marital musical chairs. Having left actress Pamela Lane and actress Mary Ure before her, he now, in 1968, after five years of marriage, left Penelope for actress Jill Bennett, whom he would in turn leave for journalist Helen Dawson, wife number five.

Osborne attributed not only his and Penelope's breakup, but all of her liaisons and subsequent breakups to "a kind of spastic ambition." No doubt, as he had the grace to concede, this was uncharitable. During her journalistic career, Penelope wrote many appreciations cum profiles of luminaries of page and screen, among the most notable those on Nabokov, Buster Keaton, Woody Allen,

Jean Renoir, Jacques Tati, and Hitchcock. Osborne attempted to link her fondness for doing articles of this kind with a penchant for "domestic involvement" in the lives of the famous men she admired.

He specified Mike Nichols and Wilson as icons on the list, asserting, "I was even privy to her selection of Nichols as an essential weapon of her ambition, although I was not aware of it at the time." Whatever the degree of truth in this, it is a fact that Penelope took up with Nichols soon after her marriage to Osborne fell apart, having visited him in Philadelphia where he was trying out a play. Soon there was a more permanent move to the United States, where she was named alternate movie critic with Pauline Kael for the *New Yorker*. Chester Square in London gave way to Central Park West. The good life continued, this time accompanied by park views and splendid parties where the British legends of theater were supplemented by those of Broadway; Betty Comden and Adolf Green and Woody Allen might all be seen arriving.

Mike Nichols had attracted Wilson's attention in his Broadway debut with Elaine May. Wilson visited their dressing rooms, arranged social encounters, and was in correspondence with Nichols when Nichols and Penelope were together. In fact, the first letters we have from Penelope to Edmund take the form of her filling the role of secretary to reply to Wilson's notes while Nichols was away making a film.

Nichols and Gilliatt did not stick, but Gilliatt stuck with her pen pal, Wilson, offering to bring him from London some cunning felt moths they both admired—the handiwork of an old gent who ran a curiosity shop across from the British Museum. These notes give way to warmer, more personal ones from her, indicating a desire to see more of Wilson and to get to know him better. At this point, after Nichols's departure, she was perhaps casting about to solace a disappointed if not broken heart. Osborne's rather bitter suggestion that her motive was career burnishing overlooks the considerable success Gilliatt's career could boast on its own. Nor does it do justice to her truly charming person, the air of excitement that any setting took on when the door was flung open and, preceded by the staccato click of her high heels, one caught a glimpse of her pixie face above her exquisite peacock blue suit, crowned by a bright red crown of hair, the whole effect guaranteed to bring the observer visual pleasure combined with the aural pleasure of her tinkling laugh.

Edmund and Penelope's courtship and affair is soon told—it progresses from those innocent transactions over the transfer and payment for the moths, through doings (still innocent) such as ritual stops at Lou Tannen's magic shop on 46th Street and Sixth, on Wilson's biannual trips to New York. These, however, took on an increasingly naughty cast as lunch and movie outings launched from the offices at the *New Yorker* gave way to more boozy lunches followed by porn flicks they attended together on 42nd Street, then included stops back at the Algonquin lounge for numbers of straight-up martinis, then extended to Wellfleet for Elena's Thanksgiving turkey, then back to more New York movie-lunch combos, and then the full-out seduction—one would have been hard-pressed to say of who by whom—on election day 1970 at the Princeton Club.

As Wilson records it, the kissing on the couch in the downstairs lounge soon progressed to the point where he was proclaiming a desire to go down on her, and she responded, "We'll soon be fucking. We'd better stop." Instead of stopping, though, they went up to Wilson's room where, "I got her to take off her clothes." His admiring catalog of her charms—"Her body was prettier than I expected"—includes, predictably enough, her ivory skin and her remarkable red hair as well as a cool assessment of her private parts. His spirits—cast down a little by her casual admission that she presently enjoys two other "fucking friends"—were buoyed up again when, upon preparing to leave the club, she says "People will know that I've just been fucked. I look like a woman who's just been fucked." "Not enough," he crows.

Of the indiscretion some people might have found in Penelope's continuing to be a guest at Wellfleet, she wrote, "Storm in a teacup." It strikes her as unlikely to be anything to get distressed about. "It'll pass." Meanwhile, she's missed him and she'd like to come up again soon. Suddenly turning politic, she suggested, however, that "perhaps you should destroy this note." That it wound up among his papers at Yale is evidence enough of Wilson's response. Now in his seventy-fifth year and between two strokes, he was not above par-laying the novelty of this situation into further gratification for him-self. He used it as a means of teasing Elena, who was left to look the other way when Penelope and her daughter came to stay under her roof; as a mode of romantic and flirtatious posturing in his cor-respondence with Clelia Carroll; and as a gesture producing in him an evident frisson, that of taking a moth from one girlfriend and giving it to another—Mary Pcolar. His recounting of this new friendship to Clelia rings with satisfaction: After running through Penelope's racy romantic history, he wrote "I have been reading her in the *Observer* for years, but never knew her till lately. She has been up to see us here, and I like her because she laughs at everything I say that is meant to be funny, besides being amusing herself."

This was not a deeply felt affair for either of them, but for a couple of scamps on the sea of love it was a last late sail for Edmund and a welcome release from sadness before the encroaching dark of all-out alcoholism for her.

What luck for both that the travail ahead was hidden from them. He knew her at a high point in her career—her reviews for the *New Yorker* and her short stories and, most excellent of all, her screen-play for *Sunday, Bloody Sunday* put her on a plane where he could feel with her the easy companionship of equals, and their exchanges were full of wit and mutual enjoyment. One of her aphorisms is prominently quoted on the Internet: "People in anger often say a lot of silly, terrible things they mean." If there was a flaw in their rela-tionship, it stemmed from the clash of his native reserve with her theatrical exuberance, which, when fueled by drink, sometimes led her to fall all over him and do so much public touching that she managed to embarrass him greatly.

She was on a periodic visit to London to visit Nolan (whose custody she had lost to Osborne) when notified of Wilson's death; it was not a lethal blow to her morale, perhaps, but a sig-nificant loss of ballast. Though in the following years she wrote as voluminously as ever — pouring out short stories, novels, movie reviews, and (unproduced) screenplays — she was slipping everywhere and, in 1979, with the discovery of (she always claimed, inadvertent) plagiarism in her *New Yorker* profile of Graham Greene, she suffered a bad fall from grace.

In the eighties she was a pathetic figure, reminiscent of Dorothy Parker who, in the last decades of her life, was often laid low by drink. In the case of Penelope, the drinking was accompanied by a very British effort to keep up a brave front—having her hair colored and coifed at the Plaza, weaving carefully from taxi to elevator to her office at the *New Yorker,* where her work was no longer welcome unless clearly labeled fiction. Still making the transatlantic effort to spend part of the year near Nolan, she was in her London digs in Westminster on May 10, 1993, when postural asphyxiation brought about her death at the age of sixty. Put plainly, she choked to death.

. . . . . .

A FOOTNOTE of sorts is called for here, and it has to do with Wilson's brief, almost nonexistent, but somehow important romance with the very young Elaine May. Never mind that it took place entirely on his side, that is what it was. (Wilson's head trip, be it noted, came before his fling with Penelope.) About as wacky as his infatuations got, this one had a forty-year gap between the principles and no encouragement (although plenty of admiration) from the new woman. The only time on record that they were ever alone together came at the end of a long evening, which included closing the Oak Room at the Plaza. It happened early in their acquaintance when Wilson offered her a ride home in his taxi—a well-worn ploy.

Elaine May was not just another performer. Like Mike Nichols, her partner in comedy at the time, she was a veteran of the University of Chicago campus theater world, someone who liked to spoof Pirandello and was fully capable of appreciating all that Wilson was. She and Nichols represented a level of literary sophistication that has vanished entirely from Broadway. Their jokes and routines were replete with references that are no longer part of a night of comedy. So it's no wonder that, in 1961, Wilson was enchanted by "An Evening With Mike Nichols and Elaine May" and saw it four times.

He records his surprised and delighted recognition of her as "perhaps something of a genius. She transforms herself so completely in her various roles that until I saw her off the stage I had no real idea how she looked. She is extremely handsome, with powerful black eyes—probably passionate and strong-willed." He cultivated a relationship with Mike Nichols, it would seem, not only because he admired him but because it provided access to his new beloved. "I told him to tell Elaine that I was sorry not to be young enough to fall in love with her and ruin my life." Nichols promised to do exactly that. But things did not fall out propitiously in a way that would allow Wilson to exercise his self-restraint. Elaine was engaged in writing a new play for Mike that roiled up the two of them and was supposedly insulting to Mike; she also fell in love, got married to a lyricist, split up, and got involved again. Wilson would have been lost in the shuffle if he had ever been in it to begin with.

So Wilson's strong attraction found its way instead into his journal. He wrote of the women from the past who came to life again in his contemplation of Elaine's dark, passionate physiognomy. When he could still share his enthusiasm for her with Nichols, the two had a conversation comparing her with Dorothy Parker. (Nichols had just met Parker and proclaimed himself "overwhelmed.") They agreed as to the terrifying sharpness of the two women. "As we were having this conversation, our tone about Elaine was mounting, both were making assertions about her and in the way that one does when some magnetic and particularly interesting person is under discussion." The delights of this scene were cut short, however, when Elaine herself walked in. Later, when Nichols and May had their falling out, Wilson, thinking of Nichols as his surrogate in a state of frustrated love for May, tried to be soothing by telling the young man that such women "were likely to end up marrying rather well-to-do middle-aged men who were not remarkably clever." He later reflected "that Mary McCarthy and Edna had, having lost their fathers very early [as Elaine had lost hers, at seven], provided themselves with father substitutes."

This reflection might have been supposed to open the door for Wilson rather than Nichols, but he remembered that he had been unable to fill this role for Mary. "I was cast as the horrid false father, her uncle, and the things that, in her hysteria, she would accuse me of were usually his crimes and not mine." This strange blend of fantasies and might-have-beens is extremely confusing. It involves Wilson displacing Nichols and then knocking himself out of the box.

Meanwhile, back in reality, Wilson recorded a tidbit from Rosalind asserting that when Nichols and May were together as a couple "they quarreled terribly." Yet, he noted, "in certain ways, she defers to him." Wilson is interested in their personal story just as the public was. But in his case a strong and beautiful female personality like May made him think of more than one woman from the past. She was the most beautiful and intelligent woman he had seen since "Mary McCarthy in the thirties." And he says that he tried, when he was around Elaine, "not to show too much interest . . . as if it had been Edna Millay." Unlike people who wanted to know the inside story of Mike and Elaine, Wilson seems to have been trying to read his own inside story through this attractive couple.

He was looking at the mystery of himself: He was figuring out that intense, creative women had torn him apart, but also made him what he was. Elaine, a wild card in his life, made him think of Edna, a woman who could make "life splendid." Elaine had passion, wit, compassion, and she added a "somber and bitter Jewish side." Like Edna, she had "pathos" and "edge." She also made him think of McCarthy, who made life hellish. He was in the grip of passion-love again—in his late sixties.

# V

## The Sum Total: Living and Writing

EDMUND WILSON WAS 5 FEET 6½ INCHES TALL (ALTHOUGH HE told the passport office he was 5 feet 8½); at age twenty-five, when his romantic life began, he was relatively slender and given to brown suits from Brooks Brothers. His own clothes meant little to him throughout life, although he remarked on men's and women's fashion in his writing. His cousin Sandy, when a patient in an insane asylum, called him up short for not having his own tailor. Glyn Morris, a friend of his in later years, remarked on the white oxford cloth shirts and loosely knotted paisley ties he customarily wore in Talcottville. Wilson himself told Alfred Kazin, "I have only one manner of dressing"—by which he meant a dress shirt and slacks (Bermudas on the Cape). He was also known for his battered and stained panamas and rumpled "ice cream" linen suits in summer.

By the time he was in his thirties and his romantic life had really taken off, he was already beginning to develop the pot belly that was likely the result of his making many bachelor meals of canned soups, processed cheeses, and every other high-saline food imaginable, followed by rich desserts. His beverages of choice (except for intermittent dry spells) leaned heavily toward the alcoholic. He favored martini cocktails, sometimes by the half dozen, and Johnny Walker Red Label scotch in similar quantities. He was seldom noticeably drunk or inarticulate in front of others, but on occasion, if he was in danger of falling, others assisted him to the nearest bed. He did not suffer from hangovers. If his liquor cabinet was in short supply, he drank anything that came to hand. During one prolonged evening alone in his house at Talcottville, he notes in his journal, he mixed

champagne, red wine, and what was left of a bottle of Old Grand-
dad, topping the whole thing off with some limburger cheese. This
way of living, he speculated, could—"in the long run"—become
unhealthy. It all helped to turn him into his characteristic adult self
—a portly figure, often gouty, with thinning, sandy (later gray-white)
hair and a somewhat rolling gait. Although his features included
an impressive Roman profile and the broad, high brow of a Roman
senator, he had jowls, too, and, perhaps least prepossessing of all,
there was the high-pitched voice. His first wife believed it to be the
result of trying to be heard by his deaf mother. When, in his brown,
boxer-style swimsuit, he rose out of the waters off Truro, he was,
as his second wife informed him in another context, no "Adonis."
And he didn't compensate for these shortcomings (as many a plain
Jane would have done, and not a few milquetoasts, too) with a mild
temper and an accommodating demeanor. His correspondence
from women and his biographers and critics (to say nothing of his
own frank journal record of personal quirkiness) is one long catalog
of instances when, instead of listening, he lectured, instead of
showing consideration for others, he issued demands with the
single-minded, roughshod purpose of a spoiled child (which, in
spite of—or perhaps because of—his loveless, lonely childhood, he
assuredly was).

Yet, this man with the underwhelming physique and overbearing
manner, once he got going, was slaying the ladies from his mid-
twenties until the day of his death at seventy-seven. He had four
wives and a couple of dozen affairs, at least a half-dozen of them
serious. He had two dates with two different women the week he
died, and both of them, accompanied by their respective husbands
—and his own wife number four—stood over his bathrobed corpse
for a six P.M. "service" as he was laid out on the bed.

The women in his life were not only numerous, they crossed
every conceivable class barrier, and numerous ethnic barriers as
well. The extraordinary thing is that he did not leave in his wake—
or at his wake—a single dissatisfied customer, sexually speaking.
With the possible exception of Mary McCarthy, wife number three,
who did in any case make literary hay out of it, they all considered

his part in their lives experience well spent. They called him, "Darling," "Dearest," "My charming old syringa," "Honeybunch, sweetspot," "Potato," and "Monkey." They signed their letters with love, with pink kisses, with Xs, and with thanks. They wrote poems to him, dedicated books to him, sent him importunate telegrams and, in one memorable instance, pursued him by telegram even into the nut house—a sanitarium called Clifton Springs where, partly to escape his entangled amours, he had checked in for three weeks in 1929. They called him the best mind, the best man, and (by implication) the best lay they had ever known.

How did this happen? One old friend, envious and not a little baffled, once asked him how he (read "you, a bookish, squeaky-voiced, hundred-and-ninety-seven-pound weakling") managed to get all those classy, good-looking dames into bed. His answer was that he "talked them into it." That's a pretty accurate answer, as far as it goes. He could be both a funny and a fascinating talker. And he had lots of funny and fascinating stories to tell, about many, in fact most, of the biggest literary lights on two continents. And women like to hear stories. But there was something else as well, something to do with who he was—a rarity in a dumbed-down world.

He was an eighteenth-century man of intellect, engrained with the code of a classical humanist, and endowed with the appetites and the stamina of a bull. Mary McCarthy thought the combination presented elements of the grotesque. She likened him to the monster in the labyrinth in Crete. But that monster exerted a strong sexual attraction over her, as she demonstrated in the fictional post-divorce seduction she records in A Charmed Life. She has her fictionalized alter ego fall onto a red couch in the fictionalized Wellfleet house she formerly inhabited with Miles, the fictionalized Edmund Wilson. In addition to displaying her attraction to his masterful behavior in the sack, she also (under the guise of nailing him as a cruel brute) has Miles deliver himself of a number of home truths. This truth telling seems to have been one of the most compelling aspects of Wilson as a lover; at least three women represent him as a breakthrough in their sexual lives, either because he was the first to take their virginity or because he was the first through whom they experienced an orgasm. Their letters record their gratitude for the pleasures he opened to them and for the self-knowledge they gained.

Any honest summation of Wilson as a critic in love must include the dark side of his behavior: the seemingly clinical self-absorption that watched and would afterward minutely record each moment of his own performance in the bedroom, the terrors of being unloved that haunted him from his early life and that would sometimes sweep over him and drive him to strike out at the partner who represented that love withheld; the selfishness and indifference to his partners' health which on occasion prompted callous disregard for pregnancies he incurred or sexual diseases he may have transmitted; the harrowing years of undeserved suffering his drunken rages inflicted upon his wives and children.

Set against this, though, the summation must show his own refusal to lie to himself or to us about these behaviors, his very real and mostly successful attempt, during his whole life, to behave decently to all. The seeming coldness and egocentricity of his journal entries about sex—not even real coldness and egocentricity as we have seen—are part of the legend of Wilson the monster. But any critical and careful look at what's going on, page by page and book by book, shows that he was trying to record the humanity of people he found attractive and loved. There is implicit tribute paid his sexual partners by the passionate attention he gave their responses as well as his own—noting with precision the linguistic, biographical, social, and even decorative points that individualized each encounter, making of each, as it were, a case of this room, this gin, and these sandwiches. The positive side of the ledger might also note his generous gifts of his time, his talent, and his money—often beyond his slender means—manifest in the many little gestures of notes, letters, Valentines, and other signs of concern he was to lavish upon women friends, former lovers or not.

Why revisit the mundane, the often graphic—and even pornographic—details of a life already lived and already copiously published by the man himself and other commentators and biographers? Because it allows the interesting women in that life to stand forth in greater clarity and poignancy, because it reconstitutes for a new generation the flavor of an important period in our American literary past, and, most important, because, by highlighting the inner struggles that accompanied Wilson's literary, critical, and journalistic accomplishments, it illuminates one more corner of the human picture.

. . . . . .

ROMANCE, LOVE, AND SEX had always been the obsessions of one of twentieth-century America's most intellectual writers. Passion was in some ways the master theme of this bookish man. His years of scholarly and literary toil were as much erotic as cerebral. This intellectual's intellectual never retreated from the life of the senses, the allure of beautiful women, nor did he fail to record his ideas of passion in his works of criticism and intellectual history. Almost like one of his literary heroes, William Butler Yeats, Wilson wanted to seek out his temperamental opposite: By nature contemplative, he wanted to break through to his active side. His life was a dialectic that began with books and isolation, moved to romance and affairs, and rose to a plane of passionate intellectualism seen in his finest work.

Along the way to becoming and expressing his true self, there were false steps, confusions, and even some ugliness. The older man who wrote an essay entitled "Sex" in *A Piece of My Mind* was not the best that Edmund Wilson could be. A crank and grouch lamenting the bred-down world of post–World War II America, he hoped that his countrymen would turn to eugenics and breed up a better species. Look what had been done with the breeding of animals! But this sourness masking as progressivism should not obscure the moving expression he had given to whole areas of the passionate life. When his brains and senses were on high alert, he was one of American literature's best writers about love.

But the trouble is that Wilson does not yield up his riches that easily, and, on first blush, the tables of contents of his chronicles— *The Shores of Light, Classics and Commercials, The Bit Between My Teeth,* and *The Devils and Canon Barham*—seem to be filled with masculine interests, canonical writers, and a plentiful lack of Jane Austen, George Eliot, and the Brontës, not to mention, in a later period, women greats like Virginia Woolf and Flannery O'Connor. Added to the problem is the paucity of essays about major female protagonists in works by men—this Dante enthusiast never discussed Beatrice; this lover of Elizabethan and Jacobean drama had little to say about Shakespeare's or Webster's heroines; this lover of French literature didn't do much with Racine's heroines or Flaubert's or Stendhal's. Now, it goes without saying that we shouldn't judge a critic by what he doesn't do, but these gaps add to the Wilson-and-women problem: What was on his mind if not the passionate sensuality of Anna Karenina or the feline deceptions of Odette? Why weren't these his topics when he was coping with them in his everyday life? This man who put so much of his own life into his works—who wrote a vast journal, two autobiographical novels, and numerous meditations on his political and social beliefs —was turning something off when it came to encountering the great tradition of women's writing and writing about women. No Laura, no Mrs. Dalloway, no Catherine Barkley. Nevertheless, while gaps tell something, they don't tell the whole story.

A closer look helps us to see what Wilson was up to, and what he was up to is by no means simple. While accident, distraction, money making, and every vicissitude of fortune play a part in what a writer —even a very organized writer—writes about, there's usually a pattern if you look closely enough. In Wilson's case the patterns can be seen once you do the sorting out. Yes, it is true that we could have a list of What Edmund Wilson Doesn't Do; and it appears that such a list would include what most other writers undertake. With a reputation as a classicist and as a strong canon man and bulwark of literary tradition, Wilson has sometimes projected a confusing sense of what he's about. He never liked to reinvent the wheel or talk about courtly love when de Rougemont could do it better, or even poach on the territory of his relatively new friend Leon Edel, or make large generalizations about love in the modern world as Lionel Trilling did in his essays on *Lolita* and Alfred Kinsey. If the others were doing it, you can be sure Wilson wasn't. Even when his essays were

a bit thin and sketchy, they were pioneering, and he was never in the
mood to put his effort into what was being copiously written about.

With the theme of love, it was the same; without making him a
man exploring the margins, we can certainly say that he preferred
the offbeat to the on beat. He always had the tendency to be
oblique and to pull out the different story in a familiar book. The
journalist in him was an artist—and he looked for a scoop that was
more than a gimmick.

His modus operandi when he went about writing on love, romance, and sex was, strangely enough, not to light upon his favorite
writers or even the best writers, and certainly not on the most popular writers. He was looking for odd perspectives and searching his
own mind and psyche for insights that were more than common-
place. Furthermore, he had no desire to twist the classics, find weird
things in Dante's Beatrice or in Shakespeare's Rosalind, or otherwise be some kind of theorist with a bee in his bonnet who found
what might not be there. He was looking for the real story that was
a new story. While it's impossible and indefensible to say that he
went about this systematically, a look at what he did do shows that
in every instance he looked for the angle and wrote with heart and
head when he found it.

The story begins as far back as *The Twenties,* and we have told
some of it as it relates to Edna Millay. But there are other instances
where he was sharply on the lookout for what was new in one of
the oldest subjects in Western literature. His piece on D. H.
Lawrence's *Lady Chatterley's Lover* in *The Shores of Light* is truly
buried in an awesome collection. But once you pull it out and look
at it closely you see that it's all about the uniqueness of Lawrence's
talent, the way that this master, a master to whom Wilson wasn't
particularly sympathetic otherwise, had done something revolutionary in this book. Lawrence's mission was colossal: nothing less
than the self-affirmation and the triumph of life in the teeth of all
the demoralizing forces of modern industrial society. Wilson, at this
period working on his Joyce essay for *Axel's Castle,* took time out
to draw the distinction between what Joyce was up to regarding sex
and what Lawrence was doing. Wilson felt that Joyce, for all his

brilliance in talking about sex, had not actually invented a new vocabulary for it. In the *Chatterley* essay, Wilson went on to say that Lawrence did something extraordinary for English fiction and for the English language; he offered genuine pioneering in the description of sexual intercourse. Wilson's essay maintains that our language never really had the vocabulary to discuss the actuality of sex: It was either romanticism or the gutter, even with a great master of the sexual life like Joyce. It was Lawrence who gave us a totally new way of talking about sex, an idiom pitched between ordinariness and poetry.

In the James Joyce chapter in *Axel's Castle,* Wilson moves from the question of erotic language to the depths of erotic feeling. He gives a profile of Joyce's characters in *Ulysses* and in so doing reveals something of his own philosophy of life. Stephen and Molly "represent extremes," the intellectual and the instinctual. Wilson wants to get these extremes in touch with each other. "In the soliloquy of Mrs. Bloom, Joyce has given another ecstasy of creation, the rhapsody of the flesh. Stephen's dream was conceived in loneliness, by a drawing apart from his fellows. But Mrs. Bloom is like the earth which gives the same life to all: she feels a maternal kinship with all living creatures." Wilson strives to connect the two extremes and to express his personal vision of the intellectual and physical through talking about Joyce's vision. In describing Molly he is describing more than the flesh. "This gross body, the body of humanity, upon which the whole structure of *Ulysses* rests—still throbbing with so strong a rhythm amid obscenity, commonness and squalor—is laboring to throw up some knowledge and beauty by which it may transcend itself." The literary-critical perception is at the dead center of Wilson's life: For Wilson, sensual things are not diversions, dissipations, and distractions, but are integral to thinking. From the time he set out to write in the twenties, this philosophy of his vocation gathered momentum. He drops hints of it in crucial essays, and, without hammering at it, makes it the current that flows through his career.

The reader of Wilson's work can find this abiding conviction in every period and rejoice in the fact that he doesn't have to see it spelled out, or in any theoretical format, or as an annoying obsession. It's there and worn lightly even at the times when Wilson's mind is immersed in very theoretical subjects to do with politics and policy. In the early 1930s when he was writing about the effects of the Depression, his own feelings of disaffection with capitalism, and his directions for a way out, he had time to write about—of all people—Jacques Casanova. This essay, which found its way into *The Wound and the Bow* in 1941, shows that a romantic philosophy of human affairs was never far from his mind; in fact, what was later called "Uncomfortable Casanova" manages to incorporate his ideas of erotic power and his visions of social protest at one and the same time.

Casanova is a transgressive observer of eighteenth-century society, someone who saw everything that was wrong, someone who had the same seat in the theater of European corruption as Rousseau or Voltaire. Despite the fact that Casanova "keeps his faculties clear" and "commands our respect," he is incapable of feeling the full force of what is before him. He sees every aspect of eighteenth-century life, but he seems to accept the good, bad, and indifferent, making no moral distinctions, protests, or calls for action. He is an observer and reporter on the scene without being a master of it. Wilson enjoys describing his exactitude, but also puts Casanova down for not knowing what to do with this meticulous description. His writing does not lead to anything larger than his own reactions.

This worrying about an uncomfortable philosopher manqué is Wilson's way of working through the project of his own career: What do a thousand observations and adventures mean? What do the romantic sieges, the successes and failures, the conquests and absurdities amount to? Wilson, never grandiose, dryly says that the real theme of it all is "the many things a life may hold." He then says that "there is even the appetite of the intellect." And he further writes that Casanova, in old age, could "still test" his "nerve and strength" with his writing. This of course is precisely where Wilson was going in 1932 and would go in later years; the crucial distinction is that Casanova adventured in a desultory way. And Wilson—of course not the household word that Casanova is—had a far more focused and comprehensive thing in mind. He wanted in one way or another to connect up man's instincts, destructive and creative, and fashion a picture out of them. The subject of his essay, however, could simply recount episodes. Wilson, in making his perhaps unfair demand on the Italian memoirist, was actually setting up a challenge for himself: hammering out a romantic-social-intellectual philosophy of life. Because he didn't work as a systematic philosopher, his vision could not be conveyed by a set of easily discernible precepts; but it could be an unmistakable attitude that stood out in his books.

Wilson's desire for connections—coherent relations between ideas and events, psychic happenings and public things—is evident in a long essay that he wrote about a high-souled, romantic American intellectual, John Jay Chapman. Without recounting the entire argument of the piece, we should notice what gives it its motivation and power: Wilson's identification with Chapman's vitality, his intense personality, and his all-or-nothing passion for justice amid the crass commercialism of the Gilded Age.

Chapman is an anti-Casanova figure, capable of the reflection and introspection that the eighteenth-century rake had no access to. Chapman, like Wilson, also knew what he wanted—a connection between his love of poetry and a beautiful woman, and the larger world of progressive politics. He had the very quality that Wilson yearned for, described in a number of places in his writings, and lamented the lack of in American society. This dream fusion of romantic instinct and high practical endeavor—something he dealt with at considerable length in *To the Finland Station*—never disappeared. In the essay on Chapman, he metaphorically says, quoting his man, that it's the desire to "play on the open strings." This of course is, once again, Wilson wanting it all. But that is part of his nature; in spite of his testiness, cynicism, and sourness in later life, the romantic idealism never died. He wanted—fantasized about, wrote about—beautiful women and a better world. (We see him, very late in life, wearing his McGovern button and telling Mary Pcolar, "But of course we must all vote for McGovern!")

But, meanwhile, the Chapman essay came out in *The Triple*

*Thinkers* at a time when Wilson was preparing his political-social masterpiece *To the Finland Station*. This epic of revolutionary ideas, ardors, and actions was a long time in the making and was finally published in 1940. Wilson had followed the romance of the Left to the Soviet Union on a Guggenheim fellowship in 1935; there he intended to do research at the Marx-Lenin Institute, was prohibited from carrying out his plan, did a considerable amount of travel and, so far as possible, had direct experience of the socialist experiment. Neither ecstatic nor nay-saying, he came away with the conviction that people did not fall apart when class distinctions fell away; yet his keen eye for what was wrong with the cultural and social picture made him suspicious of Stalin, his cult, and the emergence of a fabulous and totalized vision of how to live.

The reservations about the USSR, which were with him in full force at the time of his book's publication, were not much different from those of many other intellectuals: The Moscow trials, the Hitler-Stalin non-aggression pact, and the persecution of dissenters weighed on his conscience and made him critical. He was an unorthodox pick-and-choose sympathizer with socialism.

In spite of these doubts, his affirmations about socialist culture made the book a kind of landmark of hope and idealism; it was Wilson's biggest intellectual romance to date, containing everything he knew and believed in about the growth of the egalitarian ideal. It contains a record of reading and a record of his personal struggle to find a way out of the limiting terms of his early life—the constricted environment of his boyhood and the holdover mentality of acquisition from the Gilded Age that he so deplored. *To the Finland Station* was a kind of escape from the everyday terms of American greed, and he tried to make the book, in addition, an escape from the terms of ordinary, compromised, self-serving relationships. A dream, of course, but one that was true to his highest yearnings. In it he inscribed portraits of his heroes, and some of them were couples.

Wilson's portrait of Karl Marx and Jenny von Westphalen is among the most touching depictions in his writing. He paints it in short strokes, but when the reader puts the book down, these strokes linger in the mind. Their poignant quality is also true to Wilson's way of seeing things, unsentimental without being unemotional. Jenny and Marx essentially were wedded to each other in a disastrous yet heroic way. The girl from an aristocratic family, whose father was an Enlightenment figure and had Scottish blood from the family of the Duke of Argyle, was unlucky enough to have been captivated by a young man who wanted her to drink the poison of revolutionary sacrifice. In an early passage, in a paraphrase of a little poem by Marx, there's a lover who allows his beloved to drink poison. And Marx himself, according to Wilson, said that he "must forge on against the happiness of those he loves." This girl of many suitors, a belle of Trier, the cream of society, was to be dragged through hell—the hell of poverty, humiliation, and hardship in London.

But Wilson's Marx was by no means a heartless revolutionary; his quest to win his bride, his tender feelings for her, his respect and awe for her person were simply overwhelmed by his awe of something else. Wilson shows how Jenny was drawn into his web of ideas and revolutionary action, how she watched their possibilities for a good life vanish with the Argyle silver. But instead of showing her as the mere victim of a deluded philosopher, he depicts her as a willing party. In a quiet but titanically emotional death scene, Jenny is shown in a last meeting with her husband: Wilson quotes their daughter Eleanor to wonderful effect: "I shall never forget the morning when he felt strong enough to go into Mother's room. It was as if they were young again, she a loving young girl and he a loving young man, embarking on life together, and not an old man shattered by illness and a dying old lady taking leave of one another forever." On her deathbed, Jenny was following the first elections held in Germany "after the enactment of the anti-Socialist law, and was "delighted" with the results. Just before she died, she was cheered by a positive article about Marx. Wilson, in the paragraph that recounts these things, ends with a quote from Engels about Marx and his reaction: "The Moor is dead too."

We see the historian of ideas in Wilson come together with the portraitist, and we also see clearly that the hardness and insistence of a grand conception is the stuff of great writing when it meets the deepest feelings of individuals. Wilson made himself a master of these connections. He managed to show how single lives flowed into the larger river of action and intellectual energy. And he made the dry stuff of political economy into romantic material.

When he turns to the rush of the Finland Station itself—Lenin's story of preparing for the Bolshevik revolution—Wilson goes into high gear and makes the story of Lenin's marriage into phase two of the Marxist idea: Marx the dealer in pamphlets, arguments and propaganda; Lenin the man of action. Lenin chose as his bride someone a great deal more down-to-earth than Jenny Marx. Krúpskaya, his future wife, had felt the brutal injustices of Tsarist Russia in a way that Jenny Marx had never felt the settled prejudices and narrowness of the German bourgeoisie. Krúpskaya had been a rather unconventional girl who early on joined a Marxist circle in St. Petersburg. She'd worked as a teacher and governess, and came prepared, not simply to sacrifice and appreciate and revere her revolutionary man, but to be a revolutionary with him. She entered into the spirit of whatever tight spot they were in, fit into the most uncomfortable of circumstances, relocated when they were kicked out. She was no delicate beauty; as a matter of fact she had a strange goiter-like condition and popping eyes that caused people to say she looked like a fish. Nevertheless Wilson shows Lenin and Krúpskaya in perfect white-hot revolutionary harmony; they worked to the point of collapse, and would then sometimes seek release in mountain solitude. It's all rendered with Wilson's characteristic dramatic gifts. He's dry, direct, precise, and reluctant to slow down his narrative by censoring his characters or interpreting them unnecessarily.

His story is essentially about how a kind of idealism and a kind of humanity reached a violent peak of development. After he has told it, he shows the two comrades together with their mission accomplished. The very last page of the book—a book that earlier on has had hundreds of pages of discourse about ideas—has no reference to ideas at all. "The night of their arrival, Krúpskaya records —. . . she and Lenin 'went home to our people.'" A relative "had hung up over their beds the last words of the *Communist Manifesto:* Workers of the World Unite!" Wilson has Krúpskaya saying, "Everything was understood without words." And this is the end—Wilson's literary and historical consummation—of the socialist ideal in one writer's career. It contained all his emotion, a great deal of passionate feeling, and the learning of about ten years. It also contained his hopes, encoded in a political story, for creative workers of all kinds —that they'd find someone of like mind with whom to make their journey. In the wake of Soviet horror and the fall of Communism worldwide, there is still much value in Wilson's aspirations and craftsmanship in *To the Finland Station*. It's a book about socialism all right, and we can see around many of its vulnerabilities as Wilson himself would in 1971; but it's also and foremost a book that is a great romantic vision, an epic of people who, for more than two hundred years, yearned for something more.

The revolution signaled in *To the Finland Station* was to become a subject once again in Wilson's long reflective essays on Boris Pasternak, written at the end of the 1950s. As we have said, *Finland Station* is essentially a work of affirmation notwithstanding its excoriation of the excesses of Marxism. These new essays, "Doctor Life and his Guardian Angel" and "Legend and Symbolism in *Doctor Zhivago*" are more than affirmation: They are hymns to the life force and, at the same time, contrite reflections on the horrors of the once-noble experiment. Wilson had discovered in his later years yet another master text on which to hang his thoughts and intense feelings. *Doctor Zhivago* was the perfect work for a critic who wanted to correct his own record—and Wilson, as he tells us in numerous places, always liked to correct himself. This time we get the sense that he is correcting a massive error of perception—American intellectuals' illusions about the Soviet state. As he describes it, it is an error committed against life, passionate experience, and individualism. Pasternak the novelist bodies forth in poetic prose one of Wilson's own ideas: that our experience is worth nothing if it is tamed and beaten into shape by ideologies and political systems. Wilson had been working on this idea for years, although superficial readers of *To the Finland Station* thought that he was in the grip of doctrinaire Marxism. His big study is actually shot through with all the terrible things that happen to people under the spell of dehumanized abstractions. Wilson never had complete confidence in Marx's system, in the glory of socialist man and the iron logic of the dialectic. To him, it was a brilliant intellectual attempt with attendant disasters. It turned out that the latter were monumental and tragic, and in his later years he looked to something else. Pasternak gave him symbolic people who stood up against all the categories and all the cruelty that came from categories.

The characters in *Doctor Zhivago* who escape the Soviet system in their spirits are what Wilson calls "vital" units. Zhivago and Larissa don't work very well as social role models, and their inconsistencies, weaknesses, and failures make them something quite apart from the horrible plaster saints of the Stalinist era. They come to us with their adulteries, soiled pasts, betrayals and letdowns— which is to say, they come to us in a form that must have been very congenial to Wilson himself. Pasternak insisted that life is not "a material" to be remade; it is something that eternally renews itself. If people run according to type, if they can be moved around like chess pieces, humanity has been extinguished. Wilson goes to work on these insights, shows how Pasternak embodies them in scenes and characters, studies their antitheses, and variously shows how there's no guarantee, in the short run and in the political realm, that they will not go down in defeat.

But in the long run, Zhivago and Larissa are going to prevail, and Wilson, in "Legend and Symbolism in *Doctor Zhivago*," goes to great pains to show how Zhivago himself, named Yuri (George), is related in Pasternak's imagination to St. George, slayer of dragons, connected with the Perseus myth. He's the intellectual and idealistic force in the book. Larissa is his tarnished love, a woman who has been used and abused by the old regime and the new, and who still endures. Both of them, Wilson delights in discovering, are connected with water imagery and renewal, and this most agnostic of critics winds up celebrating "Christianity and love and art"; these have "long range importance" and hold us together in the midst of "the barbarities against which they must assert themselves." These barbarities of course are the Soviet system and all its cognates in that long period from the death of Lenin through the fifties. Wilson, not given much to enthusiasm, rhapsodizes over Pasternak and tells us "where one is" when one picks up *Zhivago*: "at home in the great literary tradition of bold thinking and original art." He's willing to become plainer, if less grand, and does so quickly; Zhivago tells us "we shall rise again in our children as well as in our work."

The two pieces on Pasternak have given Wilson the chance to set down something more permanent, less mood-ridden, disillusioned, and angry than we see in a more direct piece like "Sex" in *A Piece of My Mind*. They lead to more than the dour musings on the degeneracy of the human race, Wilson's worst kind of grousing. And they come two years afterwards. Now they don't completely cancel out that side of our critic, but they are a lot more in keeping with the whole direction of his career, the tenor of his best work.

Wilson's way of life—the clip at which he lived and loved—is not usually associated with the word *critic*. The temperate zones of surveying, analyzing, and judging literature and the arts are not generally inhabited by men and women of his will, ego, and libido. He combined the restlessness and energy and curiosity of the adventurer with the diligence and Talmudic concentration of the scholar. He was what a critic almost never is: the man of many sides, many skills, and many desires. Yet he remained a critic in his dedication to looking at a text or a person or an event and offering description and judgment rather than imaginative depiction. He was not at his best when inventing, which is not to say that he couldn't create. But his creativity was a matter of seeing relationships and revealing connections among ideas, books, and personalities. Critical writing of this kind is, as he put it, a branch of literature. He could populate a world with real people and evocations of fictional ones, genuinely and vividly drawn; he could create—out of his own erudition, inner needs, fantasies, and convictions—a world of men and women who live and breathe as we read about them.

The drama of Wilson himself—as lover, thinker, and chronicler

—is the story we have been telling. Using as our raw materials the jumpy and often fragmented backdrop of the journals, the mountainous number of letters that he wrote and received, and the literary output that didn't end, even with his death, we have tried to construct the substance of his passions and loves.

# Notes

## Introduction

page

viii "the zoo of himself": Leon Edel quoted in Edmund Wilson, *The Thirties: From Notebooks and Diaries of the Period*, edited with an introduction by Leon Edel (New York: Farrar, Straus and Giroux, 1980), xxviii.

viii "eventually have friends": Edmund Wilson, *A Prelude: Landscapes, Characters and Conversations from the Earlier Years of My Life* (New York: Farrar, Straus and Giroux, 1967), 40.

viii "something in common": ibid.

ix "eclipses": Edmund Wilson, "The Author at Sixty," in *A Piece of My Mind: Reflections at Sixty* (New York: Farrar, Straus and Cudahy, 1956), 214.

x "sympathetic": *Prelude*, 40.

x A letter to Margaret: Edmund Wilson to Margaret Rullman, née Edwards, January 1, 1962, in *Edmund Wilson, the Man in Letters*, edited and introduced by David Castronovo and Janet Groth (Athens, Ohio: Ohio University Press, 2001), 340.

x "sensitive poetic nature": *Prelude*, 32.

x "I learned a good": ibid.

xi "pitifully sparse": ibid., 31.

xi "The whole atmosphere": ibid., 42.

xii "barbarian queen": Edmund Wilson, *Galahad and I Thought of Daisy* (New York: Farrar, Straus and Giroux, 1967), 17.

xiii "remarkably uninteresting": *Prelude*, 115.

xiii "bicker": ibid.

xiii "like a Hollywood set": ibid.

xiii "They saw the clubs": ibid., 113–114.

xiii "disillusioning climax": ibid., 114.

xiv "Some people call": ibid., 127.

xiv "The Puritanism": ibid., 147.

xiv "They're hookers!": ibid, 148.

xiv "talked of other things": ibid.

xiv "sublimation": ibid., 148.

xiv "shy little scholar": F. Scott Fitzgerald, "My Lost City," in *The Crack-Up*, ed. Edmund Wilson (New York: New Directions, 1945), 24.

xv "little scholar": ibid.

xv "mellow and safe": *Crack-Up*, 25.

xvi "the little Dane": *Man in Letters*, 15 ff.

xvii "Aw, they used": Edmund Wilson, *The Twenties: From Notebooks and Diaries of the Period*, edited with an introduction by Leon Edel (New York: Farrar, Straus and Giroux, 1975), 27.

## I. Artists and Bohemians

3 "man of the twenties": Edmund Wilson, *The Sixties: The Last Journal, 1960–1972*, edited and with an introduction by Lewis Dabney (New York: Farrar, Straus and Giroux, 1993), 48.

3 "counter-memoir": Edmund Wilson, "Epilogue, 1952: Edna St. Vincent Millay," in *The Shores of Light: A Literary Chronicle of the Twenties and Thirties* (New York: Farrar, Straus and Young, 1952), 746.

3 "recklessness": *Shores*, 778.

3 "scorn for safe living,": ibid.

3 "the need to": ibid.

4 "into the void": Edmund Wilson to Edna St. Vincent Millay, August 1, 1920, Edna St. Vincent Millay Collection, Library of Congress.

4 "I don't know": *Letters of Edna St. Vincent Millay*, ed. Allan Ross Mac dougall (New York: Grosset and Dunlop, 1952), 98.

4 "lewd portrait": ibid., 99.

5 "great good fortune": Jeffrey Meyers, *Edmund Wilson: A Biography* (Boston: Houghton Mifflin, 1995), 60.

5 "somewhat heavy": *Shores*, 784.

5 "To Love Impuissant": sonnet viii in "From *A Few Figs from Thistles*," *The Collected Poems of Edna St. Vincent Millay* (New York: Harper and Row, 1956), 568.

5 "to my liking to think": *Shores*, 748.

5 "She was dressed in": ibid., 749.

6 "My candle burns at both ends": *Collected Poems*, 127.

6 "cultivate her acquaintance": *Shores*, 750.

6 "We published in": ibid., 751.

6 "was so common": ibid.

6 "one cannot really": ibid.

6 "There was something": ibid., 752.
6 "made it possible": ibid., 753.
7 "there was also a trip": ibid., 753.
7 "Here is a wound": Edna St. Vincent Millay, in *Collected Poems*, 592.
7 "for me, even rolling": *Shores*, 751.
7 "I used to take her to plays": ibid., 754.
7 "[b]etween John Bishop": ibid., 755.
7 "I was more or less . . . situation": ibid.
8–12 "Dear Edna: I must have left my pocket-book . . . wire me (collect) when I can see you": nine unpublished letters from Edmund Wilson to Edna St.Vincent Millay, n.d., June 30,1920, July 27,1920, July 28, 1920, August 1, 1920, August 12, 1920, August 17, 1920, August 25, 1920, August 27, 1920, Edna St. Vincent Millay Collection, Library of Congress.
12 "she had me and John . . . August night": *Shores*, 759.
13 "there were only two rooms . . . conveyed that idea": ibid., 764.
13 "I was not the solution, nor was anyone else she knew": ibid., 766.
13 "I saw her in Paris . . . good time": ibid., 771.
13 "found Edna very much . . . money instead": *Twenties*, 92.
14 "She can no longer . . . for her died": ibid., 94.
14 "glamour of high passion": ibid.
14 "an outlaw": Edmund Wilson, *I Thought of Daisy* (New York: Scribner's, 1929; reprint, 1968), 70.
14 "Rita Cavanaugh was": ibid., 19.
15 "boldness and austerity": ibid., 20.
15 "I had not known": ibid.
15 "on her lips . . . a song": ibid., 21.
15 "Almost like a man": ibid., 27.
15 "austere and impressive": ibid.
15 "lovely": ibid., 28.
15 "conviction": ibid.
16 "the noble magnanimity": "Give that Beat Again," *Shores*, 684.
16 "fictitious personalities . . . in her own person": ibid., 685.
16 "the old strong beat": ibid., 686.
17 "And now Edna": ibid.
17 "Yet I miss her": ibid.
17 "and with her other . . . much for her": "Epilogue," *Shores*, 755.
17 "what interests her": ibid.
17 "with a miscellany": ibid., 756.
18 "she was sometimes": ibid., 756–757.
18 "What was the cause": ibid.

18 "At that time": ibid.
18 "in the astonishing": ibid., 758.
18 "she is alone": ibid., 758–759.
18 "the demands of which": ibid., 756–757.
20 "gentility unfits people": Edmund Wilson, *Five Plays* (New York: Farrar, Straus and Young, 1954; reprint, New York: Farrar, Straus and Giroux, 1969), 225.
21 "The bedroom had been designed": Rosalind Baker Wilson, *Near the Magician: A Memoir of My Father, Edmund Wilson* (New York: Grove Weidenfeld, 1989), 29–30.
22 "a good dose of Cascara": Mary Blair to Edmund Wilson, July 15, 1922, Edmund Wilson Papers, Yale Collection of American Literature, Beinecke Rare Book and Manuscript Library (hereafter cited as Yale).
22 "great play": Mary Blair to Edmund Wilson, August 29, 1921, Yale.
22 "I had a funny dream": ibid.
24 "Mary got insulting letters": *Twenties,* 120.
24 "so low that he'd have to take": ibid.
24 "have gained intensity . . . sheared away": *Shores,* 103
25 "Winged Victory": Mary Blair to Edmund Wilson, August 15, 1921, Yale.
26 "I'm determined": Mary Blair to Edmund Wilson, April 3, 1925, Yale.
26 "I want so much": ibid.
26 "a signal": Edmund Wilson, *The American Earthquake: A Documentary of the Twenties and Thirties* (Garden City, New York: Doubleday Anchor Books, 1958), 51.
27 "The old veteran": "The Critic as Politician," *New Republic,* December 2, 1925; *From the Uncollected Edmund Wilson,* selected and introduced by Janet Groth and David Castronovo (Athens, Ohio: Ohio University Press, 1995), 99.
27 "a pair of cheap": *Twenties,* 144.
27 "one of the finest": Mary Blair to Edmund Wilson, January 5, 1941, Yale.
29 "When I finally": *Twenties,* 545.
29 "needed a girl": ibid., 33.
29 "The Rape of the": ibid., 38
30 "They all came . . . till I met you": ibid., 45.
30 "This looks like": ibid., 48.
30 "calisthenics": quoted in Mervyn Horder, Introduction to *The Best of Dorothy Parker* (London: The Folio Society, 1995), 14.
31 "Brevity is the soul": ibid., 16.

31 "I have slogged along": ibid., 12

31 "People Who Do": *The Portable Dorothy Parker* (New York: Viking, 1973), 257.

32 "if nobody had learned": ibid., 254.

32 "sliding down": Horder, 16.

32 "put all her eggs": ibid., 12.

32 "Not if it was": quoted in Marion Meade, *Bobbed Hair and Bathtub Gin: Writers Running Wild in the Twenties* (New York: Doubleday, 2004), 135.

32 "cleanly economic": *Shores*, 206.

32 "flatly brutal": ibid.

32 "disgusting jokes": *Twenties*, 346.

32 "I am cheap": ibid., 345; Meade, 101.

33 "Wherever does": Horder, 16.

33 "death of society": "A Toast and a Tear for Dorothy Parker," Edmund Wilson, *Classics and Commercials: A Literary Chronicle of the Forties* (New York: Farrar, Straus, 1950), 169.

33 "their response": ibid., 170.

33 "Listen, I can't . . . government?": Horder, 14.

34 "relief and reassurance": *Classics*, 169.

34 "imitation books": ibid., 171.

34 "I will be beyond": *Portable Dorothy Parker*, 123.

34 "she has been at some": *Classics*, 171.

35 "They all had their audiences": Edmund Wilson, *The Higher Jazz*, ed. Neale Reinitz (Iowa City: University of Iowa Press, 1998), 163.

36 "I was so sorry not . . . dress up": Elinor Wylie to Edmund Wilson, January 11, 1922, Yale.

37 "God keep you, Bunny": Elinor Wylie to Edmund Wilson, July 11, 1922, Yale.

37 "[p]robably the most remarkable . . . permanence": quoted in *Letters on Literature and Politics, 1912–1972*, ed. Elena Wilson (New York: Farrar, Straus and Giroux, 1977), 88.

37 "Roscoe N. Wingo . . . my soul": ibid., 91.

38 "Bunny is funny . . . thinking": quoted in Stanley Olson, *Elinor Wylie: A Life Apart* (New York: Dial Press, 1979), 193.

38 "quite addicted": *Twenties*, 76.

38 "living two stories above": *Literature and Politics*, 51.

38 "although rather grand": *Twenties*, 78.

38 "spontaneous . . . Shelley": Olson, 20.

38 "from a literary . . . third-rate poet": *Twenties*, 78–79.

39 "gives a false impression": *New Yorker*, March 19, 1927.

39  "live on aspirin and Scotch": ibid.

39  "Dorothy Parker, vivid, sympathetic . . . from no one else": Nancy Hoyt, *Elinor Wylie: the Portrait of an Unknown Lady* (Indianapolis: Bobbs-Merrill, 1935), 94.

40  "a moment of tranquility": *Shores*, 259.

40  "criticks": ibid.

40  "[p]osterity must be . . . the other": ibid., 260.

40  "luxuriance of phrases": ibid., 262.

41  "lovely . . . any other way?": Olson, 191.

41  "Oh, what an evening! . . . than mine, naturally": ibid., 271–272.

41  "Had you heard that . . . game of her": Léonie Adams to Edmund Wilson, October 2, 1928, Yale.

42  "Of what use . . . more magnificent poems": *Shores*, 130.

42  "How can you set up . . . believes in it": ibid., 132.

42  "the intellect that orders . . . sea without harbors": ibid., 396.

42  "by some strong . . . no study and no effort": ibid., 395.

43  "pig-headed": ibid., 396.

43  "My mother used to have . . . getting away from it!": *Five Plays,* 243.

44  "a lady poet": *Twenties,* 196.

44  "plucked one low . . . further development": *Shores,* 243.

44  "Women have no wilderness": quoted in Elizabeth Frank, *Louise Bogan: A Portrait* (New York: Knopf, 1985), 66.

45  "as for his friendship": Louise Bogan to Morton Zabel, November 5, 1943, *What the Woman Lived: Selected Letters of Louise Bogan, 1920–1970,* edited and with an introduction by Ruth Limmer (New York: Harcourt Brace Jovanovich, 1973), 258n.

45  "I don't know why": ibid., 150.

45  "I'm terribly sorry . . . remakes the world": Edmund Wilson to Louise Bogan, April 1931, *Literature and Politics,* 205.

45  "Your letter came just now": quoted in Frank, 139.

46  "Evening in a Sanitarium": quoted in *Journey Around My Room: The Autobiography of Louise Bogan, A Mosaic,* by Ruth Limmer (New York: Viking, 1980), 84–85.

46  "I have never had": Edmund Wilson to Louise Bogan, May 13, 1935, *Literature and Politics,* 269.

46  "After twenty minutes . . . piano duets": *Thirties,* 727.

47  "So come along": Edmund Wilson to Louise Bogan, July 16, 1934, *Man in Letters,* 44.

47  "I'm a professional . . . needed a teacher": *Journey Around My Room,* 132.

47 "I can't, I can't": quoted in Frank, 366.

47 "Oh-God-the-Pain Girls": *Shores*, 346.

48 "fundamental brainwork . . . I am really happy": *Journey Around My Room*, 133.

48 "Edmund is the best": Louise Bogan to Theodore Roethke, October 1935, *What the Woman Lived*, 113.

48 "a senseless and blatant": Louise Bogan to Rolfe Humphries, July 6, 1935, ibid., 93.

48 "Edmund has picked up . . . with mirth": Louise Bogan to Theodore Roethke, October 20, 1935, ibid., 112.

49 "In her new brown . . . to our signals": *Thirties*, 329.

49 "ghastly . . . Time!": April 12, 1961, *What the Woman Lived*, 328.

50 "a very remarkable book . . . of cloud and light": "The All-Star Literary Vaudeville," *Shores*, 243–244.

51 "Léonie informs us": Louise Bogan to Rolfe Humphries, December 27, 1925, *What the Woman Lived*, 24.

51 "Léonie thinks Edmund is wonderful": Mary Blair to Edmund Wilson, January 28, 1926, Yale.

51 "little moth flutterings": *Twenties*, 442.

54 "THEY WILL NOT": telegram, Léonie Adams to Edmund Wilson, January 22, 1929, Yale.

54 "horrid . . . some time before": Léonie Adams to Edmund Wilson, February 15, 1929, Yale.

55 the following August: Léonie Adams to Edmund Wilson, August 22, 1929, Yale.

55 "harrowing": *Twenties*, 495.

55 "a miscarriage after all": ibid., 492.

55 "to have a little Edmund": ibid., 518.

55 "made me be more honest": Léonie Adams to Edmund Wilson, n.d., Yale.

55 "I don't want you to feel . . . it was good for me after all": Léonie Adams to Edmund Wilson, February 15, 1929, Yale.

55 "on the whole the best": ibid.

56 "High Falcon": holograph in the Wilson papers at Yale. Also in Lèonie Adams, *High Falcon* (New York: John Day, 1929).

56 "she was so sweet": *Twenties*, 442.

57 "wouldn't know a line": ibid., 335.

57 "*jeune fille* respect": ibid, 331.

57 "improving romance": ibid., 322.

58 "I haven't the foggiest": ibid, 286.

58 "Awfully nice of you": ibid., 322.
58 "When I carried her to the couch . . . what she was not": ibid., 332.
58 "cynical, self-centered": *Twenties*, 333.
59 "her face": ibid.
59 "however unamiable the girl": ibid.

## II. Proletarians and the Bourgeoisie
60 "I told her that she was the best": *Twenties,* 441.
60 "Write me on your": Margaret Canby to Edmund Wilson, June 9, 1928, Yale.
60 "gallons of gin": Margaret Canby to Edmund Wilson, September 9, 1929, Yale.
61 "jazz high spirits": *Twenties*, 280.
61 "because the room": ibid, 139–140.
61 "stuff here for . . . big as a man": ibid., 278.
61 "with my feet on the gas heater": ibid., 29.
63 "we did not have enough": ibid., 492.
63 "a lady as none": *Higher Jazz*, 22.
63 "her piquant combination": ibid., 23.
64 "swooned away . . . miss her terribly": ibid., 179.
64 "I'm a Western girl!": ibid., 441.
64 "thought her preempted": ibid., 181.
65 "charmed and delighted . . . come": Margaret Canby to Edmund Wilson, August 16, 1928, Yale.
65 "terribly": Margaret Canby to Edmund Wilson, April 6, 1928 , Yale.
65 "prayers for a bigger": Margaret Canby to Edmund Wilson, June 9, 1928, Yale.
65 "tepid": *Thirties,* 129.
65 "feeling like Madame Butterfly": Margaret Canby to Edmund Wilson, December 22, 1928, Yale.
65 "a grand combination . . . strumpet": Margaret Canby to Edmund Wilson, January 4, 1929, Yale.
65 "When I boasted": *Thirties,* 260.
65 "a couple of washouts": Margaret Canby to Edmund Wilson, April 20, 1929, Yale.
66 "alky and water": *Thirties,* 30.
66 "than to anyone living": ibid.
66 "turtle paws": *Twenties*, 6.
66 "trim though full figure": *Thirties,* 13.
66 "a little short plumpish Venus": ibid., 21.

# Notes

66 "like a little pony": ibid., 22.
66 "her fine nobly distinguished face": ibid., 41
66 "a thoroughbred": ibid., 236.
66 "How can you worry": ibid., 235.
66 "Your great big beautiful masses": ibid., 248.
66 "You're a cold fishy": ibid., 236.
66 "Old Man Gloom Himself": ibid., 156.
66 "Why don't you take me . . . like people": ibid., 257.
66 "the silly sort of life": ibid., 245.
67 "Los Angeles (the goozly . . . beach": ibid., 132.
67 "—a pink morocco camel": ibid., 133.
67 "Perhaps I had gotten more": ibid., 248.
67 "used sometimes to make her . . . like a boy": ibid., 244.
67 "a luxury . . . cold cream on either": ibid., 237.
67 "pink prong": ibid., 253.
68 "It's very hard to write . . . Come": ibid., 600.
68 "Her nightgowns that": ibid., 260.
68 "I Picked a Lemon in the Garden of Love": ibid., 367.
68 "two Hollywood pretties . . . in Movie Crazy'": ibid., 234.
68 "happiness . . . could never know": ibid., 231.
70 "upstate Irishman named Albert Minahan": letterhead on letter from Frances Minahan to Edmund Wilson, n.d., from Oswego, New York, Yale.
70 "new boy friend": Frances Minahan to Edmund Wilson, April 26, 1934, Yale.
70 "sordid": Thirties, 298.
71 "like a fairy": ibid., 424.
72 "Fucking in the afternoon . . . rendezvous at night": ibid., 417.
72 "I asked her whether . . . over mine": Edmund Wilson, Memoirs of Hecate County (Garden City, New York: Doubleday, 1946; revised edition, 1958), 155.
73 "cold, fishy, leprous person": Thirties, 236.
73 "intelligible human terms": ibid., 298.
73 "I began to feel . . . good between us": Hecate County, 167.
74 "had brought me to her": ibid., 239.
76 "You are guileful . . . hard heart": December 7, 1933, in The Princess with the Golden Hair: Letters of Elizabeth Waugh to Edmund Wilson, 1933–1942, edited and with an introduction by John B. Friedman and Kristen M. Figg (Cranbury, New Jersey: Associated University Presses, 2000), 83.

76 "If you were just prose": ibid.

76 "stark epistolary . . . crystals": Elizabeth Waugh to Edmund Wilson, June 2, 1935, *Princess,* 101.

76 "I have always been medieval": Elizabeth Waugh to Edmund Wilson, April 1935, *Princess,* 97.

77 "Ed, dearie": Elizabeth Waugh to Edmund Wilson, November 10, 1934, *Princess,* 90.

77 "pink love": Elizabeth Waugh to Edmund Wilson, *Princess,* 84, 86, 88, 89.

77 "the flesh and the devil": Elizabeth Waugh to Edmund Wilson, February 2, 1935, *Princess,* 95.

77 "You have . . . made me": Elizabeth Waugh to Edmund Wilson, December 10, 1935, *Princess,* 107.

77 "No doubt my letters": Elizabeth Waugh to Edmund Wilson, March 20, 1936, *Princess,* 111.

77 "There are cleverer": Elizabeth Waugh to Edmund Wilson, August 3, 1936, *Princess,* 118.

77 "adolescent romantic": Elizabeth Waugh to Edmund Wilson, January 18, 1937, *Princess,* 119.

77 "Even your damn plays": Elizabeth Waugh to Edmund Wilson, March 4, 1936, *Princess,* 109.

78 "My lip is very sore": Elizabeth Waugh to Edmund Wilson, March 18, 1936, *Princess,* 110.

78 "you close up tight": Elizabeth Waugh to Edmund Wilson, June 16, 1936, *Princess,* 113.

78 "My mental agony": Elizabeth Waugh to Edmund Wilson, March 4, 1936, *Princess,* 109.

78 "Darling, After I saw you . . . good soldier": Elizabeth Waugh to Edmund Wilson, February 1937, *Princess,* 123.

78 "Don't hate me . . . agony": Elizabeth Waugh to Edmund Wilson, February 25, 1937, *Princess,* 126.

78 "I was surprised to find . . . new to me!": *Thirties,* 669–672.

79 "It was as if . . . like that too?": Elizabeth Waugh to Edmund Wilson, September 30, 1937, *Princess,* 139.

79 "the sin part": Elizabeth Waugh to Edmund Wilson, November 15, 1937, *Princess,* 141.

79 "November Ride": Edmund Wilson, *Night Thoughts* (New York: Farrar, Straus and Cudahy, 1961), 134–135.

80 "cute little red-headed . . . little society": Elizabeth Waugh to Edmund Wilson, New Year's Day, 1939, *Princess,* 146.

80 "through some difficult years": Edmund Wilson to Mary Elizabeth Jenkinson, January 26, 1947, *Princess,* 162.
81 "I gave up trying": *Thirties,* 45.
81 "vibrant and": ibid.
81 "the best sleeper-with": ibid.
81 "It seemed to me": ibid.
81 "I had some inhibition": ibid., 622.
81 "little . . . cream cheeses": *Daisy,* 80.
81 "After that we went upstairs": ibid., 623.
82 "I, having the night before . . . got up and dressed": ibid., 440.
82 "ought to be carried around . . . should be embarrassed": ibid., 450.
82 "this quince . . . won't sleep with yuh": ibid., 451.
82 "fineness and distinction . . . drawling voice": ibid., 445–446.
83 "Father James don't you know . . . didn't understand": *Twenties,* 316.
83 "literature": see *Twenties,* 421–428.
83 "obscure and meaty regions": *Thirties,* 316.
85 "always hearty . . . a real Amazon": *Hecate County,* 83
85 "tremendous cocktails": *Thirties,* 317.
85 "Lambie": ibid., 649.
85 "agitated the old ladies . . . never dreamed": ibid., 690.
86 "nonthinking": ibid., 312.
86 "not enough of one": Edmund Wilson, *The Fifties: From Notebooks and Diaries of the Period,* edited and with an introduction by Leon Edel (New York: Farrar, Straus and Giroux, 1986), 80.
86 "very Baker-ish": Helen Augur to Edmund Wilson, March 7, 1935, Yale.
87 "I've missed you": Helen Augur to Edmund Wilson, January 11, 1937, Yale.
87 "You're the only . . . all these years": Helen Augur to Edmund Wilson, January 26, 1937, Yale.
87 "affects me like my mother's": Edmund Wilson, *Upstate: Records and Recollections of Northern New York* (New York: Farrar, Straus and Giroux, 1969), 96.
87 "substitute sister": *Fifties,* 80.
87 "what's going on . . . gets it wrong": ibid.
87 "failure as a woman": *Upstate,* 97.
87 "my favorite critic": Helen Augur to Edmund Wilson, January 25, 1950, Yale.
87 "from the old hand": Helen Augur to Edmund Wilson, January 2, 1948, Yale.

87 "I'm such a stray dog": Helen Augur to Edmund Wilson, February 6, 1951, Yale.

88 "this ego-business": Helen Augur to Edmund Wilson, January 27, 1937, Yale.

88 "than just thinking . . . every sense": ibid.

## III. The Intellectual and the Cosmopolitans

90 "A man had better be feeling fit": quoted in David Laskin, *Partisans: Marriage, Politics and Betrayal Among the New York Intellectuals* (New York: Simon and Schuster, 2000), 134.

90 "boys": Mary McCarthy, *Intellectual Memoirs: New York 1936–1938* (New York: Harcourt Brace Jovanovich, 1992), 74.

91 "talk . . . I gave up the battle": ibid., 98

92 "And Philip *did*": ibid., 97.

92 "how about those letters": Edmund Wilson to Mary McCarthy, November 29, 1937, Mary McCarthy Papers, Vassar College Library (hereafter cited as Vassar).

93 "I don't expect to hold her": Edmund Wilson to Mary McCarthy, December 1, 1937, *Man in Letters,* 112.

93 "Fanny Brice's nose": Mary McCarthy to Edmund Wilson, November 29, 1937, Yale.

93 "Having just . . . a letter to you": Mary McCarthy to Edmund Wilson [ca. December 1, 1937], Yale.

93 "Such conversations": Mary McCarthy to Edmund Wilson, n.d. [ca. December 20, 1937], Yale.

94 "Philip was right": Mary McCarthy to Edmund Wilson, December 3, 1937, Yale.

94 "I have a feeling": Mary McCarthy to Edmund Wilson, December 6, 1937, Yale.

94 "Do call me or write me": Mary McCarthy to Edmund Wilson, January 7, 1938, Yale.

94 "This not-going-to . . . God!": Mary McCarthy to Edmund Wilson, January 17, 1938, Yale.

94 "though you say they mean": Edmund Wilson to Mary McCarthy, January 18, 1938, *Man in Letters,* 113.

94 "My dear, I miss you so": Mary McCarthy to Edmund Wilson, [ca. December 14, 1937], Yale.

94 "It's nice": Mary McCarthy to Edmund Wilson, January 19, 1938, Yale.

94 "I've been sleeping horribly": Edmund Wilson to Mary McCarthy, January 18, 1938, *Man in Letters,* 113.

95 "a wart-hog": *Intellectual Memoirs,* 112.
95 "a little bit in love": Mary McCarthy to Edmund Wilson, January 19, 1938, Yale.
95 "wonderful": ibid.
95 "I am surprised": *Intellectual Memoirs,* 99.
95 "Sunday was a bad day": Mary McCarthy to Edmund Wilson, November 30, 1937, Yale.
96 "skull's grin": Randall Jarrell, *Pictures from an Institution, a Comedy* (New York: Knopf, 1954; reprint, paper, Chicago: University of Chicago Press, Phoenix Books, 1986), 65.
96 "Torn animals": ibid.
96 "as a surprise": Carol Brightman, *Writing Dangerously: Mary McCarthy and Her World* (New York: Clarkson Potter, 1992), 174.
96 "How *could* you?": ibid.
97 "generally stirred-up . . . as you can stand": Edmund Wilson to Mary McCarthy, June 17, 1938, *Man in Letters,* 115–116.
98 "I haven't been doing . . . departure": Edmund Wilson to Mary McCarthy, July 31, 1939, *Man in Letters,* 117–118.
99 "I'll be seeing you soon": Edmund Wilson to Mary McCarthy, August 26, 1939, *Man in Letters,* 121.
99 "You have very strange ideas of economy": Edmund Wilson to Mary McCarthy, August 19, 1939, *Man in Letters,* 120.
99 "By all means stay . . . timetable is": ibid.
102 "first, a trick . . . happy tonight": Meyers, 207–208.
102 "We are absolutely counting": Edmund Wilson to Vladimir Nabokov, November 10, 1943, *The Nabokov-Wilson Letters, 1940–1971,* edited and with an introduction by Simon Karlinsky (New York: Harper and Row, 1979; revised and expanded edition, Berkeley: University of California, 2001), 120.
102 "We are terribly sorry about your crisis of dentistry": Edmund Wilson to Vladimir Nabokov, November 23, 1943, Karlinsky, 124.
103 "I slapped him": quoted in Carol Gelderman, *Mary McCarthy: A Life* (New York: St. Martin's, 1988), 108.
105 "note in the pin cushion": Mary McCarthy to Edmund Wilson, n.d. [ca. December 1944], Vassar.
105 "Before we married": Affadavit, McCarthy vs Wilson, February 23, 1945, Vassar.
106 "illness": Brightman, 257.
106 "I discovered shortly": Wilson's legal deposition, n.d. [ca. September, 1945], Yale.
107 "I made fewer entries": *Thirties,* 704.

107 "In her spells": Wilson's legal deposition, Yale.

107 "I am in bed": Katy Dos Passos to John Dos Passos, November 8, 1945, quoted in Gelderman, 115–116.

108 "Edmund Wilson invited me": Anaïs Nin, *Diary, Volume Four, 1944–1947*, ed. Gunther Stuhlman (New York: Harcourt Brace Jovanovich, 1971), 41.

109 "young pig": Mary McCarthy, "The Man in the Brooks Brothers Shirt," in *The Company She Keeps* (New York: Simon and Schuster, 1942), 81.

109 "it was exactly": ibid., 88.

109 "Gradually, now": ibid., 89.

109 "I like": ibid., 91.

109 "believe her a woman": ibid., 103.

109 "never failed": ibid., 104.

110 "I am myn": ibid.

110 "a little bit . . . quite sincere": ibid., 121.

110 "bitch . . . good wife": "Ghostly Father, I Confess," *The Company She Keeps*, 276.

111 "an older mold": Mary McCarthy, *The Groves of Academe* (New York: Harcourt Brace, 1952), 210.

111 "a crushing brief": *Intellectual Memoirs*, 103.

112 "the Monster": ibid., 100.

112 "she had done": Mary McCarthy, *A Charmed Life* (New York: Signet/New American Library, 1954, 1955), 78.

112 "small, pale green eyes": ibid., 27.

112 "a brilliant mind": ibid.

112 "astuteness": ibid., 47.

113 "roamed . . . might yet": ibid., 75.

113 "a stone-crusher": ibid., 83.

113 "bulldozing": ibid., 76.

113 "selfish": ibid., 75.

113 "pillaging the countryside": ibid., 206.

113 "he made his wives": ibid., 84.

113 "did not like Miles": ibid., 75.

113 "My Last Duchess": ibid., 47.

114 "Martha is a very sick girl": ibid.,32.

114 "steadying force": ibid., 76.

115 "I now think": ibid., 33.

115 "normal": ibid., 78.

115 "I'm different": ibid., 53.

115 "a mistaken premise": ibid., 82.

117 "she is tense": "The Little Blue Light," *Five Plays*, 422.
117 "with panther eyes": ibid., 476.
119 "I had definitely made up my mind": Edmund Wilson to Dawn Powell, October 4, 1943, *Literature and Politics*, 397.
120 "lively observation": ibid.
120 "About your book": Edmund Wilson to Dawn Powell, February 15, 1948, *Man in Letters*, 75.
120 "Three of her recent novels": *New Yorker*, November 11, 1944.
120 "Miss Powell has simply": ibid.
121 "All relations with Bunny": *The Diaries of Dawn Powell, 1931–1965*, edited and with an introduction by Tim Page (South Royalton, Vermont: Steerforth Press, 1995), 246–247.
121 "Freud served a purpose": ibid., 247.
123 "his comments on the woman": ibid., 215.
124 "I wish you weren't so jealous": ibid., 437.
124 "on that little back street": ibid.
125 "real embarrassment": ibid.
125 "Darling, what happened": ibid.
125 "see each other for awhile": ibid.
125 "kaleidoscopic liveliness": Edmund Wilson, *The Bit Between My Teeth: A Literary Chronicle of 1950–1965* (New York: Farrar, Straus and Giroux, 1965), 527.
125 "mind is very stout": ibid.
125 "ethereal . . . in love with you": Nin, *Diary*, 90.
125 "neurotic": ibid., 79.
126 "purely intellectual": ibid., 42.
126 "[o]lder people who fall into rigid patterns" : ibid., 65.
126 "I hate young writers. I hate them": ibid., 88.
126 "English tradition": ibid.
126 "Dutch burgher": *Sixties*, 863.
126 "a dictator": ibid., Nin, *Diary*, 98.
126 "no magic . . . no poetry": ibid., 116.
126 "the most banal of restaurants . . . wonderful": ibid., 79.
126 "To me he seemed": ibid., 93.
126 "a very good artist": *From the Uncollected Edmund Wilson*, selected and introduced by Janet Groth and David Castronovo (Athens, Ohio: Ohio University Press, 1995), 255.
126 "well-intentioned": Nin, *Diary*, 5.
127 "At no point is she aware": quoted in Meyers, 255.
127 "Wilson's writing never gathers up": Nin *Diary*, 97.
127 "I would love to be married": ibid., 89.

127 "She has worked out her own system": ibid., 86.
128 "She had not understood": *Sixties,* 673.
129 "didn't seem to look any older": ibid., 674.
129 "as if there could be such a thing": ibid., 864.
129 "the best things in our relations": ibid.
129 "I had forgotten": ibid.
129 "I don't want to cut": *Twenties,* xiv and *Thirties,* xxix.
131 "She's magnificently": Edmund Wilson, *Europe Without Baedeker: Sketches among the Ruins of Italy, Greece, and England* (Garden City, New York: Doubleday, 1947; revised and enlarged edition, 1966), 206.
131 "a handsome and voluptuous": ibid., 205.
131 "enormous old palace": ibid., 202.
131 "disorderly elegance": ibid.
131 "unshaken in morale": ibid.
131 "entirely a *female* artist": ibid.
132 "brokenness . . . physical life": ibid., 204.
132 "amused astonishment": ibid., 207.
132 "smart bathing brassieres": ibid.
132 "the Surrealists had cultivated": ibid., 208.
133 "a tough, short": ibid., 192.
133 "black bush": Edmund Wilson, *The Forties: From Notebooks and Diaries of the Period,* edited with an introduction by Leon Edel (New York: Farrar, Straus and Giroux, 1983), 109.
134 "like lumps of flesh": *Baedeker,* 200.
134 "The Neapolitans seem to me": ibid., 325.
134 "Lili Marlene": ibid., 327.
135 "Your question about heart interest": Edmund Wilson to Betty Huling, July 4, 1945, *Man in Letters,* 82.
136 "Intoxication after making love": *Forties,* 177.
136 "keep still": *Baedeker,* 182.
136 "always enchants me": ibid.
136 "added to her piquancy": ibid., 183.
136 "very fine though rather irregular": ibid., 182.
136 "her little diamond": ibid., 183.
137 "as points": ibid.
137 "disproportions of largeness . . . her complexity": ibid.
137 "British phlegm": ibid., 184.
137 "transports of delight": ibid.
137 "and read about me . . . which God forbid": *Living with Koestler: Mamaine Koestler's letters,* 1945–51, ed. Celia Goodman (London: Weidenfeld and Nicolson,1985), 62.

138 "daydreams that can't correspond": Edmund Wilson to Mamaine Paget (later Koestler), April 28, 1945, Yale.

138 "please don't fall in love": ibid.

138 "your pictures . . . feed on": Edmund Wilson to Mamaine Paget, May 22, 1945, Yale.

138 "I've never felt a natural...you": Edmund Wilson to Mamaine Paget, May 28, 1945, Yale.

138 never physically attracted: Celia Goodman quoted in Meyers, 285.

138 "idiotic": Edmund Wilson to Mamaine Paget, May 28, 1945, Yale.

139 "in spite of our snappings . . . an illusion": Edmund Wilson to Mamaine Paget, July 22, 1945, Yale.

139 "I think you live": ibid.

139 "a Greek revival . . . later installment": Edmund Wilson to Mamaine Paget, October 4, 1945, Yale.

139 "Am I the victim": ibid.

140 still in love: Edmund Wilson to Mamaine Paget, November 2, 1945, Yale.

140 "I'm going to write . . . certain times": Edmund Wilson to Elena Mumm Thornton, April 13, 1946, *Man in Letters*, 136.

140 "I'm so pleased": *Forties*, 162.

140 "r": ibid., 163.

140 "straight": Elena Mumm Thornton to Edmund Wilson, August 1, 1946, Yale.

140 seems to sign on for "cooking and...": paraphrase from a letter, Elena Mumm Thornton to Edmund Wilson, May 15, 1946, Yale.

141 "one single solitary penny": Elena Mumm Thornton to Edmund Wilson, May 22, 1946, Yale.

141 keep one hand on her knee: paraphrase from a letter, Elena Mumm Thornton to Edmund Wilson, June 7, 1946, Yale.

141 "How could you live with . . . about me": Edmund Wilson to Elena Mumm Thornton, July 31, 1946, *Man in Letters*, 141.

141 " to put it through": ibid.

142 "in a townhouse near Frankfurt": "The Admirable Minotaur of Money Hill," *Edmund Wilson: Centennial Reflections*, edited by Lewis M. Dabney (Princeton, New Jersey: Princeton University Press, 1997), 162.

142 "sad to think . . . eagerness": *Sixties*, 130.

143 "the smart people of Paris": ibid., 130–131.

143 "I love going to theaters": *Fifties*, 411

143 "Elena has really effected . . . appropriate intervals": Louise Bogan to May Sarton, June 14, 1954, *What the Woman Lived*, 288–289.

144 "hard-boiled": Edmund Wilson to Elena Mumm Thornton, May 20, 1946, *Man in Letters,* 139.

144 "you two darling ladies": Edmund Wilson to Elena Wilson, née Elena Mumm Thornton, March 17, 1954, *Man in Letters,* 172.

145 "the frank...under the sun": *Forties,* 199.

145 "We did 69 . . . expression": ibid., 203.

145 "getting slower": ibid.

145 "we made love . . . the charge home": *Fifties,* 10.

146 "reminded me": ibid., 89.

146 "romantic . . . thing": ibid.

146 "more intellectual and dignified things": ibid., 302.

146 "an elderly malady . . . get older": ibid., 303.

146 "awful dream": ibid., 305.

146 "my sexual powers": ibid.

146 "period of erotic revival": ibid., 397.

147 "One night we sat . . . a sort of excitement": ibid.

147 "It is not the family I love": *Fifties,* 388.

147 "the last lusts gutter out": *Sixties,* 642.

147 "all this fuss": ibid.

148 "getting a little old": ibid., 528.

148 "expense of spirit": ibid., 194.

148 "Afterwards, I walked around the Pond": *Fifties,* 304.

149 "hell with compensations": Rosalind Baker Wilson quoted in Meyers, 293.

149 "That we've been twenty years": *Sixties,* 561.

149 "Looking at her beautiful body": ibid., 589.

149 "a jealous scene": *Fifties,* 154.

149 "didn't have any real designs": ibid., 155.

150 "so much energy": ibid., 278.

150 "I never talked": ibid., 279.

151 "coquettish mannerisms": ibid., 146.

151 "made a pass": told to Janet Groth in conversation ca. 1970s.

151 "so much about her": *Sixties,* 30.

151 "too sexually fond": ibid., 46.

152 "the abyss": ibid., 117.

152 "spongy body": ibid.

152 "submissive, pleasant-spoken": *A Charmed Life,* 43.

152 "hovering air": ibid., 31.

152 "to efface herself": ibid., 43.

152 "all woman": ibid.

152 "manager": ibid., 35.

153 "Yes, dearest": *Near the Magician*, 134.
153 "as Wilson cringed": Meyers, 291.
153 "Oh, dearest": ibid.
153 "set about destroying . . . reaction": *Near the Magician*, 133.

IV. Endings and Beginnings
156 "she says that she has never been in love": *Sixties*, 405.
156 "Even though . . . beautifully developed": ibid.
156 "hard and solid": ibid., 118.
156 "self contained and self-sustaining": ibid., 102.
157 "Ben Franklin": Frederick Exley, *Pages from a Cold Island* (New York: Random House, 1975), 145.
157 "orange sherbet": *Sixties*, 654.
158 "*megláttam* Mr. Wilson": ibid., 55.
158 "the life of a monk": ibid., 234.
158 "While whining about": ibid., 475.
158 "I never knew a woman so armored": ibid., 816.
158 "hot and physical": ibid., 817.
158 "I want to, but I won't": ibid., 816.
159 "thanks for trying . . . bucked me up": ibid.
159 "you walk the earth . . . everything that's going": poem in Pcolar family box, Wilson papers, Yale.
159 "teaching . . . attractive": *Upstate*, 293.
159 "like to eat": Valentine in Pcolar family box, Wilson papers, Yale.
159 "Ödön Bácsi": *Upstate*, 290.
159 "I never leave Talcottville": ibid., 284.
159 "she's by far the most": letter to Roger Straus in Pcolar family box, Wilson papers, Yale.
160 "tearful . . . breathe today": Anita Loos to Roger Straus, Pcolar family box, Wilson papers, Yale.
160 "There's a cabinet particular": Valentine, Edmund Wilson to Clelia Carroll, February 1962, *Man in Letters*, 233.
161 "very nice": Edmund Wilson to Clelia Carroll, May 1,1968, *Man in Letters*, 258.
161 "Naow, . . . you know I just *love*": Clelia Carroll to Edmund Wilson, May 22, n.d., Yale
162 "untouched on the shelves": Clelia Carroll to Edmund Wilson, December 5, n.d., Yale
163 "inexplicable": Mary Meigs to Edmund Wilson, August 7, 1959, Yale.
163 "a procession": Mary Meigs to Edmund Wilson, June 11, n.d., Yale.
163 "What I feel for": *Fifties*, 551.

163 "I really love her": *Sixties,* 432.

163 "I am 41": Mary Meigs to Edmund Wilson, June 28, 1958, Yale.

164 *"Apologies to the Iroquois* presented us": Betty Crouse Mele, "Edmund Wilson and the Iroquois," *Edmund Wilson: The Man and His Work,* ed. John Wain (New York: New York University Press, 1978), 36.

165 "I was very much touched": *Sixties,* 240.

165 "a small and pretty brunette": ibid., 820.

166 "I . . . suggested her trying . . . come out right": ibid., 845.

168 "The situation has comic": ibid., 847.

168 "Sorry Answer to a Request": poem, Anne Miller folder, Wilson papers, Yale.

169 "I don't want to spoil": *Sixties,* 847.

171 "The Friendless Ones": *Queen,* April 13, 1960.

171 "a kind of spastic ambition": John Osborne, *Almost a Gentleman: An Autobiography, Vol. II: 1955–1966* (London: Faber and Faber, 1991), 180.

172 "domestic involvement": ibid.

172 "I was even privy": ibid.

173 "We'll soon be . . . Not enough": *Sixties,* 864.

173 "Storm in a teacup": Penelope Gilliatt to Edmund Wilson, March 25, 1971, Yale.

173 "It'll pass": ibid.

174 "Perhaps you should destroy this note": ibid.

174 "I have been reading her": Edmund Wilson to Clelia Carroll, January 10,1968, *Man in Letters,* 257.

176 "perhaps something of a genius": *Sixties,* 36.

176 "I told him to tell Elaine": ibid., 61–62.

176 "overwhelmed": ibid., 141.

176 "As we were having this conversation": ibid., 42.

176 "were likely to end up . . . father substitutes": ibid., 174.

177 "I was cast as": ibid., 174–175.

177 "they quarreled . . . defers to him": ibid., 36.

177 "Mary McCarthy in the thirties": ibid., 39.

177 "not to show too much interest": ibid., 42.

177 "life splendid": Edmund Wilson to Edna St. Vincent Millay, August 17, 1920, Millay Collection, Library of Congress.

177 "somber and bitter": *Sixties,* 36

177 "pathos . . . edge": ibid.

### V. The Sum Total: Living and Writing

178 "I have only one manner of dressing": Alfred Kazin, "The Great Anachronism: A View from the Sixties," in *Edmund Wilson: The Man and His Work,* edited by John Wain (New York: New York University Press, 1978), 11.

178 "ice cream": *Sixties,* 175n.

179 "in the long run": *Fifties,* 329.

179 "Adonis": *Thirties,* 441.

180 "My charming old syringa": Louise Bogan to Edmund Wilson, May 2, 1931, *What the Woman Lived,* 58.

180 "Honeybunch, sweetspot": *Thirties,* 388.

180 "Potato": Margaret Canby to Edmund Wilson, September 14, 1930, Yale.

180 "Monkey": Helen Augur to Edmund Wilson, January 11, 1937, Yale.

180 "talk[ed] them into it.": Raymond Holden quoted in Frank, 224.

185 "represent extremes": Edmund Wilson, *Axel's Castle: A Study in the Imaginative Literature of 1870 to 1930* (New York: Scribner's, 1931; reprint, paper, New York: Norton, 1984; reprint, New York: Modern Library, 1996), 224.

185 "In the soliloquy of Mrs. Bloom . . . all living creatures": ibid.

185 "This gross body . . . may transcend itself": ibid.

186 "keeps his faculties clear": Edmund Wilson, *The Wound and the Bow: Seven Studies in Literature* (Boston: Houghton Mifflin, 1941; reissue with corrections, New York: Oxford University Press, 1947; reprint, paper, with introduction by Janet Groth, Athens, Ohio: Ohio University Press, 1997), 149.

186 "commands our respect": ibid.

186 "the many things a life may hold": ibid., 152.

186 "there is even the appetite": ibid., 153.

186 "still test . . . nerve and strength": ibid, 154.

187 "play on the open strings": Edmund Wilson, *The Triple Thinkers: Ten Essays in Literature* (New York: Harcourt Brace, 1938; reprint, New York: Oxford University Press, 1948; reprint, New York: Galaxy Books, Oxford University Press, 1963), 164.

187 "But of course we must all vote": Exley, 151.

189 "must forge on": Edmund Wilson, *To the Finland Station: A Study in the Writing and Acting of History* (New York: Harcourt Brace, 1940; reprint, Garden City, New York: Anchor Doubleday; reprint, with a new introduction, New York: Farrar, Straus and Giroux, 1972), 208.

189 "I shall never forget . . . one another forever": ibid., 390.

189  "after the enactment": ibid.

189  "The Moor is dead too": ibid.

190  "The night of their arrival . . . understood without words": ibid., 554.

192  "vital": *The Bit Between My Teeth,* 430.

192  "a material": ibid., 429.

192  "Christianity and love . . . must assert themselves": ibid., 437.

193  "where one is": ibid., 426.

193  "at home in . . . original art": ibid., 426–427.

193  "we shall rise again": ibid., 428.

# Index

Abbott Academy, ix
Adams, Franklin P. (F.P.A.), 31
Adams, Leonie, 41, 50–57, 123
  "High Falcon", 56
  *High Falcon*, 56
  *Selected Poems* [of Lééonie Adams] 56
  *Those Not Elect*, 50
Alexander, Curt, 43
Algonquin Round Table, 30, 35, 160, 161,
  173; *see also* Gonk
Allen, Woody, 171, 172
Anchor Doubleday, 160
Andersen, Hans Christian, xi
  (Andersen's Fairy Tales)
Anderson, Sherwood, 22, 26
Andover, 144
Anti-Nazi League, 33
Arnold, Matthew, 83
Associated Press, 76
Auden, W. H., 17, 153, 160
Augur, Helen, 78, 81, 86–88
Austen, Jane, 34, 119. 183

Baker, Thomas, 86
Baldwin School in Bryn Mawr, 36
Bankhead, Talullah, 23, 24
Barnard College, 50, 52, 56
Barnes, Djuna, 21
  *Nightwood*, 21
Barrett, William, 121
  *The Truants*, 121
Barrymore, Ethel, 23
Barrymore, John, 23
Beckett, Samuel, 83
Bel Geddes, Norman, 21
Bell, Clive, 74
Belnap, Morris, 61
Benchley, Robert, 29, 30, 32
Benet, William Rose, 36, 38
Bennett, Jill, 171
Bennett, Richard, 6
Bennington College, 56, 169
Berryman, John, 49, 97

Bishop, John Peale, 4, 6, 7, 9, 12, 13, 17,
  21, 53, 155
Blair, Mary, vii, 13, 19–29, 43, 44, 46, 49,
  51, 53, 57, 59, 64, 66, 141
Bloomingdale's, 71
Bloomsbury group, the, 41
Boccaccio, Giovanni, 78, 158
Bogan, Louise, 43–49
  *Achievement in American Poetry
    1900–1950*, 48
  *Body of this Death*, 44
  "Evening in a Sanitarium", 46
Bogan, Madeline, later Maidie, 43
Bogart, Humphrey, 136
Bollingen Prize, 56
Book-of-the-Month Club, 122
Boop Boop A Doop girl, 63
Boston University, 43
Boswell, James, 26
Boussevain, Eugen, 13
Bow, Clara, 63
Brentano's, 43
Brice, Fanny, 93
*British Vogue*, 169
Brontë sisters: Anne, Charlotte, and
  Emily, 34, 56, 129
Brooks Brothers, 178
Broun, Heywood, 23
Browning, Peaches, 93
Browning, Robert, 79, 80, 113
  "Last Ride Together, The", 79
  "My Last Duchess", 113
Buchenwald, 132
Burke, Billie, 29
Byron, George Gordon, Lord, 26, 40, 93

Cabell, James Branch, 40
  *Jurgen*, 40
Campbell, Alan, 33
Canby, Margaret, vii, 45, 49, 50, 53,
  60–68, 88, 141
Canby, James, 64
Canby, Jimmy, 64–66, 141

Canby, Vincent, 169
Capote, Truman, 135
Carnegie Tech, 21, 22
Carroll, Clelia, vii, 160–162, 174
Carroll, Philip, 160
Casanova, Jacques, 186, 187
*Casket, The*, 32
Cassatt, Mary, 63
Catuılus, 31
Chandler, Rayrnond, 68
Chaplin, Charles, 26
Chapman, John Jay, 187
Chaucer, Geoffrey, 110
Chavchavadze, Nina, 143
Child's, 70
Chopin, Frederick, 42
Clark, Eunice, 93
Clurman, Harold, 67
Cobb, Lee J., 23
Comden, Betty, 172
*Communist Manifesto*, 191
Communist Party, 33
Condéé Nast, 31
Conning Tower, The, 31
Connolly, Cyril, 135, 140
Connor, Cyril, 169
Cornell, Katherine, 23
Covici-Friede, 92
Crane, Stephen, 26
Crowninshield, Frank, 8, 25, 29, 31,
Cummings, E. E., 26

*Daily Mail*, 171
Dabney, Lewis, 57
Dante Alighieri, xiv, 10, 183, 184
DAR, 75, 84
*David Copperfield*, 141
Dawson, Helen, 171
de Beauvoir, Simone, 92
de la Selva, Salomon, 4
de Rougemont, Denis, 183
de Silver, Margaret, 93
Dell, Floyd, 4
    *Angel Intrudes, The*, 4
Deming, Barbara, 163
*Dial, The*, 26
Dos Passos, Katy, 107, 113
Dupee, F. W. (Fred), 90, 93

Eakin, Constant (Connie), 21, 28
Edel, Leon, 44, 68, 129
Edwards, Margaret (Margaret
    Rulhnan), x
Eliot, George, 90, 183
Eliot, T.S., 17, 83
Ellis, Havelock, xi, xiv, 164
    *Studies in the Psychology of Sex*, xi
*Encounter*, 170
Engels, Friedrich, 189
Epstein, Jason, 161

*Esquire*, 166
Evanses, The, 98
Exley, Frederick, 189
Fadiman, Clifton, 102
*Fanny Hill*, 158

Farrar Straus, 85
FBI, 33
Fenton, William, 165
Ficke, Arthur Davison, 4
Fini, Leonor, 148–150
Fitzgerald, F. Scott, vii, xi, xiv–xvi, 22,
    60, 98, 123, 155
    *Crack-up, The*, 98
    *Last Tycoon, The*, 98
Fitzgerald, Zelda, 27
Flaubert, Gustave, 183
    *Madame Bovary*, 93, 150
Floradora girl, 63
Ford, Henry, 42
Fort, Louise, ("K"), 98–100
Freud, Sigmund, 121
Frost, Robert, 49

Gates, Paula, 64
Gauss, Christian, xiii, xiv, 96, 108
Geismar, Maxwell, 129
Gill, Brendan, 161
Gilliatt, Penelope, vii, 169–175,
    "Friendless Ones, The", 171
    "Sunday, Bloody Sunday", 174
Gilliatt, Roger, 170
Gimbel's, 21
Girl's Latin School in Boston, 43
Goethe, Johann Wolfgang, von, 42, 112,
    143
Gold, Mike, 48
Gonk, 30, 35, 161
Goodman, Celia (twin sister of
    Mamaine Paget), 137, 138
Goodner, Carol, 32
Gopnik, Adam, 135
Gordon, Caroline, 96
Gorey, Edward (Ted), 131, 161
Gotham Book Mart, 125
GPU, 95
Grand, Mary, 155
Green, Adolf, 172
Greene, Graham, 175
*Guardian, The*, 170
Guggenheim Fellowship, 52, 53, 70, 188

Hale, Nancy, 36
Hamilton, David, xv
Hammett, Dashiell, 68
Hardy, Thomas, 5, 6
Harvard, 36. 150, 151
Hayes, Helen, 23
Heine, Heinrich, 47
Hemingway, Ernest, vi, 22, 26, 34

Henri, Robert, 75
Hichborn, Philip, 36
Hicks, Granville, 48
Hill School, xi, xiv, xv, 18, 106
*Hill School Record*, xiii
Hitchcock, Alfred, 172
Holden, Raymond, 45
Holton Arms, 36
Horace, 31
*Horizon*, 135
Houdini, Harry, 26
Houghton Mifflin, 119
Housman, A. E., 5, 6
Hoyt, Elinor Morton, 36; *see also* Elinor Wylie
Hoyt, Nancy, 39
Hughes, Stuart, 155
Hughes, Suzanne, 155
Huling, Betty, 84–85, 108, 135, 155
Humphries, Rolfe, 48, 51
Huston, Walter, 23

IRS, 151

James, Henry, 40
*Wings of the Dove, The*, 61
Jarrell, Randall, 95
*Pictures from an Institution*, 96
Jefferson, Thomas, 145
Johann, Magda, 50, 53, 57; *see also* Katze Szabo
Johnson, Owen, xi
Johnson, Samuel, 40
Johnsrud, Harold, 115
Josephson, Matthew, 41. 42
Joyce, James, 62, 111, 126, 184–185
"Dead, The", 126
*Ulysses*, 61, 86, 185
Julliard, 169

Kael, Pauline, 172
Kane, Helen, 63
Kazin, Alfred, 151, 178
Keaton, Buster, 171
Keats, John, 167
Kennedy, John F., 158
KGB, 75
Kimball, Laura, x
Kimball, Reuel, x
Kimball, Sandy, x, xi, 154, 163, 164, 178
Kinsey, Alfred, 146, 183
KKK, 23
Koestler, Arthur, 136, 138, 149
*Darkness at Noon*, 136
Koestler, Mamaine, 135–140, 149; *see also* Mamaine Paget
Krazy Kat, 26
Krúúpskaya, Nadezhda, 190, 191

La Rochefoucauld, Francois, Duc de, 32
Lane, Pamela, 171
Lardner, Ring, 26, 41
Laski, Harold, 132
Lawrence,D. H., 94, 184, 185
*Lady Chatterley's Lover*, 184
Le Gallienne, Eva, 23
Lenin, V. I., 188, 190, 193
Lewes, Henry, 90
Lewis, Peggy, 27
Library of Congress, 56
Lloyd, Harold, 68
*London Review of Books, The*, 170
Longchamps, 126
Longfellow, Henry Wadsworth, 30
"Hiawatha", 30, 35
Looking Glass Library, 160, 161
Loos, Anita, 159
*Gentlemen Prefer Blondes*, 159
Lou Tannen's magic shop, 173
Lowell, Robert, 97
Luce, Claire Booth, 33
Lyle, Sir Alfred, 48

Macdonald, Dwight, 144
Macdonald, Michael, 142, 144
MacLeish, Archibald, 49
Macy's, 115
Malraux, Andre, 142
Marsh, Reginald, 69
Marshall, Margaret (Peggy), 90–93, 95, 123
Martial, 31
Marvell, Andrew, 142
Marx Brothers, The, 142
Marx, Eleanor, 189
Marx, Karl, 48, 50, 73, 74, 89, 92, 161, 188–192
Marx-Lenin Institute, 188
Mather, Cotton, ix
Maugham, Somerset, 123
May, Elaine, 172, 175–177
McCarthy, Kevin, 95, 107
McCarthy, Mary, vii, x, 47, 52, 67, 69, 70, 75, 79, 84, 88, 89–118, 123, 125, 127–129, 139–141, 143–144, 152–153, 162, 176–177, 179–180
Articles
"Our Critics, Right or Wrong", 90
Biography
*Intellectual Memoirs*, 92
*Memories of a Catholic Girlhood*, 91
Novels
*Charmed Life, A*, 108, 111–112, 114, 143, 152, 180
*Company She Keeps, The*, 98, 108, 110
*Group, The*, 108, 115
*Groves of Academe, The*, 108, 111–112, 118

Short Stories
"Cruel and Barbarous Treatment", 95
"Ghostly Father, I Confess", 110
"Man in the Brooks Brothers Shirt,
The", 96, 108, 110
McCarthy, Preston, 95
McGinley, Phyllis, 160
McGovern, George, 187
Medal of Freedom, 158
Meigs, Mary, 113, 162–164
Mele, Antonio Edmund Wilson, 165
Mele, Betty Crouse, 164–165
Mercantile Library, 163
Meredith, Charles, 21
Meyers, Jeffrey, 5, 127, 139, 153
Millay, Edna St.
Vincent, vii, xii, 3–19,
31–32, 43, 46, 50, 52, 56, 63, 97, 128,
177, 184
*Conversation at Midnight*, 16
*Fig from Thistles, A*, 8
*Passer Mortuus Est*, 10
*Renascence*, 6, 8, 18
*Scrub*, 10
*"To Love Impuissant"*, 5
Millay, Norma, 57
Miller, Anne, 165–169
Miller, Henry, 126
Miller, Ned, (Dr. Edgar Miller), 167, 169
Minahan, Albert, 70–71
Minahan, Frances, (Anna), 69–75, 78,
123
Miss Dana's School, 31
Montaigne, Michel de, 148
Moravia, Alberto, 133
Morris, Glyn, 178
Mrs. Flint's, 36, 38

NAACP, 33
Nabokov, Vladimir, 102, 120, 142, 171
*Lolita*, 183
Nabokovs, the (Vladimir Noldya and
Vera), 102
*Nassau Lit*, xiv
*Nation, The*, 90
Nevins, Hardwicke, 5
*New Republic*, 24, 26, 37, 50, 53, 62, 65,
84–86, 93
*New Statesman, The*, 170
*New York Sun*, xv
*New York Times*, 23
*New Yorker*, 39, 45, 47, 49, 85, 92, 102,
108, 125–126, 130, 133, 172–175
Nichols, Mike, 169, 172–173, 175, 177
Nietzsche, Friedrich Wilhelm, 45
Nin, Anaïs, vii, 125–130, 131
*Diaries*, (of Anaïs Nin), 127–129
*Under a Glass Bell*, 125, 128
Nixon, Richard Milhouse, 167
Noyes, Alfred, xv

Noyes, Larry, xv, xvii, 61
NYU, 56

O'Connor, Flannery, 183
O'Keefe, Georgia, 26
O'Neill, Agnes, 27
O'Neill, Eugene, 22–24, 27
*All God's Chillun Got Wings*, 19, 23
*Before Breakfast*, 22
*Desire Under the Elms*, 23
*Diff'rent*, 23
*Hairy Ape, The*, 23
*Marco Millions*, 23
O'Neill, Florence, 60
*Observer The*, 171, 174
Orwell, George, 137
Osborne, John, 169–172
*Hotel in Amsterdam*, 170
Osborne, Nolan, 171, 174–175

Paget, Mamaine ("G"), 108, 134–140,
149–150, 160; *see also* Mamaine
Koestler
Pallas Athene, 115
Paramore, Ted, vii, 57, 60–61, 63–65, 69
"Ballad of Yukon Jake", 60
"Virginian, The", 60
Paramount, 60
Parker, Dorothy, 29–35, 40, 46, 119,
175–176
"Arrangement in Black and White", 33
"Little Hours, The", 32
"Telephone Call, A", 34
Parker, Edwin Pond II, 31
*Partisan Review*, 89–90, 92–93, 98
Pasternak, Boris, 143, 191–193
*Doctor Zhivago*, 191–193
Pcolar, Eddie, 159
Pcolar, George, 155
Pcolar, Mary, vii, 150, 152, 155–160
Pepys, Samuel, 129
Perkins, Maxwell, 53
Plath, Sylvia, 6
Poetry Society, 37
Poitier, Sidney, 157
Pope, Alexander, 32, 167
Porter, Cole, 61
Powell, Anthony, 124
Powell, Dawn, vii, 118–125, 155
*Angels on Toast*, 120
*Golden Spur, The*, 124
*Locusts Have No King, The*, 120
*My Home Is Far Away*, 120
*Time to be Born, A*, 120
Praz, Mario, 131
*Romantic Agony, The*, 131
Preston, Augusta Morgenstern, 98
Preston, Harold, 94
Princess Margaret, 170

Princeton Club, 129, 173
Princeton, xii–xv, 4, 18, 45, 92, 108, 165
Proust, Marcel, 15, 62
Provincetown Players, 13, 19
Provincetown Playhouse, 4, 24
Pulitzer Prize, 6
Pushkin, Alexander, 96

*Queen*, 170

Racine, Jean Baptiste, 114
"Berenice", 114
Rado, Sandor, 88, 97
Rahv, Philip, 89–93, 106
Rascoe, Burton, 24, 27
Rascoe, Hazel, 27
Red Cross, 133
Redgrave, Vanessa, 171
Reinitz, Neale, 34
Renoir, Jean, 172
Richardson, Tony, 171
Rimbaud, Arthur, 62
RKO, 60
Robeson, Paul, 23
Roethke, Theodore, 48
Roosevelt, Franklin Delano, 123
Roosevelt, Theodore, 36
Rosenfeld, Paul,
Rothschild, Dorothy, 30; *see also*
    Dorothy Parker
Rousseau, Jean Jacques, 186
Rowlandson, Thomas, 133

Sacco and Vanzetti, 33, 81
Sackville-West, Vita, 41
Sacred Heart, 106
Sade, Marquis de, 132
    *Juliette*, 132
Saks Fifth Avenue, 132
Salvation Army, 24
Sartre, Jean Paul, 92
Schnitzler, Arthur, 143
Schrafft's, 70
Schwartz, Delmore, 94
Seldes, Gilbert, 26
Shakespeare, William, 22, 148, 183–184
    *Midsummer Night's Dream, A*, 119
Shaw, George Bernard, 7
    *Heartbreak House*, 7
Sheehan, Vincent, 3
    *Indigo Bunting, The*, 3
Shelley, Percy Bysshe, 36, 38
Sherwood, Robert, 30
Silone, Darina, 134–135, 142, 161
Silone, Ignazio, 135, 137
    *Bread and Wine*, 135
Siphraios, Eva, 134–135, 139, 161
Sitwell, Edith, Osbert, and
    Sacheveral, 41

Smith, Kemp, xiv
Soma, Tony, 32
Spark, Muriel, 124
*Spectator, The*, 170
St. Paul's, xi, 144
St. Stephen's, 106
Stael, Madame de, 93
Stalin, Joseph, 48, 93, 188, 192
Standish, Miles, 117
Steloff, Frances, 125
Stendhal, (Henri Beyle), 96, 108, 183
Stevens, Wallace, 26
Stevenson, Adlai, 146–147
Stieglitz, Alfred, 26
Strachey, Lytton, 22
Straus, Roger, 159–160
Streisand, Barbra, 123
Swisher, Frances, 150–151
Szabo, Katze, 50, 53, 57–58, 61

Taggard, Genevieve, 44
Tango Gardens, 69
Tate, Allen, 96
Tates, The, Allen and Caroline Gordon,
    54–55, 97
Tati, Jacques, 172
Thornton, Elena Mumm, 28, 108, 140,
    142; *see also* Elena Wilson
Thornton, Henry, 142, 144
Thornton, James (Jimmy), 141
Throckmorton, Cleon, 21
*Time*, 118
Tolley, Verna, 27
*Town and Country*, 143
Trilling, Lionel, 183
Troy, William, 56
Turgenev, Ivan, 143
Tynan, Kenneth, 171

University of Chicago, 98, 175
Untermeyer, Louis, 26, 40
Ure, Mary, 171
USSR, 188

VanDoren, Mark, 40
Van Vechten, Carl, 26, 40
*Vanity Fair*, xvii, 4, 6, 8, 26, 29–31,
    36–37, 170
Vassar Club, 116
Vassar, 22, 84, 89, 115
*Vathek*, 57
Vermeer, Johannes, 140
Vidal, Gore, 126–127
*Vogue*, 31, 132
Voltaire, 186

Walker, Leon, 61
Washington, George, ix
Waugh, Coulton, 76

Waugh, Elizabeth, 74, 75–80, 82, 86, 88
Waugh, Evelyn, 124
Waugh, Frederick Judd, 75–76
Webster, John, 183
Wedekind, Frank, 183
Wells, H. G., xiv
West, Andrew Fleming, xiv
Westphalen, Jenny von, 188; *see also*
    Jenny Marx
Wharton, Edith, 36, 42
Wilder, Thornton, 111
Williams, Tennessee, 111
Williams, William Carlos, 89
Wilson, Edmund
  Essays
    "All-Star Literary Vaudeville, 44
    "Dawn Powell: Greenwich Village in
        the Fifties", 125
    "Death of Margaret", 68
    "Doctor Life and his Guardian
        Angel", 191
    "Epilogue, 1952", 3, 5
    "Give That Beat Again", 16
    "Jumping Off Place, The", 66
    "Legend and Symbolism in Doctor
        Zhivago", 191
    "Letter to Elinor Wylie, A", 40
    "Mr. Hemingway's Dry Points", 26
    "Muses Out of Work, The", 32
    "On and Off Broadway", 26
    "Poet's Return, The", 42
    "Sex", 182
    "Toast and a Tear for Dorothy Parker,
        A", 34
    "UncomfortableCasanova",186–187
    "[Ziegfeld] Follies as an Institution,
        The" 26
  Books
    *American Earthquake The*, 26, 42,
        182, 193
    *American Jitters*, 33, 42
    *Apologies to the Iroquois*, 164
    *Axel's Castle*, 50, 62, 74, 83, 93,
        184–185
    *Bit Between My Teeth, The*, 119, 182
    *Boys in the Back Room, The*, 98
    *Classics and Commercials*, 182
    *Devils and Canon Barham, The*, 182
    *Europe Without Baedeker*, 130–136
    *Fifties, The*, 145, 148
    *Forties, The*, 133, 135–136, 145
    *Higher, Jazz, The*, 34–35, 63, 98
    *I Thought of Daisy*, 14–15, 35, 53, 60,
        62, 65, 81
    *Memoirs of Hecate County*, 69–70,
        72–74, 77, 98, 130, 143, 158
    *Notebooks of Night*, 98

*Patriotic Gore*, xvii, 147, 158,
*Piece of My Mind, A*, 147, 182, 193
*Prelude, A*, xi, xiv
*Shores of Light, The*, 3, 16, 182, 184
*Sixties, The*, 57, 182, 184
*Thirties, The*, 66, 68, 80, 82, 86
*To the Finland Station*, 46, 70, 86, 98,
*Travels in Two Democracies*, 33
*Triple Thinkers, The*, 98
*Twenties, The*, 3, 13, 28, 32, 51, 56, 60
*Undertaker's Garland, The*, 32
*Upstate*, 86, 116, 147, 154, 159–160
*Wound and the Bow, The*, 98, 186
  Plays
    *Crime in the Whistler Room, The*,
        19, 22
    *Little Blue Light, The*, 117
    *This Room and This Gin and These
        Sandwiches*, 19, 43, 52
  Poems
    "November Ride", 79
  Stories
    "Galahad", xii
    "Glimpses of Wilbur Flick", 143
    "Princess with the Golden Hair,
        The", 69, 75–80, 85
Wilson, Edmund, Sr., ix, x, 18, 25, 36
Wilson, Elena, 5, 28, 108, 124, 134,
    140–154, 161–162, 169–170, 173–174;
    *see also* Elena Mumm Thornton
Wilson, Helen Miranda, 144
Wilson, Mrs. Edmund, Sr., ix–xi, xv–xvi,
    18, 25, 28, 70, 87, 94, 99
Wilson, Reuel, 98, 103–105, 107, 144
Wilson, Rosalind, 21, 24–26, 28, 53, 66,
    98, 103–104, 107, 119, 144, 153, 155,
    167, 177
Woolf, Virginia, 41, 183
Woollcott, Alexander, 30
WPA, 86
Wylie, Elinor, 35–43, 61–62
    "Portrait in Black Paint, With a Very
        Sparing Use of Whitewash", 39
    *Jennifer Lorn*, 39, 40
    *Venetian Glass Nephew, The*, 39, 40
Wylie, Horace, 36

Yale Club, 61
Yale, 64, 162, 174
Yeats, William Butler, 17, 79, 82, 182
    "On a Political Prisoner", 82
YMCA, xii
*Youth's Companion*, 37

Ziegfeld, Florenz, 29